# TESTIMONIALS

"Great news for Jonathan Preston fans. Here comes another action-filled historical thriller from novelist Steve Doherty. *Crossroads* is an adventure story replete with spies and counter-spies, characters you'll love, villains you'll hate, set in the intrigue-filled post-WWII era. A good read."

—Robert Gandt, author of Angels in the Sky

"Doherty's *Call for Blood* is an adventure-packed military thriller with deep trenches between good and bad. The red, white, and blue hero, Jonathan Preston, is perfectly at home in this novel's patriotic World War II setting...hunting enemy agents and rescuing Allied POWs who are the test subjects in experiments with chemical and biological weapons. A cliffhanger ending will leave readers ready for the next battle."

—Kirkus Reviews

"Doherty is a master at handling surprises. *Call for Blood* exhibits that mastery as Jonathan Preston is called upon to head up missions in the Pacific Theater against some of Japan's top counterintelligence agents. However, even at the conclusion of the book, another surprise is in store for the reader, who will have to wait and wonder how the author will handle it with the next novel."

—James Marvin, US Army Counterintelligence Corps (Retired)

"Steve Doherty's *Gold Dominion* continues the kick-butt, adrenaline-soaked, action-driven WWII adventures of his larger-than-life hero, Jonathan Preston. Preston's latest saga will leave the reader breathless and wanting more."

—Robert Gandt, Author and Historian

"*Imminent Threat* is a cut above. It is filled with intrigue and keeps you wanting more. Jonathan Preston is America's answer to James Bond. He is brilliant at his job. I'm glad he's on our side!"

—Ron Knotts, Houston Police Detective (Retired)

# JONATHAN PRESTON SERIES BOOKS

Operation King Cobra

Call for Blood

Gold Dominion

Imminent Threat

Crossroads

# Crossroads

**STEVE DOHERTY**

Published by Steve Doherty Books
Muldoon, Texas 78949
www.steve-doherty-books.com



Printed in the United States of America

Hardcover ISBN: 979-8-9868106-0-7
Paperback ISBN: 979-8-9868106-1-4
Ebook ISBN: 979-8-9868106-2-1

Library of Congress Control Number: 2022911997

# ACKNOWLEDGEMENT

I want to thank the many friends and associates who continue encouraging me to write about one of World War II's most successful covert operatives. Plus, special thanks to Kyle Seymore, who has hosted four of my book launches at my favorite bar and grill.

# CHAPTER 1

*Mount Hiei, Japan—AD 1571*

In the middle of the sixteenth century, Japan was embroiled in chaos as powerful feudal lords called *daimyos* were fighting rival warlords in a battle for control of the entire country. At the same time, warrior monks were arming themselves and blocking the roads into Japan's capital, Kyoto, attacking castles, and destroying villages and farms of the warlords they despised. During the confusion, one daimyo, Oda Nobunaga, saw an opportunity to end the civil war and unite the country under one shogunate. However, doing so would mean going back to war, to conquer the warring factions *against* the changes that peace would bring to their clans and nation. To force warlords to give up their swords and embrace peace would mean forcing them to give up their samurai traditions, blood feuds with other clans, and most of all, their power. The same could be said of the warrior religious sects.

When the Tendai sect of Buddhism was initially introduced to Japan in AD 806, a monk named Saicho established a Buddhist temple and school on the 2,782-foot mountain northeast of Kyoto. Kyoto was the seat of Japan's imperial court and palace. Over the next seven hundred years, the sect grew so strong that it began to interfere with the central government. It forced its will on the Emperor, demanding more and more special privileges, and growing more powerful. Moreover, the monks who lived in Mount Hiei temples had evolved into warrior monks with martial skills equal to samurai. Shrugging change and especially foreign intervention, the monks allied themselves with warlords dedicated to keeping the ancient traditions. When that wasn't enough, they began spreading malicious rumors and creating confusion throughout the country as a means of resisting modern European ways, religion, and technology.

The leader of the Oda clan, Oda Nobunaga, was one of the daimyos leading the introduction of foreign ways, goods, and modern technology into Japanese society. He even embraced the introduction of Christianity into Japanese culture. Trying to end the decades of civil war between the various Japanese clans, Nobunaga had had enough of the seditious and conspiring Tendai monks fostering rebellion. Then, on a crisp morning in early September, traveling from Kyoto to Gifu, the report from an arquebus long gun echoed on the mountain road. As Nobunaga's horse reared in a frenzy, his retainers galloped forward and captured the would-be assassin. They soon discovered that he was a Tendai monk from the Honjanji temple on Mount Hiei. It was just one of the hundreds of temples built on the holy mountain that housed thousands of monks, along with their families and servants.

Although Honjanji was a Buddhist temple, it had been constructed like a castle. The outside walls were made of stone, and a deep moat surrounded the structure. To be a monk at Honjanji meant that you were a warrior also. No single monk was living in the fortress who did not hate Oda Nobunaga. They accused him of being an enemy of Buddhism and the destroyer of Japanese culture, for embracing European ways.

Instead of negotiating with Nobunaga, as they did with the government in Kyoto, the monks began arming themselves with guns and cannons. They prided themselves in their long-practiced traditions and enjoyed the privileges they received from the Imperial court. They were not going to change. The reports that Nobunaga received by mid-September told him the monks were digging more moats around the Honjanji fortress. He received a separate report that the monks had purchased two thousand matchlock rifles and several small brass cannons. The monks were fanning the flames of rebellion and spreading venomous lies and propaganda across Japan's provinces. If left unchecked, their actions would set off an uprising against Nobunaga's efforts to unify the clans of Japan and end decades of civil war. To indeed prosper, Nobunaga knew, Japan needed peace and foreign commerce.

The last straw for Nobunaga was a report about a messenger from the abbot of the Honjanji temple being intercepted by one of his samurai after leaving the Shogun Ashikaga Yoshiaki's palace in Kyoto. Ashikaga had regained the shogunate, with Oda Nobunaga's direct help, when he and his army marched into Kyoto and reinstalled the deposed shogun. Now, unfortunately, the small-minded and aristocratic hereditary commander-in-chief of Japan was no longer a supporter of the young daimyo, Nobunaga. In the intercepted message from Ashikaga to Abbot Sonrin, the shogun was demanding an all-out attack by the abbot's twenty thousand warrior-monks, to crush Nobunaga before he became stronger and brought more clans under his control.

The shogun had been seduced to the abbot's side because peace meant an end to his power, too. Under the circumstances, Nobunaga had no choice but to convene a war council and mobilize an army into the mountains. Everywhere Nobunaga looked, he saw enemies against his plan to unify the nation and stop the clan wars. Even the monks and priests, who were supposed to love peace and hate war, were against him. In his restless sleep that night at Gifu Castle, Nobunaga saw the whole country being devoured by flames and then awoke with a start.

"Guard! Guard!" Nobunaga shouted as he stepped from his bedroom.

"Yes, my lord," came the reply.

"Have General Hideyoshi call a war council and summon the general staff immediately." Nobunaga quickly returned to his bedroom and waited for his servants to dress him.


As the lamps in the large council room lighted Oda Nobunaga's face, it was evident how determined he was while addressing his generals who had gathered. Nobunaga wasn't requesting their input on whether it was wise to attack the renegade monks. He was asking about tactics needed to defeat them in their mountain hideouts.

While Nobunaga was worried about tactics, his generals were concerned about other clans mobilizing behind the monks before their army was ready. Their concern came to fruition when the Asakura clan moved two samurai army units from the mountains north of Lake Biwa and set up camps on the western beaches at both Karasaki and Otsu, a few miles east of Mount Hiei. Another Asakura army unit moved onto the mountains and reinforced the main Buddhist headquarters temple.

While fighting one of the Asakura armies in northeast Japan, Oda Nobunaga's younger brother, Nobuharu, was killed in the battle and his small army was routed. When the account reached Nobunaga at his camp, he was unmoved. The army that defeated his brother was now moving south to attack Nobunaga's castle garrison at Kyoto. Fortunately, Nobunaga and most of his army reached Kyoto in time to reinforce the garrison and the city, preventing the attack.

Upon arrival, Nobunaga immediately ordered the commander of the garrison, Akechi Mitsuhide, to mobilize his forces. At dawn on September 29, there was not one traveler or packhorse seen on the roads leading north out of Kyoto when Nobunaga and Mitsuhide led their armies of over 50,000 men toward Mount Hiei. As they approached the mountain, a sea of enemy banners could be seen up and down the mountain, fluttering in the stiff breeze. The combined forces of Nobunaga and Mitsuhide waited patiently while the two conversed. Their horses, sensing the coming battle, were restless. Their constantly moving feet made it difficult for the riders to remain stationary.

"I will charge straight up the mountain with my main force," Nobunaga stated. "I want you to attack the Asakura entrenched at Karasaki and Otsu. My spies tell me they number around eight thousand altogether, and they do not carry any rifles. After you route them, move up to the northern ridges. These warrior-monks disgrace Buddha, so spare no one. General Ieyasu will arrive with his army within the hour. He will protect your rear and your right flank as you move up the mountain and mop up any soldiers who escape. When you hear the conch sound once, feed your men. It will be a long day. Have your logistics team move out with extra gun powder, shot, arrows, food, and water when the conch sounds twice. When it sounds three times, begin your attack."

Three hours later, when the conch sounded three times, Mitsuhide shouted, "Attack!"

The screaming Mitsuhide forces could be heard a mile away as the 16,000 men under his banner moved closer to the Asakura front line at Otsu. Mitsuhide had put three thousand foot soldiers in the front line. Intermingled with them were three lines of riflemen, numbering a thousand per line. Following the front line were another five thousand foot soldiers with spears and swords. Finally, his five-thousand-man cavalry unit would attack through the hills on the enemy's western and northern flanks, leaving them only the lake as an avenue of escape.

"Don't panic! Don't act disgracefully. You are samurai!" shouted the Asakura general in charge, trying to reassure himself at the same time.

When Mitsuhide's army was fifty yards from the Asakura forces—who were standing resolutely behind the felled trees and palisades erected near the beach—Mitsuhide's foot soldiers and riflemen suddenly threw themselves to the ground. Then, as the confused Asakura forces looked on, the first line of Mitsuhide's riflemen got up on one knee, placed their matchlocks on wooden braces, took aim, and fired.

Struck by three bullets, the Asakura general riding on his horse was one of the first to fall, along with four hundred of his men. The remaining two thousand men, now leaderless, began to panic. Finally, a second general galloped to the line, jumped off his horse, and yelled, "Hold the line! Don't panic! Fight and die like the samurai that you are."

After the second and third volleys of rifle fire, barely six hundred Asakura warriors were standing. The newly arrived general was sitting against a fallen tree, staring at a gaping hole in his abdomen. He watched helplessly as Mitsuhide's soldiers cleared the first rampart and began thrusting their spears and swords into the second line of defense. It was hand-to-hand fighting amid the palisades, meant to keep the enemy at bay. Instead, they became a barrier to their escape. As the overwhelmed Asakura warriors panicked and began running toward the mountain, Mitsuhide's cavalry appeared out of the forest. They began driving the fleeing soldiers into the lake. Not one survived.

When Nobunaga's forces reached the village of Yamashina, the battle commenced on the mountain. The first line of warrior monks was quickly routed by his battle-hardened samurai. Enemy messengers could be seen riding north toward Mount Hiei with messages for their generals, who could hardly believe what they had heard.

"General Nagamasa!" the messenger reported, once he dismounted his horse at the Mii Temple. "Enemy forces have broken through at Yamashina. Five hundred men have died, and Nobunaga's forces are already at Keage, starting up the steep incline."

Having just received word that the forces at Otsu had fallen, General Nagamasa realized Karasaki was not far behind in the same fate. Nagamasa now realized his monks were not invincible. With regret, he shouted, "Fall back! Retreat! Back to Mii Temple."

One of Nagamasa's generals, Asakura Kagetake, shouted an order to his retainer as he mounted his horse, "Burn the peasant houses along the road after our vanguard has gone through. It may slow Nobunaga's advance."

When Nobunaga reached the Mii Temple, there was not one enemy soldier there to confront him. As Nobunaga rode along the rocky trail, the hot wind from the burning houses began scorching his brow, and sparks of burning embers tried to ignite the horse's mane and the silk tassels hanging from his saddle. Nobunaga patted out the sparks and continued, unconcerned. In Nobunaga's mind, he had become the wall of flames that were destroying the enemy's homes and fortresses. He was the immoveable force devouring the enemy.

As Nobunaga looked high up the mountain, he saw the banners of the enemy army. More than 20,000 warrior monks, priests, and peasants awaited their deaths. Tears of rage fell from Nobunaga's eyes. It was evident that what the monks were attempting was blasphemy. Mount Hiei was established to be a refuge for priests and monks—not a war zone. Of course, the priests and monks were given certain privileges. Still, the mountain's original purpose was to foster peace and harmony. Over time, the greed, avarice, and lust for power had darkened the hearts of the monks.

In his despair and anger, Nobunaga bit his lip so hard that it drew blood. He slipped from his saddle, knelt before the mountain, and said a prayer as he wept, "I fear that I have become your enemy, Holy Mountain. But I must cleanse and purify the wrong and injustice that have overpowered you. Please forgive me."

Ordering his camp stool, Nobunaga sat near the top of a hill, looking upward. As far as his eye could see, Nobunaga saw that the foothills and Mount Hiei were now covered with the banners of his men. Although the warrior monks and the Asakura army were fighting bravely, Nobunaga's forces had completely surrounded the mountain. They cut off the enemy's supply of provisions and reinforcement. *I can lessen the death and destruction by starving them into submission*, Nobunaga thought.

Nobunaga's plan was working, too. With over twenty thousand men to feed on the mountain fortress, the underground storerooms and granaries, filled with rice, barley, wheat, green beans, and sesame seeds, were quickly emptied. After nearly seventy days, the rats and birds had vanished because the monks were good at catching them. Without food or animals to catch, the warrior monks and samurai were reduced to eating the barks off of trees and any vegetation they could find. Even the dead leaves were not immune to the soldiers' hunger, and pine needles were used to brew tea. As the cold weather of winter set in on the mountain, the enemy endured more suffering.

In late December, Lord Nobunaga sent one of his retainers and four escorts to offer surrender terms to the abbot of the main headquarters temple. As the retainer spoke to Abbot Sonrin, he said, "You and your monks should lay down your weapons and return to being monks and disciples of Buddha. If you do, no harm will come to you."

"You fool," Sonrin replied. "We will resist Nobunaga's military aggression to the end and protect our traditions and the light of Buddha with our blood! Now, leave!"

"I'm afraid that you are the fool, Reverend Abbot. How are you going to protect the light of Buddha once your blood is spilled on the ground? What righteous traditions are you protecting? In reality, they are nothing more than deceptions that keep your sect strong and prospering, at the expense of the common people to whom you tell lies, whose silver and food you accept." The retainer then stood up and returned to Lord Nobunaga's camp.

Towards the end of February, several monks wearing plain robes approached Nobunaga's camp with Abbot Sonrin in the lead. "I would like to speak to Lord Nobunaga," Sonrin stated.

When Nobunaga approached, he looked down on the priest and said, "What do you want?"

"I would like to sue for peace."

Nobunaga was enraged. Now that their circumstances were desperate, they wanted peace. "Didn't you refuse my offer just three months ago? Are you and your warriors shameless?" Nobunaga said as he drew his sword.

"I come in peace! To pull your sword is an outrage!" Sonrin shouted.

As Sonrin was turning to leave, Nobunaga swung his sword and severed the abbot's head. "There is your answer. Pick up his head and leave," Nobunaga shouted to the remaining priests.

Nobunaga was sending the remaining warrior monks a clear message. They would pay for their sins with their lives. He ordered his massive force to move upwards. As his well-fed and motivated army climbed the mountain, they killed anyone in their way. They destroyed all the houses, temples, and shrines. By the time Nobunaga's army reached Enryaku-ji—the powerful and famous temple at the summit—it had been burned to the ground. Nobunaga then ordered search parties to eliminate those who had escaped the attack.

In the process, they came upon a monk wearing a purple robe and covered with soot. He was standing his ground at a burned-out shrine, shouting for Lord Nobunaga. In his hand was a magnificent-looking curved, single-edged katana. The white-headed monk went down on his hands and knees, in ashes, and bowed as Nobunaga approached.

"Lord Nobunaga, I am Hayashi Sado. This is a sacred sword given to our order by Emperor Go-Nijo, the 94th emperor of Japan. It is a sword fashioned by none other than the great swordsmith, Masamune, in the 13th century. It has never seen battle or blood. Therefore, as the protector of the sword for the last twenty years, I ask that you take it and return it to the temple at the Imperial Palace in Kyoto," the monk said, laying the sword and its black-lacquered scabbard on the ash-covered ground.

Nobunaga was about to speak and spare the monk's life, but the priest withdrew a dagger from his robe and slashed his own throat.

"Hideyoshi! Hideyoshi!" Nobunaga yelled.

"Here, my lord," General Hideyoshi replied as he sprinted towards his master, thinking he was being attacked.

"Please have some men bury this priest and place a marker over the grave stating his name, Hayashi Sado 'Master of the Sacred Sword.' This priest was a true Buddhist.

Nobunaga picked up the sword and scabbard—and admired the craftsmanship. It was in remarkable condition, and the blade was razor sharp. As he wiped the blade on his sleeve to remove the ashes, he noticed the wavy line along the edge of the blade. It was a hallmark of the swordsmith's technique of repeatedly forging and folding the steel. When he was through admiring the blade, Nobunaga placed the sword in its sheath and called for his page.

"Ranmaru! Ranmaru!" Nobunaga shouted.

The young page came running. When he reached Nobunaga, he bowed low and said, "Yes, Lord."

Nobunaga handed the sword to Ranmaru. "Guard this sacred sword with your life!"

# CHAPTER 2

*Sea of Japan—AD 1948*

Captain Rick Trejo glanced at the chronometer inset into the massive, teak navigation console, to the left of the helm in the motor yacht's luxurious pilothouse. The Thomas Mercer Marine Chronometer was one of the finest built timepieces for ocean navigation in the twentieth century. Trejo reflected that the importance of the timepiece's accuracy could not be overstated, from a paper he had written on the subject during his senior year at the Naval Academy.

Trejo, a stickler for detail and accuracy, knew that deepwater navigation relied on different positioning skills than navigating within the coast's sight. Historically, on the open sea, mariners relied on dead reckoning to determine the vessel's longitude. A navigator could estimate a ship's location, based on speed, course, and elapsed time from the last known position, through dead reckoning. The accuracy of time for these calculations was critical in determining a ship's position.

An inaccuracy of just two seconds per day could mean an error of seventeen miles—after thirty days at sea. The errors accumulating over a long period could throw a ship far off course, as it had done on the night of 22 October 1707. Due to the lack of an accurate timepiece, the navigator of the British Fleet flagship, HMS *Association*, could not accurately calculate the ship's longitude. This error drove the *Association* and four other large warships onto the Isles of Scilly's Western Rocks—a group of uninhabited rocks and skerries. Twenty-five miles off the southwestern tip of England, the archipelago consisted of six large islands and one hundred and thirty-five small rocky islets. As a result of the navigation error, nearly two thousand sailors lost their lives that night.

Thankfully, modern timepieces were exceptionally accurate. The marine chronometer Trejo was admiring was accurate to within a half-second over thirty days. Trejo wasn't anxious about his new ship's navigation errors, although calling the 126-foot luxury yacht a ship was a stretch. Set to retire from the U.S. Navy at the end of the year, Trejo was approached six months earlier by a longtime friend and Naval Academy classmate, Rear Admiral Richard Dubois.

Trejo was in his junior year at the Academy, the year Dubois graduated. In charge of naval intelligence for the Pacific, Dubois asked Trejo to accept another assignment—this one involving clandestine operations. In a secluded Navy dry dock on Tokyo Bay, Dubois gave Trejo a tour of the luxury motor yacht. Halfway through the tour, Trejo was hooked.

The twenty-two-year-old yacht, Dubois explained, had been instrumental in the war in Asia. From February 1944 to the end of the war, *Jacqueline* distinguished herself time and time again as she ferried Allied operatives into and out of Japanese-held territory. When the Japanese surrendered in September of 1945, *Jacqueline* went on a new mission to the Philippine Islands. While there, her American and British operatives helped recover gold and antiquities confiscated by the Japanese Army from the dozen Asian countries it had invaded. The treasure was hidden in caves and tunnels throughout the archipelagos' seven thousand islands. Over two hundred thousand tons of gold alone were recovered. After the mission wrapped up, *Jacqueline* returned to Tokyo harbor. She served American and British operatives on a new mission to retrieve more stolen gold in South Korea.

With her recently rebuilt, twin 305-horsepower, Winston, six-cylinder diesel engines, *Jacqueline* could cruise at twelve knots and reach a top speed of seventeen. She was still one of the fastest and most stable 126-foot luxury yachts in all of Asia. Her crew complement consisted of eight men—seven ordinary seamen and a captain. With her twenty-one-foot beam, eight-and-a-half-foot draft, and upgraded depth sounder, she could enter shallow-water ports—crucial for covert insertion and extraction missions.

*Jacqueline's* recently painted dark blue hull was built with quarter-inch lapped Norwegian steel plating. The plating was secured by countersunk speed rivets to create a smoother hull. In addition, her decks were constructed of two-inch, naturally non-skid teak decking. Teak contains natural oils that protect the wood fibers from harsh marine conditions and makes them resistant to rot and decay. She also had teak panels on the exterior and a large and extravagant teak and mahogany pilothouse. Below deck, the original seven large staterooms, paneled in white oak, were reduced to five, to give more room for the redesigned crew quarters and enlarged galley. The doors to the cabins were made of mahogany, and the hallways featured varnished mahogany panels.

The sea-blue superstructure contained three radio masts and a redesigned double smokestack, to make it look horizontally longer and vertically shorter, further reducing her profile. Permanent sunrooms were constructed on the fantail and foredeck, replacing the canvas sun covers. Navy blue canvas skirts were added to the lower- and upper-deck side railings. And a twenty-foot, partially enclosed, motorized launch replaced the older open launch. To further change her profile, the plumb bow was replaced by a clipper bow, which improved the center of buoyancy and the yacht's stability, essential for open ocean sailing.

"During the day, she is an astonishingly beautiful yacht, but at night she is nearly invisible," Admiral Dubois said, "which is what we want in this business."

After Dubois gave Trejo the background of the yacht, he told him. "As much as we tried masking her looks, she's still known in some intelligence circles as a spy ship. This will make your job more dangerous. Unfortunately, the four M2 .50-caliber machine guns won't be installed until after returning from your first mission. However, I think you will find the design quite unique. The forward gun will pop up from a built-in locker below the deck. The aft deck gun will be disguised as an equipment locker. The two on the upper deck will look like fan-driven ventilation shafts. We're working with

Browning to get ammunition belts that hold 500 rounds versus the standard belt that only holds a hundred."


By September 1948, *Jacqueline* was on a new covert mission. Her job was to infiltrate a team of Allied agents into North Korea and gather intelligence on a suspected influx of Soviet weapons and tanks. Over four days, *Jacqueline* traveled six hundred and fifty miles. She sailed south from Tokyo, passing the southeastern-most tip of Kyushu Island near its largest city, Kagoshima, and entered the East China Sea. She then proceeded north for two hundred miles before entering the Sea of Japan and turning due north toward the team's destination—near the 38th parallel.

At twelve hundred hours, one hundred and ten miles northeast of the island of Shimayama, Captain Trejo was returning to the wheelhouse after dispatching four lookouts—two to the forward and two to the aft deck. First, he gazed upward at the brilliant autumn sky, clear and pale blue—the color of a robin's egg. Then, as he entered the wheelhouse, he called to the helmsman.

"Slow to five knots," Trejo ordered.

"Aye, sir. Slowing to five knots," the first mate replied.

"Activate the ADF," Trejo said to the radio operator sitting at a small desk facing the aft bulkhead.

"ADF activated, sir," the radio operator replied after he flipped the transmit toggle switch on the automatic direction finder radio to "On." The ADF was now sending a bearing that the incoming PBY Catalina, equipped with an ADF receiver, could home in on and fly directly to the *Jacqueline.*

Captain Trejo picked up his SCR-536 hand-held radio transceiver, called a *walkie-talkie.* He pushed the 'Press to Talk' switch and contacted his lookouts, "The PBY should be due south at five thousand feet."

A few minutes later, one of the lookout stations called, "Captain, aft deck. I have an aircraft to the east, approximately six miles. Appears to be headed directly towards us. It's not a PBY, sir."

"It might be a Navy or Air Force fighter on a training flight. They have a gunnery range to the west of Iki Island. Can you identify the type of aircraft?" Trejo replied.

"Not yet, sir."

Several minutes went by before the lookout called again, "Captain, aft deck. The approaching aircraft is a single-engine, low-wing monoplane equipped with floats. It appears to be a Japanese *Paul*, sir. And she's carrying a bomb."

The *Paul* or Aichi E16A was a two-seat reconnaissance seaplane. During the Pacific War, it was operated by the Imperial Japanese Navy (IJN) Air Service. The Air Service was responsible for the operation of all IJN aircraft and conducting aerial warfare. Against a lightly armed yacht, it was not to be ignored.

The Aichi E16A was 35 feet, six inches long, and had a wingspan of 42 feet. It was powered by a Mitsubishi MK8D Kinsei radial engine. The Kinsei was a 1,300-horsepower, air-cooled, twin-row radial engine that could cruise the aircraft at 207 miles per hour (mph). Her armament consisted of two fixed, forward-firing, 20 mm, Type 99, Mark 2 machine guns mounted in the wings, and one rearward-firing, 13 mm, Type 2 machine gun for the observer. The *Paul* was also capable of carrying two 551-pound bombs.

Seconds later, the two men on the forward deck became aware of twin, winking flashes of light emanating from the aircraft's wings. Both men dived behind cover as the 20 mm bullets stitched their way on the water's surface and began pelting *Jacqueline's* deck.

One of the lookouts yelled over the radio, "We're under attack!"

"Evasive maneuvers," Captain Trejo ordered. Immediately, the first mate swung the wheel to starboard. Captain Trejo didn't wait to hear the sound of the bullets striking the yacht. He immediately picked up the ship's interphone and called, "Battle stations. Air attack!"

Everyone in the wheelhouse ducked as the 20 mm bullets struck the yacht's top and penetrated the wooden roof. Before the aircraft pulled up, the pilot released its 250-kilogram bomb. The bomb missed—but exploded dangerously close to the *Jacqueline*, sending a geyser of water 150 feet into the air.

After the aircraft passed over *Jacqueline*, Captain Trejo stood up and grabbed the radio handset, "To any Allied aircraft or warships, MAYDAY! MAYDAY! MAYDAY! This is the French vessel, *Jacqueline*. We are under attack from a Japanese fighter aircraft. Our location is one hundred and fifty miles northeast of Iki Island. I say again, MAYDAY! MAYDAY! MAYDAY! This is the French vessel, *Jacqueline*. We are under attack from a Japanese fighter...."

Before Captain Trejo completed his radio transmission, the two crew members working in the galley rushed Thompson submachine guns from the armory to the fore and aft decks. After turning them over to the lookouts, they ran back for more Thompsons and additional ammunition. As the low-flying *Paul* made a second pass on the *Jacqueline* and began strafing the ship's length, the lookouts started returning fire.

Fifteen miles to the south, a British PBY Catalina, descending through six thousand feet, heard the Mayday call. The pilot sent the radio operator to the bunk compartment to ask his two passengers to put on their radio headsets.

"Colonels, we need you on headsets. We're getting a distress call from *Jacqueline*."

Jon Preston and George Linka donned their headsets in time to hear a second Mayday call from the motor yacht that was abruptly cut short. Preston asked the radio operator, "Are the machine guns in the nose turret loaded?"

"Negative, sir," replied the radio operator.

"Is there any ammunition for the waist blister guns stored in the floor panel?"

"Aye, sir. There's a full complement of ammunition."

As part of their cover for covert activities during World War Two, Jon and George were qualified as waist-gunners on the Consolidated PBY Catalina. Now, neither hesitated. They pulled on the metal rings, which were attached to the floorboard panels beside each gun, and then removed the lids. They then pulled out several cans of belted ammunition for the two Browning M2 .50-caliber machine guns, mounted against the aircraft's port and starboard walls. Jon and George opened the blister windows and positioned the 45-inch barrels into the aircrafts slipstream. Each unlocked the bolt latch release on the gun he was loading, pulled the bolt lock's retracting handle backward, and raised the bolt cover. After releasing the retracting handle and moving the bolt forward, each inserted a cloth belt loop of cartridges into the feed tray of the gun he held and then closed the cover. When each pulled the retracting handle of the gun backward and released it, a .50-caliber round was injected into the chamber. The two guns were then ready to fire.

Despite the three years since they had touched the machine guns, both men accomplished the task in under four minutes. When Jon turned and nodded to George, they fired each weapon to make sure it worked. When the pilot heard the machine guns firing, he knew immediately what the two operatives had in mind.

After leveling off at two thousand, the pilot called to Jon and George, "The Jap aircraft is a quarter-mile ahead moving northeast, positioning for another run on the yacht. I will pull in two hundred feet above and behind the Jap, aft of its starboard wing. I'll feed in enough rudder and move the rear of the plane to the left. The port gun gets the first shot. Kill the bastard quickly. I don't want him turning on us. We don't have any cloud banks to hide in."

The PBY's parasol wing and large-waist blister opening provided excellent visibility. George put on a pair of goggles, hanging next to the gun, and stood in the port blister watching as the Aichi E16A came into view. The reconnaissance aircraft pilot was so focused on his next strafing run that he didn't see the PBY slip in behind his plane. Despite the strong wind coming through the blister opening, George held the machine gun steady—and waited. When the rear of the PBY turned enough for a clear shot, George sighted slightly ahead of the fighter's engine and began firing.

At first, the pilot of the *Paul* thought his aircraft was being struck by fire from the motor yacht. It wasn't until several rounds punctured the right side of his canopy that he looked right and saw the lumbering British PBY firing at his plane. Before he could move the control stick and turn away, a dozen more bullets punctured the cockpit's thin metal, killing him instantly. As the *Paul* flipped to port and did a nose dive toward the sea, George continued pouring .50-caliber rounds into the aircraft, igniting the fuel tanks in the thin metal wings. Seconds later, the burning plane plunged into the ocean and disappeared.

The PBY circled *Jacqueline,* trying to contact her on the radio. The pilot landed in the two-foot swells and then taxied next to the immobile yacht when she didn't respond. When the plane stopped, the motorized launch was in the water and moving toward the aircraft. As Jon prepared to disembark from the PBY, one of the yacht's armorers, Brunelle, greeted him with a smiling face while handing him a line to secure the launch to the plane.

"Make fast," Brunelle yelled over the engine noise. "We've got several bullet holes in the bottom. I don't want you gentlemen having to swim to the *Jacqueline.*"


When Preston and Linka entered the spacious main salon, Captain Trejo was treating Jim Ballangy—the British agent wounded by shrapnel. Trejo, a tall, slender man with a handsome face and slightly greying, short black hair, turned to the two agents, "He's stable for now, but I don't have the skills to remove the bullet fragment from his back. I gave him enough morphine to knock him out, but I need to put him on the PBY and have him flown directly to our naval facility at Fukuoka."

"Brunelle communicated your request before we left the PBY. I contacted Brigadier MacKenzie and received permission for the pilot to fly directly there," Jon replied. "There will be an ambulance waiting on the runway. You can use our portable shortwave until you can repair the radio."

"Thanks, but I'm afraid the radio is beyond repair. The fighter knocked it out on the second pass," Trejo responded.

"Any other damage?" Preston asked.

"Just some minor damage in the galley and engine room. A couple of holes in the hull, but there is only minor leakage. We'll have it repaired once we're in port. That bomb dropped really close. Do you guys have any idea what is going on?" Captain Trejo inquired.

"Only that it's clear the mission is compromised. Brigadier MacKenzie wants us to stay with you and head to Fukuoka for repairs and further instructions. It will take close to twenty hours to reach the port. Maybe by then, we'll have more than rudimentary guesses from the British SIS on how we were compromised."

# CHAPTER 3



General Omar Bradley, the U.S. Army Chief of Staff, sat grim-faced, listening to his Deputy Chief of Staff for Intelligence (G-2) brief on the *Jacqueline* incident. Major General Lew Miller had been in intelligence, throughout World War Two, as a Colonel with G-2, and now he headed up the intelligence organization. Lieutenant General John Renick, General Bradley's deputy and the former head of G-2, sat quietly reflecting on the situation.

"Based on information from his sources in Tokyo, Colonel Linka believes that General Uchito Tsukuda is behind the attack. As you know, Tsukuda now heads up an underground criminal organization in Japan, headquartered in Tokyo. He was responsible for planning and executing the submarine attacks on the Panama Canal and the east coast, just before the war ended. Agent Preston and his team are the ones directly responsible for preventing the attacks on Washington, Baltimore, and Philadelphia," General Miller stated.

"So, you think Tsukuda is doing this to retaliate against the U.S. for stopping the two submarines?" asked General Bradley.

"Yes, sir," Miller replied. "But more specifically, against Agent Preston and his team. It's become personal for Tsukuda—because Preston's team killed three of his nieces in Calcutta during the war. Asami Nakada, also a niece, was the second-in-command of his organization. Nakada was responsible for getting the biological weapon ashore in Virginia and into Washington. She was shot and killed by Preston's wife when she attacked them at their home near the Naval Observatory."

"Sir, we also believe that Tsukuda is colluding with both the Chinese and Soviets. He is smuggling munitions by boat into North Korea," General Renick added. "Our friend in Naval Intelligence, Admiral Richard Dubois, passed us copies of naval intercepts a month ago—when I was still in command of G-2. Those intercepts suggest the Soviets are funneling massive amounts of weapons through China into North Korea. And this week, Brigadier MacKenzie—Commander of the British Secret Intelligence Service (SIS) in Asia—provided information from his sources confirming the shipments. MacKenzie told us that Tsukuda is employing dozens of small freighters to transport weapons from Dandong, China, to Nampo, North Korea. Nampo is only 125 miles north of Seoul."

"It sounds like Tsukuda is becoming a threat to our national security, gentlemen. What are we doing to stop him?" asked General Bradley.

"We have sent an agent into deep cover in Tokyo. He is searching for Tsukuda. As soon as he finds him and contacts Agent Preston, we will strike," Miller said.

"This damn well better stay totally covert! I can't afford for MacArthur or the CIA to get wind of this."

"We understand, sir. That is why Preston, Linka, and our deep-cover agent are on temporary loan to the British SIS. Only the three of us and President Truman are aware of this mission in the States. General Sage in Tokyo, and Brigadier MacKenzie, are the only others. Sage is our inside man on General MacArthur's staff. He will be fully protected by Truman, should MacArthur find him out and fire him. Preston and Linka are under direct orders from the President to take Tsukuda down. And Truman will bear all the heat if this goes public."

"God help us if it ever does. This Congress is a bunch of hungry wolves looking for any reason to take money away from the military and make Truman look bad."


Guy Wong was a native-born Asian American and a member of Jonathan Preston's special counterintelligence team. His parents still owned and operated a jewelry store and a laundry business in San Francisco. Guy was the child of a mixed marriage. Wong's Japanese grandmother was forced into prostitution after her white merchant marine husband died from the Bubonic plague in 1908. Having a mixed daughter was worse than being full-blooded Japanese, but it didn't matter to Guy's Chinese father, who had been crippled as a child.

Growing up, learning to speak both Mandarin Chinese and Japanese proved advantageous for Wong. When recruited by Army intelligence in May 1943, Guy Wong was about to graduate from the University of Southern California with a degree in mathematics. As a condition of his recruitment, Wong leveraged the Army's need for Japanese-speaking recruits and got his mother released from the Manzanar internment camp, 250 miles southeast of San Francisco. Within a week of the Army providing documentation that she was Chinese, she was back with her husband running the family businesses in San Francisco.

From June through August 1943, Wong attended Officer Candidate School in Miami, Florida, and then moved to Counterintelligence Corps (CIC) training. The CIC training focused on uncovering treason, sedition, subversive activity, and detecting, preventing, and neutralizing espionage and sabotage activities. After completing the CIC training at Camp Ritchie, Maryland, Wong attended covert operative training, 18 miles south, at Catoctin Mountain Park, Maryland, before moving 100 miles further south to Prince William Forest Park, Virginia. Both locations were run by the Office of Strategic Services or OSS.

At Catoctin Mountain Park, Wong learned knife-fighting and close-combat techniques. At Prince William Forest Park, he was taught how to use every handgun, rifle, and submachine gun, in the U.S. inventory, as well as most weapons in the European, Chinese, Soviet, and Japanese arsenals. He also learned Morse code, ciphers for performing encryption and decryption, covert radio practices, and radio maintenance.

His training at Prince William Forest Park included making and disarming booby traps and low-level parachute jumps from aircraft.

He also learned how to operate behind enemy lines and conduct sabotage missions. The OSS training also included martial arts; however, from age five, Wong had trained in martial arts with his Chinese grandfather, a master in Wushu and Mizongyi. His grandfather received his training in northern China from a Wushu master named Huo Yuanjia. Yuanjia also specialized in Mizongyi—a Chinese martial art based on deceptive hand movements, kicks, and mobility.

Guy Wong first met Jon Preston and George Linka when they infiltrated northern China to kidnap Lieutenant General Shiro Ito during World War Two. General Ito was the Japanese microbiologist and army medical officer who commanded the infamous Unit 731.

Unit 731was responsible for creating the deadliest biological weapons in the Japanese arsenal. The unit's compound in Northeast China covered nearly six square miles and held over one hundred and fifty buildings. The ten thousand personnel who worked there included most of Japan's best and brightest medical and scientific minds. From 1937 to 1945, Unit 731 conducted biological and chemical weapon experiments. The Chinese believed that Ito personally directed the mass murder of 200–600 thousand Chinese citizens, to perfect the weapons. In addition to captured Chinese and allied soldiers, Unit 731 victims include civilian men, women, and children. Even whole villages were wiped out in the name of Japanese science.

With the help of Wong and his Chinese operative network, Preston and Linka successfully removed Ito and his wife and child from Harbin's Pingfang district. The agents ended Ito's reign of biological terror, but not before Ito shipped a new and more powerful biological weapon to General Tsukuda. Now, Wong was on the trail of the monster that deployed the two submarines, which attempted to unleash the biological weapon on American soil. He would just as soon terminate Tsukuda's life. But, Preston and the higher-ups in Washington also wanted to eliminate Tsukuda's network as well. This meant following him and collecting information on his organization.


The rain was beginning to drizzle, but the heavy, dark skies would soon open up into a torrential downfall, which was not unusual for

March in Tokyo. Wong had tailed Tsukuda on his homemade scooter, made by attaching a small two-stroke gasoline engine to a bicycle. The trail ended at a warehouse located east of the Tokyo metropolitan area, adjacent to the Arakawa River. Although American money was helping rebuild the recently renamed Koto ward, many of the buildings and warehouses in the area were still burned-out shells left over from the war.

Wong, wearing a worn, dark raincoat, parked his scooter and put on a well-worn, dark-colored diamond crown wool fedora over his shaved head. He tipped it down over his forehead just enough to hide his face but still reveal the five-inch scar on his left cheek, which gave him a menacing look. The oversized raincoat hid his muscular arms and torso as well as the MP 40 submachine gun, slung on a small leather strap hanging from his neck. The .40-caliber machine pistol carried a 32-round magazine. It was several pounds lighter than the Thompson submachine gun he carried during the war. *It is definitely more maneuverable and more concealable*, Wong thought.

Agent Wong had tracked the incognito Tsukuda from an office building near downtown Tokyo to this area near the piers. When Tsukuda got out of the 1936 Toyota AA Standard Sedan, he was escorted by two bodyguards into a rundown electrical supply store.

Wong watched from an alley across the street from the electrical supply store. The narrow passageway lay between an auto body shop and an Ososhiki, where funeral services were held. Once Tsukuda entered the shop, one of the bodyguards locked the front door and turned off the lights. Seconds later, lights were turned on in an upstairs room.

Within minutes, four of Wong's Asian counterintelligence agents, dressed like homeless people and dock workers, were stationing themselves around a two-block area of the parts store. As they settled in to watch, along with the other homeless people rummaging through the alley and trash bins, the rainfall soaked their clothes and chilled them to numbness. An hour later, when the upstairs light was extinguished, and no one exited the building, Wong contacted Preston and Linka via his handheld SCR-536 radio transceiver.

Preston and Linka were waiting in a Japanese Type 95 Kurogane 4x4, parked near the British Consulate, five miles away.

"The lights are off, but no one has exited the building. Tsukuda may be settling in for the night. I think now is the time to strike. I should be able to take Tsukuda with my four agents," Wong said.

"Negative. Stay invisible and wait until we arrive. George and I will be there with another team of agents in 30 minutes. Whatever you do, stay alert and check on your agents every 10 minutes. Tsukuda is clever and even more dangerous. For all we know, he may have men in every building around there," Preston stated.

Agent Wong did as ordered. Every 10 minutes, he conducted a visual check with his four agents by meandering through the alleys with the other rain-soaked mendicants. During the third check, Wong circled the block to where an agent was stationed. He found the agent sitting against the side of the building with his throat cut. As Wong circled the blocks around the electrical supply store, he noticed that the other vagrants were no longer there. He discovered the remaining agents were all dead. When he returned to his scooter, Preston and Linka were waiting.

"They're all dead," Wong told them. Visibly upset, he added. "Throats cut from ear to ear."

"Crap, he's out-foxed us. This is my fault, Guy. I should have anticipated that Tsukuda would be prepared," Preston remarked angrily. "Let's go ahead and enter the building. I'm certain that everyone will be gone. We'll probably find a tunnel leading to a building one or two blocks away."

"No telling where he is now," Linka stated. "Hell, he may be watching us from another building, laughing his butt off. But you can be certain—Tsukuda will try to hit us where it hurts the most. He may even send people after Camille and Katie."

"I hope not," Preston replied.

"It's a good thing you had General Miller move the girls to the Marine Barracks while we were gone. Miller should be able to protect them on the base."

"Yes, but how long will they stay cooped up? You know damn well that Katie and Camille think they can take care of themselves.

And Camille will believe she is even more dangerous now that she has Jonathan Jr. to protect."

"All the same, we should send a message and warn General Renick as soon as we get back to the consulate," Linka replied.

On the way to the British Consulate, a thousand things that could go wrong filtered through Jon's mind. However, it didn't take long for Jon to come up with a plan. He turned to George, "If Tsukuda wants to hit us, let's give him the opportunity back in D.C."

"There are no parades in Washington in February, Jon," Linka replied, making reference to their past entanglement with Asami Nakada.

"No, but we can arrange a location to our advantage."

"What do you have in mind?" Linka asked.

"Remember, our friend, Elton Fitzsimmons?"

"The fisherman, smuggler, and twice-convicted felon from the brig at Anacostia Naval Air Station?"

"Yep, that's the one."

"You think he can help?"

"He helped us find Asami Nakada's cohort, Haru Aki. Maybe he has his ears to the ground and can tell us about any new Asian visitors on the docks."

"You think he is up to his old habits?"

"A tiger can't change his stripes, but he can get wiser and make fewer mistakes. After all, we saved his kids from Aki. I'm thinking he might be grateful for that and help us out. Despite his background, he's still a patriot," Preston reminded him.

"It's worth a shot. As long as no one has found out that Fitzsimmons was the one who ratted on Aki."

"I'm pretty sure he's the type to keep his mouth closed when it comes to saving his own life. I'll have General Renick put eyes on him."

"He'll find them out within an hour," Linka said, confidently.

"I'm counting on it. Just think how relieved he'll be when we show up."

"What do we do with Guy Wong?"

"We bring him with us. He'll be a greater asset to the team, working alone, as he did in China. Plus, he knows the D.C. area from when he was doing his OSS training. He walked those streets for weeks, learning to tail a suspect. Wong knows all the Asian haunts, his uncle is still with the State Department, and he has other family and friends there. I'll have General Renick set him up with a cover as an Asian gem importer with lots of gems and cash. He'll be able to fit in and build a network of friends and informants in no time at all."

"You're planning to team him up with Elton Fitzsimmons, aren't you?"

"Let's see, gem importer with cash, and a smuggler with brains and a love of money—nothing like creating a little intrigue on the docks and in the Georgetown community. Word is sure to get to Tsukuda's informants. Plus, Tsukuda is a man of opportunity when it comes to expanding his organization with known or suspected criminals."

"You don't think Tsukuda knows it was Wong following him?" Linka asked.

"It's doubtful. Wong had been careful to disguise himself the entire time in Tokyo. He stayed in the shadows and let his Japanese and Eurasian agents follow Tsukuda. If he grows his hair back and a mustache, removes the fake pockmarks and the scar on his left cheek, gets rid of the built-up nose, and ditches the elevator shoes, he's a new entity."

# CHAPTER 4



*Washington, D.C.*

Jonathan Preston slumped in the overstuffed chair in the living room of his Georgetown house. He was worried about Camille, Jonathan Jr., and his team of agents. Uchito Tsukuda, the former Imperial Japanese Army major general and intelligence czar who had evolved into and murderous underworld chieftain after Japan's surrender, was a festering thorn in his side.

The death of the Japanese assassin, Asami Nakada, was a slap to Tsukuda's face. Despite her success in smuggling a biological weapon into Washington, D.C., Asami's plan failed when Camille put a bullet in her forehead. Preston did not doubt that Tsukuda would soon be sending assassins to attempt to take out the rest of his team and complete what Nakada failed to do. The loss of face was unacceptable to a Japanese general turned organized crime leader; it made him look weak. And weakness attracted the attention of other crime organizations. If he didn't rectify the situation, they would be coming after him. Organized crime organizations didn't like competition, and they didn't respect a weak competitor.

Jon reflected on his team's success in neutralizing the Japanese assassin and the Japanese submarine, *I-405*, over a year ago. It also presented another problem—a man by the name of President Harry Truman. President Truman wanted to go public with the mission information, which would bolster his administration's falling approval ratings. He wanted Americans to know the truth about Japan's treachery. Truman believed it would take the public's eye away from the sagging peacetime economy and rally people to his side. The President thought that U.S. citizens deserved to know about the depths of depravity that Japan would bow to—a rogue mission implemented purely for vengeance and designed to create unimaginable human death and suffering. He was convinced that people would see him as a more decisive leader and rally to his side because his actions saved millions of American lives.

President Truman was planning to recognize Jon Preston and his team members in a public award ceremony at the White House. Preston knew if Truman went public, it would jeopardize the safety of his team and their families. It would create enmity towards all things Japanese. It would endanger the safety and security of Japanese Americans recently released from relocation camps. If enough citizens complained to Congress, it could also slow down Japan's reconstruction by removing the vital funding needed to get their fragile economy on track. It would also destroy his and his team's career in counterintelligence by compromising who they are and what they did for the U.S. Army. Jon could see nothing positive coming from such a move.

Before retiring, General Dwight D. Eisenhower, the Army Chief of Staff, asked the president to keep it top secret. Unfortunately, Eisenhower's solicitation had little influence on the president. Only Preston's personal plea during a closed meeting at the White House worked. At the meeting where Jon, George Linka, Camille Dupont, and Kathleen Lauren were personally thanked for their success, President Truman began to comprehend the danger of exposing the Japanese mission.

One of the president's closest advisors, David Niles, was in the Oval Office when Preston made his case. Niles, a Polish Jew, had escaped from Russia as a large-scale wave of anti-Jewish riots began sweeping through southwestern Imperial Russia. After hearing Preston's argument, Niles told the president that a Japanese pogrom would be quite possible if the information were released.

Preston's argument to not go public struck a chord with the president. With General Uchito Tsukuda still at large, Jon's pregnant wife would be vulnerable to reprisal from the criminal mastermind. Finally, Truman relented and agreed to keep it top secret. Partially, he did so because Jon was the son of one of the president's best friends and fellow artillery officers from World War One. But mostly, because not doing so could also tarnish his presidency and threaten his 1948 presidential campaign.

"You're right, Agent Preston," President Truman replied in a private conversation after thanking the team. "We don't need more hatred against all things Japanese. As a Senator from Missouri, I had to fight to keep Missouri and Tennessee from enacting legislation to issue licenses to hunt down Japanese invaders at a fee of $2 per head after the attack on Pearl Harbor. It could have quickly turned into anyone Japanese or Asian, not just enemy invaders. Tennessee was most difficult and responded to my attempts by stating that an open season on Japs required no license."

Preston nodded. He had read about Tennessee's attempt to issue licenses to hunt Japanese in 1941. He urged the president to let him and George go to Japan and take Tsukuda down. President Truman agreed to the request, but only after Camille gave birth to her baby.

"Agent Preston, you and your team have been doing cloak and dagger work for nearly five years straight. You've earned a rest. I want you all to stand down for six months and get refreshed before going after that thug," President Truman stated.

"Thank you, Mr. President," Jon replied.

"General Miller," the President said to the newly appointed U.S. Army Deputy Chief of Staff for Intelligence, "Place Jon's team on Pentagon duty for six months in your directorate. I would recommend that you put them in charge of covert agent recruitment and training. Maybe they can create an elite cadre of agents with the same skill sets that they've acquired. Afterward, you can loan Jon's team to the British SIS and begin planning the mission to take down General Tsukuda. Just keep in mind that Tsukuda has powerful supporters in Tokyo that can cause the U.S. a lot of trouble. What you do must be done in absolute secrecy without Congress, the CIA, and General MacArthur's knowledge. This will be a mission sanctioned by me, personally, to eliminate a threat to our national security. Only you, General Eisenhower, and General Renick need to know about this mission. Perhaps you and Preston could solicit your old friend from Calcutta, Brigadier MacKenzie, for help. Tell MacKenzie, we'll give the British SIS $10 million to help."

"I'll take care of it, Mr. President," General Miller replied.

"In the meantime, I want Jon and George attending as many high-profile parties and official functions in Washington as possible, along with Camille and Kathleen, of course. I've already told General Eisenhower that I want you grooming Jon and George for a flag rank. To pull that off without proclaiming what they've done to save this country, they'll need visibility and lots of it. You can tell people that they were the two most successful and decorated covert operatives to come out of the war in Asia. Everything they did was classified top-secret for the next fifty years. That should create a buzz. They can start by attending the Armistice Day affair that I'm hosting at the White House. They will be the only officers below lieutenant general invited, and probably the only two with the Medal of Honor. That will get people's attention."

A week later, President Truman held a private ceremony in the Oval Office and awarded the Medal of Honor to Jon Preston and George Linka and the Distinguished Service Cross to Camille Dupont and Kathleen Lauren for their heroic efforts in stopping the rogue submarine attack. The reasons behind the medals would remain classified top secret for the next fifty years.


Over the next six months, Jon, George, Camille, and Kathleen spent their time developing a program for training a team of counterintelligence agents for use in covert operations. Of the four hundred soldiers who had applied for the specialized training, three hundred were cut. Those who were accepted spoke one or more foreign languages and had technical skills needed by a covert operative. Twenty-five percent of the applicants were of Asian descent and could speak and write in their native tongue. If they survived the training, those whose language skills included Japanese would work directly with Jon when they got the green light to go after Uchito Tsukuda. The others would deploy to other parts of Europe and Asia to help stop communist expansion threats.

A week after receiving their medals, Jon and George began attending one party a week. They hobnobbed with high-powered attorneys, industrialists, Congress members, ambassadors, and senior uniformed services members. On many occasions, General Eisenhower would personally introduce them to the most influential attendees and their spouses. The ruggedly handsome Preston and his beautiful wife, along with the poised and polished George Linka and his gorgeous date Kathleen, were well-received at each event.

At one party, Jon engaged in a conversation with the Under Secretary of State, Robert Lovett, and the future Secretary of State, Dean Acheson. Jon quickly ascertained that these men believed it was within their power to change world events and stop the Communist takeovers in Europe and Asia. After avoiding discussing any specifics on the subject, Jon quietly corralled Camille, George, and Kathleen and then slipped out of the party.

"What was that all about?" Camille asked.

"These damn Ivy League Washington elitists think they can control the world," Jon replied. "They are more dangerous than Stalin and Mao Tse-tung together. Some of them were OSS agents in Europe; none served in Asia. They talked about controlling French Indochina, Laos, Cambodia, Burma, and Thailand. Yet, they know nothing about Asia or the Asian mindset. If we're not careful, these idiots will get us into a war that we cannot possibly win. If I had stayed any longer, they would have involved me further in their conversation. I would have told them how irresponsible they were thinking; it would have destroyed all of our careers. I can only attempt to discourage what they are planning. I will need to meet with President Truman and convince him to stop any attempted armed force against Stalin and the Chinese."

"You think he will listen?" Linka asked.

"George, we cannot possibly stop what is happening in Asia—because we don't have the intelligence-gathering capabilities or the men and material to stop them. We don't have an army anymore, we don't know the languages, and no one comprehends how the Asians think. Truman needs to understand this more than anything. We need a larger, active intelligence organization to collect information.

Only then can we counter what the communists are planning. We all recognized this in our fight against Japan in Indochina. Still, no one remembers what was responsible for our success. Plus, we know damn well that the State Department was always clueless. They wouldn't listen to my recommendations about the Viet Minh being the strongest political force in French Indochina. Now they've taken over half the country. I just hope we can put intelligence-gathering assets in place before it's too late."

"What about Tsukuda, Jon? How do we stop him?" Camille pleaded.

"I've got an appointment with General Miller tomorrow," Jon replied. "I'm hoping he will let us go after Tsukuda and end this game."


Major General Lew Miller listened as Jonathan Preston proposed his mission to Tokyo to take down Uchito Tsukuda. General Miller thought it was a good plan, but that the timing was wrong. Despite President Truman's promise to maintain a strong military presence at a level high enough to convince U.S. enemies that we would not tolerate totalitarianism, the U.S. Congress cut military spending dramatically. It went from $556.9 million to $52.4 million, annually.

"Jon, I understand what you want to accomplish. Tsukuda and his organization need to be destroyed. Still, my budget for Asia does not have the funding needed to carry out a sophisticated intelligence operation like you're proposing. Over the last six months, Congress has decimated my funding. I'm not even certain the President can move any funding to my directorate without congressional approval. As extensive as the Tsukuda Organization is today, we would need a hundred highly trained agents. Not to mention the time and cost to develop a network of several hundred domestic agents in Japan. Plus, if word leaks to the CIA, they will rain on our parade and say it's their responsibility, which it is. And let's not forget that Japan is under General MacArthur's rule, and General Willoughby rules military intelligence with an iron hand in Japan," General Miller stated. "Willoughby would convince MacArthur to kick us out of Japan."

"Sir, the CIA knows nothing about Japan. All of the people they've posted to Tokyo came out of the European Theater, and they know nothing about Asians. Only a few speak Japanese—no more than a handful. And they sure as hell don't have the established network of Japanese citizens that George and I have in Tokyo. Nor does General Willoughby. Plus, Willoughby is as arrogant as his boss, and disregards hard-gained intelligence that doesn't please General MacArthur's palate," Preston replied.

"Jon, you're preaching to the choir. I'm just as frustrated. Because of the budget cuts, the Chief of Staff has informed me that my counterintelligence agents can only investigate crimes committed by American soldiers. Hell, my hands are tied. On the other hand, I have a request from the British Secret Intelligence Service (SIS) that might interest you."

"Does it entail going back to Southeast Asia?"

"Not at this time. The request came from Brigadier Michael MacKenzie after receiving a message from a Catholic priest in Port Arthur, China—a priest named Father William Kirkendall. I believe you worked with him when you were recovering buried gold and antiquities at the Stella Maris Catholic Church."

"Yes, Father Kirkendall was an expert on ancient Chinese art. He was responsible for saving over two thousand art pieces and other antiquities that the Japanese stole from Chinese museums, universities, and art collectors. Quite an achievement for a parish priest," Jon stated.

"Brigadier MacKenzie has asked that you and George be loaned to the SIS to handle a mission into Korea. Father Kirkendall personally passed intelligence to the Brigadier from a former OSS agent that worked with your gold recovery mission in Korea."

"You're speaking of Captain Kim Jung?" Jon surmised.

"Yes, Jung is now working for British Intelligence. He sent disturbing information about a large buildup of Chinese and North Korean forces two hundred miles north of the 38th parallel. Jung is requesting a meeting with you and Colonel Linka at Mangsang-myeon Village, fifty miles south of the 38th parallel. He's staying at the Samhwasa Temple, at the base of Mt. Dutasan, and the entrance of the Mureung Valley," General Miller said.

"Why doesn't he meet with Brigadier MacKenzie or his top agents, Miles Murphy and Henri Morreau? He worked with them on the same mission."

"The message from Captain Jung was hand-delivered by Father Kirkendall to the Brigadier himself when the Brigadier was in Port Arthur, several weeks ago. The message stated that Jung would only meet with you and Linka. Jung either doesn't trust the British—or he feels a Chinese, Soviet, or North Korean informant has infiltrated the Brigadier's organization. Brigadier MacKenzie immediately read between the lines of Jung's message and sent the request via an SIS courier directly to my office. No one in his SIS organization is privy to this information, and only you and I have seen it at the Pentagon."

"It's obvious that Jung suspects a double agent. I would handle the situation the same way. When do we leave?" Jonathan asked.

"Orders assigning you, Linka, and Wong as U.S. Army liaison officers are being cut as we speak. You will be officially assigned to the British Security Intelligence Far East (SIFE) detachment in Hong Kong. You and Linka will depart via military transport on Thursday morning. That gives you two days to smooth things out with Camille and kiss her goodbye. You'll wear your military uniforms while on the US military flights. While in Honolulu, you'll be the guest of Vice-Admiral Dubois. He's working closely with British intelligence and Brigadier MacKenzie on the Korea issue. Dubois is now in charge of all naval intelligence for the Pacific and Asia. Once you arrive at Subic Bay in the Philippines, a British aircraft will pick you up and fly you to Okinawa. A British PBY will then fly you to the Sea of Japan, where you'll rendezvous with *Jacqueline*. One of the Brigadier's most trusted agents will be onboard the yacht when it leaves Tokyo. I don't know who, but the message stated that you would recognize him. The agent will bring you up to speed on the mission."

"What about weapons?"

"Brigadier MacKenzie is furnishing everything you require. I'm hoping it will be a one-week, get-in-and-get-out mission. Whatever the Soviets and North Koreans are planning is probably just an exercise. At least that's what the CIA and MacArthur's group in Tokyo are saying. However, I had lunch with an Air Force buddy of mine, Major General Earle Partridge, the commander of the Fifth Air Force in Japan. He was in town to report on American airpower in the Pacific. He has an Air Force intelligence officer in South Korea who is providing real-time information on North Korea. The intelligence officer tells him that the leader of North Korea, Kim Il-sung, is prodding Stalin to approve an attack on South Korea. He says the Soviets are slowly sending troops, tanks, and aircraft into North Korea at night. Partridge's source expects North Korea to be strong enough to attack within twelve to eighteen months."

"Surely he's sending his information to General Willoughby?"

General Miller hesitated, then continued, "To Willoughby, yes, but it goes no further. MacArthur has the incentive to play down the likelihood of war in Korea. With all the budget cuts, MacArthur barely has enough soldiers to occupy Japan. He feels that proposing the occupation of South Korea would not get support from the Pentagon, Congress, or President Truman. In truth, Korea has been written off as a strategic interest."

"But still, if the Chinese and Soviets are backing a North Korean invasion, shouldn't Washington be concerned?"

"It should, but General Willoughby doesn't trust Air Force intelligence, and as I said, none of the intelligence has made it to Washington. General Partridge does not want to take on Willoughby or MacArthur by back-channeling the information. He asked me if there was anything I could do. That's why I'm approving your loan to the British. If there is a build-up, I want solid evidence—unit names, strengths, and locations. The SIS has two additional sources providing similar intelligence, according to Brigadier MacKenzie. Suppose you and George find out that the Chinese and Soviets are moving massive amounts of troops into North Korea, and the build-up is real. In that case, we'll let British Intelligence present it to the Army Chief of Staff. The intelligence you gather will be used only to collaborate about what the Brits present to the Joint Chiefs. It's turned into a political fight, Jon. Plus, there are a lot of MacArthur supporters in Congress that believe every word out of his mouth."

"There is a danger in what we're doing, sir. If the information contradicts what General MacArthur is reporting, it may end all our careers."

"General Eisenhower used to work with MacArthur in the Philippines. He knows how MacArthur works, and he does not like him. Plus, President Truman can't stand MacArthur. Truman and Eisenhower will protect us. Although I don't know how much longer Ike will be around. Last week, at a dinner party, he told me that he is being recruited by Columbia University to be its next President. If he accepts, he'll be retiring in a matter of months. It looks like General Omar Bradley will be the likely replacement."

"What about Guy Wong?" Linka asked.

"Major Wong will meet you in Tokyo when you return from your mission. He'll be working with Brigadier MacKenzie's team to track down Tsukuda."


Before leaving the Pentagon, Jon met with George Linka. George was not pleased with the assignment but understood the North Korean threat and the implications of a Soviet buildup.

"I was hoping we could have some more time off from this secret war crap. I am seriously considering asking Katie to marry me, this weekend. If I do, she won't want me to be trekking across Asia again. God, I hope we don't find anything. This crap with Tsukuda is bad enough. I don't want to fight another war," Linka said.

"I'm with you there," Preston stated.

"How will Camille take this news?"

"She won't be pleased, especially with a new baby to take care of by herself. And she'll be upset that I'm leaving so soon after we completed our last mission. She's still tired, hasn't lost a lot of the weight she had gained, and cries a lot because she thinks I won't love her because she's fat. I hate to leave her and Jonathan Jr., but I won't miss the crying and her feeling sorry for herself."

"So, this is what I have to look forward to when I marry Katie?"

"It's all part of the process, George. Marriage and children are great, but perseverance and patience are a must."

# CHAPTER 5

*Tokyo, Japan*

Uchito Tsukuda's great-uncle and former samurai, Hiraoka Kotaro, was a considerable influence in Tsukuda's early years. The wealthy mine owner was an influential Pan-Asianist who promoted political and economic unity and cooperation of Asian peoples. The motivating factor behind the ultranationalist Black Ocean Society he founded was resistance to Western imperialism and colonialism. Hiraoka Kotaro believed that Japanese values should take precedence over European values, which were contaminating Japan.

Kotaro's political influence enabled Tsukuda to get assigned to Japanese intelligence earlier in his career. Fortunately, the brilliant young officer needed no help after graduating at the top of his Imperial Japanese Army Academy class in 1905. By 1937, the intuitive and often charming Colonel Tsukuda was in charge of intelligence at the Kwantung Army Headquarters in Manchuria.

One of Tsukuda's responsibilities was embedding officers and enlisted agents into Kwantung Army units to spy on them as they plundered precious metals, gems, and antiquities from northern China cities. Tsukuda would pass the information on how much gold, silver, and gems the army was not reporting to General Hideki Tojo, the Kwantung Army's Chief of Staff. The thievery ended after Tojo executed over twenty officers and senior noncommissioned officers. Tojo rewarded Tsukuda for his loyalty by promoting him to major general.

When General Tojo was recalled to Tokyo in May 1938 to serve as the Vice-Minister of War, he brought Tsukuda to serve as his second-in-command. After a short tour, Tojo was made

Inspector-General of Army Aviation, and Tsukuda followed him as his vice-commander. Months before Tojo was named Prime Minister in October 1941, he had Tsukuda reassigned as one of the deputy chiefs of staff responsible for planning the invasion of Hong Kong, Singapore, and Malaysia. Although Tsukuda did well as a planner, he was not a field commander, so promotion was slow to nonexistent. Such was the life of a Japanese staff officer, no matter how brilliant. Plus, by the time Tsukuda was eligible for promotion, General Hideki Tojo began to fall out of favor with the general staff.

After the Battle of Midway, when the tide of war began turning against Japan, Tojo decided that Tsukuda would better serve the war effort back in Japanese intelligence. The intelligence community was not living up to Tojo's expectations. After several disastrous months in 1943, when over a dozen Japanese agents were lost in China, India, and Burma, the Nakano School commander committed *seppuku*—or ritual suicide by disembowelment. Tsukuda was promoted to lieutenant general and was given command of the prestigious Rikugun Nakano Gakko spy school in Hiroshima. The Nakano School was also the operations center for military intelligence operations in Southeast Asia. Within a year, General Tsukuda was graduating some of the best agents in the school's history.


Five years later, Tsukuda sat in his office in a walled, rural residence, in the Chiba Prefecture, which resembled a small Japanese castle from the 16th century. It was twenty miles from downtown Tokyo and a mile from the Naritasan Shinsho-ji Temple. As he looked out on his garden, he noticed the yellow daisies and purple orchids. The western sky was burnt orange and golden-red from the last of the sunset. *It would be a clear night*, he thought as he watched one of his servants begin to light the oil lamps with a wood shaving carried from the kitchen. At sixty-four years old, Tsukuda felt old. He sighed heavily, thinking he should go to the temple to pray. Instead, he turned to the head of his bodyguard detail.

"Raizo. Summon General Takaji Sugimoto and tell him I would like him to dine with me this evening at 1900 hours," Tsukuda ordered.

The muscular protector bowed and quickly left the room. Raizo Hata, a former Imperial Japanese Army lieutenant colonel, had been an instructor and a squadron commander at the Nakano School. He had commanded over 50 instructors with skills ranging from explosives and demolition to martial arts. Towards the end of the war, he had been the general's adjutant.

As Tsukuda focused on the maze of papers on his desk, he sighed again. The intrusion into his business by the Americans was beginning to wear on his nerves. He had been fighting the American agent, Jonathan Preston, for nearly five years and had clearly underestimated his intelligence and skills. From the moment Tsukuda discovered that his three nieces, Akemi, Akiko, and Akira Nakada, had been killed by American agents in Calcutta, he wanted them all dead.

Despite his better judgment, Tsukuda let the older sister of the triplets, Asami Nakada talk him into sending her to Calcutta to eliminate the American team. After poisoning two of Preston's female agents at an outdoor café, she attempted to take the team head-on at their motor yacht. Preston, however, aware of the threat to his team, set a trap in which Nakada barely escaped. Asami then decided to go after the American agents individually. Still, Preston prepared other surprises; and on Asami's next mission, she suffered a glancing gunshot wound to her left shoulder.

After a short recovery period, Asami made one more attempt on Preston's team. She had discovered a four-foot concrete culvert hidden in a thick group of trees and thorny shrubs, on the Hooghly River's eastern bank near downtown Calcutta. The culvert was a little less than a hundred yards from where the *Jacqueline* was berthed at the yacht basin of the 175-acre British Army base, Fort William. It was an ideal location for what she was planning.

Asami Nakada placed a note at a dead drop for her consular contact. Four evenings later, she made her way back to the drainage pipe. Inside the pipe, she found a waterproofed black canvas bag with an Arisaka Type 97 sniper rifle, scope, and ammunition. Asami had trained for hundreds of hours, firing the Type 97 rifle, at the Nakano School—and for hundreds more hours, teaching students how to take it apart, clean it, and fire it. The nine-pound bolt-action sniper rifle fired a 6.5mm reduced-charge cartridge, which improved its accuracy, limited its sound, and camouflaged the muzzle flash. The rifle's magazine held five rounds—more than enough for her purpose.

For several nights, Asami made her way to the drainage ditch, assembling the rifle and waiting for the opportunity to kill one of the American agents. On the third night, two people came out onto the back deck of the yacht. When she sighted the 2.5-power telescope, there was enough light from the soccer field next to the yacht basin to see Jonathan Preston and a young woman kissing on the fantail of the *Jacqueline*. Asami steadied her body, braced the rifle on top of the pipe, took a deep breath, and slowly let it out. At the end of her exhale, she squeezed the trigger.

When the rifle discharged, there was a muffled explosion and bright flash. Fire and debris slammed into Asami's face, and the rifle bolt struck her forehead, knocking her unconscious. When she awoke, she discovered her hands and feet were restrained. She moved her head left and right, but everything was dark.

"Your eyes are bandaged, Agent Nakada," Jon said in English. "You sustained severe damage to your right eye when the blast shattered the glass of your rifle scope. Pieces of glass entered your eye and severed the optic nerve. You'll never see with that eye again. Your left eye sustained blast damage from the explosion and small metal fragments from the bolt as it disintegrated. The doctors tell me that you may be able to discern night from day, but they're not 100-percent certain."

"Are you Preston, the one they call Cobra?" Nakada replied.

"Yes. The agent who left your rifle in the culvert didn't go unnoticed. Your rifle was sabotaged."

"Will I be shot as a spy?"

"That's up to our military lawyers. However, if it was up to me, I'd let them hang you for what you did to my two agents."


After a year in prison, American military lawyers deemed Asami Nakada a non-threat because of her blindness. She was part of a prisoner exchange for two American airmen held in Indochina by the remnants of the defeated Japanese army. Once in the Japanese consulate custody, she was moved to Japan and released into her mother's care. Three weeks after returning home, Asami disappeared and moved into her uncle's secret compound in Tokyo. For months, Asami exercised to regain her strength. Uchito Tsukuda arranged for medical specialists to treat her with oriental medicine techniques, which ultimately helped her recover her left eye vision. She then spent months working with a martial arts master to regain her skills and physical stamina. Finally, after nearly six months of twelve-hour-day workouts, she was again at the top of her game with 20/20 vision in her left eye.

When General Tsukuda briefed her on the *I-405's* mission to strike the U.S. with a biological weapon, Asami convinced her uncle to send her to America. She wanted to be the one to hit Washington, D.C., and finish what she started in Calcutta. Unfortunately, over-confident, arrogant, and blinded by vengeance, Asami Nakada underestimated Jonathan Preston's craftiness and died for her lack thereof.

It had been nearly six months since Nakada's death, and Tsukuda had not chosen a new second-in-command for his organization. That would hopefully change, tonight. He was prepared to offer the position to one of the brightest and most ruthless generals the Imperial Japanese Army produced, besides himself—Takaji Sugimoto.


Lieutenant General Takaji Sugimoto was the son of a former samurai retainer—a trusted and elite swordsman, who remained behind to protect his master's castle from enemy attacks while the daimyo campaigned with his shogun. Takaji Sugimoto specialized in Chinese studies at the Imperial Japanese Army Academy and became fluent in Mandarin and Cantonese. After serving as a military attaché to southern China from 1925 to 1927, he served in Eastern China with the IJA 6th Division. Takaji first met Tsukuda while serving as a staff officer of the Kwantung Army, from 1931 to 1932. Takaji encouraged Chinese warlords, in the region, to revolt against the

Kuomintang government of Chiang Kai-shek. The warlords were dedicated to expelling Western imperialists from China.

After becoming a colonel in 1937, Takaji commanded the IJA 44th Infantry Regiment of the Kwantung Army during the Battle of Shanghai. It was the first of the twenty-two major engagements fought between the IJA and the Chinese. Takaji became the prime instigator of the Marco Polo Bridge Incident of 1 July 1937, which led to the Second Sino-Japanese War with China. After promotion to major general, he became chief-of-staff of the 14th Army in the Philippines in 1942. He participated in the assault and capture of the American fortress on Corregidor. By 1944, Takaji was promoted to lieutenant general and commanded the 35th Army fighting the Americans on the island of Leyte. After the defeat of Japanese forces on the island, he was relieved of command and reassigned as the commander of the secret police in Hong Kong. The Kenpeitai was known for its brutality against Japanese citizens and was looked upon with distrust and hatred. For Tsukuda, this meant that the former lieutenant general was perfect for the job as his second-in-command.

Dinner with Tsukuda consisted of deep-fried pork cutlets served with cabbage, Miso soup, brown rice, pickled okra, green tea, and sake. Tsukuda kept the conversation light, inquiring about Sugimoto's family and grandchildren. It was a time for bonding. Tsukuda only conducted business after a meal.

"This is an excellent sake. Where do you get it?" Sugimoto asked.

"It's a Tokutei meisho-shu—a premium sake," Tsukuda replied. "It comes from my uncle's thousand-acre estate near Tsuchiura. Much of the loamy soil on the estate is dedicated to growing a short strain of rice called Yamada Nishiki, which is famous for its use in brewing high-quality sake."

As Tsukuda poured more sake, he continued. "The brewery complex is spread out over five acres, at the foot of one of the smaller hills on the estate, a mile from the main house. As I recall, you have been there."

"Yes, I visited your uncle's estate in 1925," Sugimoto replied. "My father and I were guests at the wedding of his youngest daughter. Unfortunately, we didn't get to tour the brewery."

"The brewery is next to a fast-running creek that powers a trip-hammer mill. The mill is used for decorticating and pounding the rice in preparation for the brewing process. The trip hammers are raised by a cam, which releases them to fall under the force of gravity. The water-mill trip hammer technology has been used in Japan for nearly 1,000 years."

Tsukuda suddenly shuttered when he recalled slipping and falling halfway into one of the hammer pits, only to be saved by his uncle before Tsukuda would have been crushed.

"Are you all right?" Sugimoto asked.

"Yes, of course. I was just recalling when I slipped and fell into one of the hammer pits during the milling process. I was eight at the time and not watching what I was doing. My uncle pulled me out before the cam released the hammer. I was fortunate he was there when I fell."

"How long is the sake aged?" Sugimoto asked deliberately ignoring the memory Tsukuda had shared.

"It's only aged for 30 days in the large casks, which produces a darker and more mature flavor. After it is bottled, it is temporarily stored in a tunnel in the hillside behind the warehouse. On average, there are 100,000 bottles there. But they don't remain long before being shipped to our clients."

"I take it that this sake does not end up on just anyone's table."

"No, it doesn't. It is sold in only a small number of geikos in Tokyo with a highly restrictive clientele. A small number of cases are sold to private individuals, politicians, and of course the royal family."

Tsukuda turned toward the door and called Raizo, "Have the servant clear the food away and bring a bottle of the Senju."

Tsukuda turned back to Takaji, "Senju is synonymous with the thousand different hands and skills it takes to produce the wine. From the planters in the field, harvesters, workers in the hammer mill, brewers, and ordinary laborers. I think you will enjoy it. It's one of our best."

# CHAPTER 6

*Hanoi, French Indochina*

Yul Butler wasn't bothered by Hanoi's incessant heat and humidity; instead, it reminded him of growing up in North Carolina. In some ways, he still felt like the kid who grew up on a farm near Swanquarter. He was eager to learn, strong-willed, and passionate. Only now, the decisions he made could lead to life or death for himself and the agents he managed. In which case, his calm and thoroughly musing personality would be advantageous.

Yul grew up without brothers or sisters on a family farm near the Pamlico Sound, where his grandfather worked as the Pea Island Life-Saving Station officer-in-charge. His mother was the school teacher of the only rural black school in the area. She taught him a love of reading. With his eidetic memory, Yul absorbed everything he read and heard. Though bright and talented, he was a lonely boy, stifled by the rural life he was born into. Yul was continually daydreaming about traveling to the faraway and exotic places he read about in books. When he visited the life-saving station, Yul devoured the many books and magazines his grandfather kept on hand, especially those which his grandfather read on architecture and engineering.

With the help of a family friend who was a former member of the Ohio House of Representatives and the current editor of the Cleveland Gazette, Yul was granted an interview with the Dean of Students at The Ohio State University. Three months after the interview, Yul received a full scholarship to study civil engineering. The scholarship included room and board, as well as a job at the school cafeteria.

When the Japanese bombed Pearl Harbor in 1941, Yul was a senior. After graduating the following year, he joined the U.S. Army. Yul was sent to the Army's Officer Candidate School in Miami Beach, Florida, where many Negro officer candidates went for officer training. After graduating at the top of his class, he was assigned to the Army Corps of Engineers 45th Engineer General Services Regiment, which was getting ready to deploy to Asia. By February, Yul was in northern Burma, commanding one of the many all-Negro units repairing the 717-mile-long Burma Road from Lashio, on the India-Burma border, to Kunming, China. It was a challenging job fraught with intrigue, disease, and constant danger from Japanese patrols—including racist U.S. Army soldiers who occasionally took potshots at the colored civil engineers as they worked on the road into China.

Jonathan Preston first met Lieutenant Yul Butler in a U.S. Army hospital in Calcutta, India, where Butler was recovering from malaria. Butler and several of his team members were captured by a Japanese patrol while working on the Ledo Road in late 1943. With his engineering background, Yul was sent to a prisoner of war (POW) camp in Thailand to work on a Japanese railroad being constructed. The railway paralleled the Kwai Noi River that ran through a hundred miles of rugged jungle and the granite canyons of the crooked east-west spine of the Bilauktaung Mountains. The railway eventually connected with an existing Japanese-controlled railway running north to south in Burma. The Japanese used a labor force of 60,000 Allied POWs and 200,000 conscripted Asian laborers to build the 258-mile narrow gauge railway. Unfortunately, malnourishment, disease, and back-breaking work attributed to a death toll of thirty percent among the prisoners.

In the summer of 1944, Butler escaped from the Hintok Station camp. For three months, Butler, aided by local natives, evaded the Japanese and made his way through Thailand and Burma, and then finally into allied-held India. He received a lot of help from Kachin tribesmen, who were working with the OSS in the region. Needing information on the Hintok camp and a nearby railway bridge, Jon Preston sought out the lieutenant's help.

Preston was explicitly interested in the one-hundred-foot gorge that created a break in a three-mile section of solid granite that the railroad was built underneath. For months, allied bombers tried to knock out the bridge that spanned the gorge. No less than nine bombing missions, ranging from four to six B-24 Liberators, attacked the railway and trestle. However, it was too well hidden by heavy foliage and granite cliffs for the bombings to be effective. When Preston showed up in his hospital room, Butler willingly obliged and gave detailed information on the camp, the railroad bridge construction, and the Kwai Noi River, where the prisoners were allowed to bathe.

The accuracy of the information Butler provided helped Preston's team determine the amount of C-2 explosives needed to destroy the bridge. When the group returned from its mission, Preston realized Butler's potential. Preston was instrumental in having Butler promoted and reassigned to Calcutta's OSS detachment. After going through several months of OSS training, the brilliant Butler, now promoted to captain, was loaned to Preston's counterintelligence team. Over the next four months, Butler was influential in uncovering and taking down a sizeable Japanese spy ring in Chittagong, Burma.

By July 1945, Major Butler was running his own covert operations and had distinguished himself in over a dozen missions. When the war ended, demobilization began. Like all reserve officers promoted quickly during the war to fill specific billets, he reverted back to his permanent, regular army rank of captain. In December 1946, Butler resigned his commission and was discharged from the U.S. Army.

The U.S. Army's loss, however, was the CIA's gain. Butler's experience in Southeast Asia proved valuable for the newly formed intelligence agency. With recommendations from General Miller and General Renick, in October of 1947, Butler was setting up and staffing a CIA station in Hanoi. His primary job was recruiting and developing a network of intelligence agents to keep tabs on Communist independence movements across Laos, Thailand, Cambodia, and French Indochina. Thanks to Agent Preston, Butler received help from four former OSS operatives—René Clairoux, his two children Renate and Jacob, and René's younger brother Jacob. René was the owner of a thriving detective agency in Hanoi, used almost exclusively by the French colonial government since the war's end.

At the beginning of World War Two, Indochina was France's most populous and wealthiest colony. Before the US dropped the atomic bombs on Hiroshima and Nagasaki, the French government in Paris fully expected the war to continue for another six months. Instead, Japan surrendered within two weeks, creating a three-month delay in French forces returning to the colony. That delay prompted an all-out indigenous insurrection across French Indochina. During the delay of French forces returning, the leader of the Viet Minh, Ho Chi Minh, established the Vietnamese Democratic Republic (DRV) in the northern part of the country. Although the French eventually reestablished control of the southern part of the colony, they could not regain the level of control in the north that they enjoyed before the Japanese takeover.

In his first meeting with René, Renate, and Jacob Clairoux, Butler was quickly brought up to speed on Indochina's political situation. It wasn't what Butler expected. While René talked, his gorgeous, long-blonde-curly-haired daughter, Renate, and handsome son, Jacob, sat obediently quiet.

"1945 was not a good year for French Indochina," René stated. "French rule, which had been in place for eight decades, was shattered when the Indochinese Communist Party (ICP) and the Viet Minh seized power and established the DRV. The Viet Minh leader, Ho Chi Minh, was proclaimed president of the new republic called Vietnam and was in firm control of most of the Northern provinces."

René paused and then began again. "Most of the political transformation took place in towns and rural villages after the Japanese coup that interred all French colonial forces in March 1945. After that, the Viet Minh and their Liberation Army squads increased in numbers. Even the emperor's royal civil guard ceased patrolling the hills and countryside north of Hanoi, with many units pledging loyalty to the Viet Minh. By the time the provisional French government of General de Gaulle got involved, nearly six months had elapsed, and Ho Chi Minh was in firm control of the north."

"Why didn't the French Army do anything to stop the Japanese when they began interring them in 1945?" Butler asked.

"French commanders discussed taking on the Japanese, but the colonial army wasn't designed to go head-to-head with the Japanese Army. It was designed strictly to ensure order among the native populations and patrol the frontier against smugglers, bandits, and dissidents fostering civil unrest. They just were not capable of engaging in modern combat operations. After four years of Japanese occupation, the tropical humidity had taken a toll on their equipment and ammunition. Plus, the Japanese controlled all of the medical and food supplies," René replied.

"What about Operation Lea? I thought that was a French victory."

"It was an attempt at a classical pincher movement to capture the Viet Minh leadership in northern Indochina. The French forces were spread too thin to stop the Viet Minh from slipping into the thick jungle. It was called off a month after it was initiated. By December, French forces were pulled back towards Hanoi.

"What about now? You have a significant number of French troops and new equipment. Can't they take the country back?" Butler inquired.

"Pride, honor, and retribution are influencing events," René Clairoux stated. "The colonial administration is under pressure from French colonists to seek revenge against the Vichy administrators for collaboration with the Japanese. They are also motivated by General de Gaulle's military pride. The general sees the maintenance of colonial Indochina and its riches as a means of reestablishing France as a world power. In other words, they would rather play politics than fight another war. Plus, the Viet Minh have the upper hand in guerilla tactics and have compromised the replenishment routes to the French forts in the north."

"How is this playing with the other French colonies?" Butler asked.

"French concessions to the DRV have set a bad example for other French colonies who are also seeking independence, especially those in North Africa. Paris is stretching her military resources too thin. It's essentially too little, too late. And unfortunately, our colonial government has only been successful in provoking a war with the DRV."

"Is it winnable?"

"It's doubtful. Our French generals are obsessed with seeking a large-scale battle to bring their firepower, airpower, and mechanized units into action for a decisive battle. The Viet Minh would never fight such a battle. They use mostly hit-and-run guerilla tactics. Plus, I doubt the government's resolve in Paris to finance and sustain a prolonged war in Indochina. France is broke. Our chief military advisor for the colony, General Humbert, warns Paris that Indochina will become a bottomless pit and exceed the French government's resources. France must now borrow hundreds of millions from the U.S. to rebuild in Europe. War in Indochina will take tens of millions away from that effort. Frankly, I believe we are on our own."

"I think that is why I am here, but Washington hasn't given me any assurances of military aid in the form of troops, weapons, or ammunition. I've been told that covert operations against the Viet Minh are not authorized. But, I do have a large budget for gathering intelligence," Butler said.

"Well, in that respect, we can be of service. We are already working with the colonial government to collect information on DRV activities around Hanoi. But, they have an extremely limited budget."

"René, I want you to gather information on Communist activities throughout Southeast Asia. If you think it would be safe and not come back on you, you are free to share the information on Indochina with your government. However, they cannot know that you are working for American intelligence."

"We can work under that arrangement, but I suspect they will know of your involvement," René replied.

"I'm not so sure. I'm here as a regional manager for an established export company out of Manila. No one knows I'm CIA. My company will be exporting gems and precious metals from Asia. Jon Preston ensures that I can trust your discretion. I will be hiring you specifically to contact, investigate, and introduce me to reputable mine owners throughout Indochina, Laos, Thailand, and Cambodia, where you already have business ties. You will no doubt need to hire additional investigators. We'll begin with a one-year contract. I'll have a courier deliver the contract to your office this afternoon. You can have your attorney review it before signing if you wish. I'll let you fill in the dollar amount that you need if that is acceptable."

"Quite acceptable, Yul. Does the CIA have unlimited resources to finance your operation?"

"Not really. But, I am authorized to provide a ten-thousand-dollar draw to help you get started. Will that be enough to get things rolling?" Butler asked.

"That is very generous. How will you finance a protracted operation? This could go on for years."

"I intend to resurrect Operation Remorse. Instead of smuggling strategic materials like rubber and tung oil, and manipulating the exchange rates of Indian rupees and Chinese yen, I'll use opium and gems and manipulate the gold and silver exchange rates. If the British could get a return of over 15 times the money they invested during the war, I should be able to get the same return, which will provide unlimited funds."

"It's a sound plan, especially with so many people involved in the black market. I'll see you in two days to finalize the contract," René replied.


On the way back to their office, Renate, who never engaged in conversation unless asked by her father, finally spoke up. "Father, if we can't defeat the DRV—how will our family and business be affected if we side with the colonial administration and the Americans?"

"In the short term, not significantly—as long as we keep up our disguise as a detective agency working for a Filipino export company. If the Communists succeed in taking over Indochina, we will move to our vacation home in Bangkok. We are already established there, businesswise, and your mother loves the area," René replied.

"The Communists know about my helping the Americans when we had collaborated with Agent Preston to capture the Japanese POW camp at Vinh Lai. So won't the Viet Minh be suspicious of our activities if we go investigating mine owners throughout the country?" asked Jacob.

"Son, we are an established business throughout Southeast Asia with a reputation for honest, reliable work. We have over a hundred investigators in six countries. If the Viet Minh get suspicious, I am certain that General Giáp—a friend who has great respect for me—will personally send a message and warn me off. When that happens, we will heed the warning and move to Thailand. In the meantime, we will take the CIA's money and build a network of investigators in Indochina, Laos, Thailand, and Cambodia. I believe we can safely work in Indochina for two or three years before we have to leave. Plus, let's not forget our British friends. Miles Murphy and Henri Morreau are already working in Indochina for the British Secret Intelligence Service. If they get wind of anything, they will inform us."

"What are your plans for us?" asked Renate.

"I'm sending you and your bother to Laos. To our office in Vientiane, run by your Uncle Marcel. You will communicate the help we need from him, to recruit investigators and uncover what the mine owners are doing. But, you will disclose nothing about our involvement with the American CIA. Is that clear?"

"Yes, sir," Renate and Jacob swiftly answered.

"Tell him, I want a dozen investigators that he trusts with his life by midsummer. Marcel married a Laotian, and she's a nationalist. I'm sure she has family that can be trusted. Regardless, he knows this business, and he knows how to recruit the right people. Everything has to be done around the theme of investigating mine owners and their business. Butler is smart in this respect—because where you will find gems, you will find opium and gold. And you will find Communists. The Communists will be trying to cash in and raise money to finance their army. You will also find arms dealers supplying the mine owners with weapons and ammunition to protect their mines. And those same arms dealers will most likely be selling arms to the Communists. That's why Butler chose gems and precious metals to export, and opium and gold as currencies to manipulate."

"Two questions, father," Renate commented. "What about Uncle Jacob? And second, what was Operation Remorse?"

"Your Uncle Jacob will continue running our office in Bangkok. I'll brief him when I travel there next week. Operation Remorse was a black market operation carried out by the British Special Operations Executive to finance their covert operations in Asia during the war. The SOE smuggled luxury items, medicine, arms, and other highly sought-after goods that the Chinese would purchase on the black market. By manipulating the exchange rates with the currency transactions, the Brits made incredible profits, which funded their covert operations."

"I guess Yul Butler is a lot smarter than I gave him credit," Jacob replied.

"Trust me, son. Jon Preston's fingerprints are all over this. Preston and George Linka trained Yul Butler as they did you and your sister. And from what Preston told me, Butler is a genius in his own right, with a photographic memory. His talents won't be wasted in Asia. Plus, Jon Preston won't leave us out to dry. I'm sure he will see to it that we will profit immensely from this. We will use the money to resettle in Thailand and start other more lucrative businesses."

"You don't think our army can defeat the Viet Minh, do you?" Jacob asked.

"I'm reasonably sure that the government in Paris does not have the resolve to fight another long and costly war. And our generals in Indochina are old-school Europeans. They do not know how to fight a guerilla war. Their arrogance and lack of preparedness are evident. When the Japanese took over our government in March 1945, only three of the thirteen French generals escaped Japanese incarceration and execution. They fell like a house of cards."

"So, you think we have already lost this war?" Renate questioned.

"Yes, simply because Paris and our colonial government will not change. The taxation policy and how badly plantation owners treat the indigenous workers have worked against us for eight decades. Most native Indochinese people are on the side of the Viet Minh. They want independence from France. So, yes, I feel it is inevitable that the war is lost, and we will have to leave Indochina."

"Then why are we staying?" Jacob asked.

"To help the Americans try to stop, or forestall a Communist takeover of our country. The Viet Minh and the ICP have been working behind our backs for over a decade. If the Americans get involved militarily, we may have a chance to get back our country. But, that depends solely on President de Gaulle. And right now, he's against any direct American military intervention, because the current U.S. administration is against colonialism," René concluded.

# CHAPTER 7

*Baltimore, Maryland*

The twice-convicted felon, and former smuggler, Elton Fitzsimmons, jumped off the bow of his fishing boat with a rope in his left hand, next to a docking cleat, at his Pratt Street Harbor berth. He looped the line once around the bottom of the cleat before sliding it over the cleat's top arm and wrapping it around the opposite arm. He then raised it over the top of the cleat and looped it under the first arm to form a figure eight.

He completed the exercise by making a small, underhand loop, placing it over the first arm before tugging the rope's end, and securing the knot. As he finished, he scanned the dock to the north and south. *Old habits die hard*, Fitzsimmons thought, looking at an unfamiliar boat, thirty yards off the bow.

As Fitzsimmons moved aft to secure the stern line, he avoided several dock workers carrying bunches of bananas, unloaded from a South American steamer. The workers took the bananas to a line of trucks parked bumper to bumper on Pratt Street. Fitzsimmons noticed an Asian man on the unfamiliar boat doing his best not to look like he was watching him. Fitzsimmons had spotted the man trailing him to his favorite watering hole, O'Neill's Pub, two days ago.

At first, Fitzsimmons thought it was a coincidence. Then, however, he was beginning to wonder if Haru Aki was alive and coming to seek revenge. Fitzsimmons knew that his betrayal of the Japanese spy to U.S. Army counterintelligence during the war might come with a price. But he was a patriot first. So he readily gave up Aki in exchange for immunity from prosecution for a third-felony theft conviction, after being caught stealing aircraft engine parts from a Navy warehouse.

After the Japanese attack on Pearl Harbor, Fitzsimmons became suspicious that Aki might be a Japanese agent. Before the war, he had brought several illegal arms and ammunition shipments from Cuba into the Port of Baltimore for the Eurasian smuggler. When the Navy Shore Patrol apprehended him, giving up Aki as a potential spy, as leverage against prosecution, seemed the prudent thing to do. Not only did Army counterintelligence take Aki down and kill him, but they also guaranteed Fitzsimmons' and his children's safety from Japanese reprisal. His teenage children were taken into protective custody by U.S. Marshalls and then were moved from their private school in Philadelphia to a new school in Boston. Fitzsimmons refused protective custody for himself, but moved his boat from Baltimore to Ocean City, Maryland, as a precaution.

In the last eight months, Fitzsimmons visited his children twice. A Coast Guard cutter would intercept his fishing boat, find contraband, and take him into custody every four months. The cutter would escort Fitzsimmons' boat to its homeport of Boston, and interrogate him on suspicion of smuggling. After a brief time in custody, a U.S. Marshall would drive Fitzsimmons to a farmhouse in the country where his children would be waiting for a brief reunion. Two days later, he was taken back to the Coast Guard base, where he boarded his boat and cruised back to Ocean City. Now, Fitzsimmons was beginning to wonder whether the U.S. government could really protect him and his family.


It was 10 p.m. before Fitzsimmons arrived home. He had walked to O'Neill's Pub, eaten, and played cards for several hours. Being cautious, Fitzsimmons exited one of the establishment's two service entrances. He stayed in the dark alleys' shadows for six blocks and then entered his house through the back door. When he flipped the light switch on, he was startled to see a bottle of Redbreast Irish Whiskey and three empty glasses on the kitchen table. As he pulled a knife from its sheath on his belt, he heard a familiar voice.

"That won't be necessary, Elton. Only friends here," Jonathan Preston said, as he and George Linka stepped from the living room shadows into the lighted kitchen.

"For crying out loud, Agent Preston. You nearly gave me a heart attack," Fitzsimmons replied.

"I thought you were tougher than that," Linka replied.

"Not when I think I'm being stalked by Japanese agents down at the docks."

"They're not Japanese agents. They are members of my team." Preston replied.

"Well, that's a relief. I was beginning to think Haru Aki was coming back to seek his revenge."

"Aki died along with every member of his team. Nothing to worry about from him."

"Then why the hell are you watching me?"

"We're just making sure that you're living as a model citizen."

"That's a bunch of crap! You know damn well I've changed my ways. I'm an honest businessman. Plus, you wouldn't expend resources on men watching and tailing me if it didn't involve national security. Now, what do you really want, Jon?"

"See, Jon. I told you he was sharp," Linka said, turning to his cohort.

"Living on the edge, like you once did, tends to leave you that way, doesn't it, Elton?" Preston replied.

"Yes. Now, if you'll cut the chatter and state your purpose, I'd be grateful."


Over the next two hours and several glasses of whiskey, Preston laid out what was happening with Uchito Tsukuda and how Preston would use Guy Wong to entrap the Japanese criminal. Fitzsimmons was not surprised that Preston was talking to him as an equal. He had been dealt with fairly by Preston during the war. And Preston wasn't acting like a government bureaucrat, demanding his help for protecting his children. The plan Preston was laying out, albeit dangerous, had been carefully thought through. Surprisingly, however,

Preston was asking Fitzsimmons for his input in the planning and execution.

"Do you think Tsukuda knows about me and what I did for Aki?" asked Fitzsimmons.

"We really don't know, Elton, but we have to assume that he does. Tsukuda had a network of spies on the east coast that reported directly to him during the war. We thought we captured or killed all of them, but we can't be certain. However, let's suppose he is aware of your past relationship with Aki. In that case, it might facilitate what we are trying to achieve," Linka replied.

"Besides revenge against your team, why would Tsukuda move into the U.S.?"

"Post-war economic opportunities," Preston replied.

"And you think that my teaming up with your agent and smuggling gems into the U.S. will appeal to his sense of entrepreneurship?"

"I believe he will recognize and take advantage of any opportunity to expand his business empire globally. Which means, if it is illegal and highly profitable, he will want in on the action."

"You think he has agents working the docks in Baltimore?" Fitzsimmons asked.

"They are probably embedded in the existing Asian population. Most likely, Eurasian, Japanese, Malaysian, and Chinese. And there is a possibility that he is using Russian immigrants. They might be working in the fisheries or on the docks or boats. And some are probably business owners whom he extorts and controls."

"Before the war, I worked with several Japanese boat owners who had double eyelid surgery before immigrating to the U.S. Most people wouldn't recognize them as Japanese."

"As I said, anything is possible," Preston responded.

"I can spot them because I've worked with them. However, the average American can't tell a Jap from a Chinaman. Since the war ended, I am seeing a lot of Russian immigrants working on the docks. Except for the language, they look just like us Americans," Fitzsimmons said.

"If you agree to help us, Elton, you will be well compensated. However, you'll be putting your life on the line as much as my agents.

But I won't let you put your life in jeopardy without your input and help in planning the operation."

"That's very thoughtful, Agent Preston, but I'm more worried about your agent than myself. It doesn't sound like he's experienced in this sort of business."

"Guy Wong is bright, deadly, and thinks well on his feet. But you're right in one respect—he doesn't have your experience with smuggling or working on boats, and he's young. So, I'm going to have to count on you to train him quickly. He knows the gem business very well. He doesn't need to know everything you know about smuggling. Just enough to help out on the boat when you're traveling to Havana and back."

"After a month at sea, he'll know the basics. But, what is his experience in the gem business?" Fitzsimmons asked.

"Wong's father is a diamond cutter and gemologist. He owns a jewelry store and a laundry in California. Guy learned the business from him and his Chinese grandfather. Wong already has a business location in Georgetown, which has been up and running for several months. And business is doing great in this economy," Preston said.

"And you need my boat to smuggle the gems in?"

"Yes. We've arranged for you and Wong to pick up gems from a reputable smuggler in Havana. We know Tsukuda had agents there during the war and probably still does. However, we don't know when or where you will be approached by someone from Tsukuda's organization. But we believe it is inevitable. You must be sure it is Tsukuda's organization, and they have to be convinced that you and Wong are willing to take risks and work with them. Tsukuda's people will probably want you to smuggle whatever they supply."

"Why are you so certain he will make contact?" Fitzsimmons asked.

"He is an opportunist, and he is relentless about expanding his organization. And as you know, from working with Aki, Tsukuda doesn't like competition. Because of your contacts and knowledge of the east coast, he would rather you work for him than someone else. And he will want you to work close to Washington, D.C., so he can get to me."

"Aki gave me a recognition code to use with his men. It may still work."

"That's great, but I sense another worry?" Preston surmised.

"The Irish mob is big on the Baltimore, Philadelphia, and D.C. docks. They won't like me teaming up with Tsukuda," Fitzsimmons said.

"As I recall, Aki took out a good portion of the Irish mob in Baltimore before the war. The Irish Mob doesn't like the violence that comes with messing with Tsukuda. I'm pretty sure they will leave you alone. Plus, you and Wong can hold your own if they try to pressure you."

"I'm going to need at least four highly qualified men for security, Agent Preston."

"I anticipated as much. I can provide four Asians to work security on your boat. They are former Marines who fought in the Pacific, and they know their way around a fishing boat. However, you're going to need a bigger crew."

"What do you mean?"

"Your fifty-foot boat only has a crew of six. Your new boat will need a crew of twenty."

"You're giving me a new boat?"

"No, you'll earn it. You and your partner just purchased the beam trawler that was converted to a U.S. Navy minesweeper, USS *Cardinal*. The navy was about to scrap her when we picked her up. She's a good boat. Built by the Bath Iron Works in 1937 and launched in August 1940. You'll re-launch her under her original name, *Jeanne D'Arc*."

"Joan of Arc. I like it. Where is she now?" asked Fitzsimmons.

"Back at the Bath Iron Works, being refitted as a fishing trawler and having her engines overhauled. I can't have you trawling the continental shelf with a Mark 22, three-inch, fifty-caliber gun on the forward deck and a pair of .50-caliber machine guns on the top of the wheelhouse. Not to mention, the two depth charge tracks on the aft deck. If you sailed her into Cuba, President Socarrás would get jealous and confiscate her."

"She must be twice the size of my boat."

"She's one hundred and thirty-six feet, four inches long, with a 21-foot beam and a draft of eleven feet, four inches."

"Displacement, engines, and speed?"

"Five hundred and sixteen tons. One 735-horsepower, Fairbanks Morse diesel engine. She'll do ten knots," Preston said.

"So, she's a single screw? A boat that size will require a crew of forty."

"Yes, but Bath is refitting her so you can run her with a crew of twenty."

"And I bet you and Wong have a crew lined up, right?" Fitzsimmons asked.

"The same ten-man engine crew and mechanics that kept her running for the navy. All are combat veterans who know how to handle themselves. The rest you will have to furnish."

"When will she be ready?"

"You'll pick her up in Bath, Maine, in two weeks. They will give you and Wong a three-day orientation before you sail."

"So, a custom refit, fit for a smuggler. That won't go unnoticed in Havana."

"I'm counting on it," Preston said.

"You don't think Tsukuda or his goons will recognize Wong as a government agent?"

"Wong spent most of the war in China as a covert operative. He didn't mingle with the Japs. During the brief time he worked in Japan, he altered his appearance. No one will recognize him now."

"Are you willing to bet my life and Wong's?" Fitzsimmons asked.

"Unfortunately, it's a risk we have to take to eliminate Tsukuda and take down his organization."

"And are you absolutely certain that Tsukuda will come to the U.S.?"

"Not Tsukuda, but his number two. Our agents in Japan have informed us that his new right-hand man is on a boat headed to Acapulco, Mexico. During the war, Tsukuda stashed a lot of gold and rare antiquities in banks there. We anticipate him picking up enough gold to begin financing a large organization from Mexico to the east coast," Linka replied.

"How will taking down the number-two guy lead to taking Tsukuda down?" Fitzsimmons asked.

"Japanese culture," Preston replied. "To be more precise, *mentsu wo tamotsu,* or saving face. It is a strong motivating force in Japan. It is one of the most essential concepts in understanding the Japanese mind."

"How does that affect Tsukuda?"

"If the other criminal enterprises in Japan learn that Tsukuda's organization was severely hurt or eliminated in the U.S., it would be unbearable to Tsukuda's pride. He would lose face. It would force him to personally take charge to redeem himself. Those other criminal organizations tolerate Tsukuda because of the business relationships he built with them in Asia during the war. He became a force to be reckoned with. Still, they tolerate him because he is doing business unrelated to their traditional roles. However, suppose they see Tsukuda as weak. In that case, they might make a move to eliminate him and take over his very profitable arms-smuggling operation."

"Then, I guess we'd better get started and make sure he loses face."

# CHAPTER 8

*São Paulo, Brazil*

Fabio Martinez was president of São Paulo's largest bank, Banco do Brasil. This deposit-taking commercial bank functioned as Brazil's de facto central bank. As he entered his office at precisely 9 a.m., his secretary handed him a Western Union telegram.

"This just arrived, sir. It's one of those garbled messages from the United States," the secretary added. "Can I get you a cup of coffee?"

"Yes, Louisa."

Louisa returned with a cup of dark black coffee and set it on her boss's desk. "Anything else, Señor Martinez?"

"No, Louisa. Just close the door on your way out."

Louisa closed the door as she exited the office, thinking that her boss must have a mistress in the U.S. sending him coded love messages.

Martinez immediately recognized the coded message signature line, which read, Château Latour. It was from General John Renick. It had been nearly two years since the general had sent him a message thanking him for his help in finding one of the rogue Japanese submarines. The submarine designated *I-14* was attempting to attack the Gatun locks of the Panama Canal. A week after her capture, a hundred thousand in American dollars and two boxes of cigars made by an obscure Russian-born Jew from Geneva, Switzerland, named Zino Davidoff, were delivered to the bank. Martinez had never heard of Davidoff, but his cigars were the finest he had ever smoked. Since then, he ordered his cigars directly from Davidoff's shop in Switzerland.

Martinez got up and went to his wall safe, located behind a picture of the founder of the Banco do Brasil, King John VI of Portugal. After opening the safe, he withdrew the black codebook delivered personally by a courier from the Pentagon nearly three years ago. After decoding the message, Martinez pulled a lighter from his desk drawer and retrieved a cigar from the humidor in the drawer beneath. After lighting the cigar and savoring the smoke, he reread the decoded message. After reading a third time, he burned both.

He recalled the message he received in late 1945. It requested his help in finding one of two Japanese submarines. One was on its way from Japan to attack the Panama Canal locks with a biological weapon. The effects of a biological weapon attack by a second submarine on New York and Washington, D.C., would have been devastating to the U.S. and the financial world. Although this message was not war-related, it did carry a sense of urgency and intrigue. If it wasn't related to national security, he knew General Renick would not involve him.

Martinez had been aware of Uchito Tsukuda, and his deposits in Banco do Brasil, since 1942. Over twenty tons of gold bullion had been deposited, which Martinez made available to secure post-war business and personal loans. The bank provided a quarter percent return on the $19 million in gold, which paid Tsukuda nearly a half-million dollars a year in compound interest. This week, one million dollars in cash was withdrawn from the interest-bearing account by a former Japanese general bearing a letter from Tsukuda.

It wasn't an uncommon practice. Tsukuda had prearranged instructions with the bank allowing anyone with a letter bearing the family crest or *kamon,* as it is called in Japan, to withdraw funds. A second stipulation instructed that the letter's bearer must display a tattoo of the kamon to the bank manager. The tattoo had to be exactly 50 by 75 millimeters and located on the inside of the left forearm. The gold and black tattoo of the Japanese quince represented the Oda family crest.

Tsukuda was a proud descendant of the warlord, Oda Nobunaga, regarded as the first *Great Unifier* of Japan. When Oda overthrew the Ashikaga shogunate in the 16<sup>th</sup> century, over half of Japan's provinces were unified, ending three centuries of feudal wars.

As Martinez considered Japanese organized crime's implications of moving into North and South America, he shook his head. Hopefully, General Renick and his top agent, Jonathan Preston, could stop the Japanese interpolation. Brazil had enough corruption. Martinez knew enough about the yakuza-style organized crime syndicates to realize it would end up with ordinary merchants living in fear of the threats imposed by the Japanese criminals. If General Renick thought he could expose and stop them with a gem-smuggling charade, it was his moral duty to help. He was anxious to meet the general's top agent, who would be arriving at the end of the week.

Jonathan Preston walked down, once the airstairs were rolled into position at the side of the chartered twin-engine DC-47 aircraft at the Congonhas Airport. He felt and looked tired. The twenty-hour flight, from Washington, D.C. to São Paulo, had taken three days, with refueling and layover stops in Miami and Panama City. As Jon walked across the dirt field towards the metal building that served as the airline terminal, he was greeted by a handsome, young man in a dark grey business suit.

"Señor Preston?" the young man asked.

"Yes," Jon replied.

"I am José Martinez," José said, extending his hand. "My grandfather, Fabio Martinez, asked me to pick you up and take you to his house. I understand that you have some cargo that needs to be unloaded and transported as well."

"Yes, there are several crates that need to be handled with care."

Jon noticed a 2½-ton 6x6 truck emerging onto the field, thirty yards east of the building. The truck, built by General Motors, used ubiquitously in World War Two, continued to be the standard medium-duty truck after the war. Fabio Martinez obviously had clout with the Brazilian military, to be able to borrow one. As the truck pulled to a stop, the cargo door on the C-47 began to open.

Six men in Army uniforms jumped from the truck's bed while four heavily armed men stood guard. The three pallets were quickly transferred to the vehicle.

"If you don't mind, I would like to ride in the truck," Jon stated.

"No problem, Señor. My grandfather assumed you would, so he directed me to ride with you."

An hour later, the truck arrived at an elegant 21,500-square-foot mansion in the Retiro Morumbi section of São Paulo. The luxury residence had a total of six different bedroom suites, including a double master suite with a large terrace overlooking the backyard's enormous pool. The truck drove up an asphalt-paved driveway that curved fifty yards up a moderate hill before turning into a U-shaped drive in front of the house. When it stopped at the east end, José exited the truck and went inside. Less than a minute later, one of the doors of the 10-car garage opened. José was standing next to his grandfather, Fabio.

"Colonel Preston, what a great pleasure to meet you," Fabio said, offering his hand. "Let's go inside. José will oversee your crates' unloading and see that your suitcase is taken to the guest bedroom. You look like you could use a cold drink."

The garage was connected to the main house by a wide, covered walkway. Jon followed Fabio into a spacious study. Occupying the entire wall opposite the double-door entrance, Jon stared at a map of South America and the Caribbean. After Jon stepped into the room and took a seat in a luxuriously padded leather chair, a butler brought in a pitcher of Caipirinha and an ice bucket.

Fabio handed Jon a tumbler and remarked, "I think this will 'hit the spot' as you Americans say. It is a refreshing drink made with cane sugar, lime, and Cachaça, distilled from fermented sugar cane juice. My father always told me it was a remedy for the common cold. Which is easy to come down with when you travel."

Preston took a sip of the drink and instantly liked it. Knowing that Brazilian businessmen wanted to get to know their guests before talking business, Preston decided to enjoy the cold beverage and listen to his host. "It is quite good, Mr. Martinez."

"Please, Colonel. Call me Fabio. I assume we will have an extensive working relationship, and I want it to be as informal as possible. We have a common enemy that must be taken down, so I want to be treated as an equal in working against this threat."

"Thank you, Fabio. Please call me, Jon."


After a four-hour nap, Jon showered. He found the wrinkled suit, from his suitcase, freshly pressed and hanging on a wooden valet stand next to a cedar armoire, where his clothes were neatly stored. Jon walked down a spacious mahogany stairway where Fabio was waiting. He followed him into a small private dining room next to the kitchen. A rectangular table was set for two people. Fabio seated himself across from Jon instead of at the end where he would usually sit. It was Fabio's way of establishing a more comfortable and informal relationship with one of America's best operatives.

Dinner began with zesty soft, tangy slices of hearts of palm and cool sweet fronds of thinly sliced, raw fennel and tomatoes. The licorice taste was unusual to Jon, but with palm and tomato slices, very tasty. Following the salad, Jon was offered the choice of two soups—*feijoada*, a rich, hearty stew made with different cuts of pork and black beans, or *moqueca*, a fish stew made with Atlantic cod, tomatoes, onions, and coriander. Jon chose the feijoada.

While they ate, Fabio talked about Brazil. Despite being prosperous, he was worried about the political direction. The current political climate was marked by instability and military pressure on civilian politicians. Fabio was afraid that a military coup would result in a fascist-influenced regime led by Getúlio Vargas. Vargas was a former Brazilian president who was deposed in a bloodless military coup in 1945.

Jon listened intently and discussed what was happening in the U. S. and the Truman Doctrine's effect in the fight against Communism. Fabio was optimistic, but Jon knew that the U.S. Congress wasn't keen on fighting another war or boosting nationalist regimes. It was more interested in spending resources needed to get the American economy rebooted. Most of the CIA's funding to fight communism came from the 200,000 tons of gold rescued by American intelligence in the Philippines, after the Japanese surrender. Although there was plenty, it was not doled out in excessive quantities. Each CIA station had to submit a plan for what they needed to spend. The exception was Europe and Asia, where the Soviets were infiltrating war-torn countries at will and meeting little resistance. CIA stations in South America and Africa were largely ignored.

Jon Preston's and Yul Butler's ingenious plan to resurrect Operation Remorse would provide unlimited funds if the French Indochina colonial government didn't find out about it. Jon's influence with General Miller and President Truman practically guaranteed unlimited funds to fight communism in Asia unless Congress decided otherwise. It also allowed him to tap into the jewels and antiquities lifted from treasure hoards in the Philippines, to fund Guy Wong's charade in Georgetown. He needed help from Martinez to legitimize the pretense. It would link the gems and antiquities to a well-connected gemologist with the right underground connection in Havana.

"I find your plan, to lure Tsukuda's organization into a smuggling trap, quite resourceful. Tell me about jewels and jade you brought with you."

"The gems will vary in quality but come in quantities of four hundred per lot. I brought sixteen lots consisting of diamonds, rubies, sapphires, and emeralds. Plus, there are three crates of hand-carved jade figurines and jadeite statues. You can pay your contact in Havana extra to grade them before he gets them to Fitzsimmons and Wong—unless you have someone here you would prefer to use."

"I have a first cousin in São Paulo that I trust. He has been a gemologist for 30 years. I prefer to have him grade the objects and gems before I send them to Havana. If we know what is going out, we can maintain positive control of the inventory. Plus, some of the gems may be fake and have to be culled."

"Do you not trust your man in Havana?"

"I trust him with my life. He was one of my best agents during the war. But regardless, it is only good business and common sense to know the exact content of your inventory."

"When can we expect the first shipment to reach Havana?"

"It will take two months to grade the merchandise. I can get the gems and jewelry there by the first week in April. The jade will take longer because I have to smuggle it in on a fishing boat to avoid the Cuban authorities."

"What arrangement have you made to pay your agent?"

"He wants a five percent commission of the wholesale value. I will pay him through an account he has at my bank. I suggest we send four lots at a time to begin. Otherwise, it might look suspicious."

"Once General Takaji Sugimoto takes the bait, how long do you intend to let it play out?" Martinez inquired.

"Long enough to drain most of the twenty million of Tsukuda's funds from your bank," Preston replied.

"And how exactly will that happen?"

"Roughly six months after Tsukuda commits to taking over the gem-smuggling operation, you will make available a remarkable cache of over 200 jade and jewelry pieces. The jewels and jade come from the Shenyang Imperial Palace, located 600 kilometers north of Beijing. My team recovered the cache in 1945 in the catacombs of the Stella Maris Catholic Church in Port Arthur, China. They were shipped to Manila and stored at the U.S. Army armory on Corregidor. But, before they could be documented and classified, they went missing. Among the imperial treasure was an ancient Japanese sword. From the photographs we took and the inscriptions on the sword, one of our experts believes the sword was made by a swordsmith named Gorō Nyūdō Masamune. He lived from 1264 to 1343 and is considered to be the greatest sword maker in Japanese history. The sword alone, which is only one of two that are known to still exist, will grab Tsukuda's attention. He will want it as a personal treasure. The jewels and jade, which are as priceless as the sword, he will seize on for profit. If sold individually, they could easily fetch $5 million."

"It sounds remarkably convenient that the cache went missing."

"Yes, I saw the value of removing them for a future operation and received approval from General Miller. They are in the capable hands of a very resourceful and discrete Catholic priest and antiquities professor at an east coast university. I have over a hundred color photographs that I will leave with you."

"Jon, you certainly know how to entice a criminal. But, how will you get Tsukuda to let go of his money without him seeing the merchandise? You can't possibly let these priceless jade pieces go through the dealer in Havana."

"I'm glad you asked. I have no clue how to pull it off. I was hoping to leave that part of the charade up to you, Fabio."

# CHAPTER 9

*Havana, Cuba*

*Jeanne D'Arc* turned south to enter the Havana harbor—an area of 800 feet wide by 4,600 feet long. Halfway to its destination, the boat was ordered to stop. It took another hour before *Jeanne D'Arc* was cleared by a Havana Port Authority official. The official had to review the boat's documents and crew manifest, and also collect the docking and entry fee. Forty-five minutes later, his crew was securing the boat at a cannery on Guanabacoa Cove. He had used the Del Fuego Cannery on his last trip to Havana in December 1945.

While he waited for the crew to unload the catch, Fitzsimmons reviewed the story Guy Wong told him about setting up the jewelry business. With the money provided by a secret fund controlled by Jonathan Preston, Wong purchased a three-story house in Georgetown—one of the earliest neighborhoods in Washington, D.C. It was located three blocks from Georgetown University—the oldest Catholic and Jesuit University in the U.S. Because of its prime location on the Potomac River, Georgetown served as a major port and commercial center during colonial times. The Aqueduct Bridge, which had connected Georgetown with Virginia until closing in 1923, was located five blocks away. Only the gatehouse remained standing.

The three-story, light-grey-painted, brick rowhouse, located at 3411 P Street NW, came with five bedrooms and three baths. It provided 2,678 square feet of living space. Cobblestone streets and charming homes dotted the federal-style neighborhood. It was more than Wong needed, but it did impart the image of a wealthy merchant. The entire bottom floor served as the showroom for Wong's rare gem and oriental antiquities business. It took some convincing, but the Georgetown community council approved the zoning change to accommodate the new store. Approval was granted once Elton Fitzsimmons was revealed as co-owner and that Guy Wong was Chinese versus Japanese.

On the house's top story, one room was converted into a private study and private showroom. Wong stored the two-hundred-plus, high-end red rubies, rare padparadscha sapphires, and the more valuable and sought-after jadeite jade pieces. It was protected with a heavy metal door and steel bars on the inside of the windows. The second story housed Wong's living quarters and quarters for two well-armed security team members. Both men were Chinese Americans and first cousins of Wong. Both served with the 1st Marine Division during their assaults on both the Central Pacific island of Peleliu and the Japanese island of Okinawa.

Four more cousins and former war-hardened Marines lived in a house next door, leased to them by a real estate corporation belonging to Wong and Jon Preston. One of Wong's uncles who owned a construction business completed all the upgrades, including a secret tunnel between the two houses' basements. Security needed to be paramount to a jewelry business, especially one involved in illegal trafficking.

To give Wong authenticity as a smuggler, Jonathan Preston worked with General John Renick to secretly set up a nefarious supply chain. One of Renick's wartime spies in Brazil made all the arrangements. Renick funneled the gems, jade, and rare gold coins provided by Preston through a cutout in Brazil to a gem dealer and former Allied spy in Havana. The rare gems, jewels, jade, and gold coins that Wong would end up smuggling came from a Japanese bounty that Jon's team recovered in the Philippines. Although Preston hated seeing the ancient Asian artifacts used in this fashion, it would be justified if it would end in Tsukuda's downfall. It was worth the tradeoff.

Preston and Linka became a silent partners in Wong's business. Jon supplied him with over 800 cut diamonds and emeralds that he and Camille had acquired during the war in Asia. They intended to start a jewelry business when they returned to Jon's hometown of Columbus, Ohio. However, Jon thought Wong could turn a good profit and earn them a good return on his investment. In April and May, Wong's business began to boom. He sold engagement rings to over 300 couples who were more than happy to spread the news about the quality and excellent service through word of mouth.

While Fitzsimmons unloaded his catch of Atlantic fish, Guy Wong met with a Cuban business owner named Jorge Serrano. His export storefront was on San Pedro Street, next door to the Hotel Armadores de Santander. A block south, the 500-foot-3-inch cruise liner HMT *Empire Windrush* prepared for her return voyage to Great Britain. It was the same ship that took Wong to India after he completed his OSS training.

The exchange of the diamonds, rubies, sapphires, and emeralds, from Serrano to Wong, was supposed to be a simple formality. Wong, cautiously playing the part of a vigilant businessman, counted each of the 400 gems in the four lots to ensure they were all there. After wrapping up his business, Wong excused himself to use the bathroom. He placed the gems in a wraparound waist pack, secured the pack under his pants, and took a cab back to the *Jeanne D'Arc*. Fitzsimmons was on the aft deck, smoking a cigarette and supervising the final stages of unloading their fish catch—when Wong boarded the boat.

"Our presence has not gone unnoticed," Fitzsimmons told Wong. "I've recognized several boats and their captains. Apparently, *Jeanne D'Arc* has caught their eye. We'll visit one of my favorite watering holes tonight after dinner. It's where most of the fishing boat captains hang out. That should further fuel the intrigue about the boat and whether I'm back in the smuggling business."

"You don't think that proposes a risk to our purpose in Havana?" Wong asked.

"Absolutely, but if we don't show up, they will become more suspicious."

"Someone followed me to Serrano's office."

"Not unusual for Havana. He's a local snitch."

"You recognized him?"

"Yes. He's harmless. Probably went to the police as well as one of the smuggling groups. They hire informants for pennies."

"Will the jewels be safe while we go out?"

"We have five guards with Thompsons, Guy."

"Do you think Tsukuda's people will recognize you?"

I'm counting on it. Our guards will be clearly visible after we leave. That alone will secure our position that we have something valuable on board. And when they find out who you visited, they will know what we are guarding."

"What if customs or the police get curious and want to inspect the boat? Won't they ask you to open the safe?"

"No doubt. They will only find the boat owner's documents and title, maps of the east coast and Caribbean, and several boxes of prophylactics that I keep on hand for the crew. I will secure the jewels in a special compartment in the bilge, below the pump intake level. It was a special modification that the Bath Iron Works added at my request."

"Does Preston know about it?"

"Of course! He had to approve the modification and pay for it."

"Damn, you think of everything."

"I didn't survive the smuggling business for twenty years by being dumb, Guy. I was never caught. What got me convicted as a thief was my own greed and listening to people I should never have trusted when I was on land. I should have stuck with smuggling."

Fitzsimmons paused, "My last bust was a crossroad for me. The only thing that saved me from life in prison was the war and Jon Preston. And, of course, I had some information on a suspected Japanese spy that helped."

"Why are you working with us, Elton? You have a successful fishing business."

"I'm nearly 45 years old. Like most fishing captains I know, I don't want to do backbreaking work for another fifteen years and die two years after I retire. Plus, I have a brain. After you take down Tsukuda's bunch, I plan to start a business."

"What kind?"

"Oil."

"What do you know about oil?"

"Quite a bit. I've been studying geology for two decades?"

"What got you interested in geology?"

"My grandfather. He lived in Texas for the last twenty years of his life. He was a smuggler, too. Taught my dad and me everything we know about smuggling. He was also a gambler. A very good gambler. On one of his trips to Havana in 1910, he got into a high-stakes poker game. He ended up winning the deed to a defunct, ten-thousand-acre cattle ranch near a town called Midland, Texas. After an oil strike in 1917, he let my father run his boat. He moved to the ranch that sat on top of a sedimentary basin between western Texas and southeastern New Mexico. It's called the Permian Basin."

Elton took a breath and continued, "It is a large oil- and natural-gas-producing area, but because grandpa had a lot of cash, he didn't do any wildcatting or much ranching. But, he did wind up marrying a widow who had a ranch next to his. She had a lot of money too, so they spent the next fifteen years traveling the world. On one of their safaris to Africa, Grandpa suffered a heart attack and died. In his will, he left his boat and cash to my father and the ranch to me."

"So, you're going to move to Texas and be a wildcatter?"

"With my knowledge of geology and the money I've saved, I think I can succeed in the oil business. Plus, I've asked George Linka and John Preston to go into partnership with me."

"What makes you think Jon and George want to go into the oil business?"

"Well, I'm pretty sure they both want out of the Army as soon as this thing with Tsukuda winds up. And George is going to put me in touch with an uncle in Dallas who has done quite well in the oil business."

"What's his name?"

"Hunt."

"You mean H. L. Hunt, the millionaire oil tycoon?"

"I'm not sure. George didn't tell me he was an oil tycoon. He just said he was a down-to-earth successful oilman who would go out of his way to help a friend. George is his favorite nephew. He's also supposed to be a math genius and a good card player. So, we should get along well."

"For crying out loud, Elton. If it is H. L. Hunt, you are indeed very fortunate."

"Well, let's hope so. I could use some good luck. Now, let's go to dinner. Afterward, we'll go rub shoulders with some salty, disreputable boat captains at the Blue Whale. And by the way, despite being my former associates, I don't trust one of them."


Dinner was not what Guy Wong had expected. Elton took him to a large, aging, multistory house in Old Havana that served dinner by appointment only. A small and barely readable sign nailed to the white picket fence read La Casa Blanca, Propietario Luis Pérez. While the outside looked run-down, the interior was modern. The four large downstairs rooms served as the dining area for as many as eighty guests, and the house was nearly packed. Large crystal rain chandeliers added pure radiance and gracefulness to the rooms. The large windows on the front and sides had alternating navy blue and red velvet curtains that reached the floor. As Elton requested, he and Guy were seated in the room at the front of the house to maximize exposure to the other guests.

"Tonight's dinner is *ropa veija*," Fitzsimmons explained to Wong. "It's made with shredded beef and vegetables that resemble a heap of colorful rags. It is traditionally made with flank steak—a beef cut from the calf's bottom muscle. It is very lean, has little fat, and has less flavor than other cuts of beef. Plus, it's notoriously tough, so here they make it with a chuck roast. Today is also a national holiday in honor of the birthday of José Julián Martí Pérez, a distant relative of the owner of this establishment. It is the only day they serve the ropa veija. I think you will find it very satisfying to your oriental palette. In other words, it is quite spicy."

Wong did find the meal delicious. The shredded beef was cooked in diced garlic, dry white wine, paprika, oregano, cumin, black and cayenne pepper, tomato, onions, and red bell peppers. The mixture was served with white rice, maduros, and black beans, and was garnished with chopped cilantro. After finishing their meal, Wong and Fitzsimmons polished off the bottle of local red wine that Fitzsimmons suggested.

"For dessert, I recommend the *flan de huevo* and a *café Cubano*. The flan is a dense custard dish made in the traditional Spanish way with eggs. It has a burnt caramel topping, which is really delicious. The café Cubano is a Cuban espresso," Fitzsimmons remarked. "It will power you up for hours."

After they finished their dessert of flan, Wong remarked, "This is something close to a custard my mother makes, except she uses only the egg whites. I like the texture of this and especially the caramelized topping. So, where is the Blue Whale located?"

"About an hour's walk or, if you prefer, a fifteen-minute cab ride."

"As full as I am, I'll opt for the cab."


The Blue Whale was a direct contrast to La Casa Blanca. Fitzsimmons stopped outside the door and turned to Wong, "Just follow me. Keep your head up and look straight ahead. Don't speak, and don't look away if someone stares at you. Stare right back. Most of the people here are hardworking and hard-drinking folks. They respect strength."

The low-ceiling bar was dimly lit and smelled of stale beer, sweat, and vomit. Fitzsimmons strode into the bar like he owned the place. He walked to the cavernous room's bar, nodded at several men he recognized, and sat at a deserted table with four chairs. Guy Wong felt totally out of place in his clean white shirt and pressed tan slacks. Nonetheless, he followed Elton and did as instructed. Elton took a chair with his back to the cinder block wall.

"Not like the bars in Georgetown," Wong commented as he took a second chair that faced the interior of the bar. Are you expecting trouble?"

"I always expect trouble. It's what keeps me alive in this business. I don't see anyone that we need to worry about."

A moment later, a plump waitress moved to the table and asked, ¿Qué estás bebiendo, Fitz?"

"Mi de siempre, Maria."

"¿Y el elegante?"

"Mismo."

As Maria walked off, Wong asked, "Did she just call me a bad name?"

"No, she called you *the fancy one*. Which means she likes you for the time being. Otherwise, she would have called you something less dignified."

"How long have you been coming here?"

"Over thirty years. I first came here with my grandpa when I turned twelve. He bought me a tequila. It was the first time I had ever drunk alcohol. After three drinks, I passed out. Grandpa had to carry me back to the boat. He told me as long as I drank the Casa Noble, I would never get sick. I've been drinking the brand ever since. Unfortunately, you can't buy it in the States."

"What's so unusual about Casa Noble that it won't make you sick?"

"It's a combination of the volcanic soil, the artesian well water, cooking the agaves whole in stone ovens before squeezing the juice out of them, not adding yeast, and triple distillation. Casa Noble has been making tequila for over two hundred years. But truthfully, I think grandpa just said that to plant the thought in my head. The power of suggestion, as the saying goes."

"How can you ferment alcohol without adding yeast?"

"They rely on natural airborne yeast. Apparently, it's everywhere. The fermentation process takes a lot longer, but they say it creates a better flavor. Plus, they age it only in French oak barrels. You'll see how smooth it is once you drink it."

As Wong sipped his tequila, a tall man with a weathered face and a slight stoop walked to the table and stared at Fitzsimmons. "When you left Ocean City, I thought you were moving to the ranch in Texas? Now, I see you have a new boat. What the hell is going on, Elton?"

Not intimidated by the big man's presence or demeanor, Elton said, "Guy Wong, meet Andrew Jackson Fitzsimmons, my father."

# CHAPTER 10

*Havana, Cuba*

Andrew Jackson Fitzsimmons sat in the chair opposite Elton. The sixty-five-year-old Irish fisherman was still lean and muscular. His once fiery-red hair was mostly white, but his large emerald green eyes appeared to be coming toward you without getting closer when he talked. His chin was accented by a thin upper lip, architecturally perfect cheekbones, and a straight-edged nose reminiscent of classical Greek artwork. Wong now saw where Elton got his good looks.

"It's good to see you too, Dad," Elton replied.

"Who's this joker?" Andrew commented. "Are you working for the Japs again? I thought you learned your lesson when the war broke out. The Nips are bad news, Elton. Are you in trouble? I saw one of their stoolies tailing this character today when he left your boat."

"I'm not in trouble, Dad. I'm just doing a little work for my friend here."

"That's not the word on the street. Wong, here, was seen going into Jorge Serrano's place. So, what—instead of guns and rum, you're smuggling jewels?"

"Mr. Wong is in the jewelry business. He owns an establishment in Georgetown and imports jewels and antiquities."

"Must have been a sweet deal to keep you from moving to Texas. All you've been talking about for the last two years is getting started in the oil business."

Andrew then turned his attention to Wong. "So, tell me, Mr. Wong. How are you going to keep my son out of prison when the Coast Guard busts him for smuggling?"

"It's easy, Mr. Fitzsimmons—when you know the right people and you have enough money."

"That won't protect you from the Japanese thugs that Elton used to work with, Mr. Wong. From what I've sniffed out, they know what you are doing, and they don't like competition, especially from a Chinaman."

"I'm also part Japanese, Mr. Fitzsimmons. That's enough to warrant a little leniency, albeit not much. I am hoping to pay them off to look the other way."

"The organization in Havana doesn't work that way. They're a bunch of bloodthirsty gangsters like those Yakuza crime syndicates in Japan. They're not as strong as before the war, but they are slowly moving back into the Caribbean. Hell, even the Cuban mob knows to stay the hell out of their way. You would do well to do the same. They're ruthless."

"Actually, I'm hoping that Elton will gain me an introduction to the syndicate, and we'll expand internationally. I have a good source of gems from Asia, and America is booming with couples getting engaged and married. Business is great, and I have plans to open more stores."

Andrew stood up and turned back to Elton before leaving. "Don't forget you have two children who depend on you, Elton. You have a responsibility to them. Anything you do with the Nips could ultimately endanger them. They don't give a crap about human life, and they will leverage them to get to you. When I found out you got another boat, I was worried about you. That's why I followed you to Havana. But I can see you're set on doing this. Just be careful, son, and stay safe."


Ten minutes after Jackson left, a smartly dressed Asian man walked into the bar. Elton immediately recognized Taro Abe. The last time he saw Abe was in April of 1941. He was the person who supplied the last shipment of guns that Fitzsimmons had smuggled into Baltimore. Two men followed Abe and blended into the shadows as the Asian gangster walked straight to Elton's table.

"I thought I would find you here, Elton. It's been a while. Can I buy you and your friend a drink?" Abe asked.

"It's been seven and a half years, Taro," Elton replied. "I expected you would be long dead. Don't you guys commit Hara-kiri when you lose a war?"

"I wasn't a soldier, Elton. I have always been in the export business. Aren't you going to introduce me to your Chinese friend?"

"Taro Abe, meet Guy Wong. He is also in the export business. Mr. Wong is my employer. And he is also half Japanese."

To be certain Fitzsimmons wasn't bluffing, Abe went into a five-minute Japanese dialogue to ferret Wong's background. After a while, Abe switched to Mandarin and then to English.

"You speak Japanese very well, Mr. Wong. Where did you grow up?"

"San Francisco's Chinatown."

"So, were you interred in an American concentration camp?"

"No, I was visiting my grandparents in China when your country attacked Pearl Harbor. However, my mother was sent to the Manzanar internment camp south of San Francisco."

"So, you escaped the war?"

"Not at all. The Japanese bombed the village where my grandparents lived. I lost a dozen family members, including my grandfather, in that attack."

"That is regretful. Do you hold animosity against the Japanese?"

"Not when it comes to profit, Mr. Abe."

"In that case, I have a proposal that may interest you and Elton."

"That depends on who you are working for, Mr. Abe. Elton has warned me about your Japanese Yakuza employers."

"I've never worked with Yakuza. They are organized criminal organizations that work strictly out of Japan. I work for a private business group. Elton worked with me before the war. It's the same export group. They have nothing to do with Yakuza."

"Does this export group have a name?

"The name is unimportant."

"Quite the contrary, Mr. Abe. Heraldry is important to all Japanese as it was to my mother. So much so, she made me study the kamons of the most important Japanese families. All the important families and their business groups have crests that distinguish them from other groups. They are much like the business logos in the United States and the coat of arms used by the knights in England, representing family lineage dating back centuries. My mother came from one of the better-known clans. If you wish to discuss business, you may avoid the organization name by displaying the kamon."

Wong could see the anger intensify in Abe's eyes and then subside as he contemplated his next move. It was clear he was not used to having terms dictated to him. As Wong waited, he noticed Abe unbutton the sleeve on his left arm and roll the shirt up to the elbow. On the inside of Abe's left forearm, there was a gold and black tattoo of the Japanese quince plant that represented the Oda family crest.

Wong turned to Fitzsimmons and said, "It probably won't mean much to you, Elton, but that is the classic crest of the Oda family. It's called the Oda Mokko. It's one of seven crests used by the famous warlord Oda Nobunaga. He was responsible for initiating Japan's unification in the mid-16th century. The Oda clan dates as far back as the 12th century."

"Is that the clan your mother belonged to?" Elton asked.

"She descends from the Taira clan. Oda Nobunaga was a descendant of the Taira. He was known to use the swallowtail butterfly kamon, which is the crest of the Taira clan," Wong stated as he rolled up his left sleeve and displayed the swallowtail butterfly on his arm. "I got this when I was 12 years old. My mother insisted that I proudly display my Japanese heritage. Unfortunately, it also got me into a lot of fights with Chinese kids."

Wong then turned to Taro Abe, "The Oda clan is well respected in Japan and abroad. I would be honored to hear your proposal, Mr. Abe. Do you mind if we take this discussion to Elton's boat?"


Wong listened closely as Taro Abe outlined the proposal in less than an hour. It was not what Wong had expected. Abe's group wanted ten percent of the value of everything that he and Fitzsimmons smuggled; in Japan, they usually extracted two to five percent. In return, Abe guaranteed them protection from the Cuban government, Cuban pirates, bandits and mobsters, and the Irish and Italian crime syndicates in the U.S. and Caribbean. In return, they would have to smuggle whatever Abe dictated.

"Mr. Abe, I am a gemologist and antiquarian. I specialize in gems from Southeast Asia and antiquities from China and Japan. I do not wish to expand beyond these two areas. The quantities of gems and fine antiquities I anticipate bringing into the U.S. can be hidden on the boat and not discovered. The gems alone should net over a million per quarter once my distribution network is in place. The Chinese antiquities that I have access to are priceless beyond belief. Collectors around the world will pay a small fortune to possess them. I will agree to a two percent fee on the gems, but only one percent on the antiquities, which will ultimately net your organization millions."

"What kind of antiquities do you have access to?"

"Over two hundred hand-carved jade figurines and jadeite statues, including a couple of dozen from the Shenyang Imperial Palace. I also have an ancient Japanese sword dated possibly to the 13th or 14th century."

"I heard a rumor a month ago about a sword for sale that was possibly crafted by a famous swordsmith named Gorō Nyūdō Masamune. Are you in possession of the legendary Honjo Masamune katana?"

"I have an ancient sword, but I have not confirmed the inscription to determine the swordmaker. However, I have never seen a sword like it before. Swords made by Masamune were made primarily for cutting human flesh. The blades are sharp, but its curved edge is the property of the blade that makes it so deadly—it could cut flesh with ease. If it is a Masamune, a record should be carved into the sword's tang under the grip. It documents the test results of the blade behavior cutting a corpse and how many bodies it was tested on."

"When will you be able to confirm its authenticity?"

"I should have an answer in 30 days."

"I would like you to cable me as soon as you know," Abe insisted, handing him a card with his business address. "If it is a Masamune, send the numbers '1534.' If not, send any other combination of four numbers."

# CHAPTER 11

*Baltimore, Maryland*

Takaji Sugimoto entered the Port of Baltimore on a freighter, as a returning businessman from South Korea, under the assumed name of Jung-hoon Kim. After negotiating customs, he faded into the Asian community and was lost among the hundreds of newly admitted emigrants. Within a week, he had re-established contact with three former smugglers who were associated with General Uchito Tsukuda before the war ended between Japan and the U.S. in 1945.

Sugimoto expanded the number of boat captains willing to work for him to six, including Elton Fitzsimmons. It was more than enough for what he was expecting to accomplish. Over the next six weeks, a half dozen emigrants under Tsukuda's command would be entering the U.S. from South Korea, Singapore, Malaysia, Burma, Indochina, and the Philippine Islands. All were former instructors, agents, and assassins trained at Hiroshima's Rikugun Nakano Gakko spy school. All were loyal to Tsukuda.

Fitzsimmons's first contact with Sugimoto at McGuirk's Bar on South Charles Street was not unexpected. He and Wong had off-loaded a haul of fish from their return trip to Havana and had tied the *Jeanne D'Arc* at a berth in the south harbor near the Federal Hill Park. In the 1800s, the underground tunnels and passageways provided storage for kegs of beer, for brewers who dotted the neighborhoods. Giant willow trees lined the riverbank in both directions, but three one-hundred-year-old live oak trees stood in the park's center.

The park also served as a defensive stronghold for Federal troops during the War of 1812. Still, it held the cannons that protected the fort during the Civil War. The once-sizeable, red clay bank mainly was a green hill, dotted with picnickers during the day—and lovers stargazing at night. However, Fitzsimmons liked the park for its panoramic view of the inner harbor and memories of his children playing on the hill when they were young.

A slender Japanese man entered the bar, walked straight to Fitzsimmons and Wong's table, and bowed slightly. Then, after removing his coat, he slipped up the sleeve of his left arm, revealing the gold and black tattoo of the Japanese quince plant, and introduced himself as Jung-hoon Kim.

Guy Wong looked at the aging man and stated bluntly, "You can cut the Jung-hoon Kim crap. You're no more Korean than I am Irish. So, you'll address me with your real name, or you can take a hike."

Taken back by the authority in Wong's voice, the man calmly took a seat. "I was warned about your audacity, Mr. Wong. I should have realized you would recognize me as Japanese. My real name is Takaji Sugimoto. I must admit, however, I am not used to people being so…impertinent."

"Americans tend to be very blunt, Mr. Sugimoto. We are not as formal, nor are we as courteous as traditional Japanese families. Although I grew up with these values, I learned quickly to adapt to the American ways, especially when dealing with white people. It was either do that—or fight every day. Now, what can I do for you?"

"I would like to follow up on the antiquities that you discussed, Mr. Abe."

"Can you be more specific?"

"The hand-carved jade figurines and jadeite statues from the Shenyang Imperial Palace are of particular interest. My organization believes that some of these may be lost Japanese national treasures."

"And your organization feels that it has a right to obtain the treasures and return them to Japan?"

"Of course, it is our duty."

"That's quite commendable, Mr. Sugimoto. Is that all you are interested in?"

"Well, the ancient katana you have in your possession is also of interest. Have you been able to verify its origin?"

"It's being evaluated as we speak. I should have the results by the end of the month. At that time, I will contact Mr. Abe as instructed."

"I understand you have access to an unlimited number of gems. The organization I work for is also interested in gems and would like to move 5,000 a month."

"That amount is beyond my control at present. But, I can let my supplier know. Plus, I don't want you competing against me in the U.S. market."

"My organization would like to act as your middleman for the Asian market. We won't interfere with your U.S. business."

"Are you suggesting that I not go through Jorge Serrano?"

"Absolutely not. Serrano is perfectly acceptable for the U.S. market. We want to be the middleman for selling gems in Japan. We also want you to use our fleet of boats to move your gems and antiquities to the U.S."

"That could compromise my supply chain, Mr. Sugimoto. If you catch my drift, if anyone but Elton moves those gems and antiquities, some may get lost in transit. This is why I am willing to pay your organization for protection on both the sea and shore."

"What if I were to guarantee the integrity of the shipments?"

"Mr. Sugimoto, can you also guarantee that you won't be shipping other contraband on your boats? Mr. Abe wanted us to ship whatever your organization put on my boat. I told him we couldn't agree to those terms because I only move gems and antiquities easy to conceal. I will not do business outside of my specialty. As far as selling gems for distribution into Japan, that is up to my very profit-minded supplier. I am certain he will agree to the quantity you mentioned. However, it will take time to get that quantity into the distribution channel."

"Very well. When may I see the jade pieces?"

"I can have a dozen figurines available for you to view at my store in Georgetown, next Monday. Will you be bringing your own appraiser?"

"Of course."

"Then, I look forward to seeing you next week, Mr. Sugimoto."

When Sugimoto left the pub, two men whom Fitzsimmons had recognized when he entered the bar, followed. He had seen the two men, along with two others, on the docks before he left the boat. That meant that Sugimoto probably had two men watching for him at his other favorite watering hole, O'Neill's Pub.

"Guy, I think you just pissed off a former Japanese lieutenant general," Fitzsimmons stated.

"Let's hope he gets over it. I would hate to have to kill him before we take his boss down," Wong replied. "All the same, we better keep an eye out for his thugs and make sure the boat is guarded around the clock."


When Sugimoto returned to his office on Park Avenue in Baltimore's downtown Chinatown district, he was still enraged at Wong's insolence. After writing out a telegram to Abe in Havana, he turned to one of his men.

"Alexei, what have you found out about Wong from your army buddy?" Sugimoto asked, in a voice that denoted authority and danger if the information wasn't immediately available.

"He was a captain in an army engineering company. He spent most of his time in China working with the 14th Air Force, building runways. He returned to California and was discharged in November 1945," Alexei replied.

"He is too cool of an operator to be just an engineer building runways. I smell a rat. It sounds like a cover for an intelligence agent. Wong is fluent in Mandarin and Japanese. It would be a hell of a waste of talent to use him otherwise. They would want a man of his skills as an operative behind enemy lines. I'm thinking he's former OSS or army intelligence. Have your friend dig deeper. Pay him whatever it takes. Plus, I want the names of any army intelligence types associated with a man named Jonathan Preston."

"Yes, sir. What about Fitzsimmons? Do you want us to rough him up?" Alexei Antonov asked.

"No, that would be a dead giveaway to my intentions. Once we have the jade artifacts, the sword, and the gem pipeline set up, you can get rid of them and their boat. Maybe an accident after they leave Havana. All hands lost at sea."

Alexei walked outside to have a smoke, and he took his brother Dimitri with him. He needed some time to think. They had only been in Jung-hoon Kim's employ for a month, and already he was talking about murdering two men. With his six-foot-six-inch frame, Alexei was willing to play a tough guy. But he wasn't sure he wanted to get involved with what was coming, and he certainly didn't want his younger brother involved.

Killing Japs for the U.S. Marines during the war was one thing; killing for hire was not what he had signed up to do. Alexei's time with the 1st Marine Division on Peleliu and Okinawa confirmed what his gut told him—Kim was not Korean. The day he met Kim, Alexei knew immediately that he was Japanese. When he had worked on the dock before the war, he had seen how Japanese mobsters had handled the Irish mob. They were ruthless and thought nothing of cutting your throat. Kim was beginning to look more and more like the Japanese mobsters he had come across in 1940.

The more Alexei thought, the more nervous he became. Suppose this Preston guy was still with army intelligence. In that case, Alexei should seriously think about *not* providing Kim the information he had requested—and walk away. And suppose Kim would have him kill Wong because Kim suspected Wong of being a former army intelligence agent. In that case, he and Dimitri, if caught, could be returned to active duty and tried for murder in a military court-martial. The sentence, if convicted, was death by hanging. Kim was definitely Japanese. But was he *organized crime,* or a Japanese spy left over from the war, seeking revenge? He would have to thoroughly think through the consequences before obtaining more information from his Army buddy or leaving Kim's employment. As Kim's hired muscle, Alexei knew too much to just walk away. To survive, he and Dimitri would have to disappear. But, how?


Sugimoto's second-in-command was one of Tsukuda's spies left over from the war. Kaito Wan had survived the debacle that killed Haru

Aki and Asami Nakada, and he had dispersed the remaining members of Aki's gang. The Japanese-Malaysian, with roots in Okinawa, had gone into hiding in the Chinese community in Baltimore. Wan's knowledge of Mandarin helped him secure a job as a dishwasher in a Chinese restaurant. He didn't make much money, but he was able to survive. It took several weeks for Sugimoto to track him down. Wan nearly killed Sugimoto one evening, as he followed him through an alley towards the restaurant. Only, the tattoo of a gold and black Japanese quince plant, which was revealed when Kaito tore a shirt sleeve off and threw Sugimoto to the ground, saved his life.

After Alexei and Dimitri left the office, Sugimoto turned to Kaito, "Were you able to make contact with anyone working in Army personnel, in Washington?"

"I have one lead I will follow up with this evening," Wan replied. "What about Alexei? Hasn't he come through yet?"

"Just the information on Wong, which I think is bogus. This Wong character is too poised and calm. He reminds me of some of the trainers I had at intelligence school. Nothing intimidates him. I want you to see what additional information you can find on Wong and the agents in Washington who worked with Preston. Double what you told him you would pay. That should be enough for your contact to take a greater risk and dig deeper."

"My contact has a big gambling debt with the people I play with—five thousand dollars."

"Tell him you'll pay off the debt if he comes through with the information. But, I want it by the end of next week."

"I'll get the information, sir."

"Have you found any more of your cohorts who worked for Aki?"

"No, sir. Not yet."

"Keep looking. There should be two or three out there. Make sure you roll up your shirt sleeves when you go indoors to eat or go to a bar. Your tattoo will attract attention, and word will spread that the black and gold tattoo is back. Then, they will find you."

"Is the second team from Asia still arriving this Sunday?"

"Yes, the fishing boat left Havana yesterday with the two men on board. It will enter the Patapsco River after dusk. The second boat will follow, four hours later."

Sugimoto paused before continuing, "Make sure everything is ready to house them at the farm. I want them to start training immediately. After years of inactivity, they may need to go through some intensive training to hone their skills."

"The staff is in place, all hand-picked by me. We will continue to operate the farm as an apple and peach orchard, as instructed. The small barn has been converted into an indoor training arena. Our first arrivals—Domen Touma and Gima Benjiro—are our main instructors. They are already training the staff. We completed the indoor firing range yesterday. I also have a location for an outdoor range that is five miles from any neighbors. With the suppressors and the reduced-charge cartridges, there should be little noise to worry about."

# CHAPTER 12

*Washington, D.C.*

Major General Lew Miller was sitting at his desk when his secretary entered his office carrying an open envelope and two paper pages. There was a troubled look on her face that Miller had seen only once before—when she thought that Jonathan Preston and his wife were dead at the hands of Asami Nakada.

"You need to see this right away, General," Nancy Brewster said, handing the letter to her boss. "I've contacted Colonel Preston and Colonel Linka. They'll be here in ten minutes."

"But, I have a meeting with Colonel Rogers at 3:00 p.m.," Miller replied.

"Sorry, sir. I rescheduled the colonel to Friday. This is more important."

"If you say so, Nancy," Miller said as she exited the office and closed the door behind her.

After reading the letter, Miller agreed. This couldn't wait. He picked up his phone and dialed General Renick's personal number. "John, I need to see you immediately! Can you come to my office?"

Renick was in Major General John Renick's office in less than three minutes. Renick and Miller had worked together in army intelligence for nearly a decade. So when Miller said *immediately*, it was implied you drop everything. Renick knew it meant life or death for someone. He just hoped no one was dead. As Renick entered Miller's office, he saw his cohort pacing near the window overlooking the Pentagon's courtyard. Miller didn't say anything; instead, he handed Renick the letter.

"You think this is on the level?" Renick asked after finishing.

"There is too much detail about Guy Wong and Elton Fitzsimmons to be otherwise. Plus, the information this guy Antonov has been asked to obtain, on our agents who have worked with Jon Preston, is disturbing. I would surmise that this Kim fellow is none other than Lieutenant General Takaji Sugimoto, Tsukuda's number-two man. I had no idea he was in the States."

"I saw the report from two weeks ago that your agents lost track of him in Acapulco. How was he able to have eluded your agents— and then vanish?"

"We're not sure. We thought Sugimoto was headed to Cuba, but when our assets there couldn't pick up a trail, we just assumed he was still in Mexico."

"Well, now he's in Baltimore, and he's after the agents who work with Preston."

"Do you want me to plug the leak with this Sergeant Knowles in personnel?"

"Not yet. Let's wait and get a take from Jon and George. They may find a use for the sergeant."

Before either man could take a seat, Jon Preston and George Linka entered Miller's office. The look on the faces of the two generals had a sobering effect. Something serious was in the works.

"Nancy said this was urgent, sir, and told us to walk right in. What's up?" Preston asked.

After reading the two-page letter, Jon handed it to George. While George absorbed the contents, Preston was thinking.

"What do we know about Alexei and Dimitri Antonov?" George asked, handing the letter back to General Renick.

At that moment, Nancy Brewster was ushered into Renick's office, where she handed General Miller three personnel folders. "I had a friend pull these while you and General Renick were talking. Don't worry, Sergeant Martin Knowles was on a break, and there is no record these have been pulled from the records department. Staff Sergeant Alexei Antonov was a sniper with the 1st Marine Division in the Pacific. Staff Sergeant Dimitri Antonov was a sniper with the 9th Infantry Regiment, part of the 2nd Infantry Division during The Battle of the Bulge. Both have impeccable records. Plus, two teams of two agents are on the way to protect Camille, at her home, and Kathleen, who is working a case at Carlisle Barracks in Pennsylvania."

"Katie won't like that, Nancy," George complained. "She thinks she's a big girl who can take care of herself."

"Standard operating procedures, Colonel Linka," Nancy replied.

"Since when?" George asked.

"Since we found out that Tsukuda's organization has plans to send people to the States and eliminate your team," General Miller replied.

"What will we do about the dozen agents that used to work for us? You don't have the resources to protect all of them," Jon stated. "There must be a half dozen that are retired and living in or around D.C."

"That's one of the reasons you and George are here," General Renick added. "We only have a dozen active agents in the Washington region, and they have to cover Pennsylvania, Maryland, and Virginia as well as D.C."

"What about the FBI?" General Miller asked.

"I don't think we want to bring Hoover into this mess," Preston interjected. "Otherwise, he'll claim the Tsukuda affair as his sole territory. Plus, he could screw up our sting operation with Wong and Fitzsimmons."

"What about Navy or Coast Guard assets?" Linka asked. "They worked well with us on the *I-405* case."

"The Naval District Intelligence Office is charged primarily with internal security. They might have the latitude to provide support," General Miller replied. "I'll contact Vice Admiral Thomas Inglis and see if he can provide some agents. John, you know Rear Admiral Jack Perkins of Coast Guard Intelligence. They have special agents that conduct criminal, personnel security as well as counterintelligence investigations. Can you check with him to see if they can lend us some support?"

"How much information on Tsukuda do you want me to give them?" Miller asked.

Before General Miller could answer, Jon interrupted, "Sir, if we want their help, I suggest we tell them everything, including what we are doing with Wong and Fitzsimmons. We wouldn't want them to keep us in the dark."

"Alright. General Miller and I will make arrangements for you and George to brief Admiral Inglis and Admiral Perkins. If they agree to help us, just make sure they keep the information in-house and on a need-to-know basis," General Renick finally said.

While Jon and George were walking back to their office, they were greeted from behind by a friendly voice. "I was hoping to catch you two while you were still in town," said Rear Admiral Richard Dubois. "Apparently, I just missed you in Tokyo when I was visiting Brigadier MacKenzie."

"Admiral, it's good to see you. How long will you be in town?" Preston asked.

"I may be here permanently. Is there a place we can talk?"

"Absolutely. Follow us, sir," George replied. "We're headed to our spacious office."

"If it's anything like the Navy gives its captains, I don't think I'm going to be impressed."

George turned right down a corridor and opened a nondescript door. When Admiral Dubois entered, he was taken aback by the size of the room. "It's not much, but it's ours," George said.

"It looks like there used to be more people. What happened?" Dubois asked.

"Reduction in force and reduction in expenditures. At one time, twenty counterintelligence agents were working here. Now, there are only six. This is where General Miller lets us hang out when we are in town," Preston said, laughing. "Now, tell us about your new job."

"I was interviewed by Admiral Thomas Hayward, the Chief of Naval Operations. He's offered me a position as his deputy."

"If I remember correctly, that's a three-star position. Are congratulations in order?"

"It still has to be approved by the President and Congress. But according to Admiral Hayward, Truman likes the work we did in the

CBI during the war, and what we did in the Philippines and Japan after the war—to secure the stolen gold and antiquities. Apparently, Truman thinks I'm the brains behind it all."

"They won't hear anything from us to make them think otherwise," Jon said, winking at Dubois.

"I hear you are looking for ONI help?"

"News travels fast. We just left General Miller's office with a task to get help from your Naval District Intelligence Office."

"Rear Admiral Inglis was visiting with Admiral Hayward and me when the call came from Miller. Hayward asked my advice."

"What did you tell them?"

"I advised him to go for it and hang his ass out in the wind," Dubois said, laughing.

"Seriously?"

"Hayward and I were roommates during our second year at the academy. He got a good laugh out of it. After I told him about what you all did during the *I-14* and *I-405* incident, he said you all can have four men immediately and another two when they come off leave. I'll introduce you all to the admiral tomorrow morning at 0900 hours. Now, why don't we have dinner this evening with those lovely girls you all hang out with, and you can introduce me to Jon Junior?"

"I would love to, but George and I have some undercover work to conduct this evening that can't wait. It pertains to what is going on with our request," Jon stated. "But, you're on for Sunday. Plus, Katie will be back in town."

At 2200 hours, Jon and George walked into a Russian restaurant in Greektown— a neighborhood of Baltimore bounded by Lombard Street to the north and O'Donnell Street to the south. Having been in business for nearly forty years, the *Stravinsky's* restaurant was an icon in the area. The owners had immigrated to the U.S. in 1908, claiming kinship to the famous Russian composer, Igor Stravinsky, whose image was hanging in a large frame behind the bar next to Pyotr Tchaikovsky's likeness. In the background, Tchaikovsky Symphony No. 5 could be heard.

Preston and Linka wore well-worn, dark-colored, wide-legged, double-pleated pants, with triple closures and cuffed bottoms. Jon wore a V-neck navy blue wool sweater over an aging yellow shirt. George had on a wrinkled white shirt and an old two-button tweed jacket with notch lapels. As Jon slipped into a booth next to Alexei Antonov, George moved into the other side, next to Dimitri.

"I'm sorry we're late," Preston said.

"Who the hell are you?" Alexei asked.

"The person you are seeking? I'm Jonathan Preston," Jon whispered.

"Oh, crap. You should not be here! This will get us killed," Alexei said.

"Who the hell are these people, Alexei?" Dimitri asked.

"Friends, Dimitri. Very good friends," George replied. "Now, be quiet and listen."

"I have agents outside," Jon said. "You and your brother will be okay. Is there a back room where we can have some privacy?"

Alexei called the restaurant owner over, who spoke in soft Russian, and the group was immediately moved to a smaller dining area behind a closed double door. George and Jon noticed a swinging door that led into the kitchen at the rear of the room. Hopefully, two of Guy Wong's cousins were stationed at the restaurant's back and another two out front. Preston didn't have time to check before entering the restaurant, but Wong assured him they would be there.

Over the next hour, Alexei explained that he and Dimitri had been hired by Kim as muscle to intimidate people, but it quickly got out of hand. Kim now expected him and Dimitri to murder people, which they did not sign on to do. Alexei admitted to Preston that he was naïve about Kim's initial expectations. On the other hand, he could not condone murder, especially of American soldiers.

"I realize I may go to jail for bribing Sergeant Knowles to provide confidential information, but I could not live with myself if someone gets killed," Alexei said. "The only information I gave him was on a former army captain named Guy Wong. And there wasn't much information on him. I thought Kim just wanted to do a background check on him because he was doing business with Wong."

"By contacting us, you may have saved yourself jail time, Alexei. It's the information on the people associated with me that worries us. Did Sergeant Knowles have a chance to get the information your boss requested?"

"No. I was supposed to ask Knowles for the information last Saturday, but thank God, he failed to show for a poker game. Why does he want this information? Just who are you, Mr. Preston?"

"If we are going to keep you and Dimitri alive, you'll need to know. For one, it's Colonel Preston and Colonel Linka. George and I headed up a team of U.S. Army counterintelligence agents during the war. We were responsible for taking down a Japanese spy ring in Calcutta, which eventually killed four female assassins. These assassins were the nieces of Kim's boss in Japan. Kim is a former lieutenant general in the Imperial Japanese Army named Takaji Sugimoto. He works for a former lieutenant general who headed up Japan's spy and assassin school. His name is Uchito Tsukuda. Now, Tsukuda heads up a growing criminal organization. Sugimoto is his number-two man. We need you two to work with us to take this guy down."

"How do you plan on keeping us alive, Colonel? We can't possibly go back to Kim."

"Your military records state you and Dimitri have no next of kin. Is that still the case? No, spouse or fiancé?"

"Yes, that's correct."

"In that case, your best option for staying alive is to be arrested for treason and placed in solitary confinement. Sergeant Knowles will be joining you."

"When?"

"Tomorrow morning, as you leave your apartment. It needs to be public, so word will get back to Kim."

"But Kim, rather Sugimoto, is bragging that he has men everywhere, Agent Preston. Even in the military police. If he knows we've been arrested, they will get to us no matter where we are. I beg you to do this discreetly," Alexei pleaded.

"Maybe he's right, Jon," George stated. "Tsukuda has had three years to infiltrate the army. And with the amount of cash and gold he has, he can buy anyone."

"Alright, Alexei. We'll do it your way. Discreetly," Jon conceded.

# CHAPTER 13

*Washington, D.C.*

At 6:06 am, Lawrence Rhett walked down his front steps and moved a garbage can made of metal, from a small recess beneath the front door of 1349 Wallach Place NW, onto the curb in front of the house. To save money, Lawrence and his twin brother Thomas had moved back into the family house after returning home from World War Two. Although trained as automobile and aircraft mechanics, both men were thieves. When they had been arrested in January 1942, they were given the option to join the Army or go to prison. They wisely chose the Army. With their breaking-and-entering skills, they had soon found themselves in the U.S. Army Counterintelligence Corps.

After eight months of training, Lawrence and Thomas shipped to the China, Burma, and India Theater of Operations, where they met Jonathan Preston. Preston was a young officer then. But, unlike any officer they had met, Preston treated them as an integral part of his team and, more importantly, as equals. They traveled with Preston to Chittagong in 1944 and helped him take down a Japanese spy ring. They were even part of the team that worked as kitchen staff when the Nakada triplets attempted to assassinate Admiral Louis Mountbatten, the Supreme Allied Commander of the South East Asia Command (SEAC), and Ralph Block, the U.S. representative to the Office of War Information in India. Thomas was stabbed by one of the three sisters while attempting to arrest her. By the end of the war, both men had distinguished themselves and each was elevated to the rank of staff sergeant.

When Lawrence and Thomas had returned to the U.S., they were again working with Preston to track down Japanese agents trying to smuggle biological weapons onto American soil. When Preston raided the Japanese agents' house where the biological weapons were stored, both Lawrence and Thomas had been part of the team. A year later, with both their father and mother dying within two months of each other, Lawrence and Thomas inherited the house. They were out of the service and, thanks to Preston, working as aircraft mechanics for the U.S. Navy—jobs they had held before being coaxed into the U.S. Army in 1942.

Lawrence, slightly taller than his twin brother, squinted his eyes as he looked east at the sun rising above the city. He gave up trying to adjust to the harsh light after emerging from the nearly dark interior of the house. He turned and walked back inside to get Thomas. They had fifteen minutes to catch the bus for their thirty-five-minute ride to the naval airfield where the Anacostia River joins the Potomac River. They worked for a civilian contractor at the airfield, repairing the PV-2 Harpoon patrol bomber and the PBY-5A/6A Catalina for a Naval Air Reserve Training Unit activated in 1946. In two months, their jobs with the navy would end when the reserve components on the base would move to Andrews Field, and the airfield would be turned over to the U.S. Air Force. The Virginia-based company they worked for received a contract to repair fixed-wing aircraft for the air force, after contributing to a representative's successful reelection campaign.

Several minutes later, Lawrence and Thomas walked out the front door and down the steps. They turned east and headed towards the bus stop, a hundred yards ahead on 13th Street NW. Lawrence put on a pair of aviation sunglasses left over from the war to ward off the sun's rays. They walked past several Yoshino cherry trees, whose blossoms were falling and being replaced by green leaves—their sweet, light fragrance lingering in the gentle breeze. The trees were the same type planted by First Lady Helen Taft and the wife of the Japanese ambassador in 1912, on the northern bank of the Potomac Tidal Basin.

"Did you tour the new hangar where the P-51 Mustang will be repaired?" Thomas asked.

"Not yet. I was too busy touring Hangar 14, where the C-69 Constellation will be housed. The Air Force went all out. This is the most amazing facility I have ever seen," Lawrence replied.

Thomas continued talking about the transition of their jobs to the newly formed United States Air Force. He had toured the new buildings where they were to work on transports and fighter aircraft, beginning in two weeks. Lawrence would be the second-shift supervisor of the transport unit, and Thomas, the second-shift supervisor of the fighter unit. With their new jobs and the great money they would make, both men planned to get married next summer.

Thomas glanced at his Timex wristwatch and was about to say they needed to pick up the pace—when he heard a loud pop. He thought it was a car backfiring until he heard a thud behind him. Thomas turned his head in time to see bright red blood pouring out Lawrence's skull onto the dirty grey concrete sidewalk. He saw a small hole in Lawrence's forehead and noticed that the back of Lawrence's head was missing. As Thomas knelt next to his brother, he went into shock.

"Oh, my God! Larry!" Thomas exclaimed as he held his brother.

Thomas didn't hear the second report of the rifle, and he didn't feel anything as the bullet entered the back of his skull. He was dead before his body pitched forward on top of Lawrence. For all their careful planning and hard work, Lawrence and Thomas Rhett would not get to go to their new air force jobs or marry the girls of their dreams. They became victims in a war of revenge being waged by Uchito Tsukuda.


Riku Nakamura and Sora Takahashi lived next door in the same duplex building on Melvin Drive in Baltimore, Maryland. The men were Japanese Americans. Both were technical sergeants in the U.S. Army Counter-intelligence Corps, assigned to the Washington Division. They fought alongside each other and gathered intelligence on Japanese positions at the Battle of Saipan, 15 June to 9 July

1944, and the Battle of Luzon, 9 January to 15 August 1945, when MacArthur invaded the Philippines.

After the war ended, they were reassigned to counterintelligence headquarters in Tokyo. They worked with a group of counterintelligence corps agents to recover gold stolen by the Japanese from the twelve Asian countries they invaded between 1937 and 1943. After the war ended, they were reassigned to Washington, D.C. They worked with the same counter-intelligence unit tasked with finding and arresting Japanese agents on the east coast.

When the hunt for the Japanese agent, Asami Nakada, moved to Baltimore, Jonathan Preston arranged the lease of a duplex for the duo and their families. After the mission was completed, Sergeant Nakamura and Sergeant Takahashi were allowed to stay in the Asian neighborhood and commute by train to the Pentagon. They now worked for Major General Lew Miller, the new deputy director of G-2.

At 6:10 a.m., Riku Nakamura and Sora Takahashi left their respective duplexes and met on the sidewalk. They began walking east to a bus stop to take them to the Camden Train Station, two miles away. As they walked into the morning sun, squinting because their field hats did not have brims, the first shot rang out.

Nakamura thought nothing of the noise, but commented, "That sounded more like a rifle shot than a car backfiring."

When Takahashi didn't respond, Nakamura turned and saw Takahashi lying on the sidewalk. Nakamura reacted instantly and went for the automatic pistol hidden in a shoulder holster. As he drew his pistol, a second bullet from the gunman struck him in the chest. Before anyone could respond or help the two men, they were both dead.


By noon, General Lew Miller and General John Renick were sitting in General Omar Bradley's office, contemplating what had happened. When Miller received word of the attacks, he immediately sent a dozen MPs to protect Camille DuPont and Kathleen Lauren at their Marine Barracks quarters. With Jon and George airborne and on their way back from the military prison at Camp Lejeune, Camille's and Kathleen's protection was up to him. Although the women said they could take care of themselves, General Miller thought it prudent to have 24-hour security at their apartments and personal guards when they left the house. He wasn't about to take a chance of losing his two favorite female agents and Jon's young son.

Despite Camille's and Kathleen's firm outward resolve, General Miller saw the doubt and fear in their eyes. The dozen veteran military policemen assigned by Miller began securing their apartments and the surrounding neighborhood.

"Ladies, this protection is not up for debate," General Miller stated. "We lost two former and two active CIC agents, this morning. They all worked on the Asami Nakada and rogue submarine case, and I will not lose more agents. So if you think you are not a target because you are a woman, you need to get it out of your mind."

"General, we are not saying we don't think we are targets. We are saying that we are well enough trained to take care of ourselves. Placing a dozen MPs around our apartment will only confirm who we are and make us bigger targets," Camille pleaded.

"Look, I promised Jon and George that I would protect you all, and I'm going to do that to the best of my ability. Especially with General Tsukuda's agents on the loose in the district. Plus, I wasn't the only one who ordered the protection. When President Truman received the news that four agents were shot this morning, he called me personally and ordered the protection. I am not about to disregard a Presidential order, nor will I disappoint Jon and George. You two, like it or not, are part of my family, and I will not let anything happen to you."

"Well, as long as you are here, you should join us for lunch," Kathleen said as she and Camille turned and walked toward the front door of Kathleen's apartment. As General Miller fell in step behind Camille, he noticed the bulge of two automatic pistols on either side of her blouse-covered dark slacks.

"You're carrying automatics. I thought you said you weren't worried about being a target?" Miller asked.

Camille turned slightly. "We may be women, but we're not stupid, General. We know when we need to be prepared."

"Watch it as you step through the hallway. I have an arsenal that's loaded for bear. I wouldn't want you to knock one over and set it off," Kathleen stated, as she held the door open for the two-star general.

As General Miller walked through the hallway, he noticed an array of Thompson M1A1 submachine guns leaning against the wall, with extra 30-round magazines lying near them. Two of the Thompsons were variants that were not issued to the military yet. As he moved into the living room, he saw four suppressed M3A1 submachine guns lying on the sofa. They were a wartime OSS special-use weapon called the Grease Gun.

"For crying out loud, where did you get the suppressed M3?" Miller asked.

"Jon picked them up at the weapons arsenal last week," Camille replied. "The old version was not truly a "silent" weapon. So, he asked a friend to rework the suppressor and develop a new low-velocity .45 cartridge. It's relatively quiet now."

"Remind me not to show up at your door unannounced."

"Don't worry, General. We know you're one of the good guys," Kathleen announced.


Despite her outward show of redhead bravado and confidence, Camille DuPont was concerned—more for Jonathan Jr. than herself. Any woman would be terrified if a Japanese underground warlord—and killer— was out to get her and all the members of her husband's counterintelligence team. However, Camille was highly trained, pragmatic, relentless, and fearless when attacked. She could see a problem and immediately know what was needed to solve it. The only way to deal with murderous thugs like Tsukuda was to kill them before they killed you. Camille was confident that Jon, George, Kathleen, and she could outwit Tsukuda's assassins and kill them. She also knew that Tsukuda was out for revenge because Jon's team killed Asami Nakada before she was able to release a biological weapon in Washington, D.C. Whether he realized it or not, Tsukuda had a red bullseye painted on his forehead. Camille was determined to put a bullet in the red, if Jon, George, or Kathleen didn't beat her to it.

Most people underestimated the gorgeous, exotic-looking, part-French and part-Thai, Kathleen Lauren. She looked more like a Paris fashion model than a deadly intelligence agent who could kill you just as quickly with her hands as a gun. She was also a master of disguise. With her lithe frame, she could imitate a man or a tramp in a back alley.

Camille knew that Kathleen was just as well trained and committed as herself. And Kathleen had no problem killing someone trying to kill her or someone close to her. She had lost her twin sister in the war to one of Tsukuda's double agents. After that, she trained and became as good as any man on the team, proving it time and time again. Taking down the intelligence czar responsible for her sister Jacqueline's death couldn't please her more. *It would bring closure to what Kathleen lost in the war. That's a good thing*, Camille thought.

# CHAPTER 14



*Washington, D.C.*

The morning after returning from Camp Lejeune, where he hid Alexei and Dimitri Antonov, Jon Preston put on a pair of light brown slacks. He added a light-colored blue shirt with button-down collars and a comfortable pair of lace-up, two-toned brown leather and tan, woven Florsheim shoes. His attire was dressy enough for the casual business meeting with Guy Wong and Father Kirkendall at Georgetown University. There was a possibility of rain today, so Jon put on his lightweight, tan overcoat.

Father Wallace Kirkendall was a tall, thin, and graceful-looking man with a thick head of all-white hair. The distinguished professor of Asian history had graduated with honors, obtaining two advanced degrees—a Master of Divinity and a Master of Asian History—from the University of Notre Dame. Three years later, Kirkendall received his doctorate in archeology and Asian history from the University of California Los Angeles (UCLA). In 1925, he was assigned to Peking, where he worked as a research assistant for the Roman Catholic Archdiocese. For twelve years, Father Kirkendall traveled throughout China, Korea, and Japan, researching antiquities. He was included on a team of two leading western researchers—Swedish archaeologist and paleontologist, Johan Gunnar Andersson, and the Canadian paleoanthropologist, Davidson Black.

When the Japanese invasion of Manchuria began on September 18, 1931, Kirkendall was working at the Mukden Palace in Liaoning, China. Two days after the Kwantung Army of the Empire of Japan marched on Liaoning, Father Kirkendall and a dozen other archaeologists were escaping toward Port Arthur on the southern branch of the Chinese Eastern Railway. The 258-mile trip took three days and was halted several times due to skirmishes between Chinese and Japanese forces. At Port Arthur, Kirkendall took refuge at Stella Maris Catholic Church, where his twin brother, William, was the diocesan.

Ten weeks after contacting the archdiocese in Peking, Kirkendall was reassigned to a private Jesuit research university in the Georgetown neighborhood of Washington, D.C. Now, fifteen years later, he was the head of the Department of History at Georgetown University.


The red brick, three-and-a-half-story, Georgian-style Old North Building stood on a raised basement. Jon took the twenty steps, two at a time, to the wooden porch with a balustrade deck, where Guy Wong was waiting. Guy greeted him with a handshake and led Jon through the arched stone doorway into the building's interior.

Father Wallace Kirkendall greeted Guy Wong and Jon Preston and then walked them down a flight of steps to the basement. He led them to a well-lighted room on the east side of the building, with only one door for access. At the back of the room stood a large Mosler safe. The 64-inch-tall, 47-inch-wide, and 37-inch-deep safe must have been 60 years old. The double doors on the outside showed minimal scuffing and scratching—a testament to Professor Kirkendall's patience and care for the things he was entrusted with.

After Kirkendall closed and locked the exterior door to the room, he bent down. He dialed the combination of the outside vault door. As the six-inch-thick door opened, he leaned in and dialed the combination on the inside lock. With a twist of the handle, the safe opened. The sword Jon had dropped off three months earlier was leaning against the solid-steel wall at a forty-five-degree angle. It was wrapped in white silk.

Kirkendall put on a pair of white cloth gloves, carefully lifted the sword from the vault, and moved to a table covered in black velvet, in the center of the room. He gently placed the katana on the table.

Next, he removed the silk cloth around it, revealing the single-edged sword in its black-lacquered, wooden scabbard.

"As a precaution, I ask that you put on these gloves," Kirkendall stated as he handed Preston and Wong identical pairs of white cloves. "The katana is in excellent condition. The gloves will keep you from scratching the lacquered scabbard and getting contaminating skin oils on the blade. However, I recommend you not touch it. It's very sharp."

"Have you confirmed its origin?" Preston asked.

"Yes."

"Is it the Honjo Masamune that went missing in 1945?"

"No, but it is a Masamune," Kirkendall said as he pulled the curved sword from the scabbard and set it on the silk cloth. "In fact, I believe it is the Oda Masamune that I saw in a private collection in Kyoto when I was doing research at the Kyoto Museum. It belonged to the Kenoe clan—an old aristocratic family with close ties to the Oda clan and the imperial family. You might remember that Prince Fumimaro Konoe was the Prime Minister of Japan who attempted to resolve tension with the United States and negotiate a peace agreement in 1941. He resigned before the attack on Pearl Harbor—after his attempt at peace had failed. He did remain a close advisor to the Emperor throughout the war. Unfortunately, he committed suicide following the Japanese surrender."

"I thought all swords were confiscated by the U.S. Army after the war," Wong stated.

"True. Many were turned over to the army, but some of the more historic and valuable ones were hidden. I understand this sword was in my brother's keeping at his church in Port Arthur, China."

"Yes, he said it was given to him by a junior Japanese officer named Fumitaka. He was afraid that the Chinese or Russians would get it if he were killed in battle," Preston responded. "Father William said he was with a group of Japanese soldiers who were storing stolen antiquities in the mission's catacombs. He must have been impressed by your brother after learning he was an expert on Asian antiquities. Apparently, he trusted him enough to care for it. Unfortunately, the instructions he left with your brother were destroyed when the church was accidentally bombed by Allied planes."

"Then, the officer could have been Konoe Fumitaka, the Prime Minister's eldest son. I met both of them at the Konoe estate. Of course, Fumitaka was just a young lad then."

"But, why would he carry such a valuable sword into battle?" Wong asked.

"It's reflective of a time in history when a Samurai rode into battle and died an honorable death. It has been the way of the Samurai for centuries. The Kenoe family evolved from the Hokke clan—one of the main branches of the ancient Fujiwara clan of the 12th century. It's been a Japanese tradition for a boy to be given his first sword around four or five years old. A sword that he wouldn't give up until his death. Fumitaka must have thought his chances of death were reasonably great for him to leave the sword with my brother. He probably realized that Father William knew the value of the sword, would keep it safe, and eventually return it to his family."

"Why a sword? The times of Japanese warlords are long over."

"To most noble Japanese families, a sword is regarded as the personification of a Shinto deity. Most Japanese believe the sword embodies the souls and the powers of former samurai who carried it. Konoe would naturally want his son to carry it in a battle to provide maximum protection. However, because Fumitaka left it with my brother, it leads me to believe that he did not share his father and ancestors' same beliefs. Or, it could mean that the rumor about the katana being a sacred sword is true, and Fumitaka didn't want to tarnish its sacredness. Otherwise, it would be in the hands of some Russian general. Earlier this week, a cable from my brother confirmed that Fumitaka died in a Russian POW camp."

"What rumor?" Preston asked.

"Two of the archaeologists I worked with were told by a museum curator that the Masamune was a sacred relic that had been captured when the warlord Oda Nobunaga stormed a Buddhist fortress on Mount Hiei, just north of the old capital of Kyoto in 1571. It was revealed to Nobunaga that the sword had never been in battle or used to kill. If Fumitaka knew this, it could be the reason why he left it with my brother."

"Interesting, but let's get back to the authenticity. How can you be sure it is a Masamune?" Preston asked.

"Three reasons, Agent Preston. First, I recall seeing this sword in 1931 when I was conducting research in Kyoto. The two researchers I was with—Johan Andersson and Davidson Black—were invited to Prince Kenoe's estate for a farewell party. The Prince was a patron of the museum. Most of the museum staff members were there as well as several of the prince's cousins. After dinner, the prince took us on a private tour of the estate, including an impressive collection of ancient Samurai swords. The most prominent was the Masamune. Information and documents on the origins of the sword were displayed with the sword. One document compiled by the Honami clan associated with the eighth shogun, Tokugawa Yoshimune, listed the sword's length as 68.7 centimeters, which matches this sword."

After pausing to catch his breath, Kirkendall continued. "Another document cataloged the designs on the blades. The wavy line along the side of the blade was created by the swordsmithing process. The high temperatures created the waves. This was because the Masamune blade featured soft and hard steel, which was blended in layers. The blending of soft and hard steel kept the sword from breaking while in battle. The Masamune I remembered seeing, at the Kenoe estate, exhibited the identical pattern shown in this sword."

When Kirkendall paused again, Preston asked, "What is the third reason?"

"The third was told by Prince Konoe himself while showing us the sword. He related how the sacred sword had been passed from Oda Nobunaga to the Tokugawa Ieyasu in 1582, after the battle of Tenmokuzan. After Nobunaga's death and receiving the title of shogun from Emperor Go-Yōze in 1603, Ieyasu presented the sword to the emperor as a show of his fealty. Then in 1860, which is the later part of the Edo Period, the sword was presented by Emperor Kōmei to the head of the Konoe clan. This blade is special because it carries a gold inlaid inscription attributing it to Masamune. Only a highly prized sword would be presented to a noble clan by a Japanese

Emperor. At the time, the Konoe clan was the most prestigious and highest-ranking noble house in the Japanese realm."

"Then, we have a big problem?" Preston asked.

"Yes, we do, Jon. This sword needs to go back to the Konoe family. It will be an invaluable foreign policy tool for President Truman to present to them. Plus, you can't possibly let Tsukuda have it. He would leverage it to consolidate more power," Wong remarked.

"I agree."

"Then, how do you plan to convince Takaji Sugimoto that we have a real Masamune?"

"I think President Truman can provide that answer."

"I believe I know where you are going with this, Agent Preston," Father Kirkendall stated. "I saw the newspaper article where General Walter Krueger presented President Truman with a 650-year-old Japanese sword from a prominent Japanese family. It is believed to be a Masamune also. But what makes you think he would give this sword to you as bait."

"First, its authenticity as a Masamune is in question, but you can solve that detail. Second, he wants Tsukuda gone from the scene. And third, he's the godfather of my son, Jonathan Junior. He listens to me."

"Really, the President is his godfather! For crying out loud, Jon. Isn't there anyone you don't know on a first-name basis?" asked Guy Wong.

"He's Mr. President to Camille and me, but he's Harry to my father. They were in the same artillery regiment in World War One. Every two years, the President and Dad get together to hunt pheasant in South Dakota and reminisce about the good old days. Truthfully, I think it's the only time that the President and Dad can get away from their wives and drink their favorite Kentucky sour mash."

"What do you want to do with this Masamune, Agent Preston?" Kirkendall asked.

"A Brink's detail should be here in the next thirty minutes to take it to a bank. I assume you have the write-up and photographs that I requested?"

"Right here," Kirkendall said. He reached for a folder on his desk and handed it to Preston. "Where is the Masamune headed, if you don't mind me asking?"

"To a vault in the Federal-American National Bank. But I'll bring it back here when our expert from Japan arrives to authenticate it. I'll bring the President's sword as well. It will need to be certified, too."

"It sounds like you have already run this by President Truman, Jon," Wong remarked.

"Yes, on Sunday, at Jon Junior's christening at the White House. The christening was delayed until Camille's uncle, Cardinal Dupont, could get here from France."

"Why did I even ask?" Wong relented.

# CHAPTER 15

*Vientiane, Laos*

After signing the contract provided by Yul Butler and filling in the amount of compensation needed for twelve months, René Clairoux did not waste any time. Within three weeks, Renate and Jacob had traveled and returned from their office in Vientiane, Laos. They briefed their uncle Marcel Clairoux on what was needed. Suspicious at first, Marcel quickly deducted that this was not a contract with the French Indochinese government because it involved gemstone mines across four countries. Although he didn't say so to Renate or Jacob, Marcel suspected the new American CIA or U.S. Army counter-intelligence involvement.

During the war with Japan, Marcel had worked with his brother as an Allied operative. René was tied into a group of OSS and U.S. Army counter-intelligence types out of Calcutta. They successfully took down a sizeable Japanese spy ring on one of the missions into Burma. The information provided by Renate and Jacob had the same feel and smell. It was large on cash but low on the identity of the employer. Marcel suspected the information requested on emerald and diamond mines was a clever cover for what René really needed—information on Communist activities in the region. Although they didn't ask, he suspected they wanted information on the number of armed Viet Minh units as well. *Classic intelligence gathering,* Marcel thought. He would collect the information as long as it didn't jeopardize his life.

Following Japan's surrender and the expulsion of Japanese soldiers from Laos in late 1945, a French-Lao force re-entered the country and freed French prisoners at Luang Phabang. That same week,

Marcel Clairoux had been second-in-command of a Franco-Laotian guerrilla regiment that entered and reoccupied Vientiane's capital, his home of twenty years.

When the French tried to regain control of the Laotian government, Vietnamese residents in Vientiane and surrounding towns began spreading anti-French propaganda to undermine French authority. The preparations to resist the French colonial rule were being directed by agents of the ICP who had established communist cells in Laos in the early 1930s. Marcel Clairoux was aware of the communist cells. He knew that they were made up entirely of Vietnamese nationals and members of the Viet Minh. The latter were escaping French persecution in Indochina. These same Viet Minh nationalist cells became allies after the Japanese took control of the region in 1941. Most worked closely with the British SOE, American OSS, and the Chinese army units of Chiang Kai-shek.

Marcel and his family chose to flee Vientiane into the Laotian countryside instead of remaining in a city under Japanese control. With his brother's help, he joined the OSS in 1944. He then became associated with Jon Preston and George Linka. They had teamed up to go after a major Japanese spy ring in Burma and Indochina. Once again, Marcel felt as though he was being drawn into the dark world of covert activities, only this time to spy on the people he fought with against the Japanese.

Despite being French, Marcel had sympathies with the Laotians and the Vietnamese after fighting with them. French colonial rule had been extremely harsh on the natives. Still, it wasn't until after he lived and fought beside them that this became evident. With French colonial forces trying to regain control, the Vietnamese agitation in Laos was instigated, once again, by the Viet Minh. Despite being masked as a Laotian national independence coalition, it was being led by Indochinese communists. Marcel had to draw a line somewhere, and communism was a line he could not step across.


In his first two weeks in the field, Marcel contacted thirty former Laotian guerillas he had fought with against the Japanese. Nearly all were relatives of his wife, Ketsana Phoulivong, a first cousin to the Laotian king, Sisavang Phoulivong. Dozens of Ketsana's relatives lived and worked in Ban Huay Xai, two hundred miles northwest of Vientiane. It was also where a significant sapphire mine was located on the Mekong River banks, directly opposite the Thai town of Chiang Khong. This area was also near the center of the opium production area, where the borders of Thailand, Laos, and Burma meet. Later in the 20th century, it would become known as "The Golden Triangle" region.

Although Marcel had fought with dozens of Ketsana cousins in northern Laos, he chose only two as his agents. The former guerilla fighters were well-respected citizens of Ban Huay Xai. Being cousins to the king had its advantages. Both men worked at the most prominent government-run mine. Noy Borom was a foreman, and Sayavong Khaek was the general manager. Wanting a dozen more agents, Marcel allowed the two men to recruit additional agents they trusted. Despite being well known in the region, Marcel was still French, and anti-French sentiments were rising in northern Laos with the Viet Minh's return. Marcel decided to limit his role in Ban Huay Xai to occasional family visits via the Stinson L-5 Sentinel his brother had obtained from a former OSS friend in Hanoi. With its 34-foot wingspan and oversized tires, the 6-cylinder, 185-horsepower L-5 was powerful enough for short field takeoffs and landings from the rough, cleared fields along the Mekong River. It was far more reliable and easier to fly than the French manufactured C.280 Phalène he had flown during the war.


For centuries, sapphires have been mined in northwestern Laos. Open-pit gem mines could be found everywhere along the Mekong River and throughout the Bokeo Province. Farmers would often dig holes in their rice fields, looking to find a small fortune in gemstones. The medium-dark-blue, green, and black-star sapphires were the most highly prized. The sapphires that were too dark or too light-colored were worth much less. But to those who sought the gemstones, less was better than nothing, and so they would dig.

It didn't take long to determine that the Vietnamese living in the region were the more ardent seekers of gemstones. In every Vietnamese community, there were open-pit mines. The gems that they uncovered were sold to the government-run mine at Ban Huay Xai. Sayavong Khaek would gather information on each seller and pass it on to Marcel. After several months, it became clear that a dozen Vietnamese settlements north and east of Ban Huay Xai were producing the most gems. Marcel suspected all had ties to the Viet Minh. The number of gemstones they were finding increased so much that Khaek's boss decided he and Borom needed to travel to the settlements to observe their operations firsthand.

On his next trip to Ban Huay Xai, Marcel received a briefing on what Khaek and Borom had uncovered. It wasn't what he was expecting.

"Because of the success with finding gemstones, the villages have tripled in size," Khaek said. "Together, the twelve settlements are producing as many quality gemstones as our mine in Ban Huay Xai. This is creating such a large surplus of product that our director wants us to scale back on our purchases."

"Have you discovered what they are doing with all the money from their sales," Marcel asked.

"I see no change in their lifestyle. No new clothes or community buildings. No new cooking utensils or upgrades to their huts. I can only assume that the bulk is going to the Viet Minh. I heard a rumor that some of the villages have been purchasing weapons from Japanese soldiers who refused to go back to Japan after the war."

"According to my brother, René, Colonel Vo Nguyen Giap recruited a group of 230 commissioned and noncommissioned officers and forty-seven gendarmes of the Japanese Kempeitai into the Viet Minh services. Apparently, they were all suspected of war crimes. The group is commanded by a Japanese colonel named Murakami. He was the Kempeitai commander assigned to the general staff of the 38th Imperial Army. Colonel Giap arranged Vietnamese citizenship for all of them as well as false identification papers. The Kempeitai confiscated over 30,000 French weapons during the coup of March 1945, and they had access to over 100,000 Japanese weapons. This is probably the source of those rumors and the munitions."

"The villagers will be upset that our mine will not purchase their gemstones. They may try to take it out on Borom and me."

"There may be another way to slow down the Viet Minh. René told me the exporter he works for in Hanoi wants to buy more gemstones. I'll contact my brother and have the two fly in next week."


Yul Butler was elated by the opportunity to purchase the sapphires from the Vietnamese villages. Since the end of the war, almost all mines in Burma, Thailand, Cambodia, Laos, and Indochina were back to full production, creating a glut in the Asian market. The overproduction quickly drove prices down. Luckily, the same was happening in the global gold and silver markets as the global economy came roaring back. Businesses were flush with cash, and banks were willing to loan to investors. To Butler, it was the perfect financial storm needed to implement his version of Operation Remorse, which he called Operation Recourse.

It didn't take long for Operation Recourse to pay dividends. From mines across Burma, Thailand, Cambodia, Laos, and Indochina, René and Marcel's agents had redirected much of the unregulated gemstone market by farmers and villages to Yul Butler's company, Asian Enterprises, Ltd. So when Preston had proposed the gemstone business, to take down Uchito Tsukuda, he was asked to brief President Truman on the extent of the operation. The president's closest advisor, David Niles, proposed setting up a limited partnership in the Philippines with Guy Wong as the primary owner and Yul Butler, George Linka, and Jonathan Preston as silent partners. Niles proposed that the company's owners could keep twenty-five percent of the profits. The remainder would go to a bank in Manila, to fund U.S. intelligence operations in Asia. However, the profit that Wong made in the U.S. could be shared by the partners. After conferring with Niles, President Truman further recommended that Camille Dupont be named the company's treasurer and placed in charge of the distributions and business operations.

"Desperate times call for desperate measures," President Truman said at the end of the presentation. "Since Congress won't fund the fight against Communism in Asia, we must continue to get creative. Just make sure that the CIA, McArthur's crowd, and Congress don't get wind of this, Agent Preston."

"I'll do my best, Mr. President," Jon replied.

Butler began consolidating the raw gemstones in Hanoi and shipping them to a corporate office in Manila, manned by a Filipino mother and son that Jon and his team had worked with after the war. In Manila, they were cataloged and sent to São Paulo. There, Fabio Martinez established a gemstone-cutting business that took the rough stones and refined them into a variety of perfectly cut and polished gems. The gems were then put into Fabio's pipeline to Havana, where fifty percent of the stones were sold directly to Tsukuda's agent for distribution to Japan. The remaining gems were picked up by Elton Fitzsimmons and smuggled into the U.S. Within a month, Guy Wong's jewelry and distribution network was starting to take on a corporate look.

When information on Viet Minh activities began flowing into Butler's office, a picture of just how organized the communists were in northern Indochina stunned everyone in Washington. The Vietnamese were not just armed with machetes, knives, spears, and old muskets like they were at the beginning of 1941. Instead, they had thousands of modern weapons given to them by American, Chinese, and British sources while fighting the Japanese. This included the two hundred thousand weapons that they had confiscated when the Japs surrendered.

René Clairoux's report revealed that there were hundreds of villages in northern Indochina with trained Viet Minh militia. Some villages had as many as two hundred soldiers. More villages were being armed and trained every month by the Japanese soldiers, who had been granted citizenship by Colonel Giap. Clairoux estimated that the Viet Minh would have three trained divisions able to take on the floundering French forces who still had not received the promised weapons and additional reinforcements from Paris. Things were not looking good in Hanoi. After conferring with René Clairoux, Butler decided to take the man's advice and open an office in Saigon, in case he had to vacate Hanoi. Before René got up to leave, Butler asked him to find a suitable location.

# CHAPTER 16



*Washington, D.C.*

Guy Wong used his family influence and network of Asian Americans to expand his jewelry business into Maryland, Virginia, Pennsylvania, and New York. For Jon Preston, the use of Wong and the Asian artifacts, to lure Tsukuda into his trap, would hopefully come to an end soon. Preston would bait Tsukuda with the priceless jade artifacts and set the hook with the Masamune sword, to ensure success.

When Preston presented his plan to his boss, General Miller was skeptical about President Truman's Masamune sword scheme. Nevertheless, Miller obtained permission from the Army Chief of Staff for his agent to pitch his plan to the president. Later that week, they met with President Truman.

"So, rather than using the sacred sword that you have authenticated as a Masamune, you want to switch it out with the sword given to me by General Krueger. Why not use the sacred sword?" President Truman asked.

"Sir, the sword was presented to the Tendai Buddhist sect by a Japanese Emperor. So, it may be more historically significant to the Japanese than the Masamune sword you were given," Preston replied. "If something unforeseen goes wrong with our operation and we lose the sacred Masamune to Tsukuda, it could help him consolidate more power and prestige in Tokyo."

"So, you are planning a bait and switch after Takaji Sugimoto and his antiquities expert view the sacred sword?"

"We hope to portray your sword as the famous Honjo Masamune katana, which was proven in battle, for over several centuries. The

Japanese believe the Honjo katana is a just-and-honorable blade that possesses magical qualities. It is regarded as the hereditary sword of power used by the ruling Shoguns of Japan for four hundred years. Its significance is unparalleled."

"How will you pull it off, Jon?"

"Simple. We stack the deck. We've discovered the name of the antiquities expert Sugimoto plans to bring to the U.S. to certify the sword. His name is Tadahisa Haruki. He is the Chairman of the newly formed Society for Preservation of Japanese Art Swords. The gentleman's only son is in a U.S. Army prison, serving a twenty-year sentence for crimes against humanity committed by the Unit 731 detachment he commanded in Mongolia. We agree to release his son and grant him U.S. citizenship for his cooperation. Tadahisa's son is the only member of his family still alive. He will agree. After he certifies the sword, Tadahisa will, unfortunately, perish in a hotel fire. Once we take Tsukuda down, we'll relocate the father to Oregon and set them up in the jewelry business."

"That's quite a plan, Agent Preston. Is that *may be the Honjo Masamune katana* going to seduce Tsukuda into accepting it as the real thing?"

"Hopefully long enough to bring him out of seclusion to take possession of the sword."

"Alright, you have my permission on all you suggested. But, what about the son?"

"We would like for you to arrange his transfer to the U.S. Army biological unit in Maryland. His only crime was being a renowned microbiologist and college professor forced by the Japanese Army to work at the Unit 731 facility. I confirmed this through other members of the unit who are now working in Maryland. They were forced to work at Unit 731 against their will also."

"Is that all?"

"There is the matter of your sword, Mr. President. First, we want the White House to announce that it is being sent to Georgetown University to determine whether it's the legendary Honjo Masamune. Next, we want you to invite Japan's leading expert from The Society for Preservation of Japanese Art Swords, Tadahisa Haruki, to complete the verification."

"Won't that simply play directly into Tsukuda's hand?"

"Yes, sir, but he won't expect our end around with Tadahisa and his son. And while he's authenticating the Honjo sword, Haruki can also certify the sacred sword, which you can plan on presenting to the Konoe family next year during your visit to Tokyo."

"So, now you're planning my diplomatic trips?"

"It's only a suggestion, Mr. President."

"And a good one at that."


Takaji Sugimoto and an elderly Asian man exited a black 1944 Ford Deluxe Coupe. They crossed the street to the Pacific Gems storefront on P Street NW. The bodyguard got out of the car after Sugimoto entered the jewelry store. He crossed the road and stood outside the house. The driver stayed in the car.

Upon entering the shop, Sugimoto shook Guy Wong's hand and introduced his antiquities expert, Professor Chen Li.

"Professor Chen was the first curator at the Palace Museum in Beijing when it opened in 1925."

Guy Wong bowed and shook the professor's hand and began a five-minute dialogue in Mandarin, asking about his family and how long he had lived in the U.S.

"I first came to the U.S. in 1904, as part of an exchange program between the New York University (NYU) and Wuhan University," Chen replied. "I received my law degree from the NYU School of Law in 1908. After my youngest daughter graduated from NYU in 1932, she married a U.S. citizen and made New York her home. When I left the museum in Beijing in 1938, I immigrated to the U.S. I eventually found a position with the Smithsonian Institute. Now that I'm retired, I work there as a docent two days a week. Mr. Takaji found me while I was conducting a tour of a Chinese exhibit."

"With your background as a museum curator, you must be very familiar with Chinese antiquities?" Wong remarked.

"As well as Japanese and many other Asian artifacts."

"I have prepared the pieces on the third floor. Are you able to walk up two flights of stairs, professor?"

"I may be 82 years old, but I walk six miles a day, Mr. Wong. I'll make it up the stairs."

Wong escorted his visitors to the third floor. Two security guards, dressed in khaki uniforms and carrying .45-caliber automatic guns in leather holsters, protected the area. One guard unlocked the heavy steel door and followed the group into the room. The other guard waited outside on the spacious landing.

Inside the room, lying on top of a glass-covered cabinet, were three sets of jade and jadeite pieces set in their own unique display. A fourth set was positioned on a separate display case at the far right of the room. It was covered with a dark silk cloth. When Professor Chen looked closely at the first set, he nodded his delight.

"Don't be bashful, Professor. You may pick these up and examine them," Wong stated.

Professor Chen reached the first display case and picked up what Sugimoto thought was an ugly, roughly polished green pendant. It was disc-shaped and had a small hole on one side.

"Rather unremarkable looking, Professor," Takaji stated bluntly.

"On the contrary, it's very remarkable," Professor Chen replied. "This is a coiled jade dragon from the Hongshan culture that lived in Inner Mongolia from 3800 to 2700 B.C. It is often called a pig dragon because it has a narrow, coiled body and long, tear-shaped eyes. If you look closely, you can see its closed mouth; however, it is without horns. It is almost as if it is an embryonic form of a dragon. Very few are known to exist. Most were in private collections before the war. It was probably used as a pendant for a member of the aristocracy. This simple-looking piece represents some of the earliest known workings of jade."

Professor Chen set the dragon down and picked up a highly polished, hollow, three-inch, beige-and-brown *cong*. It was in the shape of a square but with rounded corners. The thin one-inch corners of the jade treasure were decorated with masks. The third Neolithic artifact in this set was more to Sugimoto's liking.

"This looks like a bracelet," Sugimoto said with delight. "Is this from the Hongshan culture also?"

"No, this is a more sophisticated carving. It looks like it might be from the Lower Xiajiadian culture, which ruled from 2000 to 1600 B.C. This piece would have been worn by a chieftain who believed it endowed him with the mythical powers. But, it could also have been used as a symbol of heraldic power within their community. In fact, this period's art often depicts China's first emperor, Qin Shi Huang, wearing robes with a dragon motif. From that point forward, the dragon has been the traditional symbol of Chinese monarchs."

Professor Chen took his time going through the remaining displays of jade and jadeite. When he finished, he turned to Guy Wong.

"This is all very impressive, Mr. Wong. I'm familiar with some of these artifacts. Several are from Chinese museums, but others are from private collections that I had the honor of researching during my doctoral studies in Beijing. I assume that this next one is something exceptional."

Guy Wong moved to the second display case. He removed the dark silk cloth revealing a large, golden, lacquered rectangular box with the figures of three five-clawed imperial dragons on the lid. When Wong raised the heavy cover, it disclosed a book made of ten jade panels. Wong picked the book up carefully and laid the 11½-by-5-inch panels, end to end. The overall length of the book was over four feet.

As Professor Chen examined the book, he noticed the two outside panels were decorated with seventeenth-century-style dragons presented against a background of clouds. The clarity of the dragons and clouds was further enhanced by the incised lines filled with powdered gold. The eight interior pages, inscribed with Chinese characters, were also filled with gold dust. But the names of the ancestors to whom this book was dedicated were filled with powered lazurite. The expensive mineral would have been imported from central Asia. However, the blue color was a direct reference to the blue of heaven, where the ancestors resided.

As Chen translated the text, he said, "This is extraordinary, Mr. Wong. This book was presented in a formal ceremony by Emperor

Fu-lin in 1648 to his dead ancestors, announcing that the Empire of China had been united. It also confers the title of Empress on Fu-lin's great-great-great-grandmother. It's written in both Chinese characters and Manchu script. It must be the very first proclamation issued by the Fu-lin upon assuming the throne. From my recollections, there is no history that this book exists. This is indeed a valuable national treasure."

"Can we arrange for the purchase of these, today?" Sugimoto asked.

"For the first three sets of jade, yes. Unfortunately, this book is not for sale, but there are more where it came from. I wanted you to see this book to understand the quality of the antiquities that I can access. Do you think your syndicate can market this type of rare and high-quality product?"

"Without a doubt."

"In that case, I will have color photographs and certifications of a hundred different pieces for you to review by the end of the month, along with the asking prices. Once you have chosen the pieces you want to purchase, the items may be picked up at a bank in Washington, where they are stored. Before you take possession, you and Professor Chen will be able to examine them for authenticity. At that time, payment will be made in gold bullion or coins."

"From what I understand, Mr. Wong, it is illegal for U.S. citizens to own or trade with gold."

"True. But, we won't be revealing the trade to the government, will we?"

"What about the sword? Has its authenticity been verified?"

"Yes, it is a genuine Masamune, but not the Honjo. The authenticator thinks it is a sacred sword held by the Tendai sect of Buddhist priests of Mount Hiei until they were defeated by Oda Nobunaga in 1571. The sword was presented to the order by Emperor Go-Nijō, the 94th emperor of Japan. According to legend, it has never seen battle or spilled blood."

*Praise the gods!* Sugimoto thought. *Because of its religious significance, this sword may be just as valuable as the famous Honjo Masamune. Maybe more.*

"When can I see it?" Sugimoto asked.

"In twelve weeks, when the other artifacts arrive. However, I will have color photographs and the authenticity certificate available within thirty days. Will that be enough time for you to arrange for your own sword expert?"

"Yes, that should give me enough time," Sugimoto replied, wondering who General Tsukuda would send to verify the sword's authenticity.

# CHAPTER 17



### *Tokyo, Japan*

Uchito Tsukuda woke with a start and sat upright in his bed. The beads of sweat that formed on his forehead were now running down his cheek. It was the second time in three weeks that his grandmother, Umeko, had visited him in a dream. As a young boy, Uchito's grandfather had told him that his maternal grandmother came from a long line of seers. He said one person in every Minamoto generation was cursed with the augury of seeing what would happen in the future. It had been that way for the last 900 years.

Umeko would have dreams or visions and then council relatives and neighbors on what to do or not do. People would come from all over the province to sit with her and have their fortunes told. Most Japanese who knew her thought she was a sage. The foreigners, especially the Jesuit priests who heard about her, called her a sorceress and a witch. They told their parishioners she was possessed by a demon. Regardless, most Japanese heeded her advice.

When Uchito was fifteen, his grandmother had told him to 'beware the white samurai'—after coming out of a three-hour meditation trance. When he had asked her to explain, Umeko mumbled strange words and failed to answer his question. Later, she had told Uchito that many disasters had befallen the ancient clans because of the destructive habit of their leader's sense of pride and self-importance. Umeko had told him, "You are arrogant, Uchito. Pride will be your downfall, too."

Uchito had often wondered what she had seen in her trance. Could she have foreseen his death? If she had, how had he battled and survived the white European armies of England, Australia, and the United States, during the war? His mind had put him in positions that kept him out of danger and away from the atrocities committed by combat units. *Has the use of my intelligence and wisdom changed my karma, or is there an unknown white samurai still out there?* Tsukuda asked himself.

After his grandmother's death, his mother began having visions. In her mindless rants, she would shout, *Japan is lost! Metal birds are coming from the east. The sky is turning to fire, and children are burning!*

Unfortunately, the foreknowledge of what would happen in the future had driven her to suicide in 1938. Now that Uchito was his grandmother's only living direct descendant, he wondered whether he would inherit the prescience and go mad from the knowledge of what horrors lie ahead. Would he be tempting fate by harnessing this potential? Then again, if the prophetic abilities of his ancestors had guided the clans of feudal Japan, why couldn't they serve his purpose, in business, to avoid potential dangers? No adversary would be safe. He bowed his head and said a prayer, with gratitude for the power of prophesy that his grandmother had been given, which he believed he now possessed. But, how to access the gift?

As Tsukuda reflected on his grandmother's warning, he recalled only four foreign-born samurai of European descent. Three lived during the fifteenth and sixteenth centuries. One was Dutch, and the other was English. The third was a black man of African origin who served as a retainer to Oda Nobunaga. The last known European samurai, a Prussian, died in 1911.

Could there have been another European samurai, Tsukuda wondered? He would have Raizo inquire with the national museum in Tokyo, where the historical records of the provincial warlords and samurai were kept. If the Prussian or another white samurai had offspring, then one of their children could be the one whom his grandmother had warned him about. Tsukuda needed to know where the threat might be coming from and have it neutralized.

While Tsukuda pondered his situation, Raizo entered his study carrying a cablegram from Takaji Sugimoto. Tsukuda smiled as he digested the contents. The sword that Sugimoto was attempting to purchase from Guy Wong was verified as a real Masamune by an antiquities professor at Georgetown University in Washington, D.C. However, it was not believed to be the coveted Honjo Masamune. Instead, it was thought to be a sacred sword held by the Tendai sect of Buddhist priests of Mount Hiei. The katana was presented to the order by Emperor Go-Nijō, the 94th emperor of Japan. It had never seen battle or blood.

To further determine the identity of the sword, the university was inviting a renowned sword expert from Japan to authenticate it—Tadahisa Haruki. Tadahisa was the chairman of the Nihon Bijutsu Token Hozon Kyokai—or Society for Preservation of Japanese Art Swords. This coincided with a report he had received from a government source, two days ago.

Why invite Tadahisa to the university? To Tsukuda, this could only mean one thing—that the sword was probably the Honjo Masamune. So he picked up a pad and pen and wrote out a message to send to Sugimoto. He wanted the Masamune before Tadahisa Haruki had a chance to authenticate it. Otherwise, the government of Japan would step in and demand the sword be returned to the royal family. If that happened, he would not possess the famous sword and would not gain the prestige of secretly owning it.


Takaji Sugimoto was surprised by Tsukuda's request to obtain the sword at all costs before Tadahisa Haruki had a chance to authenticate it. "Why not let the renowned expert validate it?" Sugimoto said out loud. The message authorized him to offer Wong up to $500 thousand in gold. After considering further, Sugimoto surmised that if authenticated as the true Honjo Masamune, it would cause the price to triple. Maybe Tsukuda was not a fool after all.

When he contacted Guy Wong with the offer, Wong refused the request stating that Professor Kirkendall was adamant about having it authenticated by the representative coming from Japan. Because of the historical importance of the Masamune, its authenticity by a Japanese expert was imperative, Wong argued.

When Sugimoto countered, a couple of days later, with a one-million-dollar offer, Wong said he would have to confer with his business partner. Sugimoto immediately saw through the stalling tactic and asked his assistant to plan a way to steal the Masamune.

"The sword was moved by Brink's armored transportation services to a bank in downtown D.C.," Kaito Wan stated. "There is no way to stage a robbery on such short notice. I recommend we take the sword when it is returned to the university. The building that Professor Kirkendall is in has no security. I could easily extract the sword after the Brink's truck drops it off and their guards leave."

"You'll need at least a dozen men," Sugimoto replied.

"I have only eight that I trust. They should be enough," Kaito replied, then continued. "Can I ask why Tsukuda is so interested in this sword that he would have us steal it? It poses a great risk. Why can't we can be patient and purchase it after its authenticity is verified by the expert coming from Japan?"

Sugimoto was not without questions, himself. Tsukuda's obsession over this unverified Honjo Masamune could pose a threat to the organization. As his second-in-command, Sugimoto knew he should say something. But, knowing Tsukuda, Sugimoto's loyalty would, unfortunately, be questioned. It brought to mind a poem he had learned at the Imperial Japanese Army Academy while a first-year cadet. He recalled that *one should consider the sword to shape his own personality and stamp out evil through the perfection of his own character.*

The poem reflected the feeling of respect for the samurai sword and what it embodied. Most Japanese saw the sword as a symbol that personified the code of the samurai. Bushido represented the moral values and ethical code of samurai. It stressed sincerity, frugality, loyalty, martial arts mastery, and honor until death. Like a sword, a samurai was seen as a bright, clean, sharp, strong, and graceful individual. *The exact opposite of Tsukuda*, Sugimoto thought, who was now beginning to question Tsukuda's samurai character.

Unfortunately, the introduction of firearms in the sixteenth century changed the situation of the samurai, radically. Many samurai thought the use of firearms was a disgraceful way to kill an enemy. It eliminated the skill of the samurai's swordsmanship and bravery during battle. And it eliminated an honorable death to those the firearms killed. *What was death to a samurai if it was not honorable?*

*Anathema! Was Tsukuda's obsession for this sword honorable, or would it end up a curse?"* Sugimoto wondered, but did not dwell on it.

Sugimoto was convinced that Tsukuda was delusional in his desire for the Masamune. Pride was driving Tsukuda's desire for the blade. And pride was a double-edged sword with both positive and negative effects. It could work in his favor, or it could work against him. Sugimoto had experienced firsthand how pride could affect one's judgment. During the battle of Leyte, he did not listen to one of his junior officers. In retrospect, the officer's recommendation would have stopped the American assault on the beaches. Sugimoto believed the officer did not have the experience to warrant the request and dismissed it outright. His pride led to the defeat of his forces, and Sugimoto was relieved of command. He could no longer afford the luxury of pride. He would have to exercise extreme caution regarding this sword and how to convince Tsukuda of its dangers.

The situation reminded Sugimoto of an old Japanese proverb. If he tried to convince Tsukuda that he was wrong, it would be as effective as chanting a prayer to Buddha into a horse's ear. But, if he was to stay faithful to Tsukuda and the samurai's code, he would have to find another way to convince him of the error in coveting this sword. But, how?

Sugimoto decided to change the subject and asked Kaito, "What did you find out about Alexei and Dimitri Antonov? They haven't shown up for work in three days."

"Nothing yet. I suspect the Antonovs got cold feet when you told them they would have to kill Preston and his team members. They were soldiers during the war. Plus, Alexei was with the Marines in the Pacific. I'm pretty sure he doesn't buy that you are Korean. He may have already deduced that this is not about smuggling and muscle on the docks."

"Find and eliminate them before they decide to talk. Did you get any more information from the sergeant that works in the Pentagon?"

"He wasn't at the poker game last night, and none of the other players have seen him."

"With the Antonovs missing, is this just a coincidence, or do you think the sergeant has been compromised?"

"I have no way of knowing. However, I have another source that I will reach out to this evening."

"In the meantime, I want extra security—both at this office and at the docks. And I want to know what Elton Fitzsimmons is up to. He should be ready for another trip to Havana. Plus, I need to send one of our boats to Havana to pick up the gold bullion that Tsukuda has arranged as payment for the gems and the sword."

"Why not arrange for the exchange of gems and the sword in Havana," Kaito asked. It would be far less dangerous and better territory for us to control since we already own the police."

"That's a good suggestion. I will cable Tsukuda and propose it."

The following day, Kaito reported to Sugimoto. "Sergeant Knowles is on emergency leave, according to my source. His mother is ill, and he left for Atlanta two days ago."

"What about Elton?"

"Fitzsimmons' boat is gone, and I can't find Wong."

"That may have something to do with the cable I received from Tsukuda. He had heard a rumor that someone in the Philippines had offered $1.5 million for the sword without verifying its authenticity. But apparently, the buyer is willing to come to Havana to conclude the deal."

"That must have made Tsukuda angry."

"Yes. Tsukuda is so angry that he is thinking about coming to Havana himself to take charge of the purchase of the sword."

"He doesn't find this suspicious? What if this is a ruse to get him out of Japan?"

"I suggested that, but he is adamant. This sword means power and influence to him. It has become an obsession. I just hope it doesn't get him killed. There are organizations in Japan that want to take over his operation because it is so profitable. Tsukuda is doing the unthinkable by working with the Communists. Most of the older Yakuza organizations reject working with them because they are our enemy. Their code will not allow it. They believe the upstarts like Tsukuda don't share that code. If Tsukuda weren't so powerful, they would take him out in an instant and absorb his business."

"Did Tsukuda not ponder this?"

"He is convinced that he is strong enough that they won't attempt anything. He is also convinced the sword will make him invincible once he possesses it."

"It sounds like a formula for disaster. If Tsukuda goes down, are you prepared to step into his shoes?"

"I have enough gold set aside from my time in Luzon that I won't need to. Plus, my family was wealthy before the war and made significant profits by manufacturing war materials. They did not squander their wealth during the war. Most are secured in banks in Switzerland and South America."

"What do we tell Tsukuda about the sword?"

"We tell him what we know. Fitzsimmons and Wong cannot be reached, and the boat is gone; nothing more. I learned the hard way that you never speculate to your superiors."

# CHAPTER 18

*Saigon, French Indochina*

The week that Yul Butler established his office in Saigon, rumors swept the city that Sûreté and French military forces had uncovered and seized several sizeable caches of firearms, ammunition, and poisonous gas. The Sûreté claimed that the arms left behind by the Japanese were positioned around Saigon by the Viet Minh. Thousands of Saigon residents, mostly Viet Minh supporters, armed with machetes, knives, and wooden spears, took to the streets to protest the accusations. French civilians were assaulted and their homes pillaged by protesters. The fear of being massacred gripped French citizens throughout the city.

Two days later, a five-thousand-strong force of French troops arrived from North Africa and took control of Saigon. The Sûreté implemented a curfew from 9:00 p.m. to 5:00 a.m., and they patrolled the streets with outdated, but still effective, MAS-38 submachine guns. Despite the curfew, many Viet Minh sympathizers continued the protest. They threw bottle-based incendiaries at the French soldiers. Other protesters went into French neighborhoods, attacked and killed over a dozen French residents, and burned their homes.

The civil war that had started between French and Viet Minh forces in the Tonkin region of Indochina—Butler had noted in a report to the CIA headquarters—was now engulfing the entire country. The war initially involved a low-level rural guerrilla insurgency against the French and the Vietnamese National Army. However, Butler stated that the conflict would eventually develop into an all-out conventional war between the Viet Minh and the French Union forces. The French Union Forces entering the country included French colonial troops from Morocco, Algeria, Tunisia, Laos, Cambodia, and French Foreign Legion units. Though small in numbers, they gave the colonists hope.

Butler believed that the French were undermanned, underfunded, and too weak to win against the popular Viet Minh freedom movement. Moreover, the French Union's war-making efforts were largely ineffective due to the limited usefulness of armored tanks in the mostly jungle environment and the lack of air cover. On the other hand, the Viet Minh commander, Vo Nguyen Giap, employed effective tactics of direct-line-of-sight artillery fire. He also employed convoy ambushes and the massing of anti-aircraft guns, to impede both air and land deliveries of supplies to French forces in the field.

Butler saw that the combination of jungle tactics and guerrilla warfare was proving fatal to the defense of French forts far from their logistic bases. Within two years, Butler concluded, the French would be defeated. When his CIA superiors in Washington did not agree with his conclusions, like typical Washington bureaucrats, they asked Butler to revise his statements to favor the French. Butler was brilliant, but he was also stubborn, especially when he was right; he ignored their request. Instead, he retrieved a codebook from his safe, provided by General Renick for emergencies, wrote out a coded message to his old boss, and sent it via a special courier to the Pentagon.

When General John Renick received the message three weeks later, he asked Preston to stop by his office before going home. As Preston entered the third-floor office shortly before 1700 hours, Renick immediately handed him Butler's report on Indochina. Butler was requesting their advice.

"Butler is convinced the French are going to get their butts kicked out of Indochina. I could have told the CIA that, two years ago," Preston said with a sigh. "Most of the CIA's top echelon is former OSS types that worked in Europe during the war. They don't know anything about jungle warfare, and they don't have any clue as to the strength of the Viet Minh."

"Apparently, the CIA director thinks the French can hold their own," Renick replied.

"Most of the CIA folks I've talked to are enamored with the French and Charles de Gaulle. They seem to have forgotten that France has not won any wars, on its own, against a major nation, since 1860. The French don't know how to fight and win, and they're too arrogant to admit they can't do it by themselves."

"Jon, you and I know how inept the French Army was in Indochina when the Japanese took control. We saw how poorly their covert units performed when they supported our OSS and CIC missions. Because the operations were in Indochina, they were more concerned that French officers be put in charge than getting results. And then, when we did give them the opportunity, their officers failed to take the fight to the Japanese."

"Yet, President de Gaulle has everyone in Washington convinced the French are unbeatable in Southeast Asia. It appears both the CIA and the State Department are in bed with de Gaulle, mostly because these senior officers served in France and love French women and wine. What would you like me to do, sir?" Jon asked.

"Do you think we could convince Truman to offer the French more financial assistance?"

"Sir, President Truman can't stand de Gaulle. He thinks he's a strutting peacock. All talk and no action. Hell, the French were so unorganized that it took nearly a year to get their troops from North Africa to Indochina after the Japanese surrendered. That gave the Viet Minh enough time to gain control of the Northern provinces and get a foothold in the south. I don't see how they can turn it around. If there was an opportunity to attack and win a decisive battle, the French generals would argue and bicker until they lost the advantage. Quite frankly, I don't believe they have the will to fight a protracted jungle war, and they certainly don't know their enemy."

"What about talking to some of your friends in the CIA? The ones you had served with, in the OSS?"

"They won't risk going against the current thinking. I recommend we tell Butler to ignore the CIA's request to change his conclusions. The CIA is so busy with communist expansion in the European countries, that they probably won't realize that Butler hadn't revised his report—until French Indochina is lost. Then they'll go back to Butler's report and claim they knew all along."

"On another note, how are the gem exports working out with Butler?"

"We have a steady flow from Indochina to Brazil. So much, in fact, that we no longer need the gems we had recovered from the Japanese. We have legitimized Guy Wong as a gem exporter who can deliver what he promises. There must be five thousand carats of rubies alone moving through Tsukuda's network into Japan each month."

"How is the operation going with the Japanese sword?"

"Better than expected. We leaked information in Cuba that an unknown buyer has offered Wong $1.5 million for the Masamune. Since then, Sugimoto has been desperately trying to get in touch with Wong to secure the purchase. However, Guy has gone to Cuba with Fitzsimmons, which is encouraging the ruse. We want Tsukuda's people to panic and think that Wong is selling the sword out from under them. If it works, it may force Tsukuda to take matters into his own hands."

"Maybe Tsukuda will go to Cuba himself."

"That's wishful thinking, sir, but wonders never cease. Wong will be back tomorrow evening. George and I have a meeting with him the next day."

"When do you expect Professor Tadahisa Haruki to get here?"

"He doesn't leave Japan for another four weeks. He'll arrive by boat in San Francisco and will take a train to Washington. Plenty of time to set things up. He's tentatively scheduled to visit with Professor Kirkendall and begin the validation process on the 19th of June."

"Will the sword that President Truman is lending you be validated at the same time?"

"I had a courier drop it off with Professor Kirkendall, two days ago. He's already working on it."

"You sent it without a guard detail?"

"It was delivered in a large box of long-stemmed roses. The courier drove a florist truck and had an embroidered shirt with the name of the florist on the breast pocket."

"That was clever. Does Professor Tadahisa know about the second sword?"

"Not yet. The professor will be briefed after he checks into his hotel in Georgetown. He knows that we expect him to authenticate the current sword as the missing Masamune. I'm sure Tadahisa will be just as anxious to look at the second Masamune as he is to look at the first. After all, there are only two known to exist. This would be a third and undiscovered Masamune. Regardless, it will provide an unprecedented experience for the professor. Don't worry; he'll do what we want to get his son released from prison."

"How will you leak the knowledge of the second Masamune to Tsukuda's organization?"

"It will be accidentally revealed, when Sugimoto visits, to go over the verification of the sacred katana with the Kirkendall, Tadahisa, and Wong. Tadahisa will verify the first sword as the sacred Mount Hiei Masamune. When Kirkendall accidentally reveals the second sword, Tadahisa will mumble the word *Honjo*, feint getting light-headed and off-balance, and act like he has seen a ghost. Sugimoto will be right there, and hopefully, the professor's act will be as convincing as an Oscar performance."

"You really put some thought into planning this charade with Sugimoto. But, don't you anticipate anything untoward happening?"

"Oh, I absolutely do, sir. I expect Sugimoto's thugs will try to take the Mount Hiei sword when we move it to the university."

# CHAPTER 19

*Washington, D.C.*

George Linka signed for the Top Secret message at the window of the Pentagon's information center. It could not be decoded in the center. When he returned to his office and opened the sealed envelope, he realized it was from his deep-cover contact in Yokohama, Hattori Nozomi. He got up from his desk, walked to the olive drab Schwab safe, entered the combination, and opened the door. He retrieved a codebook and decoded the lengthy message. George smiled as he read the contents. Nozomi was living up to her name, which in Japanese meant hope.

Later that afternoon, after spending four days in São Paulo, Jon Preston returned to his office. George Linka was leaning back in his chair. Jon noticed the Duchenne smile on his face that was so characteristic of George when he knew something Jon didn't. It was a smile of genuine enjoyment which involved his mouth, cheeks, and eyes simultaneously.

Not to be outplayed by his best friend's demeanor, Preston casually asked, "Anything new?"

George took a key from his pocket, unlocked his desk drawer, removed three sheets of paper, and casually placed them within Jon's reach. "This came in this morning."

Jon read the report. When he finished, he asked, "How did you get this?"

One of my agents, Hattori Nozomi, works in Tsukuda's household in Yokohama. He apparently talks in his sleep."

"It sounds like he was communicating with someone named Umeko. Why do you think he kept asking Umeko to tell him who the white samurai is?"

"Well, it appears as if Tsukuda is worried about a white samurai. I think the clue may be in the last paragraph when he calls her *baa-baa*, which is one of the words the Japanese use for grandmother."

"Okay, you're the expert on Japan. How would you interpret this?"

"I would say Tsukuda was having a dream or a vision in which his grandmother is communicating a warning about a white samurai. There are a lot of stories in Japanese folklore where deceased relatives visit family members and give them a warning of impending danger. The Japanese take dreams very seriously. They see them as premonitions that demand careful consideration."

"Alright, but why a white samurai? There aren't any samurai left in Japan."

"In this case, I think it might mean any person with a warrior attitude or skills, or someone in the military."

"Then a white samurai could be you or me or any member of our team."

"Theoretically, yes."

"He appears to be asking his grandmother whether he will have visions."

"There are known instances in certain Japanese families where a member is a seer—someone who has clairvoyance, prescience, or supernatural insight and can see the future."

Jon remarked, "Clairvoyance, prescience. Interesting."

George noticed the faraway look in Jon's eyes just before he began pacing the office. It was as if Jon went into a trance, but George knew he was in a state of deep, careful thought. He had seen it dozens of times when Jon had a problem to solve. Usually, Jon would develop a plan of action that most would consider outlandish and impossible to implement. However, George was a thinker and wondered whether Jon's plan would be similar to what he was thinking. If so, it would be bizarre by most standards, but like in the past, he and Jon would make it work.

"I think I may have a way of getting to Tsukuda. It may be a little unconventional, but it just might work," Jon remarked. "Get your gi and practice swords. We're going to visit Master Fujiwara's dojo."

Kumiko Fujiwara was not surprised to see Jon and George. They usually visited her dojo twice a week to practice the art of Japanese swordsmanship known as Kenjutsu. It was an ancient and lethal form of Kung Fu that Kumiko had mastered. Jon and George had funded the startup of her martial arts business after she had helped Preston and his team to take Asami Nakada down. Afterward, General Miller set her up with an Army contract to train CIC agents. Other agencies with similar clandestine functions did the same. Her business was still growing.

After the death of Kumiko's first husband during the American invasion of the Philippines in 1945, her husband's childhood friend, General Tsukuda, approached and recruited her into the Japanese intelligence service. Tsukuda knew the agent training would be challenging for Kumiko, but he also knew she would endure. She was as stubborn as she was resilient. Plus, Tsukuda was recruiting her for her exceptional memory and talent with languages, as well as her existing martial arts skills—much like the skills her husband possessed.

She began training at Rikugun Nakano Gakko spy school, where Tsukuda was the commander. She quickly mastered most of the ninjutsu disciplines of espionage, unarmed combat, throwing weapons, stick and staff, stealth and entering methods, sword techniques, escape and concealment, as well as intelligence gathering, photography, bomb-making, rifle and pistol marksmanship, and sabotage. Not surprisingly, Kumiko excelled and graduated at the top of her class. In addition, she became an expert at covert methods of waging irregular warfare—a *shinobi,* which would later become known as a ninja.

After Tsukuda sent the *I-14* and *I-405* on their suicide missions in July 1945, he would infiltrate Kumiko into the U.S. to assist Asami Nakada. However, when the war suddenly ended, he quickly arranged for her to marry a United Brethren minister whose wife had been killed during a bombing raid. Tsukuda then saw that the couple was chosen to be part of the first Japanese Christians to immigrate to the United States. Thus, unknown to her new husband, Kumiko was on a secret mission along with her two teenage sons to assist

Asami Nakada in her attempt to strike Washington, D.C., with a biological weapon.

Kumiko was already familiar with Nakada from her intelligence training at the spy school. She believed Nakada was capable of anything, including mass murder, which is what this mission represented. Under the noses of the Imperial Japanese Army, Tsukuda secretly put Kumiko's twin sons through a compressed, agent-training course at his uncle's estate outside of Tokyo. The boys already had excellent skills in martial arts from their years in the military high school they attended. Now, they were proficient in bomb-making and sabotage. Outraged that Tsukuda would use her sons in his suicidal plan of revenge, Kumiko turned against him and contacted Army intelligence soon after arriving in Baltimore. Her first contact with Army intelligence was with Camille Dupont and Kathleen Lauren. The next day, she met Jonathan Preston.

After a two-hour workout, Jon and George bowed to their instructor and sat on their knees before her. "You two have certainly mastered everything I know about Kenjutsu," Kumiko told them. "But, I get the impression there is something else you want to discuss."

"Yes," Jon said. "May we speak with you in private?"

Kumiko ushered them into her windowless office and closed the thick oak door. "I take it this is official army business involving our old advisory, General Tsukuda."

George replied, "You're very perspective. How did you know?"

"Prescience is particularly strong in my family. Three nights ago, I dreamt that you and Jon would be paying me an official visit. Is General Tsukuda becoming a nuisance again?"

"His criminal organization is stronger, and he is expanding into the U.S.," Jon replied.

"Tell me about the two swords I saw in my dream. Unfortunately, my dream did not reveal any details."

"I will, but first, tell me what you know about Tsukuda. I remember that your first husband grew up next door to him, so he may have talked to you about Tsukuda and his family. Were there any members of his family that displayed prescience?"

"When Tsukuda would visit, he would talk about his mother's mother having the gift. Although, according to Tsukuda, she considered it more of a curse. Sometimes, I am of the same mind. But, regardless of whether it's a gift or curse, or if the information is wanted or not, one cannot ignore it. Tsukuda said his grandmother guarded her premonitions about family. Nevertheless, she did give him a warning."

"What was the warning?"

"Beware the white samurai. Tsukuda knew that I had the gift, so he asked me what I thought it might mean."

"What did you tell him?" George asked.

"I told him I didn't know."

"But you do know. Don't you?" Jon asked.

"I didn't know until after I met you."

"Will you help us plan his demise?"

"I will help all I can, but I want to participate. One person in each generation of Tsukuda's family has had the gift. Since Tsukuda's grandmother and mother are no longer with us, Tsukuda may yet inherit the gift. Unless..." Kumiko stopped and reflected.

"Unless, what, Kumiko?" George asked.

"In certain Japanese families, inheritance of foreknowledge is often limited to female members. Tsukuda's mother went insane and committed suicide, but he did say that his older sister developed the gift after his grandmother passed. Unfortunately, her visions drove her insane, too. She died before the war ended. In some families, both men and women possess the gift of prophecy. Unfortunately, Tsukuda had never said anything about himself—or the men in his family—having the gift."

"If you had to guess?" Jon asked.

"I would not guess, Agent Preston. I could only tell you that it could go either way. You have to assume that he has the gift. Unfortunately, seeing doesn't always lead to understanding. Because Tsukuda is independent, self-centered, and arrogant, he may not comprehend what he sees. After all, he did survive the war. He might assume that his karma has changed because he has already survived the white samurai, meaning the war against the U.S. and British. Now tell me about the swords.

Jon explained his plan of using the two Masamune swords to draw Tsukuda away from his guarded estates. However, Kumiko thought of something more sinister which might entice Tsukuda. She just needed more information.

"In my dream, one of the swords took on a dark personality, as if it was evil. I haven't been able to process what it represents. But, if Tsukuda continues his obsession with the swords, I would say he doesn't have or doesn't understand the gift. The course he is on is self-destructive. Now, tell me what you need from me."

Preston could not be sure if Tsukuda had the gift of prescience, but he was confident that Kumiko knew more than she was telling or had not thought it through. He would have to address that, but not now. Today, he needed her input into what he was planning.


Major General Lew Miller was sitting at his large oak desk talking to the assistant deputy of army personnel, Brigadier General Steve Schaefer. Miller was complaining about the quality of personnel applying for counter-intelligence positions. Miller was worried because of the lack of applicants with Japanese, Chinese, and Korean language skills.

"General," Schaefer said. "Today, CIC candidates are required to have four years of military service before they can apply. But even if the requirement was two years of service, the number of officers and enlisted personnel, with the language skills you are looking for, is extremely few."

"Steve, I need qualified candidates, and I need them now. You know damn well that Korea might blow up in our face at any time, and I'm still having trouble with a certain former Japanese general officer."

"I am very familiar with General Tsukuda, sir. I worked with Jon Preston in Calcutta. I was there when Tsukuda's assassin killed two members of Jon's team."

"What about recruiting civilians with the skills? We have a program developed by Jon and the members of his team that will train them in covert operations."

"I was not aware that the program was approved by the Chief of Staff."

"The first cadre just graduated. I intend to brief General Bradley this week. But, in the meantime, I want you to look into three individuals. They are of Japanese descent, and all are attending college," Miller said as he handed three folders to Schaefer.

"This is highly unusual, sir."

"I've already investigated the young men. A security report is in each folder. Just so you understand—Colonel Preston and Colonel Linka know these men and their parents. In fact, Preston was the one who brought them to my attention. Maybe we could expand the trial program to include these three and another dozen you can find out there."

Instead of objecting, Schaefer thought about Preston's help in his career trajectory. Jon Preston was a significant influence on Schaeffer's success, while a member of the OSS. Preston had saved his life on the docks of Calcutta.

"I'll review the files and discuss the matter with Colonel Preston, sir."

"Thanks, Steve. And congratulations on the promotion."

# CHAPTER 20

*Baltimore, Maryland*

After he visited with Kumiko Fujiwara on Friday, Jon spent the weekend with Camille, brainstorming. Then, on Monday afternoon, after he returned to his office from a meeting with the deputy director of the Smithsonian Institute, Jon took the roll of film he had shot at the institute and dropped it off at the CIC's photo lab. Since the post-war Pentagon had become a sieve with information leaking freely to anyone who inquired, Jon classified the film as Top Secret G-2 Special Projects. He didn't want any unauthorized personnel knowing the content of the photos or trying to guess his intentions. Plus, everything involving Tsukuda was classified at the same level.

"What did you discover at the Smithsonian?" George Linka asked after Jon had sat down at his desk.

"It's not going to be easy to duplicate the armor," Preston replied. "The average suit of samurai armor, consisting of a breastplate, helmet, and arm braces, will easily weigh between 50-60 pounds if it is made of metal."

"Yes, but you're talking about armor that was specifically designed for samurai who would charge into battle on horseback. Instead, you should look into the armor worn by samurai who charged into battle on foot."

"I have photographs of both. The curator of the Japanese section told me that a single suite of armor usually consists of 250 yards of silk and over 3,000 pieces of leather. Fortunately, Kumiko knows a Japanese couple who worked as costume designers for a traditional Kabuki theatre company before immigrating to the U.S. They run a tailoring business in Baltimore. She says they will be able to work from the photographs and design a suit that looks authentic. We have an appointment for a fitting with them, tomorrow."

"We?"

"You don't think I'm going to do this alone, do you?"

"I was thinking that one white samurai would be enough."

"Consider yourself as a backup in case something unfortunate happens to me. After all, we are being targeted by Tsukuda's goons."

"Which reminds me. The Coast Guard agents that Rear Admiral Jack Perkins loaned to us have identified two Asian men working on the docks for Takaji Sugimoto. They speak Malaysian and Japanese. Both illegally entered the country around three months ago. Would you care to guess their backgrounds?"

"Rikugun Nakano Gakko spy school?"

"Yep. What do you want to do about the men?"

"They are probably fanatical in their loyalty to Tsukuda and would kill themselves before being captured. Otherwise, he wouldn't have sent them. Have the Coast Guard agents identified where they are living?"

"Yes, both are on one of Sugimoto's boats. He probably thinks it safer keeping them away from the Asian community."

"It's not like Tsukuda to send only two assassins. Have the agents identified any other illegals?"

"They've photographed four others but haven't identified them. All are of Asian descent, but none are full Japanese, and they speak various languages, including English. They could be Japanese agents Tsukuda used in the Philippine Islands, Malaysia, Indonesia, or Indochina."

"I think we need to get all the photographs to Kumiko. Then, she may be able to identify them. Plus, she needs to be aware of who they are, in case they accidentally run across her."

"Do you think Tsukuda suspects that she is alive?"

"I think we have to assume that Tsukuda knows everything. Although, there is nothing in our personnel records about Kumiko, or any of the other Japanese we used, to track down Asami Nakada and Haru Aki. I think we need to assume that one or more of Haru Aki's agents survived and are working for Sugimoto."

"It's time to go on the offensive, Jon. There are too many uncertainties to account for. Plus, we need to eliminate these assassins before they screw up your white samurai plan."

"What do you have in mind?"

"The Irish mob, with a few twists."

"Do those twists include you and me?"

"Absolutely. But we will need the help of Elton Fitzsimmons and a half dozen real Irish mobsters. Maybe we need to look up our old friend, Captain Marty Schottenstein. He had several Irish mobsters who worked for him on the docks in Calcutta. One, in particular, a guy named Michael Coonan, was from Baltimore. He told me Coonan was a rising star in the mob before the war. But, maybe, he has done well for himself in the last four years."

"Calcutta was a long time ago, Jon. Do you think Schottenstein will remember us?"

"He'll remember me. We went to high school together.

The trip to Columbus, Ohio, took five days but proved to be productive. Jon, Camille, and Jon Jr. were met at the train station by Jon's mother and father. It was the elder Preston's first time seeing their grandson and only their second time seeing Camille. When Marty Schottenstein met with Jon and Camille, it was like old times. Marty invited them to dinner at his house and discussed their business in his study afterward.

"Michael Coonan was with the Irish mob alright, but he did volunteer for military service out of duty to his country. He was an excellent logistician," Schottenstein said. "Coonan knew everything about working on the docks. In fact, he ran the docks for me in Calcutta. Michael kept the material flowing to the proper places. He was very patriotic, and everyone who worked for him toed the line. He never let anyone on his civilian or military crews steal or sell war material on the black market. The ones he caught were immediately disciplined or fired. The material that got stolen was done by the Calcutta mob, controlled by an organized crime network out of Bombay. In truth, I think Coonan let them get away with just enough non-war material to keep them happy. Otherwise, it could have ended in a lot of blood being shed. Michael was clever about taking care of his men. In fact, I think you and your team stopped some of the Bombay mob."

"Yes. And a young Army lieutenant working with us was killed. Has Coonan kept in touch with you?" Preston asked.

"We exchange Christmas cards and presents every year. Coonan sends me a bottle of 16-year-old Irish whiskey, and I send him a bottle of Rothschild wine."

When Jon explained that he needed Coonan's help, Marty went to his desk and pulled out the last Christmas card he received from Coonan and handed it to him. "Show this to Michael when you see him. It may not get you his cooperation, but it will solidify that you and I are close friends. Then, to make sure Coonan doesn't think you stole it, take him a bottle of Chateau Lafite Rothschild. It's his favorite, and it's what I send him every year."

"Do you know if he is still in the Irish mob?"

"One never leaves the mob, according to Michael. So, I assume he is high in the hierarchy. He has a brilliant mind, Jon. Like you, he can recall anything he has ever heard or read. I would play to his patriotism. He hates the Japanese. Of course, you will need to offer him something in return."

"Such as?"

"He like fast motorboats, fast cars, and beautiful women."

"I think I can handle two out of the three."

"Which two?" Camille questioned, as she looked at Jon in a sultry way.

"I think that's a trick question, Jon," Marty replied with a wink at Camille.

"You have no idea, Marty. This woman is as clever as she is deadly. I'm fortunate to have her on my side."

"You might want to take Camille when you visit Coonan. Might help to serve as an…"

Camille cut him off, "Icebreaker."

"Yes. A woman as beautiful as yourself can open doors."

"In that case, we should take Kathleen also."

"Yes, Kathleen Lauren. I met her in Calcutta. Is she still part of your team?"

"One of my best and just as deadly as Camille."

"Then I pity the Japanese bastards you are going after."


Jon didn't waste time when he returned to Washington. He told General Miller what he needed, and was surprised when he delivered a speedboat and a silver convertible. The 1940 19-foot Chris Craft Barrel Back Runabout was impressive, but the 1937 Delahaye 145 Franay Cabriolet Roadster was a fantastic find.

"Where did you find the boat?" Jon asked after General Miller had handed him photographs.

"The Coast Guard confiscated it when they busted an Italian smuggling operation in D.C., two months ago."

"And the Delahaye?"

"Same raid. Both were being stored in the warehouse the Coast Guard had raided on the docks. They also took in a 1946 Triumph 1800 Roadster and a 1945 MG TC Midget. Apparently, some Italian mobster out of Palermo tried to muscle onto the D.C. docks, the old-fashioned way. The Coast Guard caught on after a few gangsters were found floating in the river. When I briefed Admiral Perkins, of Coast Guard Intelligence, and told him what I was looking for, he delivered on the boat and car."

"It's nice to have friends in high places."


Finding Michael Coonan was not as complicated as Jon had expected. When Jon mentioned who he was looking for, Elton Fitzsimmons gave him the address of his house and the bar where he could be found every evening. The tall, red-haired Coonan was in his early thirties. He was a dedicated bachelor with a trove of beautiful women vying for his attention. So when a strikingly beautiful redhead parked a 1937 Delahaye in front of the bar and walked into Flannigan's Pub with an equally beautiful friend, Coonan took notice.

"Can I offer you a table and a drink, ladies?" Coonan said with authority, motioning to his table.

"Of course," Camille replied. "But I doubt this establishment will have the wine I normally drink."

"You might be surprised. I pride myself on carrying some of the best French and German wines."

"Chateau Lafite Rothschild."

"An excellent choice. It's one of my favorite wines."

"We know," Kathleen said. But, if Michael was surprised by the revelation, he didn't show it. Instead, he motioned to one of the bartenders over and whispered in his ear.

"That's a very unique car you are driving. I saw one in France before the war. What year is it?"

"1937," Camille responded.

"If I'm not mistaken, it's a Delahaye 145 Franay Cabriolet Roadster."

"You have a good eye,"

"It is also a one-of-a-kind automobile. I also watched it win the Grand Prix de Pau in 1938."

"You certainly know your cars, Mr. Coonan."

"May I ask how you obtained it?"

"Let's just say that an Italian gentleman out of Palermo is quite unhappy with his loss."

"You're not associated with the gentleman?"

"No."

"And I take it the two of you are not here for just a drink?"

"No. It's more of a business nature."

"FBI?"

"No. Army counterintelligence."

"I am no longer in the army, Miss..."

"Agent Camille DuPont. And this is Agent Kathleen Lauren. We would like to speak with you in private about a matter of national security."

"And why would I want to do that?"

"Because you dislike the Japanese moving into your territory. And because Marty Schottenstein said you were patriotic."

"I haven't seen Captain Schottenstein since December of 1945."

"Yes, but you exchange Christmas cards and presents every year."

"Well, Agent DuPont, you've piqued my curiosity. Can I assume that the gentleman waiting in the car is with you?"

"Yes, his name is Colonel Jonathan Preston."

"Not the same Jonathan Preston from Calcutta?"

"The same."

"Well, for crying out loud! Please invite him in."


Jon spent the next hour explaining to Coonan what Uchito Tsukuda was doing in Japan, Cuba, Baltimore, and Washington, D.C. Coonan was appalled that a former Japanese general was still carrying the war to the United States. Before the war, the Japanese mob had infiltrated the Baltimore docks. Still, because of their highly violent nature, his boss recommended leaving them alone. With his boss recently deceased, Coonan was now the number-one man in Baltimore.

"Colonel Preston, I'll be more than happy to work with you as long as it stays discrete. The people I'm associated with out of New York might frown upon my cooperating with the federal government."

"We just want you to provide intelligence on the Japanese in Baltimore. My people will do all the heavy lifting. None of your men need to be involved. I just don't want your people to interfere when we take on Sugimoto's men."

"I already have a good deal of information on Sugimoto's men and the warehouse they use. Who are you using to help guide you on the docks?"

"Elton Fitzsimmons. He worked with me on a classified operation after the war."

"Ah, the Jap submarine. I heard rumors from some buddies in the Coast Guard. I also heard rumors about your exploits in Burma, China, and Indochina. It's good to know we have men like you guarding our country, Colonel."

"And women," Camille added.

"Yes, of course. I remember you and Kathleen from Calcutta."

"Now about your compensation—" Jon began.

"Colonel Preston, I do not need any compensation to help you protect my nation. If anything, it is my duty and an honor."

"Then please accept this as a token of our appreciation," Jon said, handing Coonan the keys to the Delahaye and a title with his name on it. If anyone asks, you got it from an old Army buddy."

"I am stunned, Colonel Preston. What can I say?"

"If you look out the window to your left, you'll find another token of our appreciation."

The look on Coonan's face was priceless as he saw the 19-foot Chris Craft Barrel Back Runabout on a trailer being unhitched from a one-and-a-half-ton truck. Coonan motioned for his bartender, who was watching through a narrow, rectangular window in the door. "Jon, the ladies are drinking wine. I hope you like Irish whiskey."

# CHAPTER 21

*Yokohama, Japan*

The look on Uchito Tsukuda's face was not reassuring. The leader of the underground criminal organization was tall and thick, with a constant wrinkled, frowning forehead. His piercing eyes revealed intelligence and purpose, but behind them was a constant threat of violence. Those close to Tsukuda understood the thin, jagged edge they walked—poised between privilege and sudden death if they disappointed their master. Today, because of restless dreams and lack of sleep, Tsukuda suffered a splitting headache and was even more cross.

Raizo Hata moved out of the way as Nozomi brought in a freshly brewed pot of tea and poured a cup for Tsukuda. After setting the teapot down, she picked up the breakfast dishes, bowed politely, and moved from the office. Tsukuda then wrote out a message for Takaji Sugimoto with instructions on what to do next about Jon Preston's team.

"Take this to the communications center and have it transmitted at 1000 hours," Tsukuda ordered. "Wait for a reply."

Raizo took the message and left the room. Two hours later, he returned with a sealed envelope. When Tsukuda read the reply, he threw the message on the floor.

"That fool!" Tsukuda shouted. "Sugimoto has lost two men that were gathering U.S. Army intelligence for him. He says they apparently got cold feet when he asked them to kill someone. The next day they didn't come back to work, and now they've disappeared into thin air. No one just disappears without a trace. And what's worse, Sugimoto doesn't even suspect Preston of having a part in their disappearance. How can a former field commander be so naïve?"

"I saw the same thing happen when I was with General Yamashita's staff during the invasion of Singapore," Raizo replied. "The general was actually considering surrendering to the British until I talked him into listening to what the British had to say—when they had requested a conference under a flag of truce. Within thirty minutes, General Percival ended up surrendering his forces, which totally surprised Yamashita. We were outnumbered three to one. I think Yamashita was more worried about the shortage of supplies—and failed to see how badly the British were faring."

"You're right, Raizo. Sugimoto isn't used to worrying about personnel issues. He should be relying on his second-in-command to run the daily operations. He's too used to having a staff of officers doing the mundane busywork. I need him to secure the sword before worrying about Preston and his team. He also needs more competent people. Of the agents we sent to the U.S., who are the most fluent in speaking English?"

"All can understand English, but only Domen Touma and Gima Benjiro are fluent. They both attended university in the U.S. and were assigned to the Hong Kong consulate a year before the war started. Touma and Benjiro have been assigned as the main instructors at the farm."

"Maybe they should be in Baltimore with Sugimoto. Kaito Wan is a capable undercover agent, but he doesn't have the combat experience we need to go after Preston. I think Hayashida Aoki and Enomoto Danno can perform the training functions. They were training to be instructors at the spy school when the war ended. Wait while I write out another message."

Nozomi overheard the conversation while cleaning in the next room. Later that afternoon, she left a message with one of the clerks at the store where she purchased fresh vegetables. By nightfall, the information was being transmitted to George Linka.


The first thing every morning, Nancy Brewster picked up messages at the Pentagon communications center. The envelope she noticed first was marked URGENT. It was addressed to Colonel George Linka, so she went by his office before returning to hers.

Linka was usually the first to get to the office, so it was no surprise when Nancy showed up and found him going over a weekly report submitted by Guy Wong.

"Good morning, Colonel Linka," Nancy chirped. "Here's an urgent message for you."

"Nancy, how many times do I have to tell you to call me, George?" Linka chided.

"Sorry, Colonel. Old habits never change. Don't forget your meeting with General Miller and Renick at 1500 hours."

"Anything interesting?" Jon Preston asked as he set a cup of coffee he had purchased at the downstairs canteen onto his desk.

"We'll know in a few minutes," Linka replied, as he opened the sealed envelope, noticed the ten-digit code, and went to the safe to retrieve the proper codebook. After deciphering the message, Linka read it twice to make sure he understood.

"Tsukuda has four new men in Maryland and apparently a farm where they are being housed and trained. All were instructors at the Rikugun Nakano Gakko spy school. Two attended university in the States, so they probably speak English very well."

"Just one more reason for us to recruit more Japanese-speaking agents."

"How did your meeting with General Schaefer go?" Linka asked, still staring at the message.

"He's looking at the three individuals I recommended. I hope to hear from him later today. If not, I'll bring it up at the meeting with General Renick this afternoon."

"Do you really think Eizo and Emon Fujiwara will work for Army intelligence after being trained by Tsukuda and Japanese intelligence?"

"Kumiko is convinced they will. She says they have acclimated very well and enjoyed college. Hell, they are as smart as their mom. They graduated in three years with degrees in political science. Apparently, they both want to go to law school."

"Maybe we could facilitate their wishes. I understand the Army just implemented a program to recruit capable young men who want to be attorneys. They'll go to Officers Training, first. Then the Army will pay them a monthly salary and pay for all the cost of law school."

"But first, we need them to help take Tsukuda down."

"How did your visit go with Hiroki Eguchi, when you were in Columbus? From what I remember, he was a very angry young man three years ago."

"He's changed a lot. He still misses his mom and brother but doesn't blame the U.S. government anymore for their deaths. Plus, he has continued his karate training. He found a retired Army instructor who was stationed in China and Japan before the war, who is continuing the Okinawan-style Karate that his father had taught him."

"Did you spar with him?"

"As a matter of fact, I did. Hiroki is unbelievably fast."

"So, he kicked your butt."

"In a matter of speaking, but I took him in ground tactics, thanks to the Jujutsu that Joselyn Barclay had taught me."

"Joselyn has the reflexes of a mongoose. Is Eguchi as fast?"

"Maybe quicker, but he is less experienced than Joselyn."

"Then he would make a great addition to the team. Have you heard from Joselyn lately?"

"She's still working for Brigadier MacKenzie. She's heading up his Hong Kong office while Jim Ballangy is convalescing."

"How is Ballangy?

"After six weeks in the hospital in Fukuoka, he went back to Hong Kong. From what I hear from Miles Murphy, Ballangy and Barclay are pretty close. Although, he doesn't say how Brigadier MacKenzie feels about the relationship. All the same, I wish we had a dozen agents just like her."

"Maybe, we can remedy that. Matt Whitley passed me the names of a dozen kids he knew in Honolulu; half are girls. All but one are of Japanese ancestry and speak Japanese fluently, and all have phenomenal martial art skills."

"What about the non-Japanese?"

"That would be the admiral's 22-year-old daughter, Carol. He says she has better martial art skill than the others. They're all attending the University of Hawaii and are graduating in three weeks."

"I think we may have just found our second class of recruits. Get their names to General Schaefer and have him start on the background checks."

"What do we do until then? We're still short agents."

"Admiral Dubois is providing the names of a dozen naval intelligence agents who are going to be cut from the Navy roles in the next reductions in force this August. General Renick has already received permission from the Chief of Staff to bring them onboard as CIC agents. Some are in Hawaii, but the others are in Subic Bay and Tokyo. They should be arriving in Washington by the end of the month."

"We'll need to check them out."

"I've arranged for lodging and a two-week orientation at the Marine Barracks. After that, Camille and Kathleen will head up the training."

"I'm sure they will have an attitude after being dumped by the Navy. It will be interesting to see how they adapt to female instructors. Or, is that your plan?"

"Yep. If these guys can't take orders and instructions from Camille and Kathleen, they're out. Nevertheless, they will get two opportunities to adapt; that's only because of the circumstances. After all, most have families, and all want to continue their careers in the military."

"Aren't you generous?"

"Just being frugal with scarce resources, George. These men have great records, and the admiral has personally briefed each agent on our team's success. Including the *I-405* incident. According to the admiral, they all want to be part of our special projects team."

Jon paused and then remembered something, "One other thing, I received word from Professor Kirkendall that Tadahisa Haruki, chairman of the Society for Preservation of Japanese Art Swords, has been delayed. He will arrive at the end of July. So we still have to plan the transfer of the sword with Brinks, and come up with a way to stop Sugimoto if he tries anything."

"Surely you're not going to let Brinks deliver the sword if you suspect Sugimoto will attack the vehicle?"

"No, we are substituting the driver and guards with combat-hardened Marines who fought the Japanese. I have a dozen men picked out, and they are already bivouacked at the Marine Barracks. Camille and Kathleen are seeing that they are outfitted with the latest suppressed submachine guns and semi-automatics. Plus, four are Marine snipers."

"You seem to have thought of everything!"

"Maybe, maybe not. Camille and Kathleen are taking them to the Georgetown campus to get the lay of the land."

"Not all at once."

No, two at a time. The girls started this morning. They sent the snipers out individually yesterday, and they already have a plan for where they will set up. Don't worry. They will be using suppressed sniper rifles and reduced charges. We don't want a loud gunfight."

"And how do we account for the dead bodies, if civilians see what's happening?"

"Simple. We have a fake movie camera team on the scene. All combat Marines, of course."

"Of course!"


Takaji Sugimoto was seething after reading Tsukuda's latest message. He had to sit on the tatami mat in his office and meditate before getting his blood pressure and temper under control. Kaito, seeing Sugimoto was in a lousy mood, left the office to get lunch. When he returned, he saw that Sugimoto was still red-faced, but his temper was in check. Before he was sent to the U.S. in 1937, Kaito had worked with a Japanese Imperial Army general officer. It was such a bad experience, he had hoped it wouldn't happen again, but here he was, saddled with a former lieutenant general.

"Kaito," Sugimoto said gruffly. "We need to move Domen and Gima to the team here. Hayashida and Enomoto will take their place as instructors at the farm."

Kaito asked, "What will be their function, sir?"

"According to General Tsukuda, they will be responsible for planning the assault to capture the sword and the attack to take out Preston's team. He wants combat-experienced agents whom he has trained, to lead the assaults."

"Then he must not trust us. Has he ordered us to commit seppuku?"

"Not yet. But, if this mission fails, I'm certain the order will come. Tsukuda apparently sees my defeat in the Philippines and your association with Haru Aki as reasons to warrant closer monitoring and let others do the planning. So we better make certain that we succeed, eh?"

"Hai," Kaito responded.

# CHAPTER 22



*Washington, D.C.*

George Linka knocked on the door, waited, and entered the house after Camille opened the screen door. Camille pointed to the living room and detoured left into the kitchen, where she was preparing dinner. George walked down a narrow entry made of lightly stained oak and saw Jon sitting on a worn, timber-green sofa holding his sleeping son and reading a thin book. Jon put the book down, got up and took Jonathan Jr. into his bedroom, and placed a thin blanket over the sleeping toddler. After kissing him on the forehead, Jon returned to the living room.

"He's grown," George stated.

"Twenty-three pounds and 30 inches. He's going to be tall," Jon replied as he sat on the sofa facing George, who seated himself in the same-style-and-color armchair, across from him.

"Reading Sun Tzu again?"

"Every time I read it, I pick up something new."

"Like what?"

"*The Art of War* suggests that anger and greed are causes of defeat. So I was wondering if we are doing all that we can to ensure Tsukuda's defeat?"

"It also states that good generals do not discount circumstances that make an enemy prone to defeat. And they make their stand in a place where they cannot lose."

"So, you think we are doing all we can at this point?"

"Yes."

"Can you elaborate?"

"We have limited resources, Jon."

"Therefore, we are mostly on the defensive?"

"Yes. Sun Tzu describes defense for times of insufficiency, and offense for times of plenty. We're doing a little of both, but we're mostly on defense due to our manpower issues."

"Do you feel that we are optimizing our position?"

"We have been so far. My main concern is drawing Sugimoto's goons into a firefight on a college campus. So I'm thinking we should change the location of the evaluation with Tadahisa Haruki and Professor Kirkendall."

"I was thinking that also, but I don't think his team will strike at the campus."

"You think Sugimoto will strike en route?"

"No. I believe he will strike as soon as the sword is brought out of the bank."

"Are you thinking of having Haruki and Professor Kirkendall do the evaluation, inside the bank?"

"That's one option."

"What's the other, The White House?" George asked, jokingly.

"That would be ideal, but it would be too tempting for President Truman's chief of staff to turn it into a publicity stunt to bolster the president's ratings."

"I hope you're not considering Tokyo."

"Give me one good reason why we shouldn't?"

"I'll paraphrase Sun Tzu. A wise general does not make a stand in a place where he can lose. Tokyo is Tsukuda's home ground. It's where he is the strongest."

"Sun Tzu also says that to remain invincible, you should hide your intentions and prepare enough to remain invincible. Even in Tokyo, we can do that."

"But, if we move the certification to Tokyo, Tsukuda will suspect a ploy."

"Not if we remain in Washington, D.C. and send Father Kirkendall in our place."

"You don't really intend for us to remain in Washington, do you?"

"No. We'll use doubles and leave the ladies behind. We'll be seen with them every day because Sugimoto will have his people watching.

In Nozomi's message, she said that Tsukuda wants the sword at all costs, and doubts Sugimoto's ability. So I don't think Tsukuda will strike at our team until he has the sword in his possession."

"So, how do we draw Tsukuda out?"

"You said your team in Tokyo knows all of Tsukuda's hideouts, right?"

"I hope you're not thinking of attacking him at one of his estates?"

"Why not? He feels secure in them."

"You're not telling me everything," George stated with a bit of frustration. "Spell it out."

"I'm thinking a game of psychological warfare. We know the establishments where Tsukuda conducts business, where he eats when he goes out, and where he socializes with high-ranking government officials. We also know that his grandmother warned him to beware of a white samurai. So, let's provide one."

"Alright, step me through the process."

"Before Father Kirkendall arrives in Tokyo with the sword, we play a little Kabuki theatre with Tsukuda. Tsukuda is a Kabuki enthusiast. He goes to all the good performances. And Kumiko Fujiwara knows a Japanese couple who worked as costume designers for them."

"And?"

"And their oldest son is the manager of the troupe. So, we develop a Kabuki play around a mysterious cursed sword and the white samurai who defeated its owner in a battle to the death."

"Jon, it takes time to write a play, not to mention you have to get the theater manager to go along with it. Wait! You've already started the process, haven't you?"

"It was Kumiko's idea. Plus, the couple who is designing our samurai costumes also writes Kabuki plays. They finished it a week ago, and one of our CIC couriers delivered it to their son this week. His parents have agreed to travel to Tokyo to create the costumes for the troupe and assist with the production. So the troupe will be ready to perform in time for their next appearance in Tokyo, in December."

"What mysterious sword?"

"A sword that is known for its superior quality, beauty, and lethality. The folklore about it states it is cursed."

"You're speaking about a sword created by the famous sword-smith named Muramasa Sengo. Tokugawa Ieyasu, one of the last shoguns, told everyone that all Muramasa blades were cursed because of the swordsmiths abrasive and vicious personality. It was assumed that a dark curse fell upon Muramasa, and the curse was then imbued in his swords. His blades were believed to have a thirst for blood. It's rumored that if the blade was drawn, it required blood on it before being placed back into its scabbard. If the thirst was not satisfied by the blood of an enemy, the sword would turn on its owner, possess him, and force him to commit seppuku."

"It sounds like the making of some great Kabuki theatre, don't you think? Unfortunately, Kumiko told me that most of the Muramasa swords were destroyed. However, it's rumored that one survived."

"How does our Masamune sword play into this?"

"Simple. Our expert reveals that the sword we have is not a Masamune, but a cursed Muramasa."

"And?"

"The Kabuki play will reveal that the only sword that can withstand an attack by the cursed Muramasa is a Masamune sword wielded by a white samurai. The psychological effect on Tsukuda should be interesting."

"And when Tsukuda realizes that the sword he is about to purchase is the infamous cursed Muramasa, he will want it that much more. Tsukuda is so superstitious that he will be convinced the sword will give him invincibility against his enemies because there are no white samurai anymore."

"That's right. And once Tsukuda has the cursed Muramasa sword, we arrange for numerous sightings of a white samurai, which will begin to work on his nerves."

"What's the endgame?"

"Tsukuda won't be expecting a modern white samurai to show up at his door with the only sword that can defeat the cursed Muramasa."

"He has a dozen guards at each of his estates, and dogs. And his personal bodyguard is a trained assassin."

"Between you, Wong, Kumiko, and myself, I think we can deal with them. If you don't think that's enough manpower, we could bring some of the Navy agents with us or ask Brigadier MacKenzie for some help. Plus, Kumiko is really good with a blowgun and poisoned darts. And don't forget you have a person on the inside."

"Nozomi only works at the estate in Yokohama."

"Well, let's make sure the white samurai shows up near his estates in Tokyo and drives him to Yokohama. A player on the inside could be beneficial to our plan."

"I'm not so sure. Nozomi mentioned in her last report that Tsukuda had a special wooden flooring installed in all his estates. Flooring that sings or makes a peculiar sound when someone walks across it. In ancient Japanese castles, most notably among the royal families and daimyos during the Endo period, squeaky floors were highly desired. A floor that made a loud, harsh, squealing noise or a distinctive chirp—like a Japanese bush-warbler when it was walked on—was as effective as a burglar alarm is, today. The Japanese built these singing floors in their hallways and sometimes in their great halls. An assassin trying to sneak into the castle and walk across the floor would cause the floor to chirp and alert the guards."

"Can it be defeated?"

"Legend states that only two ninjas were stealthy enough to cross the floors without making a sound, but they worked for the Tokugawa shogunate in the 1600s. Still, it could work in our favor."

"How?"

"Causing it to make noise could serve a psychological purpose. If we were to cause it to sing several nights in a row, Tsukuda's guards might start to worry and lose sleep. In the process, the guards might discover a white rat carrying a small cloth kamon, used by the last white samurai during the Tokugawa Ieyasu reign—the outline of three hollyhock leaves inside a circle."

"That's very clever. Let's run this by Kumiko and the girls."

# CHAPTER 23



*Cao Bang, French Indochina*

After receiving a series of disturbing reports from his brother, René Clairoux decided to travel to northeast Vietnam for a firsthand look. Under the auspices of a health sabbatical, René flew Jacob and Renate to a family retreat 120 miles north of Hanoi. The modified BC-12-65 single-engine, a high-wing monoplane, was built by the Taylorcraft Aviation Corporation of Alliance, Ohio, in 1944. It had an extended cab for extra passengers. In addition, it was fitted with an experimental 100 hp Continental O-200 engine, to increase power and the gross weight capacity to 1500 pounds.

Like most light reconnaissance aircraft, the fuselage was constructed of welded steel tubing covered with doped aircraft fabric. The 36-foot wings were braced using steel-tube struts, and the aircraft was fitted with oversized wheels for operating on unimproved fields. With the experimental O-200 engine, it could take off in less than 500 feet. The BC-12-65 was also modified to carry an increased fuel load which gave it a range of 420 nautical miles.

René landed in an open field at the bottom of a small mountain on the banks of the Bang River. The elegant log cabin where they were planning to stay was built by René's father in the late 1920s, in the mountains, four miles north of the village of Cao Bang. Two hundred yards away from the river, the cabin was surrounded by an evergreen forest interspersed with bamboo, teak, and star apple trees. When they reached the cabin steps, René stumbled and slumped over before he could be greeted by his Kinh caretaker, Tuan. Complaining of stomach cramps and a severe headache, he asked Tuan to fetch the village doctor.

Four hours later, an elderly Vietnamese physician from the small hospital in Cao Bang returned with the Kinh caretaker. Dr. Ping Van Chieu was in his mid-60s but still carried himself like a 30-year-old. After receiving his medical degree in France from the University of Montpellier in 1926, Ping moved to Hanoi to begin his practice of medicine. When the Japanese began occupying Indochina in July of 1941, Ping moved to a small hospital in the northeast highlands near the village of Cao Bang. While there, he became involved with the OSS and the British SIS. As a Vietnamese physician, Ping could travel freely to tend to patients, including Viet Minh, French and Japanese soldiers. In addition, the intelligence he collected on Japanese troop strengths proved valuable to Allied intelligence. Now, nearly four years later, he was just a country doctor.

When Dr. Ping entered the cabin, Renate immediately greeted him with a huge hug and a kiss on his wrinkled cheeks. She had known the doctor since she was a child. René and Jacob greeted the doctor in the same fashion.

"It's good to see you, friend," Dr. Ping said to René as he took a seat at a small table offered by his friend. "But you don't look as ill as Tuan had stated. So, I assume this is business."

"Unfortunately, yes. I'm using the excuse of a health sabbatical to visit the cabin. I was hoping to travel north," René replied.

"I'm afraid you won't like what you will find."

"That bad?"

"Chinese Communist forces are flooding the border area. So far, they have remained on their side. They are training a great many Viet Minh soldiers."

"So, you've been to their camps?"

"I've been to three of the eight camps to treat a variety of illnesses and wounds received during the training exercises."

"Do they have a field hospital?"

"Crude, but sanitary. I got to operate on several soldiers with appendicitis."

"Did you get a chance to talk to Giap?"

"Yes. I was invited to treat Uncle Ho's illness at the cave at Coc Bo."

"I take it he is doing well?"

"He is doing well for a 58-year-old man who is malnourished and still traipsing around the jungle until he drops from malaria or dengue fever. The man never stops unless he becomes bedridden."

"And Giap?"

"Well, for a history teacher, he's become an extraordinary military tactician."

"Do you think it would be safe for me to travel up north?"

"Not unless you want a bullet in your brain. The Viet Minh doesn't take kindly to French people coming into their strongholds. But, I'm sure Giap will learn of your arrival. He has a radio operator in Coc Bo that forewarns him of all arrivals, wanted or unwanted. Being a friend has its advantage."

"Do you think I can see him?"

"I'm pretty sure he will visit you. The last time we talked, he was inquiring about your curious visits to several gem mines in the west and your purchases of hordes of gemstones from native villages."

"Anything else?"

"He's convinced that the American businessman you are working for is with the American CIA. General Giap remembers him from one of the U.S. Army counterintelligence missions he participated in during the war. He said he was impressed with Captain Butler's intelligence and skill at chess."

"I'm looking forward to seeing him. Will you have dinner with us and stay the night?"

"Of course. I need to catch up on what these kids have been up to in the last year. With the way things are going, I may not see you all for a long time. I assume you have plans to move to your residence in Bangkok before the French army is totally defeated and your position becomes untenable?"

The following day, René spied the familiar form of a small Vietnamese man walking up to the house from the river. Vo Nguyen Giap was wearing khaki pants, a white shirt, and a tan French Army tropical pith helmet. On the riverbank, René noticed a flat-bottomed boat with a plank-keel that arose both fore and aft. Again, the Chinese influence was evident, but it was a well-constructed boat. Two men were waiting with the boat. One was standing aft, holding on to two long paddles. The other held what looked to be a Thompson submachine gun.

"Xin chao, my friend," shouted General Giap in Vietnamese.

"Bonjour, General," René replied, walking down the dozen steps to greet his old wartime friend.

Giap's intelligent eyes gleamed with delight as he hugged René, who was a good 14 inches taller than him. As they entered the cabin, René introduced Giap to Renate and Jacob.

"They've grown a lot in the last four years," Giap said. "The last time I saw them was at your house in Hanoi in 1944."

"It has been a while. Will you stay and join us for dinner this evening?"

"I was hoping you could travel north with me. There is someone who wishes to see you."

"I would love to. I haven't seen Uncle Ho in a long time."


The thirty-four-mile trip on the Bang River was amazingly slow against the steady current, and René was able to see things he hadn't noticed before. The astonishing eroded limestone peaks and forest mosaics provided an infinite number of shades of green. The rice paddies, tall grasses, and pine trees in the nearby hills wrote an enduring story of heavy rains of the monsoon and high temperatures of the dry season. When it became too dark to navigate the river, they camped and then started out at dawn the next morning.

They arrived at Pac Bo at noon, but it took nearly an hour to hike the last two miles to the cave where Ho Chi Minh was holed up next to a waterfall. Giap and Clairoux followed a narrow path and crossed a small stream near the entrance to the cave. There was a sweet fragrance of blossoms and wet earth. Then, René heard the sound of a waterfall. It was near but hidden by the dense vegetation. The mist was heavy, and the large rocks were darkened by moisture and speckled with green and white lichens and a deep green moss covering their base. The cave was surrounded by an ancient limestone mountain that had witnessed the evolution of human civilization for the last seven thousand years. The steep, winding path was surrounded by a thick evergreen forest filled with butterflies and songbirds.

When René and Giap walked into the cave, Ho sat cross-legged on a bamboo mat, reading a French version of Victor Hugo's *Les Miserables*. The cave was deep—hollowed out from thousands of years of water flowing through cracks and fissures. Over the centuries, spears and columns had formed, falling from the ceiling and rising from the floor. At one end, water formed a deep pool, its sides white from the limestone deposits. The water was deep and black.

Looking thin and frail, Ho rose to greet his guest with the traditional French *la bise*—a kiss on both cheeks. He was wearing a loose, indigo-colored shirt and pants—the traditional clothing of the Nung people. The Nung learned long ago that indigo dye made their woven fabrics more durable, and it saved time cleaning them.

"It's not as nice as a Paris café loaded with baguettes and strong coffee, but it's dry and comfortable," Ho commented, reminiscing his year in Paris in 1919. "Thank you for coming, René. It's been nearly three years, hasn't it? General Giap tells me that your investigation business is doing well."

"Enough to pay the bills and keep the creditors at bay, Uncle Ho," René replied. Then, noticing Ho's gaunt facial features and thin body, René moved to change the subject, "Are you well, Uncle Ho? You look tired and worn out. I can fly Dr. Park up if you require a physician."

"I've been traveling a lot lately, and I occasionally suffer from malaria," Ho replied, sensing René's reluctance to talk about his work. "I hope you're hungry. I was able to obtain a wheel of American cheese, across the border, and several bottles of wine from the Bordeaux region."

If anything, Ho Chi Minh was a gracious host. When asked by the OSS to describe Ho, during the war, René replied that he was a gentle man who was slow to anger. Ho was persuasive, undeniably patriotic, and anti-Japanese. He had a firm determination to serve the needs of his country. And not surprisingly, because he was an intellectual, Ho was always open to new ideas.

They talked for hours about the high country, the corn and rice crops, the Nung people, and Ho's philosophy. Uncle Ho believed in the inherent value of the untapped supply of individual courage and the importance of human dignity as a strategic commodity. He also recognized talent, intelligence, and the need to empower those with the capability to get things done.

"Our world is changing, René," Ho remarked. "When the Japanese attacked French garrisons across Indochina in March of 1945, it created a power vacuum that has certainly benefited the Viet Minh cause. I believe it has effectively ended French colonial rule. You and I both know that the French government has never understood the Vietnamese people. The French, for the most part, have been too egotistical to understand our aspirations of self-rule. Their greed has hardened their hearts and filled their pocketbooks at the expense of my people. The liberty that the French people value for themselves, they deny to the Vietnamese. That is why I believe that we are fighting a moral and just war, René, and, in due course, we will prevail."

René could not deny what Ho was saying. The French government and profit-driven developers had raped the country for over eighty years. However, René was different. He had seen how the native population had suffered as he fought alongside them against the Japanese. The natives had been his friends for decades. And Uncle Ho and Giap were his friends. But, unfortunately, he could not fight on their side anymore.

"Tomorrow, General Giap will take you on a tour of the area," Ho said. "I'm certain you will find it educational."


Three days later, René returned to the cabin at Cao Bang via the same flat-bottomed boat that took him north. A day later, he and his family flew back to Hanoi. With the information he had gathered on his trip north and what his brother, Marcel, had supplied, René began preparing a report for Yul Butler. He knew, without a doubt, that Uncle Ho was right. French rule in Indochina was doomed by their ego, arrogance, avarice, and unwillingness to change. The Vietnamese were indeed fighting a moral and just war. His fourteen-page report did not reflect a favorable outcome for the French. After finishing the piece, René advised his closest friends to leave Indochina. He then discretely moved his family to Saigon, where he handed the report over to Butler.

Instead of revising his statements to be more favorable towards the French, Butler's subsequent report to Washington provided an in-depth assessment from René Clairoux and his informants about the Viet Minh in northern Indochina. Most disturbing, however, was what René found across the border in China—the arrival of Chinese Communist forces. To Butler, this doomed any French chances of victory against the Viet Minh, and he said as much. The reaction at CIA headquarters was disbelief and a reprimand. Nevertheless, they ordered Butler to provide proof of Chinese Communist forces. When Butler sent photographs of Chinese Communist training camps at Nanning, via a courier, along with the names and strengths of the Chinese divisions, Washington was stunned into silence.

The photographs revealed Viet Minh battalions, fully trained and ready to cross the border into Indochina, fielding heavy mortars and pack howitzers. There were also several artillery battalions using American-made recoilless rifles and 105-millimeter howitzers. Just as alarming were the prisoner-of-war camps that held French soldiers and civilians, including women and children. A separate chapter stated that wounded French soldiers received no medical attention because captured medical officers were never allowed to treat their wounded. In fact, they were being held in a separate camp. As a result, not one French prisoner with a severe wound survived more than 60 days.

It was a photograph of a Viet Minh staff study—elaborating General Giap's plan to defeat the French—that spurred Washington to formally propose material assistance for Indochina. However, president de Gaulle, fully aware of President Truman's anti-colonial stance, quickly rejected the support, fearing the Americans would send troops and dismantle the French colony.

General Giap was well aware of America's reluctance to commit U.S. troops, to be involved in a *colonial war*. Two months after Butler's report reached Washington, Giap's fourteen battalions attacked French forts along the Chinese border. Despite being manned with over 10,000 troops, the French posts never stood a chance. In one attack, Lang-Son was hastily abandoned by French forces, leaving behind 1,300 tons of ammunition, food, equipment, and artillery. When the smoke cleared in the north, the French had suffered a stunning defeat. They had lost over 6,000 troops, 15 artillery pieces, 130 mortars, 950 machine guns, 1,100 submachine guns, 8,500 rifles, and 460 trucks. The captured material was enough to fully equip an entire Viet Minh division.

The Viet Minh guerilla groups, who had fought desperately for years to control northern Vietnam, transitioned from scantily supplied battalions and regiments into fully equipped, 10,000-person divisions—304, 308, 312, 316, 320, and 351. The 351st was a heavy division comprised of two regiments of Soviet artillery and an engineering regiment. For the French, it was only a matter of time before they would be routed. Giap, however, was not resting on his good fortune. Instead, he began planning the attack on the French outposts in their colonies of Laos and Cambodia.

# CHAPTER 24



*Washington, D.C.*

Major General Lew Miller was not thrilled with the new plan that his two agents Jon Preston and George Linka, were proposing. Although brilliant and resourceful, it was risky, and Miller did not like putting his best operatives in unnecessarily dangerous situations. However, Jon convinced him to forward the proposal to the vice chief of staff, Lieutenant General John Renick, despite his misgivings.

"For crying out loud, Lew," Renick complained. "We don't have enough agents to cover this masquerade. How can Preston possibly believe he can take down Tsukuda with just himself, Linka, Wong, and Kumiko? And this whole Kabuki Theater, cursed sword, and white samurai facade seem bizarre at best."

"It's designed to get Tsukuda out of his estate and in the open in Tokyo," Miller responded.

"And this cursed sword thing. Does Jon really believe that Tsukuda will think he is invincible if he possesses it?"

"That's what Jon, George, and Kumiko think."

"I find it difficult to believe Tsukuda is stupid enough to believe this garbage."

"Japanese society is filled with folklore and superstitions, John. A lot of the things they believe would be incomprehensible to most Americans."

"I see your point. I admit that Jon and George have really done a fine job of planning this. But, it's…it's…," Renick gasped and thought. "It's so far from conventional thinking that it just might work, but we'll need a lot of agents. Where are we with the new agents we brought on? Will any be ready in time to help?"

"Eizo and Emon Fujiwara are the readiest because of their training in Japan from Tsukuda before the war ended. Plus, they continued their martial art training with their mother while they attended college. She also taught them some skills she learned at the spy school—throwing weapons, sticks, staff, and stealth and entering methods. Therefore, she is confident that they will be great agents. Plus, the last three years in college have opened their eyes. They are fully aware of the atrocities committed by the Japanese Imperial Army and the destruction that Tsukuda planned with the submarines and nerve agent. Apparently, their enmity toward Tsukuda is greater than Kumiko's because he was responsible for their father's death. Tsukuda sent their father on a suicide mission."

"How have they performed in their training?"

"Eizo and Emon are at the top of their class in every category. Their martial arts skills are as good as Kumiko's, and they are very clever lads."

"My only worry is that Tsukuda and his bodyguards will recognize Eizo and Emon. I'm sure Tsukuda and his team got to know them intimately when they trained at Tsukuda's estate, before being sent to the U.S. to help with the submarine mission."

"They were fourteen-year-old boys then. They've grown five inches and are strapping young men now. Tsukuda would hardly recognize them."

"Maybe, maybe not. According to Kumiko, the boys look a lot like their father. I do not doubt that Tsukuda would recognize the family resemblance. So, I'm afraid it would be ill-advised to use them on this mission."

"I'll let Kumiko decide. She knows the risks, and she can disguise herself and the boys."

"What do we do for additional agents? Wong lost most of his men to Tsukuda's goons in Tokyo."

"Brigadier MacKenzie has a half dozen Japanese-speaking agents he is willing to use on the mission. In fact, officially, Jon and George are still on loan to the British SIS for another six months. I didn't cancel their orders when their mission to Korea was compromised."

"So, you're turning the operation over to the British?"

"Yes, we've no choice. Japan is under MacArthur's jurisdiction, and in Japan, CIC agents can only investigate crimes committed by U.S. Army personnel. So what we are doing is the responsibility of the CIA, but as you know, they are just getting their feet wet and still can't tell a Jap from a Chinaman."

"Will MacKenzie put Preston in charge of the mission?"

"He has assured me that he will."

"Will Miles Murphy and Henri Morreau be part of the team?"

"Unfortunately, no. Miles and Henri are busy with the chaos going on in Indochina. I take it you read the report that Butler forwarded?"

"Yes, but how did we get a copy?"

"Butler sent me a copy via courier with a note stating that the U.S. would be well advised to stay away from Indochina. The Viet Minh are a lot stronger and better organized than anyone expected. Unfortunately, a new congressman from the 11th congressional district in Massachusetts, a guy named Kennedy, believes that we should help the French. Apparently, he's planning a fact-finding mission to Indochina next year. He is convinced the French can win with our support. His wife's great-grandfather grew up in southern France. He immigrated to Philadelphia in 1815 after serving in the Napoleonic Wars, so there is some family history in play. But that's a separate matter; I don't want to get ahead of ourselves. Plus, Truman is still anti-colonial and doesn't want to commit U.S. troops to a war we can't win."

"As far as Preston's mission to Tokyo, I assume it's a go?"

"Yes, but Preston, Linka, Wong, and Kumiko will be working for the British, along with anyone else we send. It will be their show. I just hope they are smart enough to let Preston run the operation."

"Do you really think Brigadier MacKenzie would be that foolish?"

"Not as long as the brigadier is in command. There is talk that MacKenzie is being promoted to Major General."

"What if the brigadier is replaced and the new guy wants a Brit in charge?"

"Then Preston is authorized to walk away and bring his team home."

"He may walk away, but you know damn well he won't come home. He'll figure out a way to take Tsukuda down with just the four of them."

"That's what scares me. So, you better come up with a Plan B to support them, just in case."

"Admiral Dubois has a dozen Navy intelligence agents from the Asian theater that are getting released from the service due to further force reductions. Steve Schaefer is already working on their transition and getting army security clearances. Camille and Kathleen will begin training and evaluating them in a couple of weeks."

"Make sure the girls give you timely updates."

"Yes, sir. Admiral Dubois has assured us that these men are some of his best agents. Jon has Camille, Kathleen, and Kumiko doing the martial arts training and evaluations to ensure the men have no problem following women's orders. We don't want any problems with them in the field."

The twelve Navy intelligence agents who were being trained, ordered, and coached by three women were more of a mental somersault than a smooth transition to the U.S. Army counterintelligence corps. Not one had ever been trained, evaluated, or given commands by a woman, much less three women. At first, there was disbelief and resentment. Then, after three days of having their butts kicked by the women in martial arts classes, it became an embarrassment. By the end of the second week, all but one former Petty Officer First Class were singing their praises and following orders without question.

"What do you want to do with Staff Sergeant Tahara Sana?" Camille asked Jon after she briefed him on the former petty officer's evaluation.

"He scored outstanding in all the technical areas. In fact, he has scored higher than all the others," Jon replied. "I don't see how we can eliminate him."

"But, Jon. He hates taking orders from women."

Jon thought for a moment and then replied, "Okay, we can't use him in the field, but we can still use him as a trainer. Maybe after working a while with you and Kathleen, he'll change his thinking."

"Jon, he's a 30-year-old Japanese male. He was raised in a traditional Japanese household where women are subservient and don't give opinions, much less, orders," Kathleen answered.

"Yes, but he is an excellent agent. His test scores are off the chart. He'll acclimate, or he'll stay in training until he either retires or resigns."

"If we weren't desperate for people, I would fight you on this," Camille stated. "But, so help me, Hanna, if he is disrespectful one more time, I'm going to cold-cock the bastard."

"Since you and Kumiko are civilian contractors, you all have my permission to take him down a notch. But, because Kathleen is an officer, she can't touch him. So just make sure he can walk, talk and train afterward."


The next day, Jon and George made a surprise inspection at the Marine base where the training was conducted. As they approached the gym where the martial arts training was held, a Marine ambulance was driving away.

"Did someone get hurt," George asked.

"Bloody nose and concussion," Kathleen replied.

"Sergeant Tahara?" Jon inquired.

"Yes."

"Was it Camille?"

"No. Kumiko. The sergeant took issue with her theory of knocking someone unconscious with a strike to the Vagus nerve. Tahara said it was impossible and stated that she wasn't a real Kung Fu master. He challenged her to a fight, and she knocked him out."

"How?"

"Elbow to the face and then a Vagus strike."

"Damage?"

"The sergeant will have difficulty talking, drinking liquids, and pain in the ear for a couple of days. He'll pull through physically, but I'm worried about his psychological recovery."

"Damn. I wish I could have been here to see it," George responded.

"After the Vagus strike, she put him in an arm lock. I'm surprised she didn't snap it. But he was unconscious by then," Camille replied as she walked up to the group. "I just hope he's learned his lesson."

"The other men sure have," Kathleen said. "They're listening more closely to what we have to say, and all want to perfect the Vagus strike themselves. Kumiko says it takes a great deal of practice and skill to actually knock someone out. I know I haven't mastered it."

"I wouldn't rely on it in combat. We usually don't want our enemies coming back to haunt us," Jon stated. "We'll talk to Kumiko about it. I'm sure she has a bag full of moves that are more effective and decisive. I want you all to finish the evaluations today and present them to General Miller tomorrow afternoon. These men need to be on a boat to Japan within two weeks."

"What about Tahara?" Camille asked.

"After he recovers, put him to work with Eizo, Emon, and Hiroki on counterintelligence tradecraft. They need to learn how to tail suspects without being detected. From what I understand, naval intelligence knows how to do this better than any military service. They also need to be trained in the use of weapons—handguns, rifles, and submachine guns. And not just American arms. They need to learn British, Russian, Czech, Chinese, and Japanese, too. And you might as well include knife-fighting. The Marines probably have a few good instructors you can borrow."

"Would you like us to teach them how to drink and chase women while we're at it?" Camille asked sarcastically.

"They are young, handsome, and naïve, so why not. The boys need to know their limits on drinking alcohol. And, yes, they need to learn how to approach a woman and not be taken in by their feminine charms. I suggest you and Kathleen take them out to some local restaurants and teach them proper etiquette."

"And where do you suggest we find a woman qualified to teach them how to resist a woman's charm?"

"Check with Admiral Dubois. He still has a few female agents working in naval intelligence in the D.C. area. I'm sure Tahara can help, too. After all, he was a sailor."

"For crying out loud, Jon! Why not drop them off at a college fraternity house? It would be quicker."

"I'll defer to your judgment, Camille. But, yes, that's an option, too."

"Well, Katie, I guess we'd better get our fancy dresses out. These kids are going to need some serious instruction to fend-off Mata Hari. I haven't crashed a sorority party in eight years. With the school term coming to a close soon, there will be more than a few parties this weekend. It should be a hoot," Camille said, laughing as she thought of the last sorority party she had attended.

# CHAPTER 25

*São Paulo, Brazil*

After Jon Preston left São Paulo, Fabio Martinez set out to develop a way to save the priceless Chinese jadeite and porcelain pieces left in his care. The rarer and more valuable form of jade, *jadeite,* is one of two mineral species classified as jade. The other, *nephrite,* is a much more common and less costly mineral. The most valuable piece Preston left was an ornately sculptured jadeite bowl from the Qing dynasty with a delicately carved dragon wrapped around the outside. On the inside, a Chinese poem was etched. The other priceless object was a Ming Dynasty porcelain figurine of seven fairies in a boat, which stood nearly 12 inches high. Martinez couldn't bear to have them fall into Tsukuda's hands.

It would be impossible to duplicate the porcelain figurine. Still, Fabio was confident that one of his artisans could replicate the jadeite dragon bowl. Unfortunately, there was not enough time before they were to be sold. He hated to disappoint Jonathan Preston, but it was unavoidable. The alternative was to take Tsukuda down before the antiquities were shipped to Japan. Fabio was praying that Preston and his team could do it quickly—when he thought of an additional resource. He looked up a number in his card file, picked up the handset of the heavy, black Western Electric rotary phone on his desk, and dialed. After a short conversation, Fabio headed for his vehicle.

As Fabio drove up the brick driveway, lined with 40-foot tall Pernambuco trees with large rounded crowns, he gazed in admiration at the lavish, nearly 20,000-square-foot mansion. The seven-bedroom and nine-bath estate lay in the Jardim Europa neighborhood of São Paulo, and cost almost $1.25 million to build—an incredible sum in 1930.

An elderly butler opened the front door and let Fabio into the large foyer. He noticed the large multicolored skylight that levitated over a winding staircase to the second floor, as he gazed upward. After closing the large hardwood door, the butler escorted Fabio into a lavish office with an enormous carved marble fireplace that complimented the room's rustic décor.

"El Presidente will be with you in a moment, Señor Martinez. Please make yourself comfortable," the butler said, motioning to an oversized burgundy leather chair before retiring from the room.

It had been nearly six years since he had visited the lawyer, politician, and former president of Brazil. Yet, when Getúlio Vargas entered the room, he still walked with a rigid, erect military bearing that made him look younger than his sixty-six years.

"I was hoping this would be a cordial visit of a good friend, Fabio, but I suspect a bit of business will be entwined," Vargas said as he entered the room. "Can I offer you a Scotch?"

"Yes, Mr. President," Fabio responded, as the former Brazilian president hugged him and patted him on the back.

They talked for thirty minutes about family, sailing, and a possible run for a second presidency. Finally, after pouring his second glass of Scotch, Vargas relented and asked, "Fabio, what is so important that you leave the bank and visit this old politician in the middle of the day?"

"I am helping some American friends with a delicate matter, Mr. President. One involving a Japanese organized crime syndicate."

"Does it have anything to do with your new business venture?"

"Yes, sir."

"Well then, how may I be of assistance?"

"Years ago, after your inauguration, you mentioned that you had been taken in by an antiquities dealer when you had purchased over a dozen rare Chinese artifacts in the late 1920s."

"Yes, I found out years later that they were forgeries."

"Did you dispose of them?"

"Heavens, no. Despite being forgeries, they are very well-crafted pieces. They are displayed in one of my ballrooms. Why?"

"As I recall, there were many jade and porcelain pieces."

"And you need the use of these forgeries to help the Americans?"

"Yes, Mr. President."

"I heard rumors that you were actively helping the American military during the war against Germany and Japan. I also heard a story that you provided intelligence to the U.S. Navy that helped them capture a Japanese submarine off of the coast of Venezuela."

"Yes, Mr. President."

"Would this be related to a former Japanese general named Tsukuda? I understand that he deposited millions into your bank during the war. If so, I suspect this has something to do with the Japanese smugglers in Havana and your new gem and antiquities business."

"You are quite well informed, Mr. President."

"I make it my business to know what is going on in Brazil, Fabio. Much like you, I suppose. So, if what you are doing has anything to do with keeping these Japanese criminals out of Brazil, you may take whatever artifacts you need."

"Thank you, Mr. President. Unfortunately, I cannot promise that they will be returned."

"Then I will consider it an investment in the future of Brazil. So, come, let's go to the ballroom. You can choose the pieces you need or take them all. Just make sure that whatever you're doing doesn't come back to haunt you, Fabio. I wouldn't want to lose a good friend like you."

The eight pieces that Fabio chose were jadeite, nephrite, and porcelain forgeries, supposedly from the Ming Dynasty. Fabio chose seven jadeite and nephrite pieces and one porcelain figurine of a Buddhist priest. Despite its delicate look, the ivory-white porcelain was extremely hard and durable.

When Fabio's grandson gazed upon the objects sitting on the large table in Fabio's office at International Gems and Precious Metals, he found it hard to believe that they were forgeries. Even the craftsmen that worked for him marveled at the artisanship.

"Grandfather, this looks like the real thing," José remarked. "The exquisite detail of this porcelain could only be made possible by the plasticity of the clay used to sculpt it. It's much like the clay I use in my sculptures that I have to import from India. This porcelain must have been reproduced in the Chinese coastal town of Dehua, where all the super-white, fine porcelain is produced. Dehua porcelain contains a very small amount of iron oxide. This allows it to be fired to the shade of ivory that you see in this piece. It's a shame that we have to use it in our ruse to fool the Japanese."

"Yes, but President Vargas insisted that I take it. The other porcelain pieces he had were too thin and fragile. Plus, they did not have the hardness of this piece. The alternative is to use the real Chinese pieces that Agent Preston brought us. I'm just glad President Vargas let me have them. Let's get color photos taken and airmail them to Preston along with the descriptions of the artifacts."


Guy Wong met with Jon Preston in the back room of a Chinese restaurant, a half a mile from the Anacostia River and the Washington Navy Yard. The restaurant belonged to Wong's uncle. Preston was dressed in tan slacks and a long-sleeved, puckered, all-cotton fabric shirt with thin blue railroad stripes. Wong wore white slacks and a tangerine-colored, loose-fitting, lightweight, plain-weave-cotton fabric shirt.

"These came in the mail today," Preston said as he removed sixteen color photographs from a large envelope. "Fabio Martinez found some replacements for the jade and porcelain pieces. His note says they are exquisite forgeries from a collection owned by Getúlio Vargas, a former President of Brazil."

Wong countered, "I don't know if they will fool Professor Chen Li, Jon. He's one sharp 82-year-old man. If anyone can tell a fake, he can."

"I have an appointment with Professor Chen later this afternoon. His daughter has problems with the Immigration and Naturalization Service (INS) that I can make go away. But, unfortunately, some old-timers in the Department of Justice want to reinstate the Chinese

Exclusion Act, which Congress repealed in 1943. Apparently, his daughter's INS paperwork was reviewed several months back, and now they want to send her back to China."

"How did you find out?"

"I have a contact in INS who monitors certain people for us. A former OSS sergeant who worked with me in Calcutta. He keeps tabs on many people for me. When Professor Chen entered the scene, I had him and his daughter added to the list. She is on her last INS appeal. Her case is being heard next week."

"And if Professor Chen goes along with your plan?"

"His daughter's case will be dismissed."

"And what happens if he doesn't play ball?"

"I don't foresee that happening, Guy. But, if he doesn't go along, he will most certainly contract the bubonic plague and have to be quarantined."

"You've got that much clout at INS and Justice?"

"No, but General Bradley does. I briefed Bradley and his vice commander, General Renick, yesterday. Bradley is the one who suggested the plague and called in a favor with the Bethesda Naval Hospital commander, should the need arise."

"I guess I shouldn't be surprised. You pull a rabbit out of the hat all the time. So, when do Elton and I leave for Havana to pick up the artifacts?"

"You don't. General Renick sent a C-47 to São Paulo this morning with George Linka and Kathleen Lauren onboard. They will return on Saturday. That should give you and Professor Kirkendall three days to become familiar with the Chinese artifacts before you meet with Sugimoto and Chen."

# CHAPTER 26

*São Paulo, Brazil*

It was nearly noon when George and Kathleen stepped down the airstairs of the C-47 transport. They watched as a cadet-grey, Cord 812, Westchester four-door sedan, driven by José Martinez, came to a halt twenty yards from the plane. The Westchester was unique. The 289-cubic-inch, 8-cylinder engine could generate 170 horse-power with its factory-installed, supercharged engine. Like all 1937 Westchesters, the car had front-wheel drive, hidden headlights, and no running boards.

The ride north from Congonhas Airport to International Gems and Precious Metals took just under an hour. Despite the old-fashioned, tube-type rear axle and semi-elliptic rear springs, the automobile was comfortable as it negotiated the roadwork, detours, and potholes in the red gravel streets they had to travel. When George and Kathleen arrived at the business located at 684 Paulista Avenue, they were informed by José that it was in the heart of the downtown São Paulo business district.

Fabio Martinez and his cousin's International Gems and Precious Metals business occupied all four floors of the four-story, red brick building. It was built in 1899. When Fabio purchased the building, it was gutted. New electrical and plumbing were installed, and heavy fans were placed on each floor to cool the building during the sum-mer months of December through February. Raw gems were graded on the second floor—while cutting, polishing, and setting occurred on the third floor. The entire bottom floor was dedicated to business operations. The fourth floor contained Fabio's office, a large vault, and a showroom that held the finished products and the ancient artifacts. The building was guarded around the clock by a dozen men armed with Thompson submachine guns. When the car pulled to a stop under a large carriage porch, Fabio greeted the visitors.

"Señor Linka, Señorita Lauren, welcome to São Paulo. My kitchen staff has prepared a light lunch for you, as well as some refreshments. Please follow me to the dining room," Fabio said. "After you are refreshed, José will give you a tour of the establishment. Unfortunately, I have to return to my bank for a directors' meeting, but you will be my guests for dinner and stay at my house tonight. If you need anything, just tell José."

"Certainly, Mr. Martinez. And thank you for the hospitality," George replied, as he and Kathleen watched Fabio turn and get into a black sedan that whisked him away.

They turned back to José, who ushered them into a private dining room. They were soon followed by several kitchen staff members, who hovered over the visitors and described the dishes prepared for their lunch.

"I think I could get used to this type of treatment," Kathleen stated after she had tasted the grilled speckled peacock bass from the Rio Negro River.

"Uh-huh," was all George could say as he stuffed his mouth with Feijoada, a stew of black beans with pork, chicken, and vegetables that was served over brown rice.

"Maybe we should stay a couple of days to check out their security?" Kathleen questioned.

"Can't. We've got to get the Chinese artifacts to Wong. He's meeting with Sugimoto next Friday, and Professor Kirkendall needs time to familiarize himself with the pieces."

"Then maybe we should come here on our honeymoon."

"I thought you wanted to go to the Grand Canyon?"

"Can't we do both?"

"Not with all that we have going on with Tsukuda."

"Okay. But promise me you will bring me back when this is all over."

"It's a promise, Katie."

The following day, Fabio and José ate breakfast with George and Kathleen. José explained the security for transporting the five chests of artifacts to the airport. To George and Kathleen, it seemed like overkill. Still, Fabio insisted that it was necessary due to the criminal gangs in the city and the military officers that conspired with the gangs.

"Most military officers are honest and dedicated soldiers. But lately, there have been a few who have aligned themselves with political organizations that are dead set against Getúlio Vargas running for a second presidential term," Fabio said. "Since I am a friend of Vargas, my family and businesses have become targets of their unrest."

"Do you suspect word has gotten out about the rare antiquities we are picking up?" Kathleen asked.

"I always assume that someone has leaked the information. I have over a hundred artisans working for me. I try to monitor their political loyalties, but in Brazil, loyalties can change as quickly as the weather."

"Will Katie and I have access to weapons?" George asked.

"Yes. You will ride in the Cord with José and a driver. It has multi-layered bullet-resistant glass, perimeter protection of the entire passenger compartment, and battery and engine protection. In the car, you will find four Thompson submachine guns; eight, .45-caliber, Colt 1911 semi-automatic handguns; a box of Mk 2 fragmentation-type, anti-personnel hand grenades; and plenty of magazines for all the weapons."

"So, you are expecting trouble."

"When I am transporting priceless antiquities that people think are worth millions, yes. My goal is to be able to outgun anyone who attempts an attack. Plus, inside and in the back of the two trucks carrying the antiquities will be half a dozen Brazilian soldiers that I know and trust. And the jade pieces are in bulletproof containers. However, if the convoy is attacked, José will direct the car away from the fighting and get you all safely to the airport. I have already notified the crew and the Marines who had accompanied you to be ready for a 10 a.m. departure."

"Let's hope it doesn't come down to a fight," George replied, as a butler came in and informed Fabio that the car was ready.

As the Cord pulled up to the International Gems and Precious Metals building, José exited the car and went to talk to a colonel standing by one of the trucks. George noticed two 2½-ton, 6x6 *General Motors*-built trucks idling with their tailgates backed into the loading dock, at the side of the building. In addition, there were two M8 Light Armored Cars with three soldiers and a non-commissioned officer standing next to them.

"Do you get the impression we're headed for battle?" Kathleen whispered.

"Something is going on, and I don't like it," George replied, as he opened the door and walked toward José and the colonel.

Before George could ask a question, the colonel yelled and made a circle with his right arm. Soldiers began climbing into the vehicles and pulled out in an orderly fashion with an armored car leading and one trailing the two 6x6 trucks. As George rushed back to the Cord, he grabbed José by the arm.

"Quick, get in the car. I'll explain once we are underway," José said.

As the Cord took its position at the very end of the convoy and sped up to catch the armored vehicle, José turned to George and Kathleen. "We received a tip from one of our informers, early this morning, that there would be an attack on the convoy before it reached the airport. I apologize, but my grandfather didn't have time to consult with you. He was busy arranging the extra trucks and the armored vehicles."

"Then maybe we should cancel and do this another day," George countered.

"If we did, it would give more time to the people planning the attack. Our understanding is that it was a last-minute plan after they found out the antiquities were being moved this morning."

"Is one of the military factions planning to attack the convoy?"

"Not according to our informant. It's one of the local gangs, which is totally out of character. They usually aren't this well organized, and they don't have the weapons needed to pull off an attack."

"Then it's been organized by one of Tsukuda's groups. They think we're transporting the Masamune sword," Kathleen replied with urgency.

"What are you talking about? What sword?" José asked.

"I don't have time to explain," George stated as he handed Kathleen one of the Thompsons and two handguns.

George looked out the front window as they approached a road-work crew directing traffic to a side street. "That four-story building on the right. There are people on the roof. Crap, those are grenade launchers," George stated as he rolled down the window and began firing at the men on the roof.

George's gunfire caused the men on the roof to duck, but not before a grenade was launched at the lead truck. The grenade struck under the engine and exploded, nearly flipping the vehicle as it tried to swerve to avoid the grenade. Metal fragments entered the cab, killing the driver and passenger. The truck crashed into a car that was parked on the street—and came to a halt. As the six soldiers in the back scrambled from the burning wreck, three were gunned down by the fire from a submachine gun. The soldiers returned fire as soon as they reached the safety of a building across the street.

As George yelled for the driver to park and let them out, he saw one attacker slip behind an old pickup. He carried a Type 100 submachine gun with a side-mounted, 30-round, detachable magazine—a licensed version of the German MP 18. Only Tsukuda could have arranged for the weapons. As the car slowed, George and Kathleen jumped from the vehicle, carrying their Thompsons, handguns, and four grenades.

As they took cover behind a brick wall, José followed, yelling at the duo.

"Colonel Linka, we need to get you to the airport."

"Nonsense, we need to kill these assholes!" George shouted, as he fired a burst and struck an attacker in the chest. "Katie, cover me. I'm moving to the building across the street. José, have the soldiers pour fire into this building. Have the armored vehicles start putting rounds into the top-story windows. Tell them not to stop until the top floor collapses."

As George sprinted for cover, he fired another burst that took out two assailants before they could retreat into the building. Kathleen had caught another two attackers as they were about to toss German-made, Model 24 hand grenades at the remaining truck. As the stick grenades fell from their hands, three more attackers rushed to get away from the blast. José sent three bursts from his Thompson into the trio, killing them.

Kathleen fired three more bursts from her Thompson before replacing another magazine. George noticed another attacker aiming his submachine gun at her; however, Kathleen pulled the .45 from her waistband and shot a round into his head, nearly decapitating the man. Two more blasts were heard from the armored cars as 37-millimeter, anti-tank rounds penetrated the top floor. Seconds later, the top floor crumbled and fell into the third story. This triggered the collapse of the entire building.

"They're falling back," José yelled as the dust began to settle on the scene and obscured visibility for a hundred yards around.

Two more bursts came from Kathleen's Thompson, as two attackers tried to flee through the dust. As George approached Kathleen, she was kneeling next to one of the dead men.

"Eurasian," Kathleen remarked, trying to stand up but losing her balance.

George caught her before she hit the ground. As he laid her gently on the street, he realized his hand was covered with her blood.

"José, we need a doctor and an ambulance. Katie's been hit," George shouted, as he hovered over her and touched her cheek.

"It's just a flesh wound," Kathleen replied, looking deep into George's eyes before passing out.

George yelled at José, "Get the crates out of the destroyed truck, transport them to the airport, and load them onto our aircraft. Then tell the pilot in charge to take off without us."

# CHAPTER 27

*Washington, D.C.*

Jonathan Preston and General Miller sat in silence as General Renick read the cablegram from Fabio Martinez detailing the attack on the convoy in São Paulo and the injury to Kathleen Lauren. Preston was angry with himself for not expecting such a bold move from Tsukuda. He quickly realized that Tsukuda must have thought that the sword was being sold to another buyer and was part of the shipment that Martinez had put together.

"It's my job to think ahead of these criminals, General. I should have expected an attack in São Paulo," Jon stated.

"You're wrong, Jon. It was Fabio Martinez's job, and he managed it well. Fabio's intelligence network discovered the plot, and he added extra military personnel at the last minute. When they attacked, those goons were hit hard. A dozen were killed, and only two that we know of got away," Miller replied.

"Sugimoto's men will be watching the airports and bases. When will the plane arrive?"

"Tomorrow at noon. As a precaution, I had the plane diverted to Langley Air Force Base. It landed before sunrise and was taxied into a secure hangar. The antiquities were repackaged into cardboard boxes. The cargo will be flown out on a Douglas C-54 Skymaster. It will arrive at Bolling Air Force Base tomorrow afternoon."

"What about delivery to the university?"

"I've made arrangements for the antiquities to be transported to Georgetown University in six separate civilian panel vans over two days. The drivers have no idea what is in the containers, just that their contents are fragile. The cardboard cartons have logos that identify them coming from five different publishers. It will look like a normal delivery of university supplies and textbooks."

"That was quick thinking."

"Well, it was necessary. However, Professor Kirkendall and Wong can know nothing about what happened in São Paulo. Otherwise, they might appear doubtful and fearful. Or, at least Kirkendall might. Therefore, I do suggest that you arrange for additional security at the university. Make sure they are visible."

"I'll have Wong use his security guards. Sugimoto has already seen them at the jewelry store."

"I was thinking something more covert."

"Yes, I was thinking the flower beds around the Old North Building will be getting some attention starting today. That way, the ground crews will not look out of place when the meeting takes place."


Sugimoto was furious when he got word of the attack in São Paulo. Tsukuda had gone behind his back. Probably panicked, thinking the sword was being sold to someone besides him. Putting his lieutenant-general thinking cap on, he decided to send Tsukuda a message resigning his position. It was a risk to challenge his boss. Still, it was necessary to gain control of the situation that Tsukuda entrusted to him. Tsukuda wouldn't like it, but he would respect his move.

The message was short and brief: *If I am no longer trusted to complete the job you assigned to me, I regretfully request that you accept my resignation and let me return to my private life in Japan.* To make sure Tsukuda understood his predicament, he signed it Takaji Sugimoto, Lieutenant General, Imperial Japanese Army, Retired.

The next day, Hata Raizo delivered the message from Sugimoto. Tsukuda was not upset with the general's bold response to his actions. If anything, it was unforgivable on his part. Despite his fear of losing the sacred sword, he should have trusted Sugimoto and left things alone. Tsukuda picked up a pen, wrote out a reply, and handed it to

Raizo. The bodyguard took the message, bowed, retraced his steps, and took it to the communications center.

Raizo was not one to question his boss, but he wished the general would have asked for his input before ordering the attack. It was short notice, ill-conceived, and apparently poorly executed. He should have waited and struck at the university or the jeweler's place of business. Instead, Raizo thought, *I will ask Tsukuda to send our best agent, Hinata Hayashi, to the U.S. to secure the sword and antiquities. Then he can plan and kill the American agents. It is a job for a professional. A job Hattori is trained to do.*

When the White House announced President Truman's state visit to Japan, the press secretary included a brief statement that the President would be returning a special lost samurai sword to the Japanese people. After Tsukuda read the headline of the presidential visit in the Asahi Shimbun newspaper, he concluded that Wong was selling the Masamune sword to the U.S. government. The U.S. government or President Truman would return it to the Japanese government. That would explain the security around the shipment in Brazil. Tsukuda decided he could not allow this to happen.

"Raizo," Tsukuda yelled.

"Yes, General," Raizo replied as he entered the office and bowed.

"Who would you recommend to send on a dangerous assignment to the United States?"

"Hinata Hayashi, General."

"I need someone I can trust to get a job done. Someone highly trained and ruthless. Arrange for Hayashi to get into Washington, D.C., to make sure we obtain the Masamune sword. However, this must be done discretely, and Sugimoto must place Hayashi in charge of the operation. Since he's had eyelid surgery, he should be able to blend in with the Asian community and go unnoticed. Once the sword is in Hayashi's hands, his mission is to kill the American agents who killed my nieces. Make sure he reads the files on these agents and memorizes all the details. And Raizo, make sure Hayashi does not underestimate these people. They are lethal."

"Nozomi," Tsukuda yelled. "Bring tea for two."

Tsukuda offered Raizo a seat on a silk cushion and waited for the tea to arrive. After Nozomi delivered a tray with two cups and a pot of steaming tea, she bowed and backed out of the room. She had overheard the conversation with Raizo. She would pass another message when she shopped for vegetables and fish later in the day.

Jonathan Preston was in General Miller's office with George Linka, discussing the training of the new recruits. The new class consisted of half a dozen university graduates from Hawaii and six graduates from four different Ivy League universities.

"I understand there has been some friction between the trainees. Care to elaborate?" Miller asked.

"The Ivy League graduates resented having to train with the trainees from Hawaii. They called them filthy Japs," Preston replied.

"What happened?"

"Admiral Whitley's daughter took exception to the slander and knocked out one of the Ivy League trainees with a spinning round-house kick. One of his friends attempted to take her on, and he got his ass kicked. They're both in the infirmary."

"Do you see any other complications?"

"No, sir. The Ivy Leaguers were told to get along or quit."

"What about the two in the infirmary?"

"One has a broken jaw, so he is being sent home to recover. The other has multiple contusions but has rejoined the training with a fresh attitude about Asian Americans."

"Is there anything else on your mind, Jon?"

"I'm worried about President Truman's timing of his visit to Japan. I wish the White House would have scheduled it for December, as I had suggested. Now we won't have enough time to prepare for what we need to do."

"It was a State Department decision, but that may be a moot point. Berlin is becoming a hot topic for the president again. As you recall, the Soviet delegation walked out of an Allied Control Council meeting in March. This was followed by Stalin issuing orders that restricted Western military and civilian traffic between the American, British, and French occupation zones and Berlin. Yesterday it was announced that the Deutsche Mark would be introduced as the new German currency. Apparently, this was not to Stalin's liking, so this morning Soviet forces began blockading all road, rail, and water routes into the Allied-controlled areas of Berlin. Additionally, the Soviets have cut off the flow of food, coal, and other supplies."

"I hope this does not mean armed intervention."

"No, the Soviet army is too strong, and you know the condition of ours. However, this afternoon the president will announce that he plans to airlift supplies into Berlin. Since this is President Truman's first post-war crisis, the White House is announcing the delay of the state visit to Japan, later this afternoon. He's rescheduling to early December."

"That's a relief," George stated.

"Now, how will this affect your plans to take down Tsukuda?"

Preston closed his eyes to think. When they reopened, he said, "General, we were hoping to use the sword to draw Tsukuda out in the open in Tokyo. The cancellation of the president's July trip is the best thing that could happen since we wanted it to be in December. However, we just received a message from our undercover agent in Tokyo that Tsukuda is sending a trained spy and assassin named Hinata Hayashi to the U.S. If we can stop this assassin and take Sugimoto and his men down, we can continue planning the mission to Tokyo without risking our in-place asset.

"What is the implication of the assassin coming to the U.S.?"

"It means Tsukuda suspects Wong is selling the sword to the U.S. government to better relations with Japan. Therefore, he's sending a trained assassin to steal the sword. I suspect Tsukuda has also tasked him to attack and eliminate my team."

"How soon before he gets here?"

"Thirty days, minimum."

"Then I suggest you come up with a foolproof way to protect your team. What about the other issue? Have you found the location of Sugimoto's farm?"

"Not yet, but I have a local realtor who specializes in farms and ranches working on it. His entire family is in the real estate business. They have six offices in Maryland and Virginia."

"And how is Colonel Arvin doing?"

"Buck is doing great, sir. After working with his father for a year, his father retired and let him take over the realty company. He said a group of Asians will stick out like a sore thumb in a rural area. He'll locate the farm.

"As soon as he does, I'll get presidential authorization to deal with them discretely. Now, on another note. I just heard from George. Katie's surgery went well. It was a through-and-through wound, but it didn't break any bones in her shoulder. However, it did do a lot of flesh damage, and she lost a lot of blood. They anticipate her being released from the hospital next Saturday. She and George will be staying with Fabio Martinez until she is well enough to fly. After she is released from the hospital, Fabio's personal physician will stay at the estate and monitor her."

"What about security? It would be an ideal time for Tsukuda thugs to go after Katie and George."

"Fabio Martinez has tripled the security at his estate, and George has agreed to consult with his head of security to make it even tighter. Plus, President Truman has dispatched two squads of Embassy Marines to assist with the security. As soon as Katie is well enough to travel, I will send a plane to bring them home. In the meantime, I'm assigning Eizo and Emon Fujiwara, and Hiroki Eguchi to your team. I want them to work directly with you, so teach them as well as you did Camille and Kathleen. They represent the future leaders of our organization."

# CHAPTER 28



*Boonsboro, Maryland*

It didn't take Richard Arvin long to find the farm nestled in a small valley near Boonsboro, Maryland. The 120-acre farm and orchard, located twenty miles from the Pennsylvania border, mainly was dense woods except for the 25 acres on a creek bottom. The bottom held 930 productive fruit trees of apples, peaches, and pears in fifty-four neat rows. The 20-foot-wide Little Antietam Creek on the farm's southern boundary ran over a rocky limestone bottom that offered superb trout fishing. As Arvin drove his old Studebaker truck on the gravel roads bordering the creek, he noticed a small Asian man carrying a large string of fish and a fishing rod. He was walking toward a two-story farmhouse over a half-mile away.

Arvin stopped the truck and walked to the edge of the creek. As he scanned the orchard to the east, he noticed a flash of light from the farmhouse. He suspected that someone at the farm was watching with high-powered binoculars. It was not enough to confirm the presence of Japanese agents. Still, it proved that someone was suspicious and closely monitoring the comings and goings of travelers. After dipping his fingers in the cold creek, Arvin walked back to his car and drove away.

From a second-story window, Gima Benjiro followed the man's movement walking from a truck down to the creek. The Carl Zeiss turret binoculars with rotating oculars allowed Benjiro to observe the stream and focus on an object with 12x, 20x, or 40x power. The man standing by the creek was slightly overweight and in his late forties. Benjiro immediately eliminated him as a threat—just another would-be angler.

Domen Touma, watching with a weaker set of binoculars, asked, "Anything suspicious?"

"Naw, just an older man admiring the creek. He probably noticed Shiro carrying the fish from the creek and got curious. He's most likely searching for a good fishing spot," Benjiro replied.

"We can't be too careful. Sugimoto will have our heads if we screw up."

"I'm glad you convinced him to cancel the attack at the university."

"It wasn't feasible. The streets are too narrow, and there are not enough exits. We could have been trapped if law enforcement had responded quickly. Plus, Wong has his own private security company made up of Marines who fought in the Pacific. They are not your typical, overweight campus police."

"Are you afraid to fight American Marines?"

"Not at all. I just want better odds. There are only two of us with combat experience. Except for Kaito, who has never seen combat, most of the agents are old. The others are thugs Sugimoto hired off the docks. They have no skills."

"That's the purpose of the firing range and the gym. We have to train them."

"They're undisciplined and don't give a crap about martial arts. Sure, they carry knives and can use them, but we need disciplined firepower to take on this guy, Preston, and his team of agents. From what Sugimoto says, they're the best of the best, as far as U.S. Army agents go. So we need to attack them individually."

"Crap, Gima. You and I are trained assassins. We were in the field. We could take on these agents ourselves."

"Well, they certainly took care of Asami Nakada, and she was a trained assassin, as well as one of our best instructors."

"Asami was arrogant and driven by revenge. It interfered with her sense of duty and her reasoning. She got reckless and died as a result. You and I can take these agents one at a time. There is no way one of them could beat both of us."

"Still, I would prefer a highly trained six-man fire team. Right now, it's just you and me. It's a shame our other four agents were intercepted by the harbor patrol."

"Grow a pair of balls, Gima. We make do with what we are given. Once we train these old-timers to be good with a submachine gun and semiautomatic pistol, we'll be able to take on the four American agents, of which I'll remind you, two are women."

"Then maybe we should kill them first."

"Absolutely not! Don't you remember your training? American men are protective of their women. That would piss off the male agents and make them twice as dangerous. You read the report of the two female American agents Asami killed in Calcutta. The American agents were incited and bent on vengeance, and Asami paid the price. She was lucky she survived. However, I do agree with you. We do need to attack them separately."


Professor Kirkendall was surprised as he opened a reinforced, medium-sized cardboard box, delivered from one of the supply companies the university used. Inside, he found two large objects wrapped in burlap—a coarse cloth made from jute or kenaf, surrounded by a bed of cut straw. A handwritten note explained the contents.

Kirkendall carefully removed the burlap cloth, revealing two 11½-inch bluish-green jadeite cranes. As he examined the pieces, he noticed that both cranes stood straight-legged on a solid base of rocks surrounded by cylindrical stalks of woodrushes. Their delicately carved bodies were thick-fleshed with wings and head crests incised with feathers. They were exquisite examples of Ming jade.

By the end of the day, the university's five deliveries from different supply houses brought more antiquities. The last box that arrived contained a white Qing Dynasty Dehua porcelain figurine depicting an old man leaning on a writing table. At the base, below the old man, was a crane and deer lying among tall reeds. A second piece was a white Ming Dynasty porcelain bowl decorated with golden dragons chasing flaming pearls.

Kirkendall was thrilled with the Ming and Qing pieces, but at the same time, he was worried about safeguarding the treasures. The door to his laboratory had two sets of locks, but it would not deter a skilled burglar. He picked up the phone on his desk and dialed Guy Wong. After two rings, Kirkendall put the receiver down and thought about his worries. Stop overreacting, he told himself, and get busy authenticating the antiquities.

Six hours later, Kirkendall concluded that the jadeite and porcelain might be well-made forgeries. Ming clay contains an iron impurity that makes the porcelain's unglazed parts turn into a rusty iron color when fired. Usually, a rusty red color is found where the glaze stops short of the foot rim of the porcelain. However, neither the dragon bowl nor the old man leaning on a writing table exhibited any red color, which to Fitzsimmons made it suspect. Plus, there were no glaze flaws. On both pieces, the glaze covered evenly over the entire body. Also, Ming pieces usually had an overall warm look due to the iron content, which was missing from both.

After examining the jadeite cranes, Fitzsimmons determined that they were genuine jadeite. Still, the pieces did not exhibit surface deterioration common to archaeological jades recovered from burial tombs. Although Fitzsimmons found several areas at the base that showed some rough workmanship, he could not be sure that they were authentic. If they were not archaeological jades, he surmised, they were excellent forgeries. Hopefully, Professor Chen Li would be able to determine whether they were real.

After examining the jadeite and porcelain artifacts, Professor Chen Li was exuberant. The professor went into detail, explaining how each jadeite piece was exquisitely carved and how the porcelain was typical of Ming clay deposits from the town of Jingdezhen. As Fitzsimmons followed Professor Li's reasoning, he quickly understood that the professor was lying, which was confirmed by a quick wink as the professor moved on to a new piece. Fitzsimmons nodded in agreement after each exposition, knowing that Sugimoto was being hoodwinked. *Jonathan Preston, you sly dog. How did you get to the professor?* Fitzsimmons asked himself.

When Fitzsimmons opened the safe and extracted the Masamune sword, Professor Li looked in the safe and saw the second sword. "What is this? You have a second Masamune," Li said, gently extracting the sword from the safe and pulling the blade from its dark lacquered sheath.

"It just came in. I haven't had time to examine or authenticate it yet," Fitzsimmons replied, following the script that he and Preston had planned.

"It does not have the smooth wave pattern on the hamon that is characteristic of a Masamune. These are more randomized wave shapes. These waves are very long, with shallow valleys between the next clusters. This is not a Masamune, Professor Fitzsimmons. This… It can't be! It's impossible! They were all destroyed except for one that went missing in Tokyo in 1945."

"What?" Sugimoto asked. "What is it?"

"It has all the characteristics of a Muramasa blade," Chen said as he feigned staggering backward and holding on to a table behind him.

"Are you alright, Professor?" Fitzsimmons asked. "Here, have a seat. You look like you've seen a ghost."

"I…I may have. Muramasa Sengo was a 14th-century sword maker. He was renowned for the extraordinary quality and sharpness of his blades. But because of his venomous personality and sudden fits of violent rage, Muramasa was thought insane. During the Tokugawa Shogunate, Tokugawa Ieyasu came to the conclusion that Muramasa blades were cursed. Ieyasu blamed the blades for the deaths of many of his allies, friends, and relatives. He banned the Muramasa katana from his domain."

"Ancient rumors," Kirkendall protested. "Although there are known instances in the Catholic Church where artifacts seemed to be possessed."

As Kirkendall took the blade from Chen, he lifted it to insert it into the wooden scabbard.

"Stop! You cannot put a Muramasa blade back in its sheath without drawing blood," Chen shouted as he reached for the blade and deliberately cut his finger on the tip of the katana. A small amount of blood was left on the edge when he withdrew his hand.

"Professor, you've cut yourself. Here take my handkerchief," Sugimoto said, offering the soft cotton square to the professor.

"I…I had to draw blood, or the blade would have possessed me and made me commit seppuku," Chen said, trembling slightly.

Kirkendall was quick to wipe the blood from the blade and put it in its sheath before the professor did something rash. "Just how special is this katana?"

"It is rumored that the person who possessed the blade will be invincible in battle. No harm can come to the one who owns the Muramasa. Professor Kirkendall, I must insist that this blade be destroyed before it falls into the wrong hands."

"I will have to run that by the owner of the katana, professor. He is intent on selling it, once its origins are determined. But maybe we can get him to sell it to the National Museum in Tokyo."

"Professor, I have a collector who would be willing to purchase this blade. Is this not one of your blades, Mr. Wong?"

"No, I have just the one Masamune that Professor Kirkendall has authenticated. I've never seen this one before. After hearing what Professor Chen has to say, I don't think I would want it," Wong stated as he shied away from the katana.

# CHAPTER 29



*Boonsboro, Maryland*

Gima Benjiro watched with interest as the beat-up, green 1937 Studebaker, ½-ton pickup traveled north on Monroe Road, until he could no longer see it. The truck continued for another mile and then stopped at a 'T' intersection, which turned west. The passenger, who had been crouching on the floorboard as it turned north and crossed Little Antietam Creek, got out of the truck. He was dressed in camouflaged fatigues and had stripped his face, neck, and hands with alternating green, brown, and black theatrical makeup.

"Fish until dark. Whatever you do, don't panic if I'm not back when you get back here. Just continue north and come back an hour later," Preston stated.

"Are you sure you don't need this submachine gun?" Arvin asked.

"It would just slow me down. This is a reconnaissance mission. My suppressed handgun will be enough."

"Good luck," Arvin said as he turned the truck around and dove south.

When the truck returned, stopped, and parked next to the creek, Benjiro was still watching. As the driver stepped out of the truck, Benjiro noticed that it was the same man he had seen four days ago. The old man dressed in faded denim overalls, a white T-shirt, and a tattered, yellow straw hat with fishing flies stuck in the crown. After slipping on a pair of waders, the man grabbed a bamboo fly rod with a single-action fly reel and walked toward the creek. Benjiro picked up his walkie-talkie and reported he was leaving to investigate.

After Preston left the truck, he crossed the road, slipped between the barbed wire fencing, and eased into the thick woods. Deep in the forest, Preston heard the drone of the cicadas and felt the sweat dripping down his neck as he climbed a steep incline. Beneath the dense forest, it was humid and still. The path was rough and rocky as it led through a forest of beech, live oak, and evergreens. Several northern cardinals called, echoing and answering each other as they flew to a nearby dogwood.

From the reconnaissance photos, Jon knew the farmhouse was a mile to the southwest. The topographical maps Jon studied showed a steady four-hundred-foot climb for a half mile before lowering into a valley where the house and other buildings stood. Preston edged due west, following a shallow ravine to the edge of the forest. He was in luck. His position was behind one of the larger barns and was hidden from the second story of the farmhouse. Below him was a garden with beans, squash, and corn stalks nearly knee-high. Next to the barn, azaleas were blooming with a red sparkle. Around a pool that caressed the edge of the garden, red and gold carp flickered below the surface, waiting for an insect to fly near.

Preston was about to sprint to the back of the barn, thirty yards away, when he noticed smoke from a cigarette coming from the north-west corner of the structure. He waited until a medium-sized Asian man stepped around the corner, scanned the woods, and moved in a clockwise direction around the barn. *Plan A was out*, Jon thought to himself. He withdrew a Leica camera, with a screw-thread-mounted, Zeiss, 135 mm telephoto lens, from his backpack, and began snapping photos. He retraced his steps back into the woods and moved further west, and repeated the process.

When Jon completed shooting the west side of the farm, he retraced his steps into the woods and moved north and east until he had a clear shot of the east side. After taking a half dozen photos, he heard men talking. As Jon hid inside a dense cluster of Rosa multiflora, he noticed three Asian men going into the smallest of three barns. He observed through the open barn door as the men began practicing martial art techniques. Two men were obvious novices; the third man was the instructor who yelled in Japanese when they did something wrong.

Jon was about to move to a new position when he heard a noise behind and to his left. He eased his silenced .22-caliber automatic from its holster and slowly turned in the direction of the noise. As Jon raised the gun and waited, he saw Buck Arvin moving clumsily through the woods with the suppressed M3A1 submachine gun in his right hand. When he was within four yards, Jon stood up from his hidden position, startling the former CIC colonel.

"What the hell are you doing, Buck?" Jon asked in a soft voice.

"Hopefully, saving your butt," Buck whispered. "A truck with an Asian man drove north on Monroe Road while I was fishing. I assumed he was checking the woods for intruders. I continued fishing for another five minutes and then returned to the truck. I parked in an old hidden drive, a mile north of the intersection, and backtracked through the woods."

"Then we'd better leave," Jon replied.

As Preston and Arvin approached Monroe Road, they heard the noise of an engine and the squeak of worn breaks. Jon ushered Arvin to a narrow draw that sloped downward at least six feet—and they waited. They heard an anxious Japanese voice cursing. Then the man fired an automatic weapon. The bullets struck several trees where Preston and Arvin had been standing, a minute earlier. Arvin lifted his submachine gun to return fire, but Preston put his hand on the gun and shook his head. He then motioned Arvin to follow him through the draw away from the road. Jon directed them south for fifty yards before turning west, where the ground began to slope upward in three directions. They climbed the gentle slope for nearly a half mile before the woods ended near the gravel road.

As darkness overtook the woods, they heard a door slam shut, the resonant sound of an engine starting, and a mechanical grind as the vehicle shifted into first gear. The engine noise faded as the vehicle drove east and then turned south.

"How far to the truck?" Jon asked.

"Probably another hundred yards west," Arvin replied.

"Let's stay in the woods and parallel to the road, just in case this is a ruse to draw us out."

Arvin grabbed Preston's arm and pointed as they neared the hidden drive where the truck was secured; they both crouched behind a large tree. Before Preston could move closer, someone shouted.

"Hey, Buck. You out there?" a voice called.

"It's okay. It's a friend," Arvin commented as he started toward the road.

Preston grabbed Buck's arm, "It could be a trick."

"If he was in trouble, he would have called me, Bucky."

As they cleared the woods and approached the barbed-wire fence, Arvin shouted, "Over here, Sonny."

A large flashlight beam burned in the distance and scanned the fence line in Buck's direction. As Jon and Buck negotiated the fence, they heard an engine start and saw the seal beams, thirty yards to the west. As they walked toward the vehicle, a man stepped in front of the lights.

"I thought you might be in trouble when I heard gunfire," Sonny shouted.

As they came closer, Buck said, "Jonathan Preston, meet Sonny Arvin. In addition to being my older brother, Sonny is the Game Warden for Washington and Frederick County."

"Glad to meet you, Sonny," Preston said.

"I asked Sonny to patrol here, this evening, in case we ran into trouble. He's a former OSS officer and is quite capable of handling himself. He also knows when to keep his mouth shut. Plus, he told me about the abandoned drive where I hid the truck."

"I appreciate your help, Sonny, but we'd better get out of here before those Asian thugs return with more men."

"We'll take Monroe Road north to Route 68 and go into Boonsboro. I've got cold beer in the fridge, and my wife, Mary, is expecting us for dinner," Sonny replied. "Then you can fill me in on what the hell's going on in my county."


After dinner, Mary removed the dishes from the table and went into the kitchen. Jon shared what was happening with a former Japanese general and the thugs in Washington County. Sonny was alarmed, but knowing his brother, decided not to probe too deep. Jon noticed a gleam in Sonny's eyes that hinted at his love for danger and intrigue.

"Can I assume the U.S. Army will be raiding the farm and clearing out this group of Asian terrorists?" Sonny asked.

"We're not really sure, Sonny," Preston replied. "All we know is these guys are going to try to hit my team of agents and kill us. It would be a lot safer to tackle them at the farm than in Washington, D.C., but we are prepared for both contingencies. Our goal is to capture or terminate this group before they can hurt anyone. This evening was a reconnaissance mission to determine their strength and disposition at the farm."

"Is there anything you need from me?"

"Just stay clear of this area unless your duty requires otherwise," Buck remarked. "But under no circumstance should you go to that farm. These are trained Japanese assassins. They won't hesitate to kill anyone who gets curious."

As Buck drove south from Boonsboro on Route 40, Jon hoped that Sonny would not be reckless and do something stupid. However, because of his OSS background, Jon knew that Sonny would be confident in his abilities to take on anyone. Jon saw it in Sonny's eyes at the dinner table. As they drew closer to Frederick, Jon turned to Buck.

"Call Sonny when you get home and make sure he understands to say the hell away from that farm. Otherwise, he could jeopardize our plans."

"He's as stubborn as he is smart and tough, Jon. I recommend recalling him to active duty and putting him on your team. Of course, then he will have to follow orders."

"I can't bring him into this, but I will recall you."

"Like old times."

"Not quite. This time you may come under fire. Nevertheless, I want you to rent a house in Boonsboro. We'll use it as our headquarters for monitoring the farm. I'll assign two agents to you. Tomorrow, I'll contact the Maryland Department of Natural Resources and request the loan of one of their Game Warden planes and two pilots. Get with Sonny and draft a news release for the Boonsboro newspaper, informing the public of the arrival of an air unit to help stop the increase in poaching. Ask Sonny if he knows of any other former intelligence agents in the Game Warden department. We'll need two additional Game Wardens to increase patrols in the county, but I prefer combat veterans."

"How about Sonny and I arrange several arrests to make it look legitimate? The local newspapers will publish the arrests."

"Good idea. Just make sure the arrests are not too close to that farm. I don't want these guys getting suspicious or trigger-happy. The new guy that Tsukuda is sending is a real hard-ass and a former instructor at the spy school. He may take exception to the careless way these guys are reacting. If he were here, he would have sent them into the woods to ferret us out. We were lucky tonight. Next time, there will be a firefight, and people will die."

"Let's just make sure it's the bad guys who die, Jon. I don't want to lose any more friends."

# CHAPTER 30



*Vientiane, Laos*

Soon after settling his family in Saigon, René Clairoux flew north to visit Marcel in Vientiane, Laos. After reading the report that René supplied to Yul Butler, Marcel understood what this meeting was about. René was concerned for his welfare and wanted him and his family to leave Laos. Marcel called his wife, Ketsana, and explained the report.

"René feels that it is no longer safe for us in Vientiane. He wants us to move to Singapore," Marcel stated.

"I will not leave my home, Marcel. Despite the Viet Minh refugees, we are safe here. We are respected members of the royal family and this community. No one would dare harm us," Ketsana argued.

René replied, "Viet Minh forces are moving into Laos in strength and are recruiting volunteers as they deploy across the country. General Giap informed me that he will have two full divisions operational in Laos within three months. Being a first cousin of King Sisavang will not protect you, Ketsana. Because of Marcel, the Viet Minh will view you and your family as French—and enemies. You and your family members will either be killed or imprisoned. And imprisonment is certain death. Plus, Viet Minh death squads are attacking French citizens all over Indochina. It won't be long before it starts here. I beg you to leave Laos. Our business is well established in Thailand. And Marcel and I have wanted to set up a new office in Singapore for many months."

"Ketsana, General Giap, and Uncle Ho are friends to René and me. What they told René was a warning for our entire family. French people are not safe here anymore! Singapore will be a great opportunity. I have many associates and friends there. We could quickly establish our business, then prosper," Marcel said.

"Think of your children and grandchildren, Ketsana. They are at risk also," René pleaded.

"I will have to think about it," Ketsana relented, as she turned and walked away, dabbing her watering eyes with her apron.

"Ketsana has family across the border in Udon. So we can flee there if anything goes wrong, René," Marcel said.

"You need to act quickly. If Viet Minh death squads hit this town, they will be looking for anyone French; you won't be safe. So please, act quickly and move your family. And arm yourselves. I must return to Saigon and prepare to move everyone to Bangkok. Good luck, brother."


Yul Butler leaned backward in his rattan chair, trying to determine what to do next. After René Clairoux completed his report, he informed Butler that he was moving his family to Bangkok, Thailand. Butler expected Clairoux to continue helping track communist movements in Indochina. Still, René was adamant that it was no longer safe for French civilians. He had warned Butler that he should also leave, but the higher-ups at CIA headquarters insisted that the French Union forces would take back the territory they had lost to the Viet Minh.

As an alternative, René Clairoux had given Butler the names of a dozen Vietnamese loyalists whom he could hire, in the Hanoi area, to continue supplying intelligence. He provided another dozen names for Saigon and northwest Laos, which bordered French Indochina. After a while, Butler turned to the two visitors in his office.

"You're certain it is safe to keep my office open in Hanoi?" Butler asked.

"For the time being, yes. French Union forces will be mounting a large offensive against the Viet Minh in the next month—when the monsoon season is over in the north," Miles Murphy replied.

"Do you believe the report the René Clairoux provided?"

"It could be that Ho is pulling a fast one. He was known to exaggerate the strength of the Viet Minh, during the war. When we worked with him to capture the prisoner-of-war camp, north of Hanoi, he had promised over ten thousand Viet Minh, to help. From what we saw, General Giap was only able to muster 5,000 at most. It was enough to capture the camp and run the Japanese out of Hanoi. Unfortunately, the Japs recaptured the city when the Viet Minh retired into the jungle."

"Our SIS assets near the Chinese border have been able to verify several Chinese Communist divisions, ten miles north of the Indochina border. The training camps where the communists are training Viet Minh soldiers are well manned. We were not able to confirm the six Viet Minh divisions that Clairoux mentioned. But, I do not think that Clairoux would put false information in his report. If he says he saw the six divisions, then I believe him," Henri Morreau commented.

"That's exactly why I forwarded the report to Brigadier MacKenzie. I believe Ho and General Giap deliberately took René on a tour of their training camps so he would report what he saw. René even stated that Ho Chi Minh suspected that I am working for the CIA and would report the Viet Minh strength to Washington," Butler remarked.

"Did René supply the report to the French Union commander?" asked Morreau.

"I had permitted him to do so, but he said he would wait until General Salan was replaced by General Navarre as supreme commander of French forces. He has worked with General Salan in the past but does not trust him."

"Salan is an arrogant man. He sees the Viet Minh as a force of Vietnamese farmers without martial skills. That is why his forces have been having their asses handed to them when they encounter them. He wants to fight a conventional war as they did in Europe. However, the Viet Minh will not directly engage French forces. Despite the Viet Minh's success, Salan considers the hit-and-run tactics of guerilla warfare as ungentlemanly and will not adopt the tactics."

"Do you think General Navarre will be much better?" Butler asked.

"No, he is from the same school as General Salan. My sources in military headquarters tell me that Navarre has orders to ensure the troop's safety under his command so Paris can begin peace negotiations on favorable terms. I don't believe Navarre will follow those orders. Navarre is a risk-taker; he will attack in the north despite the terrain and logistical disadvantage of supplying his troops. He doesn't have enough cargo planes to supply the existing French garrisons, and the Viet Minh will ambush the overland convoys."

"Where does that leave the British?"

"The British will not enter a war that the French cannot win. Brigadier MacKenzie has wisely told London to stay the hell away from French Indochina. Plus, we have our own colonial problems with India, Singapore, and Hong Kong," Miles Murphy replied.

"How much longer will the SIS stay in Indochina?"

"MacKenzie is preparing us to withdraw everyone in July. Henri will go to Singapore, and I am being reassigned to Hong Kong. What about you?" Murphy asked.

"Unfortunately, I'm here for the duration. Is there any way I could get access to your Vietnamese operatives?"

"The Brigadier was amenable when I broached the subject, so he has authorized it. I will see that you get the list of names before I head to Hong Kong. The only problem will be that some may not want to work for the Americans because of their experience dealing with the OSS during the war. But, Henri and I will ferret those agents out."

Two weeks after René Clairoux left Vientiane, the first Viet Minh regiment entered the city. As they stormed through eastern Laos, the Viet Minh executed village chiefs who refused to bow to their will. After subjecting them to torture, they often buried the village chiefs alive while the village peasants were forced to watch.

Some fleeing Vietnamese soldiers in the French service were captured outside of Vientiane as they sought refuge with the Laotian government. After eviscerating, dismembering, and beheading the Vietnamese, the Viet Minh soldiers extracted the gold teeth and fillings from their mouths.

Marcel Clairoux and his family barely made it across the border into Thailand as the Viet Minh regiment entered Vientiane. The regiment commander met with a representative of the Laotian king and received permission to use eastern Laos as a staging point for their army and a supply corridor into southern Indochina.

After a week, a small Viet Minh force was observed crossing into Thailand. When they arrived at the village of Nong Khai, they began inquiring about a Frenchman named Clairoux. The sergeant in charge of the small force dragged the village chief into the street.

"Where is Marcel Clairoux?" the sergeant asked.

"He is not here," the chief said, fearing for his life.

The sergeant struck the chief in the head with the butt of his rifle, "Where is Marcel Clairoux?"

Wiping the blood from his eyes, the chief stammered, "He purchased supplies and fled down Route 2 in a two-ton truck, two days ago."

"What is their destination?"

"Udon, I think, Sergeant. He has family there."

"How many are with him?"

"Five adults and six children, sir."

The sergeant turned and walked to where a Viet Minh officer was waiting, and the sergeant reported his findings to him, stating, "Captain, Clairoux escaped toward Udon, which is twenty miles south on Route 2."

"Alright," the Viet Minh captain replied. "We don't have authority to go that far into Thailand. So let's return to Vientiane."


Marcel Clairoux sat inside the covered portion of a narrow, thirty-foot-long Lao riverboat. At the same time, his cousin stood several feet beyond the end of the pilothouse. The slightly V-bottomed craft cruised down the Mekong River, powered by a recently purchased two-horsepower, Model 4416, Evinrude outboard motor. Barely ten feet across in beam, the riverboat was packed with the few possession that Marcel allowed his wife, two sons, and their wives and children to bring along. In addition, the boat held food for the nearly thousand-mile journey down the Mekong River, which would take them through Cambodia before entering the far southern portion of Indochina. Once they entered the Mekong Delta in Indochina, they would be met by René Clairoux at the city of My Tho. From My Tho, they would be transported by truck into Saigon.

In villages and towns across French Indochina, French citizens were striving to combat terror attacks by Viet Minh death squads, who were throwing bombs into crowded cafés and shooting public officials on the streets. In one cruel attack, Viet Minh guerrillas burst in on a Na Nang hotel where French army officers were hosting a dinner party. With grenades and British Sten guns, they killed over a dozen officers along with their wives and children.

Throughout the countryside, from Hanoi to Na Nang, hundreds of small French forts were erected in villages, with watchtowers ringed by logs, sandbags, concertina wire, and mines to protect the major roads heading north and south. Unfortunately, these lightly manned forts had little effect in containing the Viet Minh soldiers, who carried away the mines for their own use. They quickly overran the compounds.

A week after his arrival in Saigon, Marcel and his family were on a British ship headed for Singapore. But, unfortunately, he and his family were reeling from the news from Vientiane that the two sons who stayed behind had been executed by the Viet Minh.

# CHAPTER 31



*Washington, D.C.*

After Takaji Sugimoto read the clipping from the Boonsboro News that Gima Benjiro delivered to his Georgetown address, he struck the underling with a lacquered scabbard—called a *saya*—held in his hand. The blow to the head would have killed Benjiro had it held the sword. Fortunately, the sword was being sharpened and polished in another room of the house. As it was, the blow shattered the beautifully lacquered, lightweight, wood saya—saving Benjiro's life but still knocking him unconscious.

"Wan, get him out of here!" Sugimoto ordered. "When he comes to, take him and six men to the ranch. They can practice shooting in the indoor range only. And tell them if anyone fires a shot outdoors without first being attacked, I will have their head."

"Do you want them to continue patrolling the perimeter of the ranch?" Kaito Wan asked.

"No! I want everyone staying at the ranch until we need them here. I will send supplies from here. Put them to work in the orchard. There should be grass to cut underneath the trees and dead limbs to trim. And no show of weapons outside the buildings. I do not want to give the game wardens a reason to come onto the ranch. We must look like a working orchard."

"What do you wish to do about the two katanas that Professor Kirkendall has in his possession?"

"You will break into the university tomorrow and steal them. Take one man with you."

"What about the jade artifacts?"

"At this point, they are irrelevant. General Tsukuda wants only the swords. Once we have them, we will attack the American operatives."

"I may have trouble with the safe you described."

"If you fail, you will commit seppuku. Does that give you more incentive?"

"I will not fail, General."


When Professor Kirkendall arrived at his lab at Georgetown University, he opened the safe, removed the two katanas, and carefully packed them in the flower box used to deliver two dozen long stem roses. He was careful to tie the big red bow around the box and secure the edges with tape. Kirkendall then took the box to the dean's office and handed it to a graduate student. Next, Kirkendall instructed one of the students to deliver it to Mrs. Camille Dupont at the Nursing School.

When Kirkendall returned to his lab, he took the two katanas, which Jon Preston had stowed in the box of roses, and locked the replacements in his safe, wrapped in the black silk fabric. He wasn't thrilled with Preston's plan. Still, he understood that Sugimoto's thugs would attempt to steal the swords, once it was revealed that the Muramasa sword would be returned to the National Museum in Tokyo.

The rest of the day, he worked on a report of a pair of jade statues he was authenticating for a Georgetown collector. At the end of the day, he heard a knock on his door. When he opened the door, he didn't recognize the man standing before him.

"May I help you?" Kirkendall asked as the man slipped past him.

"Close the door, professor," Jon Preston stated.

"Jon, I didn't recognize you. You're wearing a wig."

"Which is exactly my intent. I didn't want Sugimoto's goons to see me enter the building."

"So they are watching the building again?"

"Yes. Two men arrived at 2 p.m. this afternoon. They're disguised as students. One is sitting at the south of the building outside Dahlgren Chapel, and the other is to the north at Harbin Hall dormitory. I recognized them from the photographs we took of the men at Sugimoto's office. Both are trained assassins."

"So, you think they are going to strike, this evening—after the school closes?"

"No, I think one of them is going to attack in the next thirty minutes and try to catch you as you leave the lab."

"For crying out loud, Jon, I'll be killed!"

"I'm here to stop that, professor. That's why I'm dressed just like you underneath this coat. Now, take off your lab coat and put on this hat. I'm going to walk out into the hallway. You follow, shake my hand, and go to the admin office. When people start leaving work, join a group and make your way to the chapel of St. Ignatius. You can call a cab from there to take you home. I'll call you later."

Professor Kirkendall nervously removed his lab coat and accepted the hat, and put it on. When Preston walked into the hallway, Kirkendall followed, shook his hand, and left. Kaito Wan was watching through the large windows of the building as the visitor shook the professor's hand and walked down the hallway into another part of the building. Before returning to the lab, Preston reached up and pulled down a heavy white window shade on two windows, effectively blocking the view of the lab door.

Preston was watching as Kaito Wan got up off the bench and moved toward the Old North building. When Preston reentered the lab, he picked up his walkie-talkie. He called Guy Wong inside a small chapel at the Jesuit Community Cemetery next to Harbin Hall.

"Wan is on the move. Take out the other guy."

Dressed as a Jesuit priest in a dark, long-sleeved robe, Guy Wong left the cemetery and walked south on a sidewalk that took him to the east side of Harbin Hall. As Wong neared the park bench where the Asian man was observing the Old North building, he cocked the dart pistol he held in his robed hands. The man was concentrating on the building and did not hear Wong approaching from behind. When Wong was three feet away, he fired a dart into the man's neck. The effect of the nerve agent was nearly instantaneous. Before the man fell over, Wong sat down on the bench, eased him into a sitting position, and put his hand on the back of his neck to keep his head erect. Wong then began conversing about the large bed of purple, yellow, and orange Chrysanthemums directly across from the bench.

Moments later, two Jesuit priests exited the ground floor laundry room of Harbin Hall, pushing a dolly with a large steel cabinet secured to it. They stopped next to the bench, opened the cabinet door, grabbed the Asian man, and placed him inside. Then, after locking the door, they began rolling it north toward the cemetery to an awaiting truck. It happened so fast that no one took notice of the priests.

Guy Wong strolled toward Old North and entered through a door on the west side. As Wong entered the building, Wan was knocking on the door of Professor Kirkendall's lab. As Wan's head turned to see who entered, Preston opened the lab door and shot a dart into Wan's neck. The startled assassin grabbed at the dart in his neck and dropped the pistol in his other hand as the nerve agent took effect. Before Wan could slump to the floor, Guy Wong grabbed him from behind and shoved him into the lab.

"That went well," Wong stated.

"Let's hope these guys will talk when we get them to the brig at Anacostia," Preston replied.

"We can try using scopolamine. The OSS used it on German prisoners during the war."

"They used it in Calcutta, too. Unfortunately, the effects were not much different from those of alcohol. These guys are highly trained Japanese assassins. They were probably subjected to all types of chemicals during their training. Unless they want to talk, they won't. Since we know that Tsukuda rewards failure with seppuku, they might want to risk an army prison over ritual suicide."

"It's going to depend on how fanatical they still are, Jon. The war's been over for three years, but they might prefer death if these guys were trained at the Rikugun Nakano spy school. In fact, I would bet on it," Wong replied.


Jon Preston and Guy Wong drove from Georgetown into Washington, D.C., and crossed the Potomac River on the 14th Street Bridge. The south side of 14th Street was a working-class community neighborhood called Southwest Waterfront. Despite the rapid economic growth in Washington, D.C., the Southwest Waterfront was slow in making a comeback from decades of economic and social decline. Despite the post-war boom, it lagged behind the rest of the area.

A mile east, Jon turned south on 11th Street and drove by the Washington Navy Yard. In 1797, it was home to an eight-story sugar refinery and was Washington's earliest industrial neighborhood. During the nineteenth century, the Yard was a bustling wharf, serving ships that brought a multitude of raw materials to the capital. Over time, the Yard evolved into shipbuilding, and later the production of finished ship products and the manufacture of ammunition during times of war. By mid-1945, the Yard housed over 130 buildings and employed 26,000 workers.

After crossing the 11th Street Bridge and entering Anacostia, Jon turned west on a recently paved road that paralleled the river. The road wound north before turning south into the Anacostia Naval Air Station (NAS). Jon and George Linka had interrogated Elton Fitzsimons here during the submarine crisis. After showing their military identification at the guarded gate, Jon and Wong drove to the base operations building. They parked the military staff car in a spot designated for senior officers. As they walked up to the front of the building, a large Shore Patrol NCO opened the door from the inside and greeted them.

"It's been a while, Colonel Preston. I'm Chief Petty Officer Mike McCormick."

"I remember you, Mike. But you weren't a chief two years ago."

"No, sir. I was promoted six months ago. Your agents brought the two Japs in, an hour ago. They're in the same place as your last visit."

Chief Petty Officer McCormick led them out the back door of the base operations building and walked them twenty-five yards to a nondescript two-story, brick building. Jon noticed the heavy round bars still covering the windows on both floors. Over the top of the heavy steel entry door was a nameplate that needed repainting. It read, "Anacostia NAS Brig."

Jon remembered the military jail. A tall, thick-necked Seaman in a white uniform in the reception area waved them in when he saw

Chief Petty Officer McCormick walking behind them. After taking their pistols and locking them in a secure storage bin, Jon and Guy were escorted through a heavy locked door. They were greeted by another pair of seamen, who accompanied them to an even more secure section of the jail.

There was a small office farther down the hall with a lieutenant's name written in bold white letters on the upper glass portion of the door. Further down the hall was a steel door with a heavy lock and a sign that read, "Armory." A husky seaman stood in front of an interrogation room. As Preston and Wong got closer, the seaman opened the door. Inside, Kaito Wan was sitting at a table with shackles on his ankles and wrists that allowed him no movement. When he saw Preston, his eyes began burning with anger.

"I should have killed you three months ago."

"Yeah, but you didn't, and now I have you. Care to discuss your situation, or would you prefer the hangman's noose?"

"You've got nothing on me. So you can't charge me with anything!"

"Let's see…illegal entry into the U.S., carrying a suppressed weapon without a permit, and smuggling jewels and antiquities. Oh yeah, and how about being a Japanese assassin wanted for war crimes, murder of four army agents in Washington, and conspiracy to murder another five army agents and a renowned Georgetown University professor. That would be enough to get you a quick walk to the gallows. Then there is the conviction for war crimes by the military tribunal in Tokyo. You were sentenced to hang."

"Humph," Wan grunted.

"I have a presidential letter stating that I can execute you on the spot, Wan. But that would be too easy. So instead, I think I'll take you to Yokohama. Then, after your confession is published in a Tokyo newspaper, I'll chain you to the front gate of General Tsukuda's villa. Hell, you might get a chance to write your death poem before he tortures you with the death of a thousand cuts. I hear a victim can linger for days without dying."

Wan's face sagged as he thought about the deaths of the two women who were American spies whom he had killed in the same manner, three years before, on orders from Tsukuda.

# CHAPTER 32

*Boonsboro, Maryland*

After Takaji Sugimoto reached the farm, he was suffering from nervous anxiety and pacing in the barn, which had been converted into a gym. His number-two man—Kaito Wan, a highly trained Japanese operative—and one other field agent—Hino Goro—had been missing for over 72 hours. Sugimoto couldn't imagine Wan not reporting about the success of his mission. He surmised they saw an opportunity to sell the swords themselves, or they were both captured. Regardless, the two men were as good as dead. If the Americans hadn't killed them, *he* would—as soon as he got his hands on them.

Sugimoto was walking back and forth across the gym—when a dozen operatives entered the building. All were aware that Wan and Goro were missing, and the operatives were silent as they stood waiting for instructions. Domen Touma was the first to speak.

"All men are present, sir, except for Gima Benjiro. He is still suffering dizziness from his concussion. However, before Dr. Ishida left for the city, he instructed the cook on preparing an herbal remedy that would help relieve the pressure on the brain. Consequently, the doctor expects Benjiro will be able to resume his duties by the end of the week," Touma explained.

"Let's hope his common sense returns, too. If he does anything foolish to jeopardize our mission, kill him. That goes for everyone else, too. Some of you are highly trained assassins and operatives. Even though it's been several years since you were in combat, I expect you to follow orders and exercise common sense and make sure we stay undetected. What Benjiro did last week could have exposed our entire operation. So, unless you see someone infiltrating the farm with the intent to capture or kill, do nothing. People in the U.S. are used to crossing fences and wandering onto other people's property to chase game or ask about purchasing fruits and vegetables. Therefore, we must look like a working farm and orchard. If anyone comes on the property inquiring about anything, send them to Touma. Tell them he is the farm foreman," Sugimoto stated.

Touma wanted to remind the general that a mission of this magnitude was complex and required extensive planning and preparation, but he felt reluctant to explain it. Sugimoto was used to soldiers following his orders and not making excuses or calling his judgment into question. He knew he should, but he was reticent to do so because of the general's agitation.

Instead, Touma said, "Yes, sir. Would you like to go over the plan for surveillance of the farm, General?"

"I want an account on surveillance, training, weapons, and vehicles. Since I assume that Wan and Goro are captured or dead, you will be my second-in-command. So, pick the best man here to command the farm after we leave for Washington. You have one week to develop a scenario to take down Preston and his team of agents. I suggest you utilize the men here to help. They all have field experience. Don't get too fancy because it will be more to screw up. I want a simple, get-in-and-get-out operation with maximum kill power. I expect you to hit Wong and Preston at the same time. We can't give them time to recover and strike back."

Touma bowed deeply and replied, "Yes, General. Now, if you will follow me, I will explain our preparations."


George Linka clasped Kathleen Lauren's right arm as he guided her down the airstairs of the C-54 cargo plane. The injury to her left bicep and shoulder still required her to use a sling. She had undergone surgery to repair the tissue damage to the muscle, in São Paulo, and spent four days in the hospital before being released. Fabio Martinez insisted that she and Linka stay at his residence until the doctor released her to travel. Plus, he could protect them there.

The three weeks went slowly for Kathleen. She was anxious to return home and resume her duties. With the help of the former Brazilian President, Getúlio Vargas, the Brazilian government hosted an award ceremony in the Catete Palace in Rio de Janeiro. President Eurico Gaspar Dutra awarded George and Kathleen the Combat Cross First Class, at the presidential palace, for their bravery and for saving the lives of over a dozen Brazilian soldiers caught in the crossfire at the ambush. For being wounded in action, Kathleen also received the Blood of Brazil Medal.

After expressing their appreciation to the Brazilian President and the Minister of Defense, Fabio Martinez gathered the duo. He drove them to Santos Dumont Airport, where a Curtiss C-46 twin-engine transport aircraft was waiting to fly them to Mexico City. In Mexico City, a U.S. Air Force cargo plane would be waiting to fly them to Washington, D.C. After five days of travel with over thirty-two hours in the air, George and Kathleen were exhausted. As they set foot on the tarmac at Anacostia Naval Air Station, an army staff car driven by Camille Dupont pulled to a stop, thirty feet away. Camille got out of the car and sprinted to Kathleen.

"God, I missed you," Kathleen said as she hugged her best friend.

"Thanks for bringing her back safely," Camille whispered to George as she kissed him on the cheek.

"Anything interesting happening?" George asked.

"General Miller wants you all to get a good day's rest before reporting. We have a meeting with him on Thursday to go over the events here in Washington."

"Come on, Camille. Tell us what's been happening," Kathleen stated.

"Well, okay. I'll fill you in on what Jon and Guy have been up to on the way to your quarters. Jon is grilling steaks for us this evening. You can get all the details from him on the other happenings."


General Miller treated George and Kathleen like returning heroes as they gathered in his conference room. Admiral Dubois welcomed them home along with Colonel Arvin, which drew a questionable look from George. Lieutenant General Renick greeted them like family and gave them a brief note from President Truman expressing his appreciation for a well-done job. After everyone left, General Miller asked everyone to take a seat, then turned the meeting over to Jon.

"As you know, we have two of Sugimoto's assassins, Kaito Wan and Hino Goro, in custody. Wan is not talking, despite my threats of taking him back to Japan and leaving him chained in front of General Tsukuda's estate. When I threatened Goro, he panicked and wanted to make a deal."

"Has he given you anything useful?" George asked.

"Just the number of men that Sugimoto has, and their intentions to attack us as soon as the two swords were secured. With Wan and Goro missing, it is unclear what Sugimoto's intentions will be. That is why Colonel Arvin has been called back to active duty. He is heading up a group of CIC agents in Boonsboro. With the help of a couple of game wardens assigned to our task force, they are keeping tabs on the people at the ranch. Since the incident where they tried to attack me while I was doing recon on the farm, things have gotten unusually quiet."

"There are at least eighteen operatives at the farm, and six cooks and cleaning staff. They have been confining themselves to the farm and are working in the orchard. I was able to infiltrate the area and photograph their combat training. They are very skilled in martial art techniques and throwing weapons—knives, spikes, darts, and *shuriken* or throwing stars," Arvin stated.

"It appears they are going to attempt to attack us without automatic weapons," Jon remarked. "Probably in a public place where we shop or eat."

"What is our plan to prevent this?" Kathleen asked.

"Camille and I have been working with Kumiko to train everyone using darts and throwing knives. I would like to hit them at the ranch in the next forty-eight hours."

"How many agents do you plan to take?" George asked.

"Including Kumiko, nine. Kumiko's two sons, Eizo and Emon, Hiroki Eguchi, Camille, Guy Wong, two of the new CIC agents that transitioned from the navy, and myself."

"Alright, what's the plan of attack?"

"Kumiko and I will infiltrate the ranch and conceal ourselves in the forest near the orchard. We will wait for the afternoon shift and strike at dusk. Only four men are working at a time. We have a new $CO_2$ propellant dart gun that is accurate up to a range of twenty yards. The neurotoxin we use will render them unconscious for six hours. Once we take them down, we'll drag them into the forest and secure them. Then we'll hit the remaining men while they are preparing to eat dinner."

"Sounds risky, Jon. Only you, Camille, and Kumiko have combat experience. Are you sure Eizo, Emon, and Hiroki are up to the task?"

"I forgot to mention, we'll be backed up by a squad of Marines and three snipers."

"Do they have many men patrolling the area?" Kathleen asked.

"As of this morning, they have four teams of two men that patrol the fence line from sunrise to sunset. It takes three hours to walk the property. They alternate teams, every four hours. They are not carrying weapons that we can see, but each team has a radio. At night, three guards are patrolling close to the house and barns. Buck and the two new CIC agents are tasked to take care of the fence patrols. One of our Marine snipers will be in charge of taking out any snipers in the second-story rooms."

"I don't like it, Jon. If they're not patrolling at night, they must be using concealed traps in the forest," Linka stated. "If someone sets one of the devices off, the entire operation will be blown."

"That's why we were going in the day, and we need you along, George. You are great at finding concealed traps like punji sticks, tripwire grenades, bamboo whips, and toe-popper cartridge traps. Your sharp eyes saved my life, in the Philippines, on two occasions."

"I would like to recommend that George take Eizo and Emon with him. They have eyes like hawks. They are very disciplined and thorough," Kumiko said.

"It's your call, George," Preston replied.

"I'll take them, but if we go through with this attack, I want Camille and Kathleen to stay at the Marine barracks with additional protection."

"Why?" Buck Arvin asked.

"Frankly, I smell a setup. The last time I talked to Fitzsimmons, he mentioned that Sugimoto had over fifty men working for him at the docks in Baltimore and another dozen in Washington. So Sugimoto could have thirty or more men at the ranch and another dozen in D.C. prepared to follow us and hit us from behind. Let's not forget that we believe most of Sugimoto's men are trained spies. Like in São Paulo, they are probably watching our every move."

"What are you suggesting, George?" General Miller asked.

"I suggest we have INS and Coast Guard raid the Baltimore and Washington docks and arrest as many of Sugimoto's men as possible. That way, we'll have a good idea of how many men might be at the farm. Sugimoto would then be forced to move people from the farm to the docks to cover his illegal enterprises."

"I think that ambush in São Paulo has heightened your intuition, George." General Miller replied. "Jon, can we delay the mission and do as George recommends?"

"If George's gut is telling him it's a trap, I think it is a terrific idea. It will give me time to go back to the brig at Anacostia and interrogate Hino Goro. Unfortunately, I'm beginning to think he has played us."

# CHAPTER 33



*Baltimore, Maryland*

When the INS struck the Baltimore and Washington, D.C. docks, they apprehended thirty-eight illegal Asians and five Russians who worked for Takaji Sugimoto. The Coast Guard impounded four of Sugimoto's fishing boats which contained contraband. Among the illicit items collected were sixty, Mark VI, Sten-suppressed submachine guns, twenty thousand rounds of subsonic ammunition, four kilos of opium, and half a ton of gold coins. Unfortunately, the boats were registered in the name of one of the fishermen apprehended, so Takaji Sugimoto could not be arrested.

It took two days for the news of the raids to reach Sugimoto at the farm in Boonsboro. When the information did arrive, he raged at the man who delivered the news. As Sugimoto returned to the barn where Domen Touma was instructing the men in Okinawan Karate, he was pale and nervous.

"The INS has raided our boats in Baltimore and Washington. Almost all of our men were arrested. Fortunately, Fukumoto Haruto was away from the docks when they struck. He got away and brought the details. All but one of our boats have been impounded by the Coast Guard. The one that wasn't is still in Havana," Sugimoto stated.

"What do you want us to do, sir?" Touma asked.

"I must go to Georgetown and get a message to General Tsukuda. You will come with me. Once I report to the general, he may demand my life, and you will have to take charge."

"But, General. This is not your fault. The INS is always looking for illegals. General Tsukuda cannot possibly hold you responsible."

"Unfortunately, I am in command. The commander is always responsible for what happens, whether it's an act of the gods or not. I would be surprised if U.S. Army counterintelligence does not have something to do with this."

"Sir, if we are under attack, we should strike back immediately! It is the only solution that will save face with General Tsukuda."

Despite being depressed, Sugimoto looked at Touma with hope in his eyes. Touma had a high forehead that crinkled when he talked, suggesting insolence. His bulging black eyes appeared to have no pupils. His abnormally long arms and big hands made him seem awkward, but he was just the opposite. Sugimoto suddenly realized how intelligent an operative he had working for him. *Better put him to good use*, Sugimoto thought.

"Touma, you are absolutely correct. You would have made a great field commander in my army in the Philippines. We must counter-attack immediately. Have all the men move out tonight. We have enough vehicles to put four per vehicle. Make sure they are armed to the teeth. We will meet at the house in Hyattsville."

Sugimoto paused, then asked Touma, "Is there anything I missed?"

"Sir, Gima Benjiro is not well enough to participate."

"What do you suggest?"

"I recommend we place him in charge of protecting the farm and the household staff."

"Good thinking. It will allow him to save face. Now tell me, what's your plan for attacking and killing the American agents?"


Three nights later, at 2 a.m., Sugimoto's team of operatives struck Guy Wong's house. Wong and half a dozen guards were waiting on the house's second floor when a silenced round broke the glass in the upstairs window and struck a guard in the neck. A second round followed and creased Wong on his right cheek.

Wong ducked below the level of the window sill and contacted one of his men outside the house.

"Sniper firing into the front of the house," Wong said over the walkie-talkie in his hand.

"On it!" came the reply.

As Wong and his men waited, more rounds penetrated the second-floor windows, and another guard was wounded in the arm. Wong crawled quickly to a room on the far side of the house and grabbed a sniper rifle with a night scope. He stayed in the recess of the darkness of the room and aimed the rifle toward the shattered front window.

When the sniper fired again, Wong saw the muzzle flash. He breathed in, let his out slowly, and fired. Wong noticed a dark figure fall backward from a forty-foot tree as his bullet struck him in the forehead.

"Sniper's down," came over the walkie-talkie. "But I think there's a second out there."

The conversation was cut off as another sniper began firing through the second-story window of the other upstairs room facing the street. Wong was about to charge down the stairs when the front door crashed inward, and three hooded men rushed through. They were firing Mark VI, suppressed submachine guns that had been captured in Indochina in 1945 when a British plane had dropped them in the wrong location. The Sten utilized a system of twenty-seven metal washers with baffles and rubber seals fitted over a 12½-inch-by-2-inch barrel. The only thing audible was the soft blowback, open-bolt retracting after a round was fired.

Wong threw himself to the floor as a storm of subsonic bullets passed, striking a guard behind him. He grabbed the guards M3A1 submachine gun and fired three short bursts down the stairs. The .45-caliber rounds tore the head off one of the hooded assailants and wounded a second. The wounded man raised his Sten to fire again, but Wong fired first, nearly decapitating the assailant.

As Wong waited for the third assailant to show himself, his walkie-talkie informed him that three more assassins were in the alley and would be attempting to enter through the back door. Wong cursed. He had had enough. He grabbed the body of the dead man next to him and tossed him down the stairs. When the third assassin fired, Wong returned the fire—emptying the clip of .45 ACP rounds and cutting the man in half. Wong then grabbed a fresh clip from a wounded guard and rushed into a room overlooking the alley.

Guy Wong saw three hooded gunmen from his second-story window as they detoured toward the rear door. In the faint light, he recognized the Mark VI, Sten-suppressed submachine guns they were carrying. Wong had used the same model during the latter part of the war against Japan and was familiar with it. However, he did not expect the assassins to use it on full automatic, because it made the gun louder. Instead, Wong assumed they would be well-disciplined and use the Sten in semi-auto mode. As Wong continued to watch, he noticed one of the gunmen on a portable two-way radio. He was probably coordinating with another sniper in the alley.

In the alley, the three Japanese assailants noticed the windows were so high off the ground that the only option was the back door. Wong was watching from the upstairs window as the assassins began edging toward the door. Before they could set foot on the concrete steps, Wong's men in the adjacent house fired through the windows, cutting the three assassins down. *Thank God something went right!* Wong thought.

Two blocks west, two of Wong's men fired their sniper rifles at the men waiting in the cars that delivered the assassins. The well-placed shots struck them in the head and slammed them against the side window of their vehicle. As the two men watched for the movement of other assailants, they heard the screech of tires further down the street as a car raced away. There had been someone else monitoring the assault.

As Wong surveyed the destruction, one of his men remarked, "Not like we planned it, boss."

"No, it wasn't. We lost a couple of good men tonight, and now I have to give the news to their families," Wong replied. "Call for the army ambulances and take care of our wounded. Let's take the assassins' bodies out the back door and then start cleaning this mess up. I'm sure someone heard all the commotion and has called the D.C. police."

Over the last twelve weeks, Jon, Camille, George, and Kathleen trained diligently under Kumiko Fujiwara's supervision. Jon was in some of the best physical conditioning of his life. Camille trained harder than anyone to lose the weight she had gained during her pregnancy. As a result, her lithe and agile body was more muscular than it had been during her career as an OSS agent. Even George and Kathleen were in the best physical shape of their careers—when they flew to Brazil. With Kathleen out of action, Jon hoped it would be enough to stop what Sugimoto was planning.

Despite the objections of General Miller, Jon and Camille moved from their Marine Barracks apartment back into their 900-square-foot, one-story Georgetown house. Jon had been planning the move, for months, in hopes of luring Sugimoto into a trap. Two months ago, Jon had Guy Wong rent two apartments in a duplex directly across the street from his house. Fifteen days before Jon and Camille had moved back into their home, a pair of Marine snipers had settled into one of the apartments. Alexei and Dimitri Antonov had moved into the other.

Alexei and Dimitri Antonov were unrecognizable. After moving the brothers to Camp Lejeune, they had grown full beards and trained with a group of CIC recruits who arrived from Honolulu. Both men had lost thirty pounds and were muscled-up from the four-hour-a-day martial arts training classes. They had spent two hours a day at the shooting range, honing their skills with the Springfield M1903A4 sniper rifle. Another two hours were utilized for training them in counterintelligence tactics. When they had returned from Camp Lejeune, both were brought back on active duty as undercover U.S. Army counterintelligence agents at the rank of technical sergeant.

During the day, the marines and the Antonovs played the part of blue-collar workers, leaving their apartments before sunrise and returning after sunset. The marines drove to Anacostia Naval Air Station, where they were employed as civilian guards. Alexei and Dimitri went to the Marine Corps Base, Quantico, where they worked as postal workers. At both locations, Jon Preston had set up martial arts training. The men continued practicing four hours a

the left arm. I pulled him from the car, cuffed him, and laid him on the sidewalk. I must have hit him in the brachial plexus; he bled out and died within minutes. Dimitri is watching over the bodies until an ambulance arrives."

"I contacted George," Arvin reported. "He and Kathleen were monitoring the area near the Causeway estate. They report no activity to the north. And Kumiko is reporting it's clear to the south."

"I get the impression that this was not the A-team we were expecting," Jon said.

"I think you're right. This was too easy. These guys appeared to be out of their element. Then again, assassins are not generally taught combat tactics and how to storm a house."

"We got lucky, Buck. If this had been a trained assault team, it might have turned out different."

"Six ambulances are on the way to take the bodies to the Marine Barracks morgue. I'll hang around and get this scene cleaned up if you and Camille want to check on Wong."

Jon and Camille arrived at Guy Wong's house just as three army ambulances were pulling away. After they got out of their car, they walked to where Guy Wong was talking with a Washington, D.C. policeman. The policeman had been patrolling the neighborhood when Sugimoto's team struck.

"Good timing," Wong said to Preston. "Lieutenant Isreal, this is Colonel Jon Preston and Major Camille Dupont. Jon is the head of my counterintelligence section at the Pentagon."

Jon withdrew his army counterintelligence badge, showed it to the lieutenant, and shook his hand. "Any problems here, Lieutenant?"

"No, sir. Major Wong was explaining that six Asians attacked his residence with submachine guns. It's a little disturbing, but it appears that you all were expecting trouble and dealt with it quietly. I realize that this is U.S. Army business, but do you need any help from the D.C. force?" Isreal asked calmly.

"Guy, what do you think?"

"We did wake several neighbors, and they are quite disturbed. I believe it might help them feel more comfortable if you could send a patrol car through every thirty minutes until the sun comes up. You can tell them it was an attempted robbery," Wong replied.

"I'll see that it is taken care of, Major Wong. I'm the night supervisor in this area, Colonel Preston. Is there anything else I need to be aware of?"

"You may be hearing about another attack near the naval observatory. Eleven Japanese assassins attacked my wife and me at our home. All were dispatched, and their bodies are being taken to the Marine Barracks to be identified. We've been monitoring this group for months and have been expecting an attack for several days. Fortunately, they struck at night when no civilians were out. I'll have General Miller call your chief of police tomorrow morning and explain the situation."

"As a former Marine commander, I assume you want to keep this classified secret. If you agree, I will give the chief a verbal report in the morning before I go off duty, and will inform him that General Miller will be calling him personally."

"Thanks for understanding, Lieutenant."

"Guy, we'll be meeting at 1300 hours in General Miller's office. He'll want a detailed report. Did any of your men get hurt?"

"Two dead and one wounded. These goons surprised us with a sniper attack. My men, however, performed admirably."

"Were any of the men CIC agents?"

"No, sir. They were all members of my security business."

"I'm sorry for your loss, Guy. I know they were your cousins."

"I'll be leaving shortly to inform their families."

"Alright, I'll see you at 1300."

# CHAPTER 34

*Washington, D.C.*

"I don't get it," General Lew Miller stated. "We've wiped out Sugimoto and his goons, and you still want to go to Japan and take on General Tsukuda? For crying out loud, Jon. We've dealt him a blow from which he probably won't recover. Let's let the damn Yakuza organizations take him down. With this embarrassment, he will lose face, and that will make him vulnerable."

"Sir, Japan is still suffering economically, and so are the Yakuza organizations. Tsukuda has enough hidden gold to buy them off. So he won't stop trying to kill us. He's like a cornered leopard; he's more dangerous now than ever. Plus, he is not the type to give up, and there is one more assassin on the way to the U.S.!" Jon said reprovingly.

"I was hoping I could talk you out of it."

"Not a chance, sir. This man has tried to kill us on five different occasions. It's his time to die!"

Taken back by Jon's upbraid, General Miller sat down at his desk and shook his head, wondering where it all would end. He sighed and then retrieved a folder from his desk drawer. Looking pensive, he handed it to Jon.

"This is a Presidential Order that authorizes you to go after Tsukuda in Japan," Miller stated. "Since you insist on using the Kabuki theatre troupe to entice Tsukuda, I'm assuming you're planning to take the swords with you to Japan?"

"Yes, sir. The swords are the bait that will draw Tsukuda out. So we will continue the charade with the cursed Muramasa sword and the priceless Masamune. But, first, we'll let Tadahisa Haruki examine the swords at Georgetown University. He arrived earlier this week, but I'll have Professor Kirkendall feint illness and delay the exam two weeks. Then, once Tadahisa validates the swords, he and Professor Kirkendall will formally announce the finding at a university reception with Japanese embassy officials and a select group of reporters. At the reception, President Truman will make an unscheduled visit and announce his intention to give the swords back to the Japanese people during his state visit in December."

"How will you draw Tsukuda out of hiding?" Miller asked.

"The president will announce that he is making arrangements with Tadahisa Haruki to have both swords displayed at the Tokyo National Museum. First, the President wants to allow the Japanese public to view the swords for a month. After that, President Truman will turn the Masamune over to its rightful owners, the Konoe family, and explain how we came by the sword during his state visit. Then he will present the Muramasa sword to the National Museum. I'm fairly certain that Tsukuda will do everything in his power to obtain the swords when they are displayed at the museum."

"And how will Tsukuda be enticed to go see the Kabuki theatre troupe?"

"He won't be able to pass up a historical play about a white samurai—especially after the warning he had received from his grandmother. In fact, George's sources in Tokyo tell us that Tsukuda has hired several prominent history professors to research the white samurai of Japan. He wants to know if any of their relatives are alive. He fears that one will be responsible for his death. Therefore, I'm going to give him something up close and personal to worry about."

"That might not be enough to get him out of hiding,"

"It will if the two katanas are used in the Kabuki play, and if the white samurai is wielding the Masamune and the evil samurai the Muramasa."

"That would certainly entice him. Wait! You're not planning to play the part of the white samurai in the Kabuki play, are you?"

"As a matter of fact, I am. And George will be the other samurai."

"Jon, that is most clever. Dangerous, but clever."

"Even better. My dad and I used to go to Wisconsin to fly-fish. He taught me how to cook a trout on an open fire. We also caught a rabbit in a snare and cooked it, too."

"Considering I have had neither, it had better be delicious."

"Trust me, it will. We'll get some fresh vegetables and cook them in a cast-iron pot. It will be grand."

"I hope you will get as excited about me as you do eating."

Jon reached around his wife's back, pulled her close, and kissed her deeply as Jon Jr. squirmed to get a hug and kiss.

"That's a warmup for later tonight, babe."

"All this excitement with Sugimoto has left you amorous, Jon. Maybe we need more bad guys in our life?"

"You're all I need to get excited, Camille," Jon said, as he kissed her again.

"The roast has another hour to cook. Maybe you should put Jon down and head to the bedroom with me," Camille responded, taking his hand and leading him to the bassinet.

Camille lifted her arms after they entered the bedroom, allowing Jon to pull her dress over her head. Underneath, she was totally naked. In her excitement, she nearly tore Jon's shirt off and began kissing his strong, muscular chest. As Jon pulled her close, he felt the rock-hard nipples of her firm breasts against his bare skin. As his mouth caressed hers, Jon saw the raw lust in her eyes. After a deep kiss, Camille unfastened his belt, took his pants off, and pulled him to the floor, which was covered by a new Persian rug with geometric designs of red, yellow, gold, and blue.

"I've been dreaming of this all afternoon," Camille whispered.

Jon didn't say a word but thought, *I love it when she does this.*

# CHAPTER 35

*Hanoi, Indochina*

Yul Butler was having lunch of noodles and shrimp in a small café within the block-long Cha Lon Marketplace, where vendors sold fruit, vegetables, fish, and meat. It was the middle of the monsoon season, hot and balmy, and he was sweating profusely. Butler was wearing khaki pants and a loose-fitting white cotton shirt, stained under the arms. His new pair of Jarman saddle, brown and tan Moc-San shoes, which he had ordered from Sears and Roebuck, looked out of place in the muddy enclosure.

As he was finishing his lunch, the owner approached and asked if he needed anything else. Butler shook his head and gave him a handful of Indochinese piasters. Unfortunately, the piasters were becoming increasingly worthless due to the Japanese army's decision to print thousands of 500-piaster notes in March 1945, triggering widespread inflation. Still, most Vietnamese businessmen preferred the piaster to the French franc because the Viet Minh would destroy a shop if a merchant was discovered accepting the franc.

After Japan surrendered in 1945, the Chinese government issued a formal decree, increasing the exchange value of the Customs Gold Unit issued by the Central Bank of China, from one to 1.5 piasters. A devaluation of the piaster by 50 percent meant higher prices for all Vietnamese and an open market for currency trafficking.

Butler was acutely aware of the effects of inflation, particularly on the Vietnamese economy. A currency trafficker could purchase 350 francs in France for one American dollar. He could smuggle the francs into Indochina and buy 52 piasters on the local black market. He could then take the piasters to the Bank of Indochina and redeem them for 884 francs—doubling his initial investment. Hundreds of French and foreign visitors were playing the franc trafficking game.

In November 1945, in an attempt to reassert their economic and political authority in Indochina, French authorities announced that the Bank of Indochina would no longer redeem the large notes. Because of this, thousands of merchants and families who held the notes faced significant losses. This caused the Viet Minh to organize a massive demonstration outside the Hanoi office of the bank. Panicking bank guards, pelted by rocks and bottles, fired on the crowd, killing many demonstrators. The public was so enraged in Hanoi that merchants and workers went on strike. All were refusing to provide services or sell food and dry goods to anyone French.

The food merchant took the wad of cash that Butler handed him, turned toward his cash drawer, and retrieved change. When Butler held out his hand, he noticed a note written on rice paper was included in the exchange. Butler quickly put the money and note in his pocket, thanked the restaurant owner, and walked casually back to his office, four blocks away.


When Butler returned to his office, he was distracted by a phone call from Jacob Clairoux. Unfortunately, he forgot about the note.

"Mr. Butler, this is Jacob Clairoux, René's younger brother. We met in Chittagong in 1944."

"Yes, I remember you, Jacob. How may I help you?"

"I'm here at my brother's request. It's imperative that I see you. Can you meet me at our office at 9:30 p.m.?"

"Yes. Are you here to pick up the second payment?"

"No. René will send you instructions on where to wire it."

"You sound a little stressed. Is there anything I should be aware of?"

"You might want to bring a weapon. Hanoi is becoming very congested with foreign operatives."

"Alright, thanks for the heads-up. I'll see you this evening."

Butler was disturbed by Jacob's warning. Usually, he didn't carry a weapon because American businessmen were left alone in Hanoi. However, the foreign operative's statement could mean many things. He had noticed a lot of new faces in the last two weeks—Chinese, Russian, and British. He mused that they were capitalizing on currency trafficking. However, Jacob's warning might mean trouble for his gem business. Or, someone has discovered that he was an American agent and knew his real mission.

At 9 p.m., Butler unlocked his safe and withdrew a shoulder holster with a .45-caliber, Colt M1911A1, semi-automatic pistol and an ankle holster with a Walther PPK. He stuffed extra cartridge clips in the pockets of his cream-colored sports coat. He locked the office as he left and began walking west.

As Butler neared Clairoux's office, he became aware of someone following him. He stopped at a storefront, watched the reflections in the glass, and saw a tall, dark-complexioned Chinese man duck into an alley across the street next to the Quan Thanh Temple. Another well-dressed Chinese man was standing next to a two-wheeled rickshaw half a block to the east. He had seen him at the International Hotel a week ago with a delegation of Chinese diplomats. *Damn! Chinese intelligence. What the hell do they want?* Butler thought.

Butler entered the Clairoux Detective Agency office and closed the door behind him. A cheerful-looking Asian woman in her mid-thirties was seated at the receptionist's desk. "Go right in, Mr. Butler. Mr. Clairoux is expecting you."

As Butler was about to enter Clairoux's office, he heard a small click of a gun's safety being flipped behind him. Butler grabbed his holstered weapon and dove toward the floor. Two rounds, fired from an FN Browning M1900, missed Butler by a fraction of an inch. Next, Butler fired at the woman, striking her in the chest. The .45-caliber round knocked her halfway across the room.

Butler jumped up and kicked in the door to Clairoux's office. A startled Chinese man raised his pistol, but Butler fired first, taking off half of the man's head. Then, Butler rushed to Jacob Clairoux, unconscious and tied to the chair behind his desk.

Before attending to Jacob, Butler locked the front door. When he walked back into the office, Butler noticed blood trickling down the left side of Jacob's face and heard a soft mumbling from his lips. Yul untied the barely conscious detective, laid him on the floor, and used his sport coat to support Jacob's head.

Butler was about to pour a glass of Scotch when he heard two taps on the front door followed by three quick taps. Butler opened the door and let the British agents into the office.

"Glad you're okay," Miles Murphy stated.

"And I'm glad you were still in town," Butler replied.

"How's Jacob?"

"Took a nasty hit on the head, but he's coming around. What happened out there?"

"Two Chinese chaps came running down the alley with pistols drawn when they heard the gunfire. They're with their Taoist gods now. Henri and I put them in the boot of his auto. We'll get these two in my car and dispose of them in the Red River. With these heavy rains, they'll be in the South China Sea by this time tomorrow night."

"You don't think the Chinese will miss them?"

"Chinese intelligence usually works without informing anyone at their consulate. Henri and I picked up on this team a week ago. One of our Chinese-speaking agents overheard them talking about gems. I believe they were here to take over your enterprise. Which could mean they are former Chinese intelligence agents, gone rogue."

"Or, the Chinese communists are making a move into Indochina and want to take down my intelligence-gathering operation."

"Either way, Yul, you're screwed."

Yul and Miles heard a soft moan and saw Jacob trying to get to his feet. Miles grabbed his right arm and helped him to a rattan sofa as Henri Morreau walked through the door.

"I figured you were okay when I heard that big-ass gun of yours go off. Two more dead Chinese operatives for the river, I see," Henri stated.

"Thanks for the help, Henri," Yul responded.

"I'm sure Miles told you that these are the same four we've been monitoring for a week. They've been living too high to be Chinese intelligence. We figured they were after your gem operation, so we got the Brigadier's permission to hang around a bit longer. Glad we could help."

"Yul…Yul. Are you alright?" Jacob mumbled as he tried to stand.

"A lot better than you, friend. How about some Scotch to shake the cobwebs loose?" Butler asked.

"There's some Gin in the cabinet if you don't mind."

Butler poured half a glass and handed it to Jacob. "Tell me why you wanted to see me?"

"Didn't you get my note?"

"Crap, I forgot all about it when I got your call."

"We lost three detectives last week in northern Indochina, near the Laotian border. One of our teams was ambushed. According to the sole survivor, these guys are former Chinese army officers looking to make big off the gem business you struck up. They've taken over the mining operations of at least three villages and are forcing the villagers to work for them."

"How many soldiers are we talking about?"

"At least a dozen heavily armed men. They must have obtained the name of our agency from one of our detectives, probably under torture, or they threatened his family. I'm glad you came prepared. Shortly before dusk, that woman entered my office, wanting our agency to follow her husband and catch him cheating. Before I knew it, she struck me on the head and knocked me unconscious. I assume she is part of the Chinese gang looking to take over your gem operation. God, this hurts," Jacob said, rubbing the knot on his head.

"Do you have wireless communications with any of your detectives?" Miles asked.

"Only six of the two dozen."

"Better start contacting them, and warn them of the threat."

"I'll do one better. I'll have them inform the Viet Minh in the area. General Giap and Uncle Ho don't tolerate rogue Chinese soldiers on Vietnamese soil."

# CHAPTER 36

*Yokohama, Japan*

Uchito Tsukuda stood staring at the message he had received earlier in the morning from one of his operatives in Havana. Thirty-eight of his agents had been arrested by INS in Baltimore and Washington, D.C., and four of his five boats were seized by the U.S. Coast Guard. All the weapons, ammunition, opium, and gold were in American law enforcement's hands. *That sonofabitch, Sugimoto, will pay for his incompetence,* Tsukuda said to himself. While Tsukuda was seething, his bodyguard entered his study and bowed deeply.

"This just came in, General. It's from Hinata Hayashi," Raizo said. He handed the message to his boss and waited for Tsukuda to dismiss him. Unfortunately, it was more bad news.

"Thank you, Raizo," Tsukuda replied, "You're dismissed."

Tsukuda sat at his desk and began reading with anticipation, thinking that the American agents would be dead. Instead, he started trembling with rage as he read the brief message: I arrived too late. Sugimoto has failed in his attempt to kill the American operatives. Seventeen agents were dead, along with Sugimoto. Awaiting instructions, Hinata Hayashi.

The general sat motionlessly, slumped in the heavily padded chair, feeling emotionally and physically exhausted. His head was throbbing with a dull ache, as he tried to review the circumstances that led up to the disaster with Sugimoto. His brain was numb, and he couldn't think clearly. He had a distinct feeling that something was wrong. The answer was there but out of reach. Suddenly, Tsukuda had a vision in which he was twelve years old again and his grandmother was saying, *beware of the white samurai.*

Tsukuda stood up at his desk, wrote out a reply, and called for his bodyguard. "Raizo!"

"Yes, General," Raizo said as he entered.

"Send this to Havana immediately."

As Raizo retrieved the message, he bowed low and backed out of the office. As he made his way to the communications center, he wondered if the Americans would strike in Japan. He was a young operative on his first mission in Calcutta when he first encountered Jonathan Preston and the American team. He had barely escaped capture when Asami Nakada's triplet sisters attempted to assassinate a high-ranking British general and an American diplomat. All three sisters were killed that night. Later, he worked with Asami Nakada when she was deployed to Calcutta to take out the team of American operatives.

During one attempt, Asami barely escaped with a gunshot wound to the arm. After making her way back to her house, Raizo had dressed Asami's wound and nursed her back to health. He was well aware of the skills of the American agents, especially Preston, the one they called *Cobra*. However, over the last two years working as Tsukuda's head of security, Raizo had become lax in his martial arts. So, he decided he would begin training more diligently. *It was only a matter of time before Preston would bring his team to Japan,* Raizo reflected.

When Raizo returned to Tsukuda's office, the general was pacing between the desk and the door to the garden. When Tsukuda saw Raizo, he barked loudly.

"Gather all the men for a meeting at 1900 hours in the great hall, and have the chef and staff prepare a meal for everyone. Make certain we have plenty of tea and sake for the men. It will be a long evening."

"Yes, General," Raizo replied.

"On Friday, we will travel to Tokyo and meet with all the men there, the following day. Same arrangements. The American agents will be coming to Japan, Raizo, and we must be prepared to deal with them."

As Raizo bowed and retreated from the office, he noticed that Tsukuda's face looked pallid and nervous. A small tick had developed on his lower right eyelid and at the corner of his mouth. Raizo knew that Tsukuda had not been sleeping well. He had caught the general pacing his office at 3 a.m., on several occasions over the last month, when Raizo had taken the late-night watch so that one of the guards could be with his sick wife. During the war, Raizo had witnessed what had happened to sleep-deprived soldiers; many had gone insane. *This is not a good sign*, Raizo thought.

That evening, the thirty men were treated with rice with miso soup, fresh and pickled vegetables, grilled Pacific cod and salmon, and Kansai-style sukiyaki. The sukiyaki was made with thinly sliced beef that was slowly cooked at a large table. It was served with Udon noodles, long green onions, and shiitake mushrooms, cooked in a shallow iron pot in a mixture of soy sauce, sugar, and mirin. Tsukuda spared no expense on the meal and provided the best quality sake from his family's vineyard.

After the dishes were cleared from the tables, Tsukuda stood up and addressed his men. All were former assassins and intelligence operatives with the Japanese Imperial Army. They were highly trained as assassins, but few had actual combat experience. He informed them that they would be drilling at an abandoned JIA Special Forces training camp over the next couple of weeks. It was located in the heavily forested hills, east of Mount Kumotori. The camp was shut down in February 1945, when all the select soldiers were sent to Okinawa to defend the empire against the impending Allied invasion.

Of the six hundred Special Forces soldiers deployed to Okinawa, four had survived the invasion. Three were wounded so severely, that they would never work again. The fourth, Furutani Hinata, one of the instructors, was on the way to the camp with a dozen select veterans to prepare the facility to receive sixty of Tsukuda's men. For two weeks, they would work on conditioning, martial arts skills, and small-arms weapons. Then, two more weeks would be dedicated to close-quarters combat, involving multiple combatants at short range, using the wakizashi and tanto swords. Tsukuda was going to make damn sure his men were prepared to take on the American agents, if and when they attacked him at one of his residences.

As the general made the rounds, shaking hands and slapping agents on the back, he prayed to the Shintō god of war, Hachiman, for protection. Four times, Tsukuda had sent agents to kill Preston and his team of agents. On each occasion, his agents had underestimated the American operatives and failed. However, this time, the Americans would be on Japanese soil, and Tsukuda was making sure he had the advantage. If the Americans got past the nightingale floors he had installed in his mansions, they would face a force of hardened killers with samurai skills.

George Linka left Washington and flew to Tokyo. He met with his agents and gathered intelligence on Tsukuda's current activities. Over the two weeks that he was there, he collected evidence that Tsukuda was preparing for a major confrontation. George's agent in Yokohama, Hattori Nozomi, sent information that Tsukuda was training men at an abandoned army base in the hills east of Mount Kumotori. In addition, several of George's agents from small isolated villages in the area returned home, to visit relatives and spy on the activities.

When the agents returned, they reported that Tsukuda was training over sixty men in close-quarters combat, using suppressed submachine guns and pistols, as well as wakizashi and tanto swords. George wired the information to Preston before flying back to Washington.

Preston showed the message to General Miller, who immediately determined that the nine agents Jon planned on taking to Japan wouldn't be enough. The general cleverly asked Jon his thoughts.

"Well, general, we can't hit Tsukuda at his estate without a better plan. When George returns, I'll ask him if we can use Nozomi in some capacity to disable the men by putting a sedative in their food or sake. If we use her, she will be at great risk unless she takes the sedative herself to remove all suspicion," Preston replied.

"She's a great asset. But, we don't put agents in a no-win situation," General Miller said. "Even if she took the sedative, she would fall under Tsukuda's suspicion if he somehow managed to escape. Knowing Tsukuda, all of the staff would be interrogated under torture."

"We may be able to use a nerve agent to incapacitate everyone at the estate. The major problem will be with the gas dispersion. There are over sixty rooms and three levels. We would have to fire canisters through the windows on each level. The guards in the gardens and the periphery of the estate would have to be dealt with separately. We would need a dozen snipers to cover all the areas."

"What about incapacitating Tsukuda and capturing him during the Kabuki play?"

"Too many civilians, sir. The theater holds up to three hundred people."

"When George returns, I want you to brainstorm and come up with a new plan. We have to take Tsukuda down before we can dismantle his organization."

"Maybe we don't. Instead, we could start hitting Tsukuda's enterprises. He is still shipping arms into Korea. So that would be a good place to start."

"It would have to look like an accident, Jon. We can't afford a confrontation with the Chinese. It might accelerate whatever timeline they have for Korea."

"Maybe an accident on the docks where they are unloading the munitions. I think we need to talk with the air force intelligence officer who works for the Fifth Air Force commander in Japan—Major General Partridge, the agent who has been collecting intelligence on North Korea."

"I get a monthly report from General Partridge. Unofficially, of course—because it does not go through MacArthur's staff. The Chinese are still moving men and arms into the north."

"Maybe we could team him up with Brigadier MacKenzie's agent, Captain Kim Jung. Can you discretely contact General Partridge and set up a secret meeting with his man on his base?"

"It's worth a try."

"If General Partridge agrees, have Nancy book me a flight to Japan. Then contact George and tell him to meet me at Yokota Air Base."

"Is there anything else you want me to arrange?"

"Yes, sir. I would like to meet with Brigadier MacKenzie, Colonel Ballangy, and Captain Kim while I am there."

"You've got that faraway look again. What are you thinking?"

"That this would be a great opportunity for the white samurai to come to life."

"To do what?"

"To hit Tsukuda where it hurts, by destroying the ships along with the material they are funneling into North Korea."

"What you're suggesting could be construed as an act of war, Jon."

"Only if we are exposed, sir. But that won't happen. Plus, these are civilian boats smuggling illegal arms. We'll make it look like an accident. As you know, ammunition can be very unstable. If one ship explodes, others could very well be damaged and destroyed if they are tied up close together. We'll need the Brigadier's intelligence on when the shipments are coming, along with one of his special mission submarines to get us in close. I will only take George, Captain Kim, and Partridge's agent."

Jon paused and thought for a second. "And unless you want us doing this on our own, we'll need President Truman's authorization."

"I'll inform General Renick and arrange the meeting to discuss it with the chief of staff. You'll have to conduct the briefing."

# CHAPTER 37



*Yokota Air Base, Japan*

The 12,700-mile flight from Bolling Air Base to Yokota Air Base took four days. When Jon walked down the airstairs of the C-54 Skymaster, he looked tired, and the flight suit he was wearing was chaffing his legs. He was met by an air force corporal in a blue staff car and a young major in a khaki uniform who looked vaguely familiar.

"Welcome to Yokota, Colonel Preston. I am Scott Bayless. You probably don't remember me. I was just a young first lieutenant in Algiers when you landed there in 1944 on your way to Calcutta," Bayless stated.

"It's been a while, Scott. You worked for the OSS Commander, Colonel Farrington. I take it you are in Air Force intelligence now?" Preston asked.

"Yes, sir. I'm General Partridge's assistant deputy director of intelligence. As soon as the corporal retrieves your bags, I'll take you to your room. You're already checked in. Colonel Linka is in the room next to yours. After you take a shower and change, the driver will take you and Colonel Linka to the Officer's Club for dinner."

"I suppose we will be meeting with you, your boss, and General Partridge tomorrow morning?"

"Yes, sir. Afterward, I'll take you all to our intelligence center, where you will meet Captain Jacob Ikestead. Although I'll warn you, he prefers to be called Jake. I've also been informed that Brigadier MacKenzie and Lieutenant Colonel Ballangy of the British SIS will be landing this evening after dark. The Brits have a compound on the north side of the base. The general wants you to remain hidden.

Therefore, you and Colonel Linka will be given a temporary office in the Brits' facility."

"Scott, you seem to have covered all our needs. I assume you've been told that this mission is Top Secret and that I, Colonel Linka, and the brigadier's team have never been here."

"Yes, sir. All the rooms are registered under the names of cousins of mine back in the states."

"I hope you will join us for dinner tonight."

"Unfortunately, sir, I have plans. But, I will pick you all up and take you to breakfast at 0700 hours tomorrow morning. Brigadier MacKenzie and his men will be eating separately. To keep a low profile, they are posing as British journalists. We'll meet with General Partridge at 0830 at the intelligence center, before his 0900 staff meeting. From what I understand, it is just a courtesy call and a welcome to South Korea, to a visiting colonel. He wants to know nothing about your intentions."

"Yes, General Miller said as much. Plausible deniability, in case he is questioned by General MacArthur."


Four days later, Jon Preston, George Linka, and Jake Ikestead were on a C-47 headed to Fukuoka, the capital of Fukuoka Prefecture, which sits on the northern shore of Japan's Kyushu Island. They landed at Ashiya Air Field, which served as an air defense force base for the Japanese Army Air Force. After deplaning, they were picked up by a U.S. Army, Model 3D staff car, driven by a stiff, untalkative British corporal. He drove them to a nondescript hangar on the north side of the base.

Before the men exited the sedan, the corporal said, "Show your credentials to the nice sergeant inside that hangar door, chaps."

As they entered the hangar, they were greeted by a tall, muscular staff sergeant dressed in the uniform of a Special Air Service (SAS) paratrooper. He wore a maroon beret, bashed to the right, with the parachute regiment beret badge above the left eye. Two more members of the SAS were standing behind the sergeant, holding Thompson submachine guns at the ready.

After checking each man's credentials against what was in his folder, the staff sergeant said, "Brigadier MacKenzie is expecting you, gentlemen. Please follow me."

Brigadier Michael Patrick MacKenzie arose from his chair as the sergeant escorted the Americans into his office. Captain Kim Jung rose from a chair in the far corner of the office. As the sergeant left, MacKenzie offered all four men a choice of iced lemonade or hot tea. The Americans accepted the lemonade, but Jung selected the tea.

"This is good timing, gentlemen, so let's get down to business. You'll have plenty of time to get to know each other later. I just received a report that eight of Tsukuda's small freighters and a larger supply ship will be leaving Tianjin for Nampho, in two days. My sources say the freighters are carrying small arms, ammunition, artillery, and mortar shells. The larger ship is an old 650-ton, *Nosaki*-class supply ship. It's carrying approximately 2,200 barrels of gasoline and 300 barrels of kerosene, presumably for cooking purposes," Brigadier MacKenzie stated.

"That's convenient. Let's hope they berth the ships close together. An explosion on the large freighter could wipe out the entire lot," Jon Preston said.

"Captain Jung's sources have provided photographs of freighters unloading at the docks at Nampho. Most of the ammunition is offloaded by hand and is stored in a guarded area next to the port. The tanker has two cargo cranes. However, it took three days to load the ship in Tianjin. And, yes, they are berthing them close together."

"I have a team of three agents working the docks in Nampho, Colonel Preston," Jung said.

"Do they have radios?" Preston asked.

"Yes, sir. They listen for instruction, each night, at 2300 hours. When they receive a message, they acknowledge it by sending a prearranged single Morse code alphabet letter. In addition, the communists have a network of radio listening stations in the area, so under no circumstance will they break radio silence."

"What about security at the port?" George Linka asked.

"The North Koreans have two regiments of infantry bivouacked a half a mile inland. They have a minimum of two companies, or around 100 soldiers, guarding the docks and the surrounding area, day and night. When ships are in port, they usually double the number."

"We'll need a diversion," Captain Ikestead replied.

"One of my men is prepared to start a fire in the mess tent, near the docks where the guards and dock workers eat. They've had several fires already due to the poor quality of their cooking stoves, which leak profusely. And they have several barrels of kerosene and gasoline stored next to the mess tent, which will create a nice explosion and a large blaze," Kim responded.

"It would help if some of the nearby command tents caught fire, too," Preston stated. "We need a large blaze to diminish their night vision."

"That won't be a problem, Colonel. Those tents are within twenty feet of the mess tent. One of my agents is a cook, and he works in the mess tent each night."

"Gentlemen, we need to feed you and get you to your quarters," Brigadier MacKenzie commented. "In thirteen hours, you will be getting on a PBY and be flown to a rendezvous with the HMS *Storm,* a hundred miles northwest of Jeju Island. Since this is a British SOE mission, Captain Kim will be in charge. Do you chaps have a problem with that?"

"None whatsoever, Brigadier," Preston replied. "We just want to make sure we hurt Uchito Tsukuda's organization."


The British PBY landed on the Yellow Sea, as the sun was rising in the eastern sky. It taxied to within a hundred feet of the waiting submarine, where sailors were launching a twelve-man life raft powered by a small outboard motor.

The sky in the east turned from yellow to light blue, as the PBY lifted off for its return flight to Fukuoka. Several sailors were standing by, to receive the gear and help the four men onto the submarine's deck. As Jon and the others stepped on the deck of the HMS *Storm,* they saluted the British officer standing above them on the conning tower.

The captain of HMS *Storm*, Commander Larry Mercer, was standing near the forward gun—when the life raft pulled up to the port side behind the conning tower. Not seeing an officer on the deck, Preston said in a loud voice, "Colonel Preston and company requesting permission to come aboard, sir."

"Permission granted," Commander Mercer yelled in reply from the far deck. "I thought I had seen the last of you in 1945, Jon."

Jon Preston instantly recognized the gruff voice and replied, "Is that you, Larry?"

"Good to have you back on board. Hurry up and get below. I want to be underway in ten minutes," Mercer said, as he climbed the ladder to the conning tower.

"Aye, aye, Captain," Preston replied.

After Preston and his team hurried to climb up the ladder and down through the conning tower, they were escorted to the crew mess. A minute later, Commander Mercer gave the order to dive the boat.

"Dive! Dive! Dive!" the chief of the boat repeated over the ship's intercom. The announcement was followed by two loud blasts from the sub's klaxon, "Ahoooga, ahoooga!"

The men outside on the bridge hurried down the ladder into the conn. The last man down was the executive officer, or XO, who closed the hatch and yelled, "Hatch secured!"

"Green board," the COB reported seconds later over the intercom, followed by "Pressure in the boat," as the interior lights switched from red to white. The "Green board" notification informed the crew that the boat was sealed, watertight, and ready to dive.

"Take her down to four-zero meters and turn to a heading of 350 degrees," Captain Mercer ordered.

Before the 218-foot HMS *Storm* began its dive, the agents sitting in the mess heard the main air-induction valves slam shut and the irregular gurgle of water entering into the ballast tanks. The two eight-cylinder, 950-horsepower diesel engines stopped. The boat switched over to the battery-powered Metropolitan-Vickers electric motors for its underwater propulsion.

Several minutes later, the diving planesman called out, "Level at four-zero meters, heading 350 degrees, Captain."

When Captain Mercer was satisfied that everything was under control, he turned the boat over to the XO. He made his way to the galley where Preston, Linka, Kim, and Ikestead were enjoying a cup of tea and going over a nautical map of Taedong Bay.

Jon looked up as Mercer entered the small mess. He was shocked at what he saw. The six-foot-three-tall submariner, whose muscles usually rippled under his khaki uniform shirt, was a shadow of the man Preston remembered from 1945.

"What the hell happened to you, Larry?" Preston asked.

"Pour me a cup of tea, and I'll tell you all about it," Mercer replied.

# CHAPTER 38

*Yellow Sea*

Jon Preston poured a cup of hot tea and set it in front of the submariner. He estimated that Captain Mercer had lost over sixty pounds since the last time he had seen him on the HMS *Storm,* in December of 1945. Mercer's cadaverous features reminded Jon of the emaciated Allied prisoners he had rescued from several Japanese POW camps.

"About fourteen months ago, the *Storm* was ordered to return to Trincomalee, Ceylon for rest-and-relaxation and an engine overhaul. Shortly after we arrived, there were outbreaks of malaria and dengue fever. I came down with dengue," Mercer stated with a sigh.

"You must have become seriously ill to lose so much weight," George Linka said.

"I came down with the more severe form, dengue hemorrhagic fever. I had the typical symptoms: high fever, headache, muscle, and joint pains, and skin rash. After I was admitted to the hospital, severe belly pains began. I was vomiting blood, passing blood in my urine and stool, and bleeding from my gums and nose. I couldn't eat or drink, and I soon became dangerously dehydrated. The only thing that saved me was the intravenous solutions the doctors put me on," Mercer said, pausing to take a drink of tea before resuming.

"After seven weeks, I began to recover. I was able to eat soup and bread, and drink tea. In the eighth week, I was finally able to get out of bed and into a wheelchair, so the nurses could take me outside to get fresh air and sunshine. Unfortunately, just as I was recovering, I became very ill again—this time with shaking chills, and later, with a high fever. During those short outside visits, I must have been bitten by a mosquito carrying malaria. In the end, I was in the hospital for nearly fifteen weeks."

"How long before you were able to go back to sea?" George asked.

"This is my first mission in fourteen months. After I was released from the hospital, I had to convalesce for six months. I lost a lot of weight, and my muscles were still very weak. Before I became ill, I weighed two hundred and forty-five pounds. By the time I was released from the hospital, I had dropped to one-eighty. I started lifting weights, eating a diet high in fish protein, and jogging on the beach. I was away from the *Storm* so long that I had to recertify. That took four months."

"You're still quite thin," Jon replied.

"Hey, I've put on twenty pounds, but I like myself at this weight. I look and feel a lot sexier."

"I suppose you have more stories about those twin sisters?" George asked.

"Not anymore. I met a beautiful nurse in Trincomalee. I married her, four months ago."

"Congratulations, Larry," Jon stated. "Now, can you tell us the plan for getting to Nampho?"

"We'll stay submerged for another hour to make sure there is no surface ship shadowing us. The Russians have several trawlers in the Yellow Sea that we suspect they are using to monitor the British and American presence. When we surface, we'll cruise at 12 knots. That should put us abeam Weihai, China, in twenty hours. We'll submerge before dawn—because the Chinese have a naval air unit at Weihai. It's made up of a dozen older Soviet, Yakovlev, Yak-4 light bombers that were purchased by the Chinese from their new communist friends. They have been flying reconnaissance missions from Weihai for the last two months. But, according to our intelligence sources, they are having problems maintaining them."

"Probably keeping an eye on the freighter missions," Captain Jung added.

"That, too. But, naval intelligence and the Brigadier believe that the Chinese are purchasing the bombers to support their ground forces when they invade South Korea. Weihai is only 250 miles from Seoul, so it's not unreasonable."

"That is plausible if they are purchasing more bombers. Nevertheless, Captain Jung and I believe that the north won't be in a position to invade for another 24 to 36 months," Captain Ikestead said.

"Why is that?" George asked.

"Training and logistics, Captain. The North Koreans have the manpower, but their men are not well trained. Nor do they have the supplies built up in their country to support an extended campaign into South Korea. Granted, they have brought a lot of equipment into the north. Still, they do not have the trained technicians needed to maintain the equipment or the experience. They will, however, learn over the next two to three years as they train—especially during the winter months, which will be critical to their overall success. Maintaining equipment in cold weather is a must."

"You really believe that they will invade South Korea, Jake?" Preston asked.

"Absolutely, sir. I have agents inside the palace in Pyongyang. Kim Il-sung is hell-bent on taking the south, and Stalin is behind him one hundred percent."


After twenty-two hours of running on the surface, the HMS *Storm* submerged. Once Mercer was confident the *Storm* was under control, he ordered a shift change. He turned the boat over to the XO, Lieutenant Commander Bob Carpenter.

"You have the helm, Bob," Captain Mercer ordered. "At 38.45 degrees north latitude, and 123 degrees east longitude, put her in an east-to-west, racetrack pattern. We should have the first contact with the freighter convoy by 1800 hours. At 1700 hours, take her up to thirty feet and raise the radar. Four sweeps, then take her back down. Do it again at 1730. I'm going to get some sleep. Wake me, if necessary. Otherwise, I'll see you at 1800 hours."

Before Captain Mercer went to bed, he pulled out his journal and began to reflect on the last four months. Bob Carpenter had been a torpedo officer on the *Storm* when Larry's best friend Admiral Don Cowan was its captain. When Cowan was promoted to flag rank, Mercer became captain, and Carpenter moved to navigation before becoming the plotting officer. When Mercer returned to the *Storm* after his illness, he knew Carpenter was ready—and chose him as the new XO. When Mercer opened his journal, he wondered whether Captain Cowan had reflected on his performance. He smiled and shrugged the thought off, as he wrote: "MEMO: August 16, 1948. Lieutenant Commander Bob Carpenter, XO, HMS *Storm*, is ready to become captain of his own boat."

At 1600 hours, Commander Carpenter told the COB to have the mess crew bring food and hot tea to the men at their stations. He wanted them fed and alert when contact with the convoy occurred. Carpenter also wanted the men to know that he was thinking about their needs. He had served on one boat where the captain was the opposite of Captain Mercer—a real jerk. Well, *he* wasn't a jerk, and he swore he would never become one—because he needed the men to have his back.

"Sonar contact, Skipper," the sonar operator reported. "Bearing 270 degrees. Multiple screws. Possibly, one high-speed screw."

"They must have picked up an escort," Carpenter replied.

Carpenter looked at his watch—1650 hours. Next, he looked over the navigator's shoulder. The navigator pointed at the far western edge of the racetrack and said, "We should be turning east in six minutes, Skipper."

"Skipper, one high-speed screw confirmed. Bearing 260 degrees, approximately 10,000 meters," the sonarman stated.

"We should start toward the surface if we want to get our 1700 sweeps, Captain," the radar operator informed the captain.

"Not until we know what kind of escort is out there," Carpenter replied. "Sonar, any idea of the type of contact?"

"It could be a destroyer or destroyer escort, sir."

"Helmsman, take us to periscope depth."

"Level at eighteen meters, Skipper," the helmsman replied a few minutes later.

Carpenter picked up the phone and said, "Engine room. Slow to four knots." He placed the phone in its cradle and said, "COB, raise the periscope, but only break the surface. Report what you see."

The COB raised the periscope and squatted close to the floor. Three-foot waves were obscuring the view, so he raised it higher and changed to the ten-power setting. After five seconds, he brought the scope back down.

"One destroyer, 6,000 meters. Bearing 269 degrees, Skipper. Appears to be an old World War One Russian Imperial Navy *Orfey*-class destroyer. Unless it was modified, it wouldn't have sonar or radar."

"Radar, four sweeps, please," Carpenter ordered.

"Aye, sir, Four sweeps," the radar operator replied as he flipped the switch and raised the radar mast. "Skipper, there are nine ships total. Seven small craft and two larger ones."

"Very well, Helmsman. Depth 60 meters." Carpenter picked up the phone. "Engine room. Speed six-knots."

Captain Mercer had been standing at the back of the conn, watching and listening to all the activity. The COB noticed the captain and was about to announce him to the conn crew, but Mercer shook his head, turned, and went down the ladder. He returned to the mess where the cook was preparing his tray of food. When he entered the mess area, Jon Preston was sipping on a cup of coffee.

"How is the XO handling things?" Preston asked.

"Extremely well. Carpenter is ready for his own boat," Mercer replied.

"You and Cowan trained him. Did you expect anything less?"

"Not with Carpenter. He's as bright as they come."

"What are your long-term plans?"

"Admiral Cowan has offered me a position on his staff."

"Promotion to Captain and a land job... Sounds like an ideal job to begin a marriage and start a family, Larry."

"It does seem rather appealing. Plus, Cowan is in charge of designing the next generation of submarines. So I could put my mechanical engineering skills to good use."

"I think you've already made up your mind, friend."

"What about you? You're a colonel now. You shouldn't be roaming all over the world, chasing bad guys."

"Well, I do have a one-year-old boy and a beautiful wife to think about."

"So, what are your long-term plans, Jon?"

"Not sure, I'm at a crossroad. George and I have been contemplating leaving the Army and going into the oil business in West Texas. He has an uncle who is willing to help us get started."

"Sounds like you've pretty much made up your mind."

"Pretty much. But there's one last bad guy to take down first."

"And these freighters, moving the arms and ammunition, are his, I take it?"

"Yep."

"Then I'll get you all close, so you can wallop him good. I assume you have an exit strategy should you be unable to make it back to the sub?"

"Yes. A small junk, ten miles south of Nampho."

"Then I'll keep an eye out for you should the worse scenario happen."

"Thanks, Larry."

# CHAPTER 39

*Nampho, North Korea*

Nampo was a small seaport village in South Pyongan Province, lying on the northern shore of the Taedong River, nine miles east of the river's mouth. Two and a half miles across the bay, on the south shore, was the smaller settlement of Nampho. There, the North Korean Army encampment housed nearly two thousand soldiers and civilian dock workers. The docks, built in a natural one-mile-wide and two-mile-deep indention of the south shore, provided excellent protection from the storms coming off the Yellow Sea.

The Yellow Sea is considered a marginal sea of the Western Pacific Ocean, located between mainland China and the Korean Peninsula. The Yellow Sea covered 150,000 square miles and is approximately 600 miles in length and 430 miles wide. Its maximum depth is 499 feet. However, its average depth is 144 feet. Captain Mercer was well aware of its depth as he navigated the HMS *Storm* closer to Taedong Bay.

It was pitch black when the HMS *Storm* surfaced, two miles south of Ch'o-do Island. The sliver of the quarter moon was barely visible between the intermittent cover of low, rain-heavy clouds. Captain Kim Jung was on the forward deck sending Morse code with a flashlight fitted with a red lens. Minutes later, a small junk edged alongside the starboard side of the submarine.

While several *Storm* sailors secured the junk next to the submarine, Kim and Preston began handing gear and explosives to one of the Korean men in the junk. The other Koreans held the rudder steady to keep the boat as still as possible. Minutes later, the gear and all four men were in the junk, rowing toward shore. While onboard the sub, Preston, Linka, and Ikestead had made use of the OSS theatrical kit to color their skin the dark, injong shade of a North Korean.

The junk took them to a shallow inlet six miles west of Nampho, where they were met by two Korean men dressed as peasants. As they moved their gear from the boat to the shore, one of the men handed each agent a dark-colored, loosely woven, and roughly finished cotton *jeogori* to put over his clothes. The jeogori covered each agent's arms and upper body and was loose enough to hide the thirty-three-inch Soviet PPSh-41 submachine gun with a 71-round drum magazine, carried by each. The dark-colored wide-brimmed hats he handed them were made from straw and hung low over their faces.

Captain Jung had chosen the PPSh-41 because of its simplicity and reliability. During World War II, it was one of the principal infantry weapons of the Soviet Armed Forces. Now, the Chinese Communists and North Korean armies made use of the weapons. It was a magazine-fed submachine gun that used an open-bolt, blow-back action. After a round was fired, the bolt was forced to the rear, ejecting the empty cartridge. The bolt remained in place at the back, ready for the next shot. The trigger's pull then pushed another round into the chamber. It automatically ignited the round once it was fully seated in the chamber. It was a simple design, made mainly of stamped steel, and fired a 7.62 x 25 mm rimless pistol cartridge. Jung had loaded his and Preston's drums with alternating armor-piercing and incendiary rounds.

The Tokarev TT-33 semi-automatic pistols they carried were loaded with hollow-point bullets, according to Jon Preston's instructions. Preston wanted the maximum kill power should they encounter any close resistance. Plus, each man carried a V-42 fighting knife. The V-42 had a double-edged blade that could slash an opponent with a forehand or backhand stroke. The blade was so sturdy that it could easily penetrate a steel helmet with a single thrust.

As the agents approached Nampho, the Koreans broke off and headed to their quarters at the main camp, south of the docks.

Captain Jung led the rest toward the southwest section of the port, where the fuel drums were being offloaded. As they drew closer to their destination, they were stopped by a North Korean guard.

"Halt! What are you doing here?" the guard demanded.

"We are heading to work at the docks. We live four miles south in the village of Unryul-up," Jong answered.

"You are late. The third shift started an hour ago."

"I am very sorry, sir. The village headman delayed us because his donkey broke out of its pen when a lightning bolt struck near it. The donkey ran a short distance and got stuck in a bog next to the village. You might have heard it. It was bellowing as loud as a winter storm. We had to help him pull the donkey out, or our village would lose its only plow animal. You see, our ox died last winter. We are going to be even later, sir, if you don't let us proceed."

The guard grunted a chastising remark and motioned them onward. Withdrawing a small pouch of tobacco from his coat pocket and a packet of rolling papers, he rolled a cigarette. He turned his back to the wind and lighted it with an old Park Sherman cigarette lighter. He had traded a good pocket knife to get it. Reflecting back, he thought kitchen matches were more reliable. He took two deep drags on the cigarette before continuing his assigned route, thinking nothing of the peasants, and wishing he was back home in Pyongyang.

The lights of the docks in the distance were becoming more visible as the agents continued their eastward trek. Preston estimated they were still two miles away. When Jung looked back, Preston motioned for him to come near. Jung slowed his walk and let Preston come up beside him.

"Shouldn't we split up soon?" Preston asked in a low voice.

"We need to wait until we get past all the guards and into the holding yard, so I can speak for the group if we get stopped again. Otherwise, we might get in a fight before we get the opportunity to hit the ships and ammo dump," Jung replied.

Jon nodded his agreement and followed Jung, three paces behind. They climbed through a stretch of barbed wire with two broken strands, when a guard appeared out of nowhere and halted them again.

"Halt! You're supposed to use the south gate," the guard shouted.

"Sorry, sir. We are an hour late for work, and I was trying to make up some time," Jung replied, bowing deeply.

The others halted as they caught up and bowed deeply in response to Jung's action. The guard yawned. He was obviously tired.

"The headman of our village detained us to help him free his donkey from a bog. That's why we are late, Corporal Kim. By the way, where is your buddy, Corporal Park?" Jung asked, using the two most common surnames in Korea.

"He was sick tonight," Corporal Kim replied. "It's just me."

Corporal Kim was about to let them go when he changed his mind. "Wait, I need to see your work permits. Otherwise, the sergeant will get pissed if he finds out I let you through without checking them."

"No, problem," Jung replied, pulling a packet of papers from under his jeogori with his left hand.

As Corporal Kim reached for the papers, Jung thrust his fist into the corporal's solar plexus with his right hand. As the corporal stumbled backward, Preston hit him with a large rock, smashing his skull.

"Quickly, drag him to that swamp and put him behind the tall reeds. Pull some reeds and grass to cover him," Jung said.

While Jung stood guard, Preston and Ikestead dragged the body behind the reeds taking care not to step into the swamp. While Ikestead pulled reeds and grass and placed them over the dead corporal, Preston began laying rocks on top—to hold the grass in place. When they joined up with Jung, they continued eastward. Jung slowed to talk to Preston.

"You handled that quite well," Jung stated.

"So did you," Preston replied.

"I didn't want to stab him because of the blood."

"Let's hope we don't encounter any more guards. This is exciting enough as it is."

"Another twenty minutes, and you'll have more excitement than you can handle. Let's hit the boats first and then the ammo dump."

"What time does the fire start in the cooking tent?"

"At 0200 hours. That gives us a five-minute margin to get to the docks."

"Better pick up the pace. I would rather be early than late."

When Jung reached a group of Korean dock workers squatting in a circle around a small cooking stove, he motioned for the others to join him and sit facing away from the group. Jung, however, squatted next to a small building looking directly at the group of Korean men. Trying to blend in, Jung made a joke in Korean, and the other agents laughed. The smaller freighters were berthed in neat rows, thirty yards away, with stacks of ammunition boxes lining the narrow dock. The large supply ship was setting broadside at a newer dock built specifically for larger vessels. There were hundreds of barrels of fuel crowding the large dock.

When the fire alarm sounded, the group of Koreans stood and began staring and chattering as the flames shot skyward 200 feet to the south. Jung walked around the building and saw a group of guards running in the direction of the fire.

When he returned to the group, Jung said, "Time to go. Cover our tails while Preston and I hit the boats. When you see us run back here, light up the ammo."

Linka and Ikestead moved to within fifty yards of the ammo dump and squatted like many Korean dock workers. As the first shots were fired, many workers paid no attention and kept staring at the fire to the south. However, when a large explosion rocked the farthest freighter, the Korean workers began to panic. Having seen accidents happen on the dock before, many started running toward the west to get away from the exploding ordinance.

While Linka and Ikestead remained squatting, two North Korean guards rushed toward the workers, urging them to move as much war material off the docks as possible. When they refused, the guards lowered their rifles and shot two of the workers. Before the guards could get off another round, Ikestead flipped the selector to single shot, raised his PPSh-41, and killed the two guards. In his nearly flawless Korean, he told the worker to flee. They immediately began running to the safety of the hills to the west.

When Linka saw Preston and Jung stop and fire at the large supply ship, he nudged Ikestead. They both got up and began strolling toward the small building where a pot of rice was still simmering on the tiny cookstove. Ikestead grabbed the pot, drained the water, and tossed the rice in a small burlap bag.

When Linka looked at him strangely, Ikestead commented, "We might get hungry during our retreat. And rice is nourishing and very filling."

Ikestead and Linka saw Jung and Preston sprinting toward them. As they ran, tracer rounds could be seen flying in all directions—which meant live rounds were among the tracers. Ikestead and Linka quickly raised their submachine guns and began spraying the ammo dump. After he emptied his drum, Linka tossed two grenades and then turned and ran to catch up with the others. As the four agents reached the top of a small knoll, a colossal explosion rocked the docks. The fire on the supply ship had finally ignited the fuel. Another explosion nearly knocked them down as the ammo dump went up.

"Let's get the hell out of here. I don't want to be a casualty of a stray bullet or a mortar round," Linka said.

Looking back at the burning inferno reminded George of one of the poems written by the renowned twelfth-century, poet-priest, Saigyo Hoshi. In the poem, Saigyo describes the paintings of hell that he viewed in an ancient temple.

"Six miles to the junk. Better walk at a good pace, but not too fast. We don't want to draw attention to ourselves. There are still guards posted out here," Jung stated.

"I've still got two drums of ammo. Should I keep the burp gun or ditch it?" Ikestead asked.

"Keep the guns. We may need them yet. Does anyone need ammo?" Preston asked.

Everyone shook their head.

# CHAPTER 40

*Yokohama, Japan*

Tsukuda sat in stunned silence, as he read the message his bodyguard brought him from the communications center located at the back of the large estate. He reread it to make sure he wasn't imagining it. The message was brief, stating that all the freighters and the supply ship were destroyed in what appeared to be an accidental fire. He removed his reading glasses and rubbed his eyes. He hadn't been sleeping well, and just last night, his grandmother, Umeko, visited him in another dream—warning him once again to beware the white samurai.

"Raizo, get hold of our Chinese contact in Tokyo. I want to know whether it was a careless accident—or a deliberate attack on the docks. And if it was an attack, who do they suspect? I can replace the boats, but I cannot tolerate an attack."

Raizo bowed and said, "Yes, General."

"Nozomi," Tsukuda shouted. "Bring me a bowl of rice and vegetables and some hot sake."

Nozomi entered Tsukuda's office, a few minutes later, and set a food tray on a small table near the wall. After she placed a bowl of rice and steamed vegetables in front of the general, she returned with a cup of sake.

Nozomi bowed and asked, "Will there be anything else, General?"

"Yes, when I'm done, bring some wagashi with my tea. I seem to have a sweet tooth today," Tsukuda replied.

As Tsukuda devoured his breakfast, he couldn't help but think that the disaster at Nampho had been orchestrated. *But, by whom?* Tsukuda asked himself. It could be one of the more aggressive yakuza organizations. The Yukako-kai had approached him to take over his trade with the Chinese and Koreans. Stating that they would take all the risks and share a thirty percent split with him. He politely refused, saying that his arms business was not within the parameters of the yakuza's organizational business model. Shipping arms and ammunition was a legal and legitimate commercial enterprise. He wasn't going to share when he could take a hundred percent of the profit.

Tsukuda wasn't worried about the money. Once the ships reached Nampho, he was paid. Fortunately, his freighters and supply ship were insured. The report to the insurance company would state that an accident caused the initial explosion, which led to the destruction of all the berthed ships. Nevertheless, he needed to get to the bottom of this disaster. Since the North Koreans were not at war with the south, he had discarded American or British involvement.

There were several incidents of subversive organizations in North Korea. And it was believed that Kim Il-sung had squashed the movements. But, still, he couldn't get the thought out of his head that a foreign power was behind it. *Of course, I would think that,* Tsukuda thought. *I have been battling them for decades. But, could the Americans or British really be behind the disaster, or am I just paranoid?*

Nozomi returned with the dessert and tea and began removing the other dishes from Tsukuda's desk. As she turned to leave, something fell from her sleeve. Tsukuda reached down and picked it up. It was a flyer for a Kabuki performance.

"Nozomi, you dropped something," Tsukuda said politely.

As he held the leaflet out for her, he froze as he read the title of the play, *Legend of the White Samurai.*

"When is this play?" Tsukuda asked.

"Oh," Nozomi stated in surprise. "I forgot it was still in my sleeve. I believe it will be in December, General. I picked up the flyer at the grocery store, this morning. The grocer said that it was a historical play. Apparently, there were two foreign-born samurai of European descent in the late-1500s. I had never heard of a white samurai in Japan before, so I thought it would be fascinating. I plan to visit my mother in Tokyo and take her to the play."

"I am very interested in the subject, too. Please keep me informed so I may purchase tickets."

"Certainly, General," Nozomi said. She retrieved the flyer, bowed deeply, and left the room with the tray of dishes.

Tsukuda quickly returned to his thought of the Americans and British. Both had very efficient, intelligent organizations. But, could his grandmother's warning have anything to do with the Americans and British? Or was it simply a warning to stay away from the public eye and the Kabuki Theater?

Before Tsukuda could dwell on the problem, Raizo entered the room and bowed. Then, as he handed the message to Tsukuda, he said, "Here is a message from Taro Abe in Havana, General. It's good news."

Tsukuda took the message and dismissed Raizo. He read the contents and smiled. Abe had discovered the source of the gems being shipped to São Paulo and the American Guy Wong. An export company in Manila received gem shipments from Vietnam and forwarded them to São Paulo for grading and cutting. The gems were then shipped to a middle man in Havana who sold them to Wong. Abe had traced the source to a former U.S. Army officer living in Hanoi. The officer had captured the gem market after the war ended.

"Raizo," Tsukuda shouted.

"Yes, General," Raizo said, bowing.

"I want you and Asahi Tanaka to go to Hanoi. Find out as much as you can about this former U.S. Army officer, Yul Butler, and how he operates his gem export business. Once you have all the information, eliminate him, take over the operation and leave Asahi in charge. After that, we won't need to go through the middle man in São Paulo, and we certainly won't need that half-breed Chinaman, Guy Wong. Asahi has a good business mind. Plus, he used to operate in the region and speaks the languages."

Raizo smiled. He was going to get work as a field agent again. He loved the general for his decisiveness. The general was action-oriented. When he ordered his subordinates to do a job, he trusted them to get it done. There was no what-if thinking. No, let's come up with a plan and execute it. Tsukuda had absolute faith in his operatives. He believed in their capabilities. After all, he was responsible for designing their training and ensuring they were the best-trained operatives in the world. And now, after three years of living through the humiliation of Japan's defeat, Raizo would strike the very men who were responsible for Japan's humiliation. They may not be the men at the top, but it would be a victory, nevertheless.


Three days after rendezvousing with the HMS *Storm*, Preston, Linka, Jung, and Ikestead were picked up by a British PBY in the Yellow Sea and then flown directly to Yokota Air Base. After the PBY landed, it taxied inside a large hangar with a small British flag flying on the rooftop. Before the passengers deplaned, the hangar doors were closed. The same untalkative British corporal who picked them up on their first visit to Yokota met them as they stepped from the plane. This time, he was dressed in the uniform of an SAS paratrooper.

"Good day, gentlemen. Brigadier MacKenzie is waiting in the conference room. Jump in, and I'll drive you to the door," the corporal stated.

"Are you really an SAS paratrooper, or do you have numerous uniforms from other services that you switch between?" George Linka asked.

"Yes," the corporal replied as he led them deeper into the British complex.

"Well, Jon, I think we have just met another counterintelligence counterpart within the British Secret Intelligence Service," Linka stated.

"Or, at least one of them," Preston replied. "But he doesn't have the personality of Miles Murphy or Henri Morreau."

"I heard that, Colonel," the corporal replied. "You will find both those charming characters in the Brigadier's office."

"For crying out loud," Linka stated. "He does talk, and he does have a sense of humor in a British sort of way. I think I like him."

"Don't get carried away, Colonel. You haven't met my dark side yet."

"Now, I'm sure I like him, Jon. Can we take him on our next assignment?"

"Only if he speaks fluent Japanese," Jon replied.

The corporal replied, "Watashi wa anata no yanku no o shiri o nihongo o fukumu 4 tsu no gengo de keru koto ga dekimasu."

"Did he just swear at us?" Jon asked.

"No. The corporal said he could kick our yank asses in four languages, including Japanese," George replied laughingly.

"Do you still like him?"

"Definitely."

As they entered Brigadier MacKenzie's conference room, Miles Murphy and Henri Morreau were leaning over a map along with the Brigadier. MacKenzie motioned them over. Preston looked at the map of French Indochina and then at Murphy and Morreau.

"I thought that you all had left Indochina," Preston remarked.

"Henri is in Singapore, and I'm in Hong Kong. But, unfortunately, things are getting nasty in our old stomping grounds in French Indochina, which Uncle Ho wants us to call Vietnam now," Miles Murphy replied.

"How is Yul Butler fairing?"

"Struggling. After René Clairoux and his older brother booked, he moved his operation to Saigon. Butler managed to save René's younger brother's life. After that, however, he's moved back to Hanoi to be closer to gem mines. Or, so he said."

"What's really happening?"

"A Chinese gang was trying to take over his business. We helped him take them down."

"And with the French?"

"The French are getting their asses handed to them every time they go after the Viet Minh. They are trying to fight a conventional land war in a damn jungle. But, of course, the Viet Minh won't play the Frenchies' game. They're using hit-and-run guerrilla warfare tactics—as they had used during the war against the Japanese," Murphy stated.

"How much longer can they hold out?" Linka asked.

"Two, maybe three years." Henri Morreau replied. "It will take a significant defeat before they capitulate."

"Do you think Butler will be safe?"

"So far, Uncle Ho is doing nothing to intimidate the British or the Americans. Regardless, we're staying clear. However, if they go after the French civilians, it might be the tipping point needed to bring you Yanks into the war."

"God, I hope not. I told the Pentagon and the State Department that we should let the Viet Minh take over in 1945," Preston said.

"Did they listen?" Miles asked.

"Only the Pentagon. The State Department is run by a bunch of Ivy League idiots. They think they can rule the world from Washington by swinging a pencil. It's a war that would be unwinnable."

"I don't mean to disturb this conversation, but we just found out that Tsukuda has purchased two dozen more freighters and three large supply ships. Apparently, he plans to double his shipments from China into North Korea," Brigadier MacKenzie interrupted. "His other ships were insured, and because there is no war, the fire on the docks was declared an accident."

"So, he's back in business," Jung stated.

"I have an encrypted message for you, Jon. It's from General Miller. The packet you left in my safe must contain the codebook you need, so you can come with me, collect it, and use my office to decode the message."

When Jon returned to the conference room, he handed the message to George, saying, "It's for you."

George read the message forwarded from Hattori Nozomi and stated, "Tsukuda took the bait."

"Care to explain, Jon, or is this a Top Secret, U.S.-only operation?" Brigadier MacKenzie asked.

"No, it's certainly something we need your help with to take Tsukuda down. One that has presidential authorization, and one for which you received funding already," Jon replied.

"Tsukuda stays in virtual seclusion behind the walls of several large estates in Tokyo, Yokohama, and Tsuchiura. Hardly ever goes out. Yet, he wields tremendous power over politicians and rivals. They come to his estates when he summons them," George stated.

"So, what's your plan to lure him out?" Henri Morreau asked.

An hour later, Jon stopped talking and sat down at the large conference table. Brigadier MacKenzie, Henri Morreau, Miles Murphy, and Kim Jung were astonished but believed it was achievable. They had worked with Jon during the war against Japan and knew he was brilliant at out-of-the-box thinking. And this proved it once again. The proof, however, would be in the execution of the plan. And execution was Preston's strength. And he was the best at what-if thinking, on the fly.

George Linka knew the capabilities of his teammate, Jon Preston. Jon had taught Linka that the places they were going were extremely dangerous and full of wicked men. After the first two missions with Preston in World War Two, Linka realized that he and Jon were the scary guys. George felt they had been terrifying when they had worn the shrunken heads in the jungles of Southeast Asia. The shrunken heads had been given to Preston by a Kachin chieftain.

That knowledge motivated George, which instilled confidence and determination to get better and better at his trade. And the more dangerous and alarming, the better. The purpose of Jon's plan with the Kabuki Theater and the White Samurai play was to create panic in Tsukuda's organization. The key, however, would be the timing at the Kabuki play and the assault on Tsukuda's hideout.

# CHAPTER 41



*Vinh Yen, Vietnam*

On his return from visiting several mining villages along the Red River near Bac Cuong, Yul Butler stopped his bright yellow 1942 Citroën, Type 45 flatbed truck on the side of the road next to a French army post. The post, surrounded by rusting barbed wire, was located on a small hill on Route 6, near a village market, eighteen miles north of Hanoi. Sitting behind the wire, beneath France's tricolor flag waving in the gentle breeze, sat a Vietnamese soldier named Binh Phan.

Binh usually fashioned toy cars from empty butter tins and bottle caps, to sell at the market or give away to the many children who would sit and listen to his tales of battling the Japanese. The middle-aged soldier would point to a long scar on his right leg, which he had received in a Vietnamese partisan unit charge at a place called Marble Mountain. Today, he was singing a sad French love song in his deep baritone voice, encouraging the children to join in.

"They sing pretty well, Binh," Butler said as he squatted next to the man.

"How was your trip north, Yul?" Binh asked.

"It went well. Are you staying safe? I understand there has been some Viet Minh activity hereabouts."

"Just a Viet Minh patrol, six miles to the east. They were ambushed by a French regiment patrolling the Red River. All but one got away. What about you, Yul? Are you staying safe?"

"Of course. Why would you ask?"

"As you traveled through here last week, you were being followed. When you stopped at the market, two men stopped and watched you. When you drove off, they followed."

"Viet Minh?"

"No. Japanese dressed as Vietnamese. They were riding bicycles."

"What makes you think they were Japanese?"

"I recognized one of the men. During the war, he was an intelligence officer. He was one of the Japs who interrogated me after being wounded and captured at Da Nang in January 1944."

"Are you sure he isn't one of the many hundreds of Japs that went over to the Viet Minh after Japan surrendered?"

"Not, this guy. He was a hotshot major when he interrogated me. Then, six months before the war ended, he was promoted to lieutenant colonel and transferred to some spy school in Hiroshima to be a commander of some sort. The Japs had a big going-away party for him at the POW camp. His name was Raizo Hata."

"You don't mean the Nakano Spy School, do you?"

"Yes, that's the name it was called."

Knowing Binh wouldn't take money for giving him information, Yul picked up one of the toy cars, pulled a ten franc note from his pocket, and handed it to him. Yul thanked the soldier and left. As he strode back to the truck, he was wondering why he was being followed—and why by a former Japanese intelligence agent. *I need to contact Jon Preston*, Yul thought. *This could be related to his mission against Tsukuda.*


Jon Preston sat in a comfortable chair, reading the message from Butler. Then, after reading it a second time, he leaned forward and handed it to George Linka. Linka did not like the look on Jon's face.

"What do you know about a Japanese guy named Raizo Hata?" Jon asked.

"Only what Nozomi reported," George replied. "He's Tsukuda's personal bodyguard and head of security."

"That can only mean one thing, George. Tsukuda has information on our involvement in Vietnam. He could also be guessing that we are behind the attacks on his ships, and he wants to strike back at us."

"Well, his thugs did attack Jackie and me in São Paulo. If the attackers that got away were able to identify us, it could tie us to you. And suppose he's guessing that you're behind the gem business. In that case, he's going after Butler to eliminate him, take over his business, and cut out the middle man in Havana."

"And if he's smart enough to figure that out, he may suspect that our team is behind the White Samurai play."

"If he has, Nozomi hasn't heard a thing."

"She was the one who dropped the flier and got Tsukuda interested in the play, George. Tsukuda may suspect her. She could be in danger."

"Nozomi is smart enough to know when to get out, Jon."

"I hope so. I don't want Nozomi to have to go through what Yumiko and Takara had to endure. Death by a thousand cuts is a long, drawn-out, brutal form of torture. It's intended to see how many cuts a person can withstand before dying."

"What are you going to tell Butler?"

"I sent him a message right after I picked this message up at the communications center. I told him that Raizo Hata was there to assassinate him. He'll know what to do if he hasn't figured it out already. I'm betting that Butler already has him in his rifle sight."

"Do we have any assets in place to support him?"

"I sent Brigadier MacKenzie a message asking for support. I assume he will send Henri or Miles to help out. But hell, MacKenzie has been recruiting agents in the area for the last three years. He may have a dozen agents watching out for Yul already."

"I think you're right about Butler. As soon as he sent you that message, he already had a plan."

"Let's hope so. Otherwise, our operation with the sacred sword and Guy Wong's role in Georgetown could be blown to hell. In fact, I want you to send Nozomi a message and warn her of what we suspect."

"Already ahead of you," George replied, handing Jon a handwritten draft.

Nozomi Hattori was choosing more vegetables when the clerk walked through a cloth curtain that hid the back room of the small store and nodded. Nozomi walked to the counter, reached in her purse for money, and waited to pay Mr. Ishida.

"I received a shipment of nagaimo yams this morning, Nozomi. I saved you a dozen," Ishida said.

"Thank you, Mr. Ishida. My master will appreciate these," Nozomi replied.

"I assume you use them as a garnish on soup noodles when they are fresh? But, tell your cook they can be dried and easily stored so they won't go to waste."

"Yes, our master likes them as a garnish with his noodles and stir-fry chicken and vegetables."

Ishida knew from discrete inquiries that General Tsukuda was using the versatile yam to treat dry cough and frequent urination. Moreover, it was apparent the general smoked heavily and drank far too much sake.

Nozomi paid, walked to a shelf containing canned goods, and then paused. Inside the bag of yams was a message written on thin rice paper. After reading the note, Nozomi put it in her mouth, chewed, swallowed, and left the shop. She was worried. It had obviously been a mistake to drop the Kabuki play flier in front of Tsukuda. She had to make a decision. *Stay or leave. Your decision, Nozomi,* she said to herself as she walked back to the only remaining eighteenth-century shiro in Yokohama constructed during the Edo period.

It should be a museum, Nozomi reflected as she walked through the back entrance. One of the guards she liked smiled and nodded. She smiled back at him and went through the door into the kitchen. After she set the burlap bags filled with vegetables on the counter, she walked to her room. She heard a sharp thump as she moved the sliding doors open. Nozomi froze. A guard was searching the room.

"What are you doing, Fuji?" Nozomi asked cautiously.

"Weekly search. I usually finish before you come back from the market," Fuji replied.

"How long has this been going on?

"Ever since I became the chief of security for the general, Nozomi. I thought you knew?"

"No, I didn't."

"I apologize, Nozomi. I must have startled you."

"Yes, well, I should have expected it. After all, I do work for a retired general."

"Yes, ma'am," Fuji replied. "It goes with the territory."

"If there is anything you need from me, just ask. I have to be getting back to work," Nozomi said, ending the conversation by grabbing her notebook.

As Nozomi walked from the room, her heart was racing. *I really need to leave. But if I do, it might compromise Colonel Preston's mission. So I will need to be much more careful. Next time I go to the market, I will request a new way to communicate. I should also accept Director Yano's employment offer. That would give me a good reason to leave,* Nozomi thought.

# CHAPTER 42

*Yokota Air Base, Japan*

Brigadier Michael MacKenzie handed a folder with the latest intercepts from Vietnam to his new deputy director, Lieutenant Colonel Jim Ballangy. Ballangy, a seasoned intelligence agent who had worked in China, Burma, India, and most of Southeast Asia during the war, was worried. A Japanese team was stalking Yul Butler, which might compromise one of Mackenzie's agents, Binh Phan. Phan wanted to take the Japs out.

"Binh wants revenge from the interrogations and torture that Raizo Hata was responsible for when Binh was a prisoner," Brigadier MacKenzie stated.

Ballangy remained quiet, acting like he was thinking. He knew to let the general talk when he was worried. The brigadier was concerned about Butler as much as Phan. He knew he needed to help Butler, not only because of their friendship but because this Jap could jeopardize three years of recruiting and undercover work.

"What wetwork asset do we have in place that can take Raizo and the other Jap out quietly?" MacKenzie asked, using the Russian criminal slang term for assassination.

"Just one—Albert Collins. Eleven agents have already been shifted to our counterinsurgency campaign in Malaya, sir. Collins is scheduled to depart for Singapore in two weeks," Ballangy replied.

"Put him on this problem. But warn him that Raizo is extremely dangerous."

"Shouldn't be a problem, sir. Collins has been in Southeast Asia since he was a young lad. He fits right in. Plus, he is half Japanese and was born in Japan. He moved to Hanoi in 1940 when his father was transferred there with Shell Oil. He speaks French, Japanese, Mandarin, Thai, and nearly every dialect of Vietnamese."

"I need this done quickly and quietly. And I need Collins in Malaya on schedule before this Malayan Emergency gets out of hand. Our tin mines and rubber plantations are getting attacked by communist guerrillas. My tail is on the line to search out their leaders and eliminate them, and Collins is the best we have to get the job done."

"I'll get the instructions to him immediately, sir. Should I tell Binh to stand down?"

"No, tell him to be cautious. Only intervene if Butler is in imminent danger."

"Do you want me to inform Colonel Preston of our plans? I can go see him this evening."

"Won't be necessary, Jim. We're having lunch with him, George, and General Miller tomorrow."

"I wasn't aware that Miller was in town?"

"General Renick sent me a message thirty minutes ago. Miller lands at midnight. He's on a covert fact-finding mission for President Truman, on the Korean situation. Even General MacArthur is unaware, and they want to keep it that way."

"Will I be meeting him at the plane?"

"No, I've asked Major Bayless to meet him in one of our medium Lorries. Miller will be dressed as an Air Force Master Sergeant named Smith. Have Bayless take him directly to our off-base bungalow, and make sure he takes a paratrooper uniform for the general to change into on the way. I've already alerted our security team."

"You suspect that MacArthur has placed spies on our base?"

"You know my motto, Jim."

"Yes, sir. Trust no one. Suspect everyone."

"That's right. And General MacArthur's chief of intelligence, Major General Willoughby, has spies everywhere. Willoughby doesn't trust the Major General Partridge to play his game or go along with MacArthur's view that the Chinese will not start a war in Korea. Especially since Partridge has his own intelligence sources telling him a different story."

"I still don't know how the U.S. can ignore what is going on at the Yalu River and in Nampho."

"Well, it's a good thing Jon Preston is involved. He has direct access to President Truman because of the General Tsukuda thing. Plus, Truman is Jon Junior's godfather. And now that we know for certain that Tsukuda is smuggling arms and munitions into North Korea, President Truman will know the truth. But, unfortunately, he can't fire MacArthur without causing a lot of political turmoil in Washington."

"At least he knows the truth."

"Yes, but without truthful estimates of what is going on in North Korea from MacArthur, Truman won't be able to get additional funding for troops and equipment. Hell, Willoughby's even got the CIA bamboozled. They believe everything he tells them."

General Renick sat on a sofa next to General Omar Bradley, facing President Truman, pacing back and forth in front of his desk. Renick had just briefed the president on the latest situation involving Uchito Tsukuda and shipping arms to North Korea.

"Dammit, Omar. Why is General MacArthur refusing to believe North Korea is amassing troops and munitions?"

"I'm certain that General Willoughby knows the true picture, sir. It's just that Willoughby is succumbing to MacArthur's political belief. MacArthur desperately wants to believe that China will not enter into a war against South Korea. Therefore, he believes if he says so publically, it will keep the Chinese and North Koreans at bay," General Bradley replied.

"Do you believe that?"

"No, sir. I believe the intelligence that Colonel Preston's team has gathered in cooperation with the British SIS."

"General Bradley, how many more troops can we get into Japan?"

"We're at our maximum strength now, sir. MacArthur won't request additional troops because it would be upsetting to the Japanese. Furthermore, I don't have a budget to move a division to the Philippines to get our forces closer should a conflict arise. I talked with the budget committee chairman eight weeks ago about sending two divisions to Manila, and he laughed in my face. He said that nation-building was not a priority."

"General Renick, it looks like we will have to put onto your shoulders the responsibility of stopping more arms shipments into North Korea. Tell Colonel Preston to take Tsukuda out! Take all of his ships out! And he has to do it without getting us into a war with China and pissing off the Japanese when Tsukuda is dead. If anything, it should look like he had an accident or died of a heart attack."


Jon Preston was not surprised by the request that came through General Renick from the president. The political situation in Washington was all nationalistic —keeping America first—and he understood it. Politicians didn't want to hear of another threat of war. The U.S. had lost four hundred and twenty thousand soldiers in the war that ended in 1945. The American public wanted peace and prosperity. They don't like sending their sons off to be killed in another foreign country.

"Well, do we go after the ships, first—or Tsukuda?" George asked.

"The ships. It will put more strain and stress on Tsukuda and make his organization look weak," Jon replied.

"You're hoping one of the stronger yakuza organizations will go after Tsukuda. But, the yakuza has a code of not deliberately starting a war with another yakuza organization."

"Yes, but Tsukuda is not yakuza. His organization is an independent intelligence-gathering source. Political and industrial espionage. He's an opportunist. And he's doing things the yakuza would never attempt by involving himself in international politics."

"Eventually, the yakuza will see that war is all about money and opportunity, Jon. So they will change their code to match the times," Brigadier MacKenzie stated.

"We will need to plan this carefully. I think it would be best to stage an accident at the Chinese ports where the ships are being loaded," Preston stated.

"That will require Chinese resources that we don't have, Jon," General Miller replied.

"Guy Wong had a network of agents near Harbin during the war. Maybe we can get them to sabotage the trains that are shipping the arms to the coast. That could slow the process," Ballangy stated.

"That would also alert them to our plans," Preston responded. "If we are going to hit a Chinese port, we cannot give them any indication that we might be coming. So it has to be a total surprise."

"Why not do both?" General Miller asked.

"Right now, the communists believe we are toothless. MacArthur is acting like we will do nothing. He doesn't want a war, and he wants the Chinese to believe it. That means they will be unprepared. They won't be guarding the docks with several regiments of troops. They won't be inept, but they might be lax in their security. And that is an opportunity for us."

"I assume you are suggesting a team of my Korean agents?" Captain Kim asked.

"That and as many Chinese agents we can muster," Preston countered.

"And that also means you will need the Royal Navy to get them there," Ballangy acknowledged.

"Well, gents," Brigadier MacKenzie said. "We need to get this planned before the winter storms hit the Yellow Sea. That means we need this mission to hit the docks in six weeks. So, let's get cracking."

# CHAPTER 43

*Yellow Sea*

The 217-foot HMS *Storm* plowed through a squall, ten miles southeast of Ershan Island. It was 2300 hours, and Captain Mercer was on the bridge conning the submarine. There were two lookouts above him—one on the radio loop tower, and another on the radar antenna tower. Two more stood on the bridge on either side of Mercer, scanning the surface ahead and behind with their night vision binoculars. Despite being clothed in rain gear over his royal navy deck jacket, Mercer was shivering from the cold wind and the rain that drenched his clothing.

Ershan Island was the northernmost of three islands belonging to the Qiansan Island chain, located six miles due east of the port city of Dalian near the southern tip of China's Liaoning Province. Before the communists took over, it was called Port Arthur.

Mercer picked up the handset and called to the conn, "Sonar, report."

"Single contacts, two screws, sir," the sonarman reported.

"Radar, two sweeps."

"Single boat, ten thousand meters, bearing 300 degrees, Skipper."

"XO, have the teams get ready. We're thirty minutes out. I want them off as soon as we rendezvous with the fishing boat."

"Aye, aye, Skipper," Lieutenant Commander Carpenter replied.

Captain Kim and ten men were ready. The dozen waterproof bags were filled with explosives. Their thirty-three-inch, Soviet PPSh-41 submachine gun had four extra 71-round drum magazines. Although the gun had been modified with a German-made suppressor, Kim didn't want to take the submachine guns. However, Jon

Preston insisted, just in case they were discovered while entering or leaving the docks. Kim agreed but decided he would leave them on the fishing boat after they got close to their departure point. They were too much extra weight and would be hard to cover up while dressed as a Chinese dock worker. The Tokarev TT33 semiautomatic pistols they carried would be enough. A special branch with U.S. Army counterintelligence had fitted it with a suppressor—a modification of a suppressor designed in 1936 by Hiram Maxim. The subsonic-speed, 9 mm, Parabellum cartridges they developed were good at further reducing noise while retaining accuracy, range, and effectiveness.

"I can come with you if you want," Preston said.

"No, Jon, you would be a liability. This isn't rural Korea, where you can escape into the darkness and make your way across a deserted countryside. This is a Chinese city, and you would stick out like a sore thumb, as you Americans say."

"But, I've been here before. At the end of the war, I spent three months in Port Arthur securing the gold and treasures the Japanese hid in the hills and at the Catholic mission. So, I know these docks," Preston argued.

"Yes, but these people are living under communism now. They live in fear. They won't protect you, and they sure as hell won't help you escape should we be discovered. You'll do more good here on the sub if things go awry."

Jon felt guilty for not being able to go, but he knew Kim was right. If anything did go wrong, which was highly likely, he could advise Captain Mercer on what needed to be done to rescue the team. On the other hand, Preston knew Mercer would not jeopardize his boat and men if the Chinese launched destroyers or PT boats. If that happened, Kim was on his own, because this mission did not involve U.S. or British forces—which was why a fishing boat was anchored off the isthmus that connected Ershan and Dashan Island.

The 96-foot boat was an old Japanese, No.1-class, auxiliary patrol boat. It had been purchased by a private firm in 1946 and converted to a fishing trawler. The firm outfitted it with the latest navigation and radio electronics, as well as SJ radar, to provide directional and highly accurate distance information on surface contacts and low-flying aircraft. The SJ radar was the standard system used on British and American submarines during the Second World War. Its hull and superstructure had been painted blue-grey to blend in with the waters of the Yellow Sea. Its propulsion system had been modified from a single-shaft, 400-horsepower engine, to duel 400-horsepower engines with two screws, which could power the boat to 18 knots. On the stern, a red flag with a single yellow star waved in the stiff breeze.

Fifteen Chinese men operated the boat. They were the first group of expatriates that fled to Taipei when the communist forces of Mao Zedong took firm control of northern China. Many of the men had formerly worked as Allied agents under Guy Wong—when he had operated out of Harbin. All had lost family members during the communist takeover. For now, they were in the employ of U.S. Army counterintelligence under the command of Jonathan Preston. Preston had worked with most of the men when he had run an operation in Harbin in 1945. They trusted Preston because they trusted their cousin Guy Wong, who was in Taipei when they had sailed north.

The twelve-hundred-mile trip had taken six days. For the last week, they had been fishing thirty miles southeast of Ershan Island. The boat had been stopped once by a Chinese gunboat. Still, after seeing the makeshift communist flag and talking with Captain Fang Wong—who said they were out of Dongwanggou—the gunboat captain let them go. The communists may have taken over northern China, but they had no official document system. That wouldn't come until late 1949.

Earlier that afternoon, Captain Wong's boat anchored on the seaward side of the isthmus. The captain and the crewmen, who were sleeping, were awakened when the second mate fired up the engines at 2200 hours. They had been motoring south-southeast at six knots for an hour when the crewman manning the radar yelled, "Contact, Captain."

Captain Mercer flipped the power switch to 'on,' on his signal lamp, which had a red cover over the lens. He flashed a Morse code signal and then received the correct reply from the trawler.

"Positive ID on the fishing boat," Mercer said into the handset. "Get the men moving."

"Forward hatch is open, and agents are proceeding to the deck, Skipper," the COB replied.

As the fishing boat pulled alongside the HMS *Storm*, sailors tossed lines to the fishing boat. Once the explosives, equipment bags, and eleven men were aboard, the sailors aboard the fishing boat threw the ropes back to the submarine and saluted. Captain Wong then ordered the boat to twelve knots and drove into the darkness.

The *Storm* turned northeast, and the XO relieved the captain on the bridge. She remained on the surface for another four hours. Finally, forty minutes before the sunrise, the XO gave the command to submerge the boat.

At 0200 hours, the fishing trawler came to a halt—two miles east of Port Arthur. Five small flat-bottomed boats with pointed bows and square sterns were lowered into the water. Each boat was powered by a small outboard motor with a muffled engine. Two men entered the skiffs. Captain Kim joined two of his men in the last boat.

The first boat pulled under the pier on the southwest side at 0220 hours and then moored to one of the pilings. The other boats each took a dock where one or two of Tsukuda's freighters were moored. They were easily recognized because of the gold swallowtail butterfly kamon painted on either side of the bow of each boat. One man stayed with the boat while the other would board the freighter. They had forty minutes to get on the ships, place their charges, and get back to their boats. Captain Kim found a nearby dock crane, climbed into the control cockpit, which was twenty feet above the dock, and kept a lookout with his suppressed sniper rifle.

The freighters had only one revolving guard, which the attackers successfully avoided. After they got onto a freighter, the black-clad men would place their charges and set the timers. One hundred and eighty minutes later, after they were back on the trawler and well into the international waters of the Yellow Sea, the small incendiary charge would ignite the ammunition and barrels of fuel. The ensuing explosions and fires would hopefully damage the docks and delay further shipments to North Korea.

As Kim watched his men board the freighters, he noticed movement in the wheelhouse of the tanker. He raised his rifle and saw through his Kassel, '4 x 81' magnification scope that the captain and three men were in the wheelhouse. As he continued to watch, he heard a low rumble of a diesel engine starting and then noticed that grey smoke was beginning to roll upward from the single stack. *Crap, she's preparing to get underway*, Kim thought. Unfortunately, without any way to contact his man on the freighter, Kim would have to rely on the agent's instincts.

Five minutes later, Kim saw his agent exit a hatch on the starboard side of the ship. Before he could make his way down the side into the water, a roving guard confronted the agent. Kim noticed an animated conversation between his agent and the guard. Kim was about to shoot when his agent grabbed the guard, and both went over the ship's side into the water.

When forty minutes had elapsed, Kim made his way down the ladder and returned to his boat. The guard he had watched was already there. The agent who had remained in the boat was treating a knife wound to his left shoulder.

"Time to leave. Take us out to a hundred yards, and we'll cover the withdrawal," Kim ordered.

# CHAPTER 44

*Washington, D.C.*

Lieutenant General Jon Renick sat across the table from General Omar Bradley, as Major General Lew Miller gave a comprehensive briefing on the raid at Port Arthur. According to Miller, it was a total success, and Tsukuda was put out of business again.

"Brigadier MacKenzie provided a detailed report on the damage at Port Arthur. The tanker and four of the five freighters were destroyed. However, there was minimal damage to the Chinese docks. Colonel Preston believes there could have been a timer failure on the freighter that survived, or a crew member could have found the explosive and dumped it overboard. Regardless, it has put Tsukuda out of business for the time being," Miller concluded.

"Do we have any information on the reaction from the Chinese?" General Collins asked.

"Dong Biwu, the representative for Communist China in North Korea, filed a protest at the British and American Consolate in Tokyo demanding that Great Britain and the U.S. cease attacking China. Naturally, the British and our representative denied any involvement."

"Have we heard anything from the Japanese?" General Bradley queried.

"Nothing, yet, sir. If we do, it will probably come as an informal request through our consulate or the British consulate," General Renick replied. "They like to use a junior member of their Finance Ministry, Kenta Wanatabe, as a go-between on delicate matters. He's been on several Japanese delegations that visited the U.S. over the last three years. He was responsible for negotiating the long-term lease of several Japanese military installations to the U.S Navy and Air Force."

"What about MacArthur?" Collins questioned.

"Douglas has been exceptionally quiet so far," General Bradley replied. "Then again, he doesn't usually consult with me on anything. MacArthur thinks that the fifth star on his shoulder gives him immunity from orders or from having to report to anyone but the President. He believes he is totally autonomous in his Japanese kingdom."

"And we've heard nothing from General Willoughby in his weekly intelligence updates," Renick stated. "It's as if they haven't heard of the disaster in Port Arthur."

"No, he's ignoring it because it doesn't fit MacArthur's agenda. As foolish as it seems, Douglas MacArthur still believes that China will not help North Korea attack South Korea. By the way, you and Lew are briefing President Truman tomorrow morning before his cabinet meeting. He'll want updates on the operatives you've recruited and trained as well as Preston's next actions. We'll drive over in my car at 0700. I'll pick you up at your quarters," General Bradley stated as he rose from his chair, effectively ending the meeting.


Jonathan Preston was relaxing in the temporary office at the British SIS facility on Yokota Air Force Base. He was drinking a cup of coffee with George Linka and discussing Operation White Samurai—when there was a knock on his office door.

"Enter," Preston replied.

"Sorry to disturb you, Colonel, but General Partridge wishes to see you and Colonel Linka ASAP," Major Bayless said.

"Any idea what this is about, Scott? Preston asked.

"Not a clue, but the general is upset about something."

"Alright, we'll be there in five minutes."

As they were ushered into the general's office, Partridge was shouting through the handset of his phone, "Dammit, MacKenzie, if this is your doing, I want to know how this leaked out. General

Willoughby says it's on the front page of the Yomiuri Shimbun—one of the major newspapers in Tokyo."

As he hung up the phone, Partridge said, "I guess you can figure out what that was about. Today's lead story is about an American-led sabotage mission into Port Arthur. So, you don't have to guess why you are here, do you? I'm catching hell from General Willoughby, who thinks I let a covert mission be staged from my base."

"It's probably a story planted by General Tsukuda, sir. He obviously suspects the U.S. involvement and specifically my team because we have been battling each other for the last five years. And we have recent history. Four months ago, his men attacked my agents in Brazil and Georgetown. When we got the chance, my team and the Coast Guard, in Washington, D.C., and Baltimore, took out his entire east-coast operation. We captured two dozen Japanese operatives, killed a dozen more, and confiscated four boats filled with arms, ammunition, and a half-ton of gold bullion. So he's pissed at my team and me. And now he wants to put the blame on the U.S. Army."

"Well, he's doing a damn good job of it. General Willoughby just ordered me to Tokyo to brief General MacArthur tomorrow afternoon. He wants to know where the missions to North Korea and China were staged from, who authorized them, and who led the missions."

"As I recall, General Hoyt Vandenberg is your boss—not General Douglas MacArthur. Therefore, I suggest you tell General Willoughby that you are respectfully denying his request."

"I already did that, Colonel Preston. Plus, I've sent a message informing General Vandenberg. I'm sure he will communicate with General Bradley, as well as your friends, General Renick and Miller."

"That makes sense. Just so you understand, what I am doing is totally Top Secret and off the books. My missions are authorized by President Truman under Executive Order EO480602. Neither you nor General MacArthur has a high enough clearance to access. So, everything in that newspaper is pure speculation, General. It is designed to make America look like a nation-building bully."

"It's still got my dander up, Colonel."

"You knew this might happen when we came to you, asking for cooperation from Captain Ikestead. Your chief of staff was briefed by General Bradley ahead of time. So I wouldn't worry about MacArthur and Willoughby. I would, however, worry about what General Tsukuda is going to do next— because he apparently has placed spies on your base."

"What are you suggesting?"

"Three things, General. First, double security immediately. Second, have your base information officer draft a press release to give to the American and foreign press when they come calling. But, first, get General Vandenberg's approval on the press release. Both will make you look like you've got things under firm control, which will ease General Vandenberg's mind, as well as the President's, considerably."

"And the third?"

"Support us when we ask, deny knowledge of everything asked about a covert mission and our presence on your base, and stay out of our way. We are going to put an end to General Tsukuda and his criminal organization in ninety days."

"You don't leave me much choice, Colonel. And I was going to do those things anyway. It's not every day we get to take down a bad guy. So, I suggest you secretly have Major Bayless transferred to your team and read him in on the mission. He will still have my full cooperation and access to base resources. I just need deniability of what you are doing. So, tell me nothing.


After General Miller concluded his presentation, President Truman stood up and paced the Oval Office. He looked at General Miller and asked, "Are you aware of the front-page headline in one of the major Japanese newspapers in Tokyo, accusing the U.S. of attacking China and North Korea?"

"Yes, Mr. President. I received a heads-up message early this morning from Colonel Preston. He suspects that General Tsukuda planted the story," General Miller replied.

"Well, this is not the kind of publicity I need, General. I had a call from the House Majority Leader before you got here. He stated that the Republicans in Congress are starting to request information on covert military activity from the intelligence committee. Therefore, I suggest that you take this criminal down as quickly as possible before more arms make their way into North Korea and before Tsukuda manages to damage my foreign policy in Japan."

"According to Colonel Preston, the problem will be resolved within ninety days, Mr. President," Renick replied.

As the three generals walked from the Oval Office to their staff car, General Bradley said, "Make sure Colonel Preston follows through on his promise, gentlemen. He and Colonel Linka are on my radar to become flag officers before retiring at the end of next year. We need men like them to prepare our intelligence corps for this next war and what's happening in Southeast Asia. I also want two hundred more counterintelligence agents trained by next summer—which means those three badass ladies of yours are going to be very busy."

"Don't worry, sir. Those ladies are on top of it. We expect fifty agents will be fully trained by the end of October. The next class will have close to 300 recruits. We are winding up the negotiations with Admiral Whitley, to put a training facility at Subic Bay in the Philippines. We have been working with British SIS and are screening over four hundred applicants from Taiwan, Thailand, Cambodia, Laos, Burma, French Indochina, and Malaya. Twenty of the agents who will graduate in October will be the initial cadre of instructors."

"Well, done. Just make certain that Jon and George have the support they need to end the Tsukuda problem."

"Yes, sir," Renick and Miller said in unison.

# CHAPTER 45



*Yokota Air Base, Japan*

After reviewing the latest information provided by Nozomi Hattori, George Linka began to have doubts about the Kabuki theater operation and attacking Tsukuda at his residence. Tsukuda had tripled the number of guards at his four estates and increased his bodyguard detail to ten. As a result, Linka calculated that they would need an additional thirty agents to pull off the operation.

"George's information matches ours. You can't pull off the operation with only a dozen agents. You are outnumbered ten to one. You will need to come up with another plan," Brigadier MacKenzie stated.

"I was thinking the same thing, sir," Preston replied.

"Tsukuda has to have other vulnerabilities that we can exploit, but I haven't found any yet. Has your agent provided a schedule of his comings and goings over the next couple of weeks?"

"Tsukuda has clamped down on information across the board. So, Nozomi doesn't find out what he will be doing until fifteen minutes before he leaves his estate—when his car is brought to the front door. And even then, she isn't told where he is heading," Linka replied.

"What about his dealings with politicians and the various Japanese ministries? We know he has numerous shipping contracts with the Japanese government. Surely he has to visit their offices?" Preston asked.

"Our only sources in the Japanese government are Minister Masao Yano and Kenta Wanatabe," MacKenzie said. "Our other source was a high-ranking attorney in government, who was contracting within the Ministry of Commerce and Industry. But he had a heart attack and passed, last month."

"I may be able to get some information from an old friend," George said, "one whom I haven't seen since December of 1945."

"One of your father's United Brethren parishioners?" MacKenzie asked.

"No, sir. A man named Morihei Ueshiba. He founded the Japanese martial art of Aikikai. When my father pastored the United Brethren Church in Tokyo, he enrolled me in martial arts training at the Aikikai Hombu School. I was six years old."

"Is he reliable?"

"Yes, sir. After I graduated high school and went to college in the U.S., we corresponded monthly. Ueshiba began warning me of the Japanese military's movement toward blind nationalism and racist contempt for outsiders. He traveled extensively in China in 1940. He saw what was happening during his visits to Kenkoku University in Manchuria. He was invited to teach his martial art. The Japanese military was turning into merciless brutes, killing captured civilians and military prisoners."

"Does he have contacts in the Japanese government?"

"Yes, Ueshiba still teaches most of the children of high-ranking ministers and directors. He's become the most sought-after martial arts instructor in Japan. Ueshiba has always believed his martial art was not just about physical fighting. He believed the power and grace of Aikikai could be used to prevent violent actions and not hurt anyone. Before the war, he taught that taking a human life should be avoided as much as possible, even in war. He preached that it was a sin to kill and that you should give your enemy every opportunity to surrender and make peace. That's why, in 1941—when Japan pursued a course of military dominance—he retired and moved to a small country town."

"I'm surprised the Japanese military didn't arrest him and throw him in prison."

"He had well-established relationships in the Japanese government. He was an instructor to members of the Emperor's family, cabinet ministers, and most of the top military officers. Ueshiba's art was taught in dojos throughout Japan during the 1920s and 1930s. Despite his unorthodox beliefs, he was later recruited to teach his martial arts at the Imperial Japanese Army Academy and Nakano Spy School. He probably taught Asami Nakada and her sisters while in grade school and later at Nakano."

"That's quite a résumé. Ueshiba taught you well, George."

"He is a great instructor. He was schooled in jujutsu, judo, sumo, swordsmanship, spear, knives, and staff, before developing his martial art style of Aikikai. So I was well prepared when I did my OSS training in Ceylon under Major Bill Fairbairn and Sergeant Raymond Westerling. Fairbairn's "win at all costs" hand-to-hand combat methods helped keep me alive during the war."

"Maybe he can help us. Can you and Jon go visit him today or tomorrow?"

"I will have to go by myself, Brigadier. Two Europeans would raise concerns, and Tsukuda has spies everywhere. Word would eventually get back to him. With our OSS theatrical kit, I can disguise myself to look Eurasian. Plus, I speak the Shitamachi dialect of Japanese, a working-class dialect. I'll fit right in and go unnoticed."

"While George visits Morihei Ueshiba, I'm going to go talk to Captain Ikestead. He's been in Japan since the war ended. So if he has an established network of spies in Korea, he most likely has a network in Japan also," Jon stated.

After George left, Jon stayed in the chair across from Brigadier MacKenzie with a faraway look on his face. MacKenzie knew that look. Jon was in deep thought, so he waited until his expression returned to normal.

"What's on your mind, Jon?"

"We need extra men to take on Tsukuda. We need experts in stealth, and men who are extremely violent—not just any run-of-the-mill soldiers. So, are you still in contact with the group of Lin Kuei warriors we used at Tsuchiura Naval Air Base?"

At first, MacKenzie looked disturbed. Then, after reflecting, he said, "Yes, there are six platoons of Lin Kuei warriors in Hong Kong and four platoons in Singapore. But they are so violent that

I use them mostly for the consulate and special detail security for high-ranking military and government officials."

"In that case, I'm requesting that you bring in three of those platoons to Tokyo, sir. I'll see that you are compensated for the transportation and their services. They would give us the edge we need against Tsukuda's thugs."

The Lin Kuei warriors are not welcome in Japan, Jon. They are a clan of ninjas that the Japanese aristocrats considered outcasts, once they moved from Japan to Hong Kong in the late 1500s. Shortly afterward, the warlord Oda Nobunaga attacked and tried to eradicate them."

"Yes, but they are still Japanese. The Lin Kuei did not intermarry with the Chinese, at least not all of them. They speak multiple languages, sir. If they keep their mouths shut, they will be indistinguishable from most Japanese. They are trained in disguise, concealment, explosives, escape, poisons, hand-to-hand combat, and most forms of weaponry, including swords. It would be a group of warriors worthy of the leadership of the White Samurai."

Brigadier MacKenzie's eyes lighted up, and a smile emerged across his thin lips, "You plan on using them as actors in your Kabuki play. Outstanding! Won't that surprise the hell out of General Tsukuda? Are you sure you need only three platoons?"

"I'll take more if you can spare them, sir."

"I'll have four platoons flown over by the end of next week. That will give me time to get their quarters arranged on base and large tents erected for a— let's say, a combined SIS/U.S. Army martial arts training class."

"I'll arrange for forty extra Samurai costumes with the Kabuki theater company. Thanks, Brigadier. This will give us an added element of surprise."


It took George Linka two hours and five bus changes to reach East Shinjuku, where the Aikikai Hombu School was established in an old one-story commercial building that had survived the bombing of World War Two. George walked four blocks from the bus stop and reached the school at 5 p.m., as students were arriving for class.

When George walked through the door, he scanned the dojo. He instantly recognized the sixty-nine-year-old martial arts teacher, the son of a landowner near Osaka, 250 miles southeast of Tokyo. The white-headed teacher had the same goatee that George had remembered. It was neatly trimmed and hung down three inches below his chin.

When Ueshiba noticed the newcomer, his keen eyes locked momentarily with George's. An instant later, Ueshiba's eyes widened with recognition. He walked briskly across the floor to greet his old friend. When he came to George, Ueshiba embraced him with a bear hug.

"O'Sensei," George said as he clung tightly to his longtime friend.

"Joji, it has been nearly three years. You look well. But I take it this visit is rather clandestine. Let's go to my office," Ueshiba said, pulling George along by his arm.

Ueshiba closed the door and offered George a cushion on the sparsely furnished office floor. When they were seated, Ueshiba stroked his beard and said, "Talk in English, Joji. No one here speaks it. I take it you need some help with your enemy, General Tsukuda?"

"Yes, O'Sensei. It's rather urgent; otherwise, I wouldn't bother you."

"I heard that he was transporting arms and ammunition into North Korea. I also read in the paper last week that many of his ships were destroyed in Port Arthur. Is that what this is about?"

George nodded. My team has been tasked to take Tsukuda down and try to stop a war. Unfortunately, he is more powerful than he was a three years ago. It is difficult to determine his location and movements. I thought that you might be able to provide some insights."

"General Tsukuda has a first-rate criminal organization. He has very quietly won over several high-ranking politicians to his side with his commercial enterprises. Apparently, gold bullion entices officials to look the other way, and Tsukuda, I hear, has plenty of gold to spread around."

"We estimate he got away with over thirty tons during the war."

"He's a bad person, Joji. What he is doing in North Korea will be responsible for the deaths of hundreds of thousands of innocent people. So, yes, I will do what I can to help. Just promise me that you will at least try to capture him and put him in prison."

"I will try, O'Sensei, but I cannot promise. He is extremely violent. And he has over sixty armed thugs working for him. However, I will tell you that we are tasked to do this quietly and efficiently. No one must know of our involvement. It needs to look like one of the Yakuza clans has taken him down."

"I have been invited to a dinner tomorrow evening that Naruhiko Kinmochi is hosting. He's the new Deputy Chief Cabinet Secretary and a member of the lower house of the National Diet. I was going to decline the invitation, but now I must go. Tsukuda may attend. There is a rumor that he had a hand in Kinmochi's ascent. He will no doubt remember me from the Nakano Spy School, so I will make a point to say hello."

"I am grateful for your help, O'Sensei."

"I will mingle and listen, Joji. The sake usually flows heavily at these parties, and people talk freely. Is there anything specific I should listen for?"

"It would be helpful to know who he is meeting over the next few days and weeks, and where he is traveling. The more information, the better. Unfortunately, for my team to remain unnoticed, we have to be very flexible and invisible—which, as you know, is hard for a European to do in Japan."

"Your disguise is rather ingenious. Except for your eyes, I almost didn't recognize you. You have learned your craft well, Joji. Just be careful. Tsukuda has some thugs who are well-trained in martial arts. Not as good as you, but still formidable."

As George got up to leave, he hugged his teacher. "I will come back in three days, O'Sensei."

# CHAPTER 46

*Tokyo, Japan*

Uchito Tsukuda stood pacing his office in his elegant estate in a northeast section of Tokyo. He had just finished a dinner of mackerel marinated in rice vinegar, rice, sweet potatoes, sweet-and-sour squid, and plenty of his private estate's sake. As usual, Tsukuda was silent during most of the meal. His guest, Nobutake Kojima, a former admiral in the Japanese Imperial Navy and commander of the 2nd Fleet, had just paid him a compliment on the wine.

"It's from my uncle's estate and brewery, north of Tokyo. It's the finest sake in Japan," Tsukuda mentioned.

"Did I hear correctly at the minister's party that you had purchased your uncle's estate, Uchito?" Kojima asked.

"Yes, earlier this year. My uncle is getting on in years; he's 87. I am his favorite nephew, and I have always loved the estate, so he made me an offer I couldn't refuse. Although, I would have gladly paid twice as much as he had asked."

"You didn't invite me here for small talk, Uchito. We are good enough friends to get straight to the point. What do you need from me?"

"As you know, I lost a few freighters and tankers, recently. I need to replace those ships, and I want to put armaments on them, discretely, of course. Something like the German raiders did during the war."

"So you want me to be your intermediary in purchasing a dozen ships and find a shipyard that will discretely install the armaments. What kind of weapons do you have in mind?"

"On each ship, I want six fifty-caliber machine guns, two sets of tube-launched torpedoes, K-gun-type depth-charge projectors, and a sonar detector for each ship."

"Crap, Uchito, are you planning to go to war?"

"Something like that. I'm convinced the Americans and British are sabotaging my ships. The only way the saboteurs can be inserted is by submarine. So I want to make certain that they cannot attack my ships directly again without reprisal. Plus, we'll need to register the ships in a neutral country; otherwise, I will violate the formal peace treaty and alliance. With your contacts, this should be a simple task."

"Even with my influence, no shipyard in Japan will touch it, Uchito. However, I have contacts in Vietnam, Malaya, and the Philippines who can do this, but it will not be cheap. Finding fifty-caliber machine guns won't be a problem. There is plenty of surplus for sale. The tube-launched torpedoes and K-gun depth-charge projectors will be more difficult but not impossible. The U.S. Navy has several dozen destroyers and destroyer escorts in storage in the Philippines and Liberty freighters. Stuff disappears off them all the time."

"How much?"

"At least 100 thousand American dollars per ship, for the armaments, and another $10 thousand for installation. The freighters and tankers will cost around $400 thousand each, which is cheap considering they cost $2 million to build. Moreover, because of the Merchant Ship Sales Act of 1946, I can purchase them from the U.S. government through my business in Manila; they have hundreds stored near Subic Bay."

"What kind of commission do you want?"

"Twenty percent. I will have to bribe a great number of officials to get this done quickly."

"I'll have one of my bodyguards deliver the name of my banker, at the Philippine Central Bank in Manila, by noon Friday. Do you have an account there?"

"Yes. But are you sure you want to go ahead with arming the ships, Uchito? This could end up coming back on you in a horrible way."

"I'm certain, Admiral. I can stay well-hidden in Japan. I only go out for a few special outings, and then I have a dozen bodyguards protecting me. So, no one will find me."

"I'm not worried about our people finding you. I'm worried about the Americans. They will come after you with a vengeance."

"Not your worry, Nobutake. I can vanish in minutes. But, I'm going to make the Americans and British pay dearly for what they did. According to my sources, the Brits have two special mission submarines that rotate out of Ceylon for duty in the Sea of Japan and the Yellow Sea. One has been there for three months and is due to rotate back in another thirty days. So, I would like you to get all the ships ready as quickly as possible."

"I'll do my best, Uchito. But faster costs more money."

"Cost is not a problem."


George returned to the dojo in East Shinjuku at 9 p.m. on Monday, as Ueshiba was ushering out his last students. Ueshiba's keen eyes noticed him in the shadows of a two-story apartment building across the street. As he turned back into the building, Ueshiba turned both the outside and interior lights off. Ten minutes later, George slipped unnoticed into the building.

"You're quite the stealthy agent, Joji," Ueshiba stated.

"And you still have eyes like a hawk, O'Sensei. Nothing gets past you." George replied.

"Sharp eyes are what have kept me undefeated in martial arts for so many years. And they probably help you, too. Your reflexes were swifter than any student I have taught, past or present. But, you're not here to be flattered. So, let's go into my office. I have a fresh pot of tea steeping."

As Ueshiba poured the tea, he explained to George about the dinner party, "Uchito Tsukuda was there, accompanied by two body-guards in the house and another half a dozen outside, each heavily armed. The whispered scuttlebutt in the room was that the new Deputy Chief Cabinet Secretary was deep into Tsukuda's pockets. Otherwise, he would never have gotten the job."

Ueshiba paused, then continued, "Tsukuda was quite talkative. He was bragging about his commercial projects on the Tokyo docks. Tsukuda has purchased most of the property located east of the Tokyo metropolitan area, adjacent to the Arakawa River. Many of the buildings and warehouses in the district are still burned-out shells. The few that are standing were partially destroyed but usable with a bit of rehab. They are near the docks that Tsukuda has rebuilt over the last two years at Koto City."

"I bet he wasn't bragging about his destroyed ships."

"No, not a word. However, Nobutake Kojima, a former admiral in the Japanese Imperial Navy, was at Tsukuda's side, most of the night. Kojima's family owns shipyards in Japan, Manila, and Southeast Asia."

"You suppose the admiral is doing something nefarious for Tsukuda?"

"When he was on the fleet staff, he was in charge of procurement."

"Procuring what?"

"He specialized in armament for fleet ships. His family supplied most of the guns, torpedoes, and depth-charge launchers that went onto destroyers and destroyer escorts."

George replied, "He's using Kojima to procure new ships, and then arming them in some obscure shipyard in the Philippines or Malaysia."

"I believe I'd read recently that his family had purchased a ship-building company in Vietnam."

"O'Sensei, this is totally irrational. It sounds like Tsukuda is building merchant raiders, like the Germans and Italians built in World War Two. If he can procure the right technology, he will be able to sink our merchant vessels or go after our submarines in the Yellow Sea."

George paused to think, and then asked, "Did you find out about any of his travel plans?"

"Yes, he plans to visit the Ministry of Finance next week. And then he is heading to the estate he purchased from his uncle."

"The one with the brewery, northeast of Tsuchiura Air Base?"

"Yes, they make the best sake in Japan there."

"I was there in 1946, on a covert mission, of course. It must be close to a thousand acres, half of which is wooded. There is a half-kilometer-deep, underground bunker where they store the wine."

"Yes, I was invited to a wedding there in 1935. I remember it was enormous. The house must be close to twenty thousand square feet."

"This is great information, O'Sensei. I cannot thank you enough."

"Come to visit, Joji, when this is all over."

"I will. I promise. And I'll bring my best friend."


Jonathan Preston was not surprised by the information Morihei Ueshiba had supplied. He figured Tsukuda was out of control with rage after the last disaster. However, the raider ships were an unwelcome twist. Tsukuda was going tactical, probably wanting to sink the British submarine that brought his teams into play. *Well*, Jon thought, *if Tsukuda wants a war, I'm prepared to bring one—only it will be far deadlier than he expects.*

"George, get a message off to General Miller," Preston said. "Ask him to brief Admiral Dubois and get his input. We may be able to stop the freighters before they are fitted with weapons. I'll set up a meeting with Brigadier MacKenzie for tomorrow. He may have some insight into the facilities in Southeast Asia that can handle the weapons' retrofits. It looks like we will have additional work for his Lin Kuei warriors—and for Henri Morreau and Miles Murphy as well."

"Anything else, boss?" George asked.

"Yes. Get a message off to René Clairoux, in Singapore. We are going to need his agency as well. We'll need a list of shipyards in Singapore, Malaysia, and Vietnam. And ask him to look up our old friend, Andy Larned. He might be the best source for that kind of information."

"What about Admiral Whitley in Honolulu? He might have intelligence on the Philippines."

"Yep; him, too. Additionally, tell General Miller that we will need all of the Japanese-speaking agents that Kumiko, Katie, and

Camille just graduated, including Kumiko—if she is willing to return to Japan."

"Are you planning to go to war, Jon?"

"Yes—a 'first, strike; kick ass; and then get-out-quick' war, in multiple locations, George. Just like President Truman ordered. Only not as loud."

Jon got up to leave and go see Captain Kim—when he noticed something in George's demeanor. Something was bothering George, so Jon sat back down.

"I can see that something is troubling you, George. What's on your mind?" Preston asked.

"It's what has happened in Japan since the American occupation. The culture of defeat in Japan has given way to opportunism in every possible form. The most shocking and repulsive is the Japanese government's formal embracing of prostitution to service the Allied soldiers occupying the country," George stated.

"You saw this when you visited your friend, Ueshiba?"

"Yes, ordinary people are living in despair, hunger, and poverty. Jobs are scarce, factories are not producing yet, and job opportunities for women are nearly nonexistent, according to Ueshiba. He told me that when the government set up comfort facilities for the occupation army, the responsibility for staffing and oversight had fallen to the local chiefs of police and businessmen. They created recreation centers across Japan that recruited teenage girls and women to be prostitutes. In addition, GIs come bearing gifts of nylon stockings, lipstick, nail polish, makeup, tins of food, and colorful clothing—which enamors the women even more, to the soldiers."

"Yes, Brigadier MacKenzie mentioned that Tsukuda owns several dozen of these centers in Tokyo and Yokohama."

"For crying out loud, Jon. Because of the starvation and shortages, every woman in Japan is a potential prostitute. The entire country is being taken in by the illusion that this creates prosperity. What was once a spiritual and religious society is being transformed into a new society so desperate, that it now accepts the legalized sex trade as a normal part of everyday life! It's morally appalling."

"It's unfortunate, George. Just one more reason to get this Tsukuda business over and done with. Let's plan a reconnaissance trip to Tsukuda's brewery on Saturday night. We'll take Kim and Ikestead. They can serve as snipers and guard our rear."

# CHAPTER 47



*Washington, D.C.*

Lieutenant General John Renick reread the message that George Linka had sent, before handing it to Major General Miller. Miller took a minute to digest the information before handing it back. He picked up the porcelain coffee cup of dark rich coffee and took a sip before saying anything. It gave him a few more seconds of careful reflection to choose his words.

"We have to let Jon and George handle this, John. The President won't allow open involvement with our navy unless our vessels are attacked directly. And suppose we put additional warships in the Yellow Sea. In that case, Tsukuda may suspect we have found out about his plans," Miller stated.

"It will also upset the Chinese and North Koreans," Renick replied quickly, "which worries President Truman. He fears it might prompt an invasion of South Korea. Truman says if South Korea comes under communist control, other countries in Asia and world-wide will fall like a line of dominoes. It's why Congress approved $400 million in military and economic assistance for Greece and Turkey last year. But, unfortunately, Congress doesn't want to fund aid for South Korea because of the fear of another war in Asia. Truman also believes that too much aggression on our part will bring the Soviet Union into the fracas. So, we need to find a way to stop the arms shipments, that doesn't involve striking Tsukuda on Chinese or North Korean soil."

"I'll run this by Admiral Dubois today. I have lunch with him every Tuesday. I'm certain he won't have a problem with Admiral

Whitley cooperating with us. I know Matt would do it without his permission, but Dubois will expect us to keep him in the loop."

"Are you sure that it's wise to send all our newly trained agents to Japan? What if something cataclysmic should happen, and we'd lose all the agents? It would be another six months before the next class would be ready."

"I think we have to defer to Preston's wisdom on this, John. He's the commander in the field, and we need to support his request. But, how many times has Jon Preston been wrong?"

"None that I can recall. But there's always a first time, Lew. And Tsukuda is clever and ruthless. If he knows that Preston's team is in Japan, he would certainly attempt to strike them."

"Regardless, we must trust Jon. If he had any doubts, he wouldn't have asked for all of them."

"When do they depart?"

"They leave tomorrow morning and will arrive in Yokota on Sunday morning, at 2 a.m.—if the weather holds out. There's a cold front moving through Anchorage, but it should be through by the time they land."

"What other kind of help has Jon requested?"

"None. Jon is working exclusively with Brigadier MacKenzie and his SIS group, which is what the President wants."

"You don't think this article in the newspaper will ruffle MacArthur's feathers?"

"Ruffle, yes. But with the CIA, Air Force, SIS, and us, all agreeing that the story was planted by Tsukuda, he'll do nothing. Of course, that won't keep General Willoughby and his spies from snooping around."

"And if Willoughby discovers Preston's team at Yokota?"

"Well, say that the new CIC agents are there for training in British SIS counterinsurgent tactics—since the SIS has the most experience."

"And if Willoughby doesn't buy it?"

"We'll tell him to take it up with General Bradley—which he won't do; because he knows that MacArthur wouldn't approve."

Camille Dupont and Kathleen Lauren were finishing up teaching a class on Jujitsu to a dozen new recruits in one of the gymnasiums at the Marine Barracks. The students were from all over the world—India, Burma, French Indochina, the Philippine Islands, and Australia. Most were young adults whose American parents had migrated back to the U.S. at the end of World War Two. They were too young to fight in the war then, but now they were eighteen or older and eager to serve. Another dozen, recruited from across the U.S., came from mostly Asian families. General Renick had specific requirements for the new recruits. They had to speak an Asian language—preferably Japanese, Mandarin, Cantonese, Korean, Tagalog, Malayan, or Vietnamese. Many of the recruits were fluent in two or more.

After class, Camille and Kathleen departed the Marine Barracks base in Camille's '42 Ford sedan. Camille noticed a Buick following her car, a mile north of the base, after she casually turned east on D Street SE and to the left on 9th Street SE—a technique Jon had taught her, to spot a tail.

"Can you crawl over the seat and retrieve the grease guns and .45s under the back seat?" Camille asked.

"What's wrong?" Katie asked as she slipped into the back seat.

"Fifty yards behind us…a dark green Buick with three men. Maybe they are just tailing us, but I want to be prepared if something offensive happens. You know, just in case."

"Sure. Just in case."

After Katie pulled the seat free, she retrieved two suppressed M3A1 submachine guns and six 32-round detachable box magazines, along with two .45-caliber semiautomatic handguns and four extra clips. After inserting a magazine in each and loading the guns' chambers, Katie placed an M3, pistol, and additional clips on the seat next to Camille. Next, she put the seat back in place, slipped a handgun in her slacks behind her right hip, clutched the submachine gun in her left hand, stayed low in the back seat, and rolled both windows down.

"I'm going to turn left on Independence Avenue and speed up, to see how they react. There's a used car lot, three blocks down the road on the right. If they try to overtake us, I'll whip in there. It'll give us some good cover," Camille said.

"Go for it," Katie replied.

When Camille turned the corner, she pushed the accelerator to the floor and hit 50 mph. The green Buick did likewise.

"Looks like they got a radio," Katie shouted. "Are you sure these aren't guards from the base?"

"Positive," Camille replied. "These guys look like European thugs…Russian or Romanian."

"Well, they're catching up. How far…? Crap, they're firing at us!"

Camille swerved, but several rounds hit the trunk. She was doing fifty-five through a red light and nearly hit a car that had crossed in front of her. The Buick was getting closer.

"Half a block, then I'm turning into the car lot," Camille said.

Katie looked out the right side window and braced herself. As Camille slowed and turned right, Katie fired a three-second burst into the Buick, injuring the front passenger and causing the driver to swerve left. Camille slammed on the emergency brake, and the Ford skidded to a stop. Camille and Katie leaped out of the car, hustled behind a black 1939 Cadillac LaSalle, and waited for the men to empty their weapons.

The driver tried to follow Camille into the lot, but the car was too wide to the left and going too fast. The Buick slid sideways and clipped a telephone pole with its left front bumper, putting it into a 360-degree spin. It skidded to a stop against an abandoned brick building, effectively blocking the driver-side doors. The lone passenger in the back seat threw his door open, exited the car, and began firing a German-made MP 40.

Camille and Katie ducked as a hail of bullets struck the Ford and began to ricochet in the direction of the Cadillac. Katie hit the pavement and looked underneath the Cadillac. She saw one of the assailants grabbing a fresh clip from the Buick, thirty feet away. She pulled the .45 semiautomatic from her slacks, aimed, and fired. The man with the MP 40 was struck in the knee and went down on the pavement. Katie fired a second shot and hit him in the chest.

"One down," Katie said. "Do you see the others?"

"They're retreating, Camille said. "I don't want to fire at them because there are civilians on the street."

As Camille and Katie watched the two men sprint down the street, a tan sedan with two men came to a screeching halt, twenty yards in front of the men. In a flash, the men were out of the car, aiming their M3A1 submachine guns at the two assailants. One of the assailants raised his gun to fire but was immediately cut down. The other man dropped his weapon and raised his arms in the air.

Camille and Katie sprinted to where the two men had the surviving assailant on his belly and were handcuffing his hands behind his back. Camille knew both men. They were two of the intelligence agents Admiral Hayward had assigned to Jon's team. Jon later had assigned them to protect Camille and Katie.

"Agent Briscoe, Agent Nelson, I thought I had dismissed you two before we left the base?" Camille asked.

"Sorry, ma'am. We're following our commander's orders. If anything happens to you two, it's our fault, and we'll suffer the consequences," Briscoe explained.

"We're grateful," Katie stated, extending her hand to Briscoe and Nelson.

"I need you to get this guy to an interrogation room at the Marine Barracks in thirty minutes," Camille stated.

"As soon as the base ambulance arrives and the Marine MPs show up, we will be able to leave. Plus, someone has to deal with the D.C. police and inform them this is a military matter," Briscoe replied, as sirens were blaring in the distance.

"We'll meet you at the Marine detention center. Make sure you check him for hidden weapons and empty his pockets. And leave him handcuffed. I don't want him taking any poison pills. I need him to talk."

"Aye, aye, ma'am."

As Camille turned to walk back to her car, she stumbled and fell to the pavement. Briscoe and Katie were at her side in an instant. As Katie rolled Camille over on her back, she noticed blood streaming from her left temple.

"She's been hit. Get your first aid kit out of the car and call for an additional ambulance. Have them transport her to George Washington University Hospital. It's the closest trauma center," Katie ordered, as three Washington, D.C. police cars came to a screeching halt, ten yards away.

Agent Nelson pulled his badge and turned toward the police cars, "I'll deal with the police. You call for the ambulance, Briscoe."

Katie took a blanket that Agent Briscoe offered, and placed it under Camille's head. Katie opened the first-aid kit and pulled out a bottle of iodine, and a small, white bandage. She poured the iodine liberally onto the wound, applied a bandage, and held it in place with the field tourniquet.

Camille moaned softly and looked Katie in the eyes, "Tell Jon… tell Jon and Jon Jr. I love them. Tell Jon I'm sorry I let him down.

"Tell him yourself. You're going to live through this. You've got a flesh wound and concussion from a shell that bounced off your damn hard head. Don't worry. You'll be toting Jon Jr. around in a couple of days. Just stay awake. Don't close your eyes, Camille. Stay with me, girl. Tell me about Jon Jr.," Katie replied urgently as she gently slapped Camille's cheeks, trying to keep her awake.

# CHAPTER 48

*Yokota Air Base, Japan*

Brigadier Patrick MacKenzie had just received a message from General Miller and was deliberating whether to let Jon Preston see it. He didn't want Jon distracted by the attack on Camille and Kathleen. In the end, MacKenzie realized that Jon would be better off knowing what had happened and that Camille would fully recover. He called for his jeep and driver to take him to where Jon and George assisted the civil engineers in erecting a temporary training facility. When he arrived, the engineers were installing a triple concertina wire fence. The fence consisted of two parallel concertinas joined by twists of wire and topped by a third concertina.

As the brigadier's jeep pulled up, George walked over to greet the general. Jon was a quarter-mile away, directing the engineers. George noticed the grim look on MacKenzie's face.

"What brings you out today, Brigadier?" George asked.

"News from D.C. It's not good," MacKenzie replied. "I think it might be best if you took the message to Jon."

George read the message and remarked, "You're right, Brigadier. I'll handle it."

In the distance, Jon noticed the jeep and the brigadier. When he saw George walking his way, Jon assumed the brigadier wanted to see him. So, Jon began walking toward the jeep.

"What's up with the brigadier?" Jon asked.

"You need to read this," George replied, handing the message to Jon.

Jon read the message twice before commenting. "Looks like Tsukuda is taking the war to the U.S., first. Apparently, he wants to make this personal."

"You're not upset?"

"Of course, I'm upset, but there is nothing I can do, George. Camille is recovering, and Katie is okay. That's all that matters. Plus, General Miller has them guarded 24/7. From the interrogation of the surviving assailant, we know it was Tsukuda who had ordered the attack. What do you think we should do about it?"

"It might be a good time for the white samurai and a few of his trusted warriors to strike Tsukuda's brewery, destroy some premium sake, and cut off a few heads."

"Well, we are planning a reconnaissance mission on Saturday before Tsukuda arrives. Let's talk with the brigadier first. Then I want input from Major Bayless, Captain Kim, Captain Ikestead, and Kumiko Fujiwara. We'll need a map and aerial photos of the estate. If there are none, I'll have Bayless arrange for a photo recon mission later this afternoon."

After discovering that no current aerial photos of the brewery were available, Major Bayless arranged for a reconnaissance mission over Tsukuda's estate. The F-5A photo reconnaissance plane, affectionately called "Photo Joe" by most pilots, was a variant of the P-38G. It was powered by twin, 1,400-horsepower Allison engines. The F-5 could carry from three to five powerful aerial cameras in its nose, which were operated by the pilot using a remote control from the cockpit. Other than the .45 the pilot carried, the F-5A carried no armament, making it much lighter and faster than the standard P-38. In addition, this F-5A was painted light blue to better camouflage it against a clear sky.

The F-5A took off on a scheduled training mission at 1600 hours. It then flew north for thirty miles before turning due east and heading straight toward the 2,877-foot peak of Mount Tsukuba. Ten miles east of the mountain, the pilot started the cameras and flew one pass over Tsukuda's estate, at five thousand feet. After passing the estate, the pilot climbed the aircraft to eight thousand feet, feathered the starboard engine, declared an emergency to Yokota Tower, and returned to the base. Two hours later, Preston, Linka, Kim, Ikestead, and Fujiwara were going over the photographs in Jon's temporary SIS office.

Half of the thousand-acre estate that Tsukuda had purchased from his mother's brother was loamy soil dedicated to growing a short strain of rice called Yamada Nishiki, which was used in brewing its famous high-quality sake. The other half was hilly—and forested with beech, evergreen, oak, and red pine trees.

At the bottom of one of the smaller hills, a mile from the main house, the sake brewery and a large warehouse stood. Next to the brewery was a fast-running creek and a water-powered trip-hammer mill, used for decorticating and pounding rice in preparation for the brewing process. The trip hammers were raised by a cam, which released them to fall under the force of gravity. The water-mill trip hammers had been used in Japan for nearly 1,000 years.

Jon recalled the brewery complex was spread out over five acres of the property. Concealed directly behind the warehouse was a half-kilometer-long tunnel, dug into the hillside. It was used to store the sake after it was bottled. The entrance to the tunnel was directly through the large double doors in the front of the building. A separate tunnel exit had been constructed on the western slope of the hillside, through another large building.

"The last time George and I had visited the estate, we had dropped from the back of a slow-moving truck onto a gravel road, west of a Shinto shrine leading to Mount Tsukuba. We had entered a thick forest of beech and evergreen trees," Jon said, pointing to the shrine in the photograph. "After hiking for thirty minutes, we came upon the first of Tsukuda's guards. We went around them and hiked another mile before we reached the warehouse. That was when we discovered that Tsukuda was building the underground warehouse."

"It appears that there are guard towers on the estate," Captain Kim said as he pointed to several structures.

"Yes, but since Tsukuda is not at the estate, they probably will not be manned," George remarked. "At least we hope not."

"So, how many guards might we be facing?" Kumiko Fujiwara asked.

"Unknown," Jon replied. "But, if I were Tsukuda, I would have at least a half a dozen men on-site, with two guards on rotating eight-hour shifts."

"If that's the case, the men will be lax, possibly bored because the boss is not around," Captain Ikestead said. "I see the same thing happening with our guards here at the base."

"Kumiko, I would like to bring several of the new agents on the mission. Who would you recommend?" Jon inquired.

"My two sons, Eizo and Emon; Hiroki Eguchi; and Carol Whitely," Kumiko replied quickly. "They are the cream of the crop. All are highly skilled in stealth tactics and martial arts—and are the best shots of the lot. However, of the four, Carol is the most skilled."

"Kim—you, Bayless, and Ikestead will be responsible for guarding our rear after we are dropped off. George will take Eizo, Emon, and Carol—and head to the warehouse. I'll take Kumiko and Hiroki—and go to the brewery. George and I will carry five charges of C-3 and 120-minute pencil detonators, which will allow us plenty of time to get away. We don't want to be noticed. Therefore, we will avoid all contact with guards. However, if we are unfortunate and encounter a guard, I want him incapacitated—not killed. So, we'll have to bring him out with us when we leave. We'll leave an empty sake bottle and his weapon behind, so it looks like the guard got drunk and went AWOL."

"Do we want to let one of the guards see someone dressed as a Samurai?" George asked.

Jon replied, "It might show our hand too soon. I wouldn't want to screw up the Kabuki theater scenario. What does everyone else think?"

"It might explain the disappearance of a drunk guard," Kumiko stated.

"I think it would create a lot of fear. Most Japanese are superstitious, anyway, so I say let's do it," Ikestead added.

"Kim, what are your thoughts?" Jon asked.

"As long as it doesn't detract from the mission, I agree. My only reservation is the costumes may be noisy, or the cloth might catch on a bush and tear."

"I tried on one of the costumes. They are made mostly of silk and cotton. The iron plates, armored skirt, and arm and shin protectors are made from soft leather. The sandals are made from rice straw and rope. The chain-mail chest protector is made from silk-screened cotton." George stated. "I think we'll be okay."

"Let me think on it overnight," Jon stated. "You'll have all day Friday to brief the others and rest. We'll move out in four vehicles, Saturday, at 9 p.m., and we'll rendezvous at the Tsuchiura Naval Air Base. I have a team of MPs already in place and a secure building where we can go over final preparations and any new intel."

As the meeting broke up, Jon pulled Ikestead aside. "I have a special request that only you can handle."

As Jon told Ikestead what he needed, his eyebrows lifted, and a smile crossed his face. "I think I know where to get them. I'll have everything you need, at the naval base tomorrow evening."

# CHAPTER 49

*Tokyo, Japan*

As the Minister of Finance, Masao Yano was a key player in leading the charge for fiscal change in Japan. However, when he was first appointed in 1946, he was frustrated mainly because his talents were minimized by the American minions whom MacArthur had placed in charge. They knew nothing about how Japan's economy worked, and they implemented policies that would never work. He eventually determined that the American bureaucrats cared little for Japan and more about their careers.

Masao Yano was distracted and feigned interest at the weekly security meeting on Tuesday with five other SCAP-appointed cabinet members and their American security counterparts. After the meeting, Yano asked General Jim Sage to remain behind, to go over the proposed security procedures for the Port of Tokyo, to help counter a large amount of theft occurring after the offloading of cargo. General Sage answered Yano's questions, but he knew there was an alternative agenda. While Sage talked, Yano carefully slipped an envelope into General Sage's open file folder. Sage pretended that he didn't notice the envelope, and he continued explaining what the military was planning, to secure the docks and prevent theft without interrupting the flow of products. When he finished, he asked, "Minister, if there is anything else I can do to be of assistance, please don't hesitate to contact me."

"Thank you, General Sage," Yano replied formally. I may have additional areas that need clarification since I have to fund the Japanese security personnel working with your security forces. Would it be too much trouble to have lunch one day and discuss the numbers of personnel I will need over the next twelve months? I am worried that we may run short of funds to pay them. I may have to ask Washington for more monetary assistance. Therefore, I would like to work with you to develop a better strategy to see that our security team is deployed efficiently. Our government does not want to pay overtime."

"I am free this Friday, Minister. Could you make it to the American Embassy at noon? There is a great lunch buffet. We could make it a working lunch."

"That suits me fine, General Sage."

General Sage left the sixth floor of the Dai Ichi Insurance Company building and walked down three levels of stairs toward his office. Instead of going directly to his office, he went to the men's bathroom and entered an empty stall. He took the envelope from his folder, read the contents, tore the letter into tiny pieces, and flushed them down the toilet. Sage then walked down three flights of steps to the lobby, where a staff car was waiting to drive him to the American Embassy.

Sage told his driver, "Change of plans today, Jimmy. Take me to Yokota Air Force Base."

After passing through the base's main gate, he directed his driver to the northeast side—to the British SIS offices. Before he exited the vehicle, Sage handed his driver a five-dollar bill and said, "Take a long lunch break, Jimmy. Pick me up at 2 p.m. I'll be lunching with the Brits, and you know how long they take to eat."

Brigadier Michael MacKenzie was about to leave his office to go to lunch—when the phone rang at his desk. He considered ignoring it and leaving the office, but abruptly changed his mind and answered on the seventh ring.

"This is Sergeant Billingsley, sir. A General Jim Sage is requesting to see you, sir. He says it's extremely important."

Despite its elegant rooms and displays of fabulous art treasures that had been strategically placed to enhance their beauty, Nozomi did not enjoy living and working at Tsukuda's luxury estate in Yokohama. She was doing the job of an undercover agent for a foreign government. At any moment, she could be discovered. Despite her training and skills, she was always on guard. Whenever she left the estate, she was constantly followed. When she was allowed days off to go to Tokyo to see her mother, she had the feeling she was under continuous surveillance.

The estate served as a constant reminder of the wealth and power that Tsukuda projected. Nozomi had to constantly remind herself that all the artifacts were spoils of war, taken from museums, universities, or private collections during the invasions of China, Malaysia, and the Philippine Islands, or taken from Japanese families accused of treason. And when Tsukuda was there, it was a place of pure evil.

Throughout the day, she would listen to Tsukuda issuing directives to his muscular bodyguard and lieutenant. She didn't know how a man could be so calm and confident in the face of Tsukuda's outbursts when the information didn't please him. At times, she would be on the receiving end of Tsukuda's tantrums when the tea wasn't hot enough or if she didn't move fast enough to please her master. It was disturbing when Raizo would notify his master that someone had been killed and disposed of in the river or bay because he had failed to follow orders. Tsukuda had begun wearing clothing reminiscent of feudal Japan in the last month and had ordered all his staff to start calling him 'Lord Tsukuda.' Even before Raizo was ordered to Vietnam, he began to look uncomfortable and concerned over the changes he saw in the former general.

At times, Nozomi would catch Tsukuda watching her as she worked. Despite doing everything in her power to hide her looks, he still noticed. She wore her hair very short, refused to wear makeup, and would wear loose-fitting kimonos to hide her lithe, muscular figure—a figure that stayed toned and hardened from the ju-jitsu classes that everyone was required to practice under Raizo's supervision. Still, she would catch Tsukuda, in her peripheral vision, leering at her. She could sense his lust. Nevertheless, Tsukuda remained professional, did not chat casually with her, and did not approach her for favors. She shuttered as she wondered what might lie in store if she were to be revealed as a spy.

The only family member who might know of her occupation was her uncle, Hozumi Eguchi. Eguchi had moved to the United States five years before the outbreak of war between the two nations. After entering the U.S., Army intelligence agents interviewed Hozumi and learned about his relatives in Japan. So, through an intermediary named George Linka—the son of a United Brethren minister living in Tokyo—Hozumi's niece Nozomi was recruited into army counterintelligence and secretly trained. The year before Japan had attacked the U.S. in 1941, Nozomi was hired as a secretary in the Japanese War Ministry. While there, she met a charming naval aviation lieutenant and married him a year later. Unfortunately, he died at the Battle of Midway in June of 1942.

As the widow of an IJN aviator, Nozomi did not fall under suspicion of the secret police. On the contrary, she had provided intelligence to two female agent contacts that amazingly went undiscovered throughout the war. When the war was over, Nozomi secretly met with Linka. She was asked to continue her secret mission with Jonathan Preston's team. When Tsukuda went looking for someone to work in his estate in Yokohama, the young widow came to his attention through a former Imperial Japanese Army officer—a high-level official with the Japanese Ministry of Finance and a former Japanese major general in the Imperial Japanese Army named Masao Yano. With a solid recommendation, a background with the War Ministry, and a top-secret security clearance, Tsukuda hired Nozomi. Still, he watched her like a hawk, as he did all his employees, except for his most trusted bodyguards.

Months back, Tsukuda took additional measures to ensure security at his estate, which resembled an ancient Japanese castle. Constructed with extreme beauty and skill, a new type of flooring, commonly known as the *uguisu-bari*— or nightingale floor, to master carpenters—was installed in the hallways of the Yokohama estate. The carpenters placed planks of thick white pine above a framework of supporting beams, secured underneath with nails and metal clamps. The pine floor and flooring clamps, constructed in an upside-down V-shape, would move up and down against the clamp nails that were secured into the floor joist—when the floor was trodden upon. The friction between the nails and clamps would create chirping sounds similar to a Japanese Nightingale. Thus, there was no way a person could silently tread through the halls.

During the day, the chirping was pleasant, and after a while, Nozomi got used to it. At night, Tsukuda forbade his guards to walk on the hallway floors unless it was an emergency. Apparently, Tsukuda hadn't researched how guards and sentries, during the Edo period, were known to have individual gates or rhythms, as they traversed the floor. And when they did walk the floors at night, each guard's unique rhythm would create a song separate from the other guards. Over time, the guards could distinguish one guard from another. If another tune was heard, they would immediately recognize it as an uninvited guest and would sound a warning.

At the vegetable market today, a note from Nozomi's old boss at the War Ministry was waiting. Masao Yano's message was a warning that Tsukuda suspected someone in his organization of leaking information. Furthermore, Tsukuda had once again asked Yano's advice on the loyalty of Nozomi when she worked for him. Yano's response was brief—unquestionable. Still, Yano thought Nozomi should be warned.

General Jim Sage shook the brigadier's hand and had a seat in a mahogany frame chair in MacKenzie's office. Sage was not one to exchange pleasantries like the Brits, so he got directly to the point of his unexpected visit.

"I have a message for George Linka," General Sage explained. "Because of what happened in North Korea and China, I suspect he and Jon Preston are on this base, and you know his whereabouts."

"Would you like me to deliver it, or do you need to talk to him in person?" MacKenzie asked.

"I prefer you deliver the message. It's for George's eyes only. For obvious reasons, I do not want to be seen with either Jon or George. But, the person who passed the message said it was life-or-death urgent."

"I'll make sure he gets it in the next twenty minutes. Now, will you stay and have lunch with me?"

"As long as it isn't boiled fish, yes."

# CHAPTER 50

*Tsuchiura Naval Air Base, Japan*

Preston's team left Tsuchiura Naval Air Base at midnight and traveled northeast to the Tsukubasan Shrine, a mile south of Mount Tsukuba. It was the same route they had taken in 1946 when they had foiled Tsukuda's plans to recover 24 tons of gold, secured in hidden tunnels at the base. The former IJN 'special attack force' training base was once the home to four thousand young pilots training for kamikaze missions.

George, Eizo, Emon, and Carol were dropped off first. A waning crescent moon provided enough light to move stealthily through the thick forest of conifers and deciduous trees. Finally, after thirty minutes, they were near the warehouse. Suddenly, George held his hand up. Everyone froze. A single guard was standing near the entry door to the warehouse office, smoking a cigarette. Obviously, he was bored, tired, or both, because his rifle was resting against the side of the building. In his hand was a small bottle of what George suspected to be sake.

*This is better than I had expected*, George thought. George showed his palm to the others, telling them to stay put while he moved from tree to tree and inched closer to the east side of the warehouse.

In the dark, by the side of the building, George said aloud in Japanese, "I thought you were going to wait for me before you started drinking sake?"

"Hiroki," the guard replied. "You're not supposed to be here for another forty minutes. So, what are you doing here?"

"I got thirsty."

"You scared the daylights out of me!"

"You'll have more than that scared out of you if the boss catches you drinking."

"No one will be here until Monday. You know that."

"Regardless, you were supposed to wait for me."

"I've only had two bottles. There is plenty for you."

"Quick, bring two bottles to me. After that, I must head back to the brewery. It will be another hour before I'm back."

The guard reached into a burlap bag and retrieved two brown bottles, and walked to the edge of the building. Before he could turn the corner, George clubbed him with his pistol. Then, after he was sure the guard was unconscious, he motioned for the others to come out of hiding.

"You two secure his hands and feet and put a blindfold on him," George said to Eizo and Emon. "Carol, check to see if the door is unlocked."

Once the guard was secured and blindfolded, George directed Eizo and Emon to stay in the shadow of the building and stand watch. "Carol and I will go inside to set the charges," he instructed.

Before they went into the warehouse, George said to Eizo and Emon, "We only have twenty to twenty-five minutes before the next guard arrives on his patrol. So, move this guard to that stand of birch trees, fifty yards away. We'll take him with us when we leave."


A mile farther down the road, Jon, Kumiko, and Hiroki slipped from the back of their truck. They were at least a mile away from the brewery. Jon anticipated it would take thirty minutes to safely negotiate the woods. However, he knew from his previous visit that there was an empty field that he didn't want to cross, so he would lead everyone to the creek and his team would then work their way to the hammer mill. Hopefully, the mill was running fast, which would mask the sounds of their approach.

Before they left the road, Kumiko asked, "Where is Captain Ikestead? I didn't see him with Kim and Bayless."

"He's on a special assignment. But, he'll be along, before we leave the brewery."

Jon led his team along the creek until they came to the hammer mill. It was located at the bottom of one of the smaller hills, a mile from the main house and ten yards from the brewery. Next to the hammer mill, the creek gurgled and tumbled down a ten-foot water-fall. The noise it created would hide the sounds of their footsteps, but it would also hide the sound of an approaching guard.

The old water-powered trip-hammer mill had been used in Japan for nearly 1,000 years to *decorticate*—or remove the husk—and pound rice, in preparation for the brewing process. When in use, the trip hammers were raised by a cam that was powered by running water. At the apex, the hammers would be released to fall under the force of gravity to crush the rice. At present, the trip hammers were locked in place. Jon admired the old technology and decided not to destroy it. After posting Kumiko as a guard, he and Hiroki entered the brewery to set the charges.

As Jon and Hiroki crept through the brewery, he began looking for the koji processor, where *koji-kin*—a mold used to ferment rice—is added to the seed mash to make alcohol. However, after seeing the old brewery, Jon decided he couldn't destroy such a historic site. Instead, he made his way to the storage tanks, where the raw sake is immersed in hot water, heated to between 140-149 °**F for** 30 min-utes, and pasteurized. Jon then opened the valves of the dozen metal tanks and let the clear liquid drain.

"Let's get out of here," John said as he led the way back to the hammer mill.

Before they left the hammer mill, Jon said, "Stay here, Hiroki. I've one more thing to take care of."

When Jon returned, they collected Kumiko and made their way back to the road, in time to see two horses with riders dressed as samurai racing down the road towards them.

"Don't shoot. They're our people," Jon assured Kumiko and Hiroki.

When the riders stopped in front of the group, Kumiko rec-ognized Ikestead in the pale blue, yellow, and red samurai outfit. Each rider had a *sashimono*—a small banner with a triple hollyhock kamon extending from a four-section bamboo pole—attached to the saddle. The kamon was the crest of the Tokugawa clan. Tokugawa Ieyasu was the founder and first shogun of the Tokugawa shogunate. Kumiko didn't recognize the second rider dressed in orange and purple, but Jon did. Jim Ballangy wore a red mask with a three-pronged mustache of golden animal whiskers that extended eight inches in length.

"How did you get Ballangy into this?" Jon asked.

"Simple, we ride together all the time. So, Jim was a logical choice. Plus, he speaks Japanese," Ikestead remarked.

"Okay, the entrance to the estate is one hundred yards ahead. Make one pass—by the house, brewery, and warehouse—with your swords out. Scare the hell out of the guards, and haul ass back to the trailer. Then get out of here and head back to Yokota or to wherever you got the horses. I'll see you tomorrow."

Ikestead and Ballangy touched the brims of their *'ten-hell-judges-hat'*-shaped helmets. Then, they rode west at a gallop, waving their katanas, as George and his team returned to the road with their prisoner. The petrified Japanese guard was still blindfolded and shaking. He had no idea what was happening or what would happen to him.

"I thought you had decided against the samurai stunt," George stated.

"I changed my mind. It's time for Tsukuda to start believing in ghosts," Jon replied.

"Well, let's hope that Ikestead and Ballangy don't get shot."

"I think the chances are slim. First, the guards will be in shock when they see the horses and riders brandishing swords. Then, when Tsukuda comes to interrogate them, he will believe they were drunk."

"Well, at least one guard was drinking," George said, pointing to their prisoner. "He was probably bored out of his mind. He was standing around smoking and drinking when we arrived at the warehouse. We hid his bag of sake bottles near the east side of the warehouse. That should solidify Tsukuda's case against the guards. How will the presence of horse hooves be explained?"

"Tsukuda had three horses in a paddock behind the hammer mill. I saw them in the aerial photo. I let them out before we returned."

"Clever."

"Tsukuda will not be convinced at first. But when he realizes that his horses are shoed, and the ones Ikestead and Ballangy were riding were not, he just might begin to believe in ghosts. Or, at least, begin to have doubts about his conclusions."

# CHAPTER 51

*Tokyo, Japan*

Tsukuda sat quietly in his sparsely furnished office as the brewery manager gave his report on the destruction at the warehouse and the loss of sake from the koji tanks. His inventory of premium sake was destroyed, and ten thousand gallons of sake, awaiting pasteurization, were gone. Tsukuda wondered whether one of the Yakuza families was sending a message—or if the Americans had struck again.

Tsukuda decided against the Americans because they would not have spared the brewery. He would, however, have to find out which Yakuza clan had attacked the brewery—because this appeared to be a warning shot across the bow. Obviously, they knew his ships had been destroyed, which made him look weak. He wouldn't put it past one of the two new communist clans to attack him. They were becoming bolder, and they were jealous of his move to help the North Koreans. They didn't think a non-communist should be getting the business. If he didn't strike back soon, he would lose face in the eyes of every clan and be even more vulnerable.

What was more troubling to Tsukuda was the manager's reporting that one guard was missing. The manager had found a bag of empty sake bottles and the guard's gun leaning against the building.

"Of course, he could have been scared off by the samurai on horses," the manager stated.

"Say that again?" Tsukuda asked.

"The other two guards on duty reported seeing two men on horses dressed as samurai warriors. They were quite shaken up. The mounted samurai came out of nowhere, rampaging past the house and brewery, waving their swords. When I asked him where the other guard was, he said that he must have gotten scared and then ran off."

"Are you certain they weren't drunk, too?"

"Absolutely, General. One of the guards was shaking uncontrollably as he told his story. I think he must have fallen asleep and had a vision or thought he had seen a ghost, and then he convinced the other guard that there were mounted samurai charging across the field. He swears that one of the riders was a *gaijin*—a white man."

"Gaijin, samurai on horses—preposterous! There has to be another explanation. Plus, if there were horses, then there would be hoof prints in the dirt."

"Yes, sir. There were horse signs all over the place. But, unfortunately, the three horses behind the hammer mill had gotten out. I found them grazing near the house and brewery, so I have no way of validating his story."

"Go back to the brewery. Send the guards home for three days and tell them to sober up. Then, I want you to get the brewery up and running, back to full production in one week," Tsukuda ordered.

"Yes, General. However, it will take us two weeks to fix the tunnel. The ceiling has collapsed in two places," the manager said.

"Just get the job done," Tsukuda said, waving his hand and dismissing the manager. "Samurai on horses, jihi!"

"Fuji, I want an inventory of our supplies of sake in my warehouse in Tokyo. Tell the warehouse manager to double the price of our stock. There will be a significant shortage for a while." Fuji bowed and turned to leave, but Tsukuda called his new head of security back.

"And Fuji, send a case of premium sake to Professor Tadahisa Haruki, along with an invitation to have dinner with me at 8 p.m., tomorrow evening. He's the Chairman of the Society for Preservation of Japanese Art Swords. Sugimoto used him to validate the Masamune katana that Guy Wong is selling. And I understand that while he was at Georgetown University, he validated the Muramasa sword that the American President will present to the Tokyo National Museum. So I want to hear his story firsthand."

"I will see to it, General."

"Nozomi," Tsukuda called. "Bring me a fresh pot of tea and some sweets."

"Yes, General," Nozomi called from the other room.


Two days later, George read the brief note Nozomi had sent about Tsukuda's meeting with Tadahisa Haruki. *Tsukuda is up to something nefarious*, George thought. *But what?*

After mentioning the meeting to Jon Preston and Brigadier MacKenzie, George asked, "Is Tsukuda planning to steal the swords from the museum?"

Jon replied, "It's more likely that he wants Tadahisa to invalidate the Muramasa once he has it at the museum. If he does that, it won't matter if the sword is misplaced and goes missing from the museum."

"Do we need to confront Tadahisa?" MacKenzie asked.

"No. Let's let it play out. Tadahisa will undoubtedly inform Tsukuda that both swords will be used by the famous Kabuki troupe putting on *The Legend of the White Samurai*. That will certainly entice Tsukuda to go to the theater."

"You don't think Tsukuda would steal the swords and blame the troupe for losing them?"

"No, sir. Each night, after the play is over, they will be placed in an armored truck and transported back to the museum for safekeeping. However, I'm thinking that after the night of the last performance, Tsukuda could arrange an accident, where the swords are switched out with fakes and end up being destroyed when the truck catches on fire and explodes. Then all Tsukuda would have to do is have Tadahisa validate what's left of the swords as the original pieces."

"And Tsukuda ends up with the Masamune and the Muramasa, and Tadahisa is a hundred thousand yen richer."

"Probably a hundred thousand in American dollars. Tadahisa is no fool."

"Clever. How would we stop the heist?" MacKenzie asked.

"We don't. If Tsukuda actually attempts it, we let him steal the swords from the truck."

"You can't be serious?"

"We can if we switch out the swords with fakes before the armored transport picks them up. Remember, Tadahisa is our man. I'll get him to make fakes that can be used for the switch. I'm sure there are plenty of swords at his disposal for such a ruse."

"Won't you be placing Tadahisa in jeopardy? If Tsukuda finds out he possesses fake swords, Tadahisa will be dead within 24 hours."

"If Tsukuda does pull off a heist, Tadahisa and his son will be on a U.S. Air Force transport to the United States, once Tadahisa validates the remains of the fakes as the real swords. He won't play into Tsukuda's hand. He values his own son too much."

"Won't Tsukuda be suspicious if Tadahisa ends up missing?"

"I'm pretty sure that Tsukuda will be gloating over his new possessions and won't think of Tadahisa again. Especially if Tadahisa suffers a heart attack and is confirmed dead."

"You think of everything, Jon. Remind me to hire you if I need to disappear."

"Anytime, Brigadier. But I imagine Miles Murphy and Henri Morreau could do the same for you."

"On another subject. I wish you would have informed me that you were using Lieutenant Colonel Ballangy in your mounted samurai scheme. He could have been killed, Jon."

"I had no idea that Ballangy was coming. It was Jake Ikestead who recruited him. Apparently, they ride horses together, and Jake thought he would go along with the plan."

"Ballangy was laughing and bragging about it to me. I wanted to get upset with him, but I was laughing too hard. It was a brilliant plan to introduce your white samurai."

"He did a great job, Brigadier. If anything, he and Ikestead deserve a medal."

"Unfortunately, they do. But it created a bigger problem."

"How so?"

"Most of my paratroopers want in on your next operation. Your samurai act has them all motivated to kick ass on the bad guys."

"To tell the truth, Brigadier, I could use them. Unfortunately, I'm short of experienced soldiers. And when we take on Tsukuda at his Tokyo residence, I could certainly use the extra firepower."

"I thought this was going to be quiet—in and out quickly, totally covert."

"That's the plan, but Tsukuda and his men might have other ideas. They've been practicing their skills in a hidden location for a month. If there is shooting, your paratroopers would be an excellent team to have in reserve. Plus, I need some good snipers."

"Alright, you've convinced me. So I'll have Ballangy cycle the men through the firing range and start working on their hand-to-hand combat techniques, and I'll fly in four of my best snipers from Hong Kong. Is there anything else you need?"

"I could go for a couple of bottles of that single-malt scotch that we used to drink in Calcutta. That is—if you have any extra?"

"I just had ten cases of Macallan 25 shipped from Calcutta to my office in Hong Kong. They were left over from the barges we had moved from Singapore and had hidden from the Japs, in the marshes on the Indian coast. So, I'll have two cases brought in when the snipers arrive this weekend. But, you don't drink that much, Jon. By the way, why do you need two bottles?"

"I want to buy Tsukuda a drink at the Kabuki Theater."

# CHAPTER 52

*Yokota Air Base, Japan*

George Linka was concerned about Nozomi because Tsukuda suspected someone in his organization was an informant. She had been working for Tsukuda for nearly three years. During that time, George had only met with her twice while visiting her mom in Tokyo. The last time was over six months ago. George realized how vulnerable Nozomi was because Tsukuda was the hard-driving force behind his criminal organization that punished failure and rarely rewarded success.

Although still young and very fit at twenty-eight, Nozomi had shown signs of deep stress. However, Nozomi would be in Tokyo in December visiting her mother and was planning to take her mother to the Kabuki play. Then, finally, she would have a chance to relax. Nevertheless, George wanted to pull her out of harm's way. But Jon Preston mentioned the timing was wrong. It would alert Tsukuda and make him suspicious right before the Kabuki performance. Unfortunately, the only safe way to pull Nozomi out of the game without jeopardizing her mother would be to help Nozomi fake her death and then make her disappear—which would break her mother's heart. *Thank God this is coming to a close,* George thought. *Only four more weeks and this will be over.*

Earlier that morning, a messenger had delivered a packet of information and photographs of Tsukuda's estate in Yokohama. A second package was due on the following day, with details on the estate in Tokyo. George and Jon agreed that Tsukuda would most likely reside in Tokyo for the winter, because the Kabuki play, *The*

*Legend of the White Samurai,* would premier at the end of December during President Truman's visit to Tokyo.

George had flown over Tsukuda's Tokyo estate, once, because there was only one road to the castle, guarded around the clock. The estate sat on a hill between two rivers. The Nekona River turned southwest and traveled past Tsukuda's estate, a hundred meters north of the hill. At the same time, the Tokko River bifurcated and flowed east. A ten-foot rock wall surrounded the estate. It resembled a small Japanese castle reminiscent of 16th-century Japan, often called the Golden Age of Japanese castle building. The ten-acre estate was in the far northern part of Chiba Prefecture, twenty miles northeast of downtown Tokyo. A mile south was the Naritasan Shinsho-ji Temple—a three-story Buddhist pagoda that Tsukuda would frequent twice a week, when there.

The castle was three stories high. It consisted of the three cluster towers. Unlike most Japanese castles, the main keep was on the first level, including offices, storage rooms, the kitchen, and a large reception hall. The second floor held Tsukuda's master bedroom, bath, and quarters for three guards. Finally, the third level was a watchtower with quarters for four guards.

The south side had a compound gate made of two separate entrances placed at right angles, which were joined by walls to create a square enclosure. Anyone entering the castle would be trapped in a box while his or her identity was verified.

The ten-foot rock wall surrounding the castle was built in a curved profile, increasing stability during an earthquake. No mortar was used to join the stones, so each stone could move without the wall cracking. Instead, the wall was built using a 'disordered pilling' technique, consisting of large numbers of small stones packed tightly together that were chiseled to a smooth finish. The result was a wall that left no footholds and was challenging to climb.

If Jon's team were to attempt an attack, three teams would be required. Two teams would have to negotiate the Nekona and Tokko rivers before climbing over the rock walls. The third team would have to cross a two-hundred-acre rice field to the south. Attempting this could prove disastrous if they were discovered. The trick was to get Tsukuda and most of the guards away from the estate and deploy the teams while they were out—which was the reason behind the Kabuki play.

Most times, Tsukuda would only have ten guards for protection when he traveled. Maybe two would join him inside at the Kabuki play, while the remainder would be stationed outside the theater. Jon told the team that attacking Tsukuda at the theater was out of the question: first, because of the number of civilians; and second, because Jon and his team could easily be identified as Americans—which would create a political shit-storm for President Truman, who would be in Tokyo on a state visit. The purpose of Truman's visit was to formally hand over the treasured Muramasa katana to the Tokyo National Museum—and to return the sacred Masamune katana to the head of the Kenoe family.


On Tuesday morning, Tsukuda sat discussing security with Fuji Takahashi— when a guard knocked on the office door.

"Please forgive the intrusion, General," the guard said. "The head cook has informed me that three of our servants and a secretary have taken ill and are in the hospital with food poisoning. Apparently, they went out to eat together last night and had pufferfish as one of their courses. On the way home, they began having symptoms of paralysis. They were rushed to the hospital and diagnosed with tetrodotoxin poisoning. They will recover, but they will be out at least ten days."

"Don't we have anyone to substitute?" Tsukuda asked.

"No, sir. Two are in their last month of pregnancy and are off. So our only option is to bring servants from other estates—because they have all been vetted."

"Alright, make it happen, but make sure one of them is Nozomi Hattori. She's in Yokohama. She was coming to Tokyo in December to visit her mother. So this would make it convenient for her. Plus, I have purchased tickets to a Kabuki play for her and her mother."

"Aren't you being a little too gracious?" Fuji asked. "She's only a servant."

"Her husband was a naval aviator. He was killed during the war. I don't see where a little charity will be too decorous. Remember, we take care of our own, especially widows. Now, tell me of your plan to attack the armored truck and secure the swords."

"We'll block the primary and alternate routes the vehicle normally takes, which will make them proceed across the Sumida River at Azuma Bridge. Our truck will have an accident in front of the armored truck, which will block the bridge to the west. Another truck will follow and then wreck, trying to avoid the accident, effectively blocking the bridge's east side. Our men will attack the truck and fill it with knockout gas, which will incapacitate the guards. After removing the swords and replacing them with the replicas, we'll move the guards to safety and place explosives under the gas tank. It will look like the armored truck was rammed from behind, causing a fire, eventually exploding the gas tank."

"For good measure, after the fire and explosion, why don't you cause the armored truck to roll off the bridge into the river? That will make the recovery more difficult, if not impossible."

"Not a problem, General. I estimate no more than ten minutes to get it all accomplished."

"How far to the nearest police station?"

"Four miles. There is one station to the north—and one south. But, there will be road construction on both routes to the bridge. So, it will take the police at least fifteen minutes or more to respond to the accident scene."

"Very good, Fuji. Now, tell me what you have discovered on this missing guard from the brewery and our suspected informant issue."

"I'm leaning toward the belief that the missing guard was in on the operation to sabotage the brewery. If it was one of the communist Yakuza factions, they might be a group from Arakawa City. It's close to where the guard was raised. Unfortunately, there is nothing in his file to indicate he has ties with the communists. He was in the 222nd infantry division—a mobile reserve division attached to the 11th area army. He was twenty-one when the war ended. He saw minimal action. We interviewed a sergeant from his company who said he was a dedicated soldier."

"Is it possible that he was drunk, scared, and went AWOL after the so-called white samurai showed up on their horses?"

"It's possible—if you really believe that ghost story, General."

"According to the brewery manager, there were two types of horse tracks—shod and unshod. My horses were shod. And unshod horses' tracks were found leading into the forest to the east. So, maybe they weren't ghosts. On the other hand, maybe someone wanted the guards to think they were ghosts."

"We searched the roads to and from the brewery but found no trace of horse hooves."

"Hell, Fuji. If someone had brought a trailer with the horses, they could have trailed a log with burlap bags behind it and wiped out the signs when they left."

"Sorry, sir. I'm not familiar with horses or how they would be transported."

"What about the guard?"

"We've canvassed the area where he grew up, but no one has seen him. For all I know, he could have run scared for miles in the woods, passed out, and got eaten by a pack of wolves known to frequent the forest."

"We'll go with that theory for the time being. What about the informant?"

"Three possible suspects. One cook in Yokohama, and a guard and a servant girl here in Tokyo. All are under surveillance. The guard and the servant girl are having an affair. But, so far, nothing suspicious or out of the ordinary."

"Is the servant one of the girls in the hospital?"

"Yes, sir."

"See that she doesn't recover and then kill the guard."

"What would you like me to do about the cook in Yokohama?"

"Keep him under surveillance. Good cooks are hard to find. Have your informants at Yokota Air Base discovered anything?"

"Just a bunch of new American MPs who were flown in from Hawaii for a joint training exercise with the British MPs. Pretty standard stuff, these days. Practicing martial arts, counterinsurgent tactics, and boning up on their Japanese. Although, according to our informant, some speak our language quite well."

"Any sign of American counterintelligence agents?"

"None so far. After what happened to Agent Preston's wife, I imagine he is in Washington, D.C., helping her recover and taking care of his kid."

"I wouldn't go that far, Fuji. If he's deployed, his superiors may not even tell him about the attack. Obviously, our man in Cuba screwed up. The two women he attacked should be dead."

"Would you like me to sanction another attempt?"

"No, they are probably guarded day and night. It would be a waste of men."

"What about the swords?"

"Let's proceed with Operation Katana. However, I want at least a dozen practice runs before the performance, from the theater to the bridge, so the men are intimately familiar with the route and what you expect of them. And make sure they practice at night."

# CHAPTER 53



*Singapore, Malaysia*

Andy Larned was working on the pilot console when he heard a hail from the dock. He looked out the side window of his fishing boat and saw a rather tall, distinguished man with greying hair and a sharp nose, wearing khaki slacks and an expensive cotton shirt. He had never seen the man before, but he called him by his Army rank in a prominent French accent. With the man was a beautiful curly-haired blonde who looked like she might be his daughter. But with the French, you never knew.

"Major Larned, may I come aboard," René Clairoux shouted.

"Who the bloody hell are you?" Larned shouted back.

"A friend of Brigadier MacKenzie and your friend from America."

Larned waved his arm and motioned the man to come aboard. Then, skeptical, Larned removed his pistol from under the console into his right hand. *If the man is a foreign agent,* Larned thought, *he will pay the price for anything untoward.*

René Clairoux and the blonde girl walked up the boarding walk onto the deck and moved toward the wheelhouse. He stopped below the open window to address Larned.

"Major, I would like to discuss working with you on a project that Jon Preston and Brigadier MacKenzie would like us to collaborate on.

"Do you drink coffee?"

"Of course, I'm French."

Larned climbed down a ladder and escorted Clairoux and the curly-haired blonde into the boat's large galley. Andy poured three cups and set them on a small table with bench seats on two sides.

He put cream and sugar in the middle of the table. Clairoux and the girl sat. Larned stood.

"Do you have any identification, Mr. Clairoux?"

"Just a driver's license and my business card. I'm a private detective. My family and I moved to Singapore, six months ago, from French Indochina. This is my daughter, Renate. She's a detective, too. I have a message I received from Brigadier MacKenzie via courier. In the first part of the message, which is in plain text, he said you would be able to decrypt the second part."

Andy took the message and said, "Wait here, please."

After taking the message, Andy went to his cabin and locked the door. He didn't worry about Clairoux following him and firing through the door. It was bulletproof—a precaution that seemed well worth the expense when he had initially purchased the boat. He unlocked the small safe under his writing table and pulled out a dark green codebook. Twenty minutes later, he returned to the galley.

"I apologize for the cold shoulder, Mr. Clairoux, Miss Clairoux," Larned said as he sat down on the bench seat. "In my business, you can't afford to trust anyone you don't know."

"I understand, Major," René replied.

"As of ten days ago, it is Lieutenant Colonel. But, just call me Andy. I'm in the reserves, and I'm not on duty."

"Can you help with the project, Andy?"

"Outfitting a dozen freighters with sonar, fifty-caliber machine guns, tube-launched torpedoes, and K-gun depth-charge projectors is serious armament. This Tsukuda character must want to start a war."

"Apparently, he believes that the Americans are responsible for the losses he sustained in North Korea and China."

"Yes, I read about it in the newspaper. I know Jon Preston, and I wouldn't put it past him to be the one who planned and executed both attacks. He's a wizard when it comes to covert operations. But, to answer your question, yes, I will help."


Larned spent the next week putting out feelers with his network of ship captains and first mates who had helped him collect intelligence on the Japanese in the past. After, a week a picture began to emerge. Six wartime Liberty ships had been seen steaming into Dung Quat harbor, sixty miles south of Da Nang. Another six were moving up the Bach Dang River to a shipyard at Haiphong. All of this had been occurring in the last ten days. Both shipyards were located in Vietnam.

"Apparently, they want shipyards that are as far away from Japan as possible—so that no one would notice," René remarked.

"That, and the cheap labor. The only thing complicated is installing the sonar detectors. It's reasonable to assume they had sent technicians from Japan to do the installations. I'm guessing the teams were in place well ahead of the ships arriving," Andy replied.

"I have detectives in Haiphong. So I'll find out for certain and get an estimated completion date."

"You do that—and I'll send a message to the Brigadier. It should take at least forty-five days to complete the retrofits. I'm assuming the Brigadier will want to sabotage the ships."

"Yes, I thought the same. But I have no experience in that type of work."

"Well, I do. But, I know the Brigadier. He will have several teams close by and ready to do the job. He just needs intelligence on the locations, to pull it off—which is where we come in."

"What do you need me to do?"

"Do you have a way to send coded messages?"

"Certainly. One of the Brigadier's agents in Hanoi delivered code books to me before I left Indochina. I have detectives in Hanoi, Haiphong, Da Nang, and Saigon, with similar copies."

"Contact your detectives in Da Nang and Haiphong and tell them we need the names of the ships, their sizes, tonnage, maps of the shipyards, and their locations. Then we'll fly to Da Nang. I'll arrange for a boat for us to use to travel to Dung Quat and Haiphong. We can leave the day after tomorrow, which will give your men time to collect information. We'll fake engine trouble and stay in Dung Quat for two days and do a thorough reconnaissance on the ships. Then we'll move on to Haiphong and do the same."

"Can I bring Renate and my son Jacob? They both speak several dialects of Vietnamese. They are trained in martial arts and are very good at undercover work."

"How old are they?"

"Renate is twenty-five, and Jacob is twenty-three."

Larned was surprised. He had thought Renate was only seventeen. But, instead, she was only four years younger than him.

"Yes," Andy replied, "as long as they can follow orders. I know there are still a lot of Europeans in Vietnam, but we will most likely stick out. There won't be many Viet Minh in Dung Quat, but with its close proximity to Hanoi, Haiphong is another matter. I have a theatrical kit provided by Jon Preston. You and I can tint our skin to look part Asian. What color hair does your son have?"

"Blond, like his sister."

"They will have to go without the tint. Otherwise, they will stick out even more. I've never seen a blond Asian."

"Neither have I."


The 600-by-1,700-foot Dung Quat shipyard was small, compared to the shipyards in Singapore. It could handle only two of the 441-foot Liberty ships at a time and would require more time to do all the refits. The information Larned obtained during his visit to the shipyard gave the Brigadier ample time to devise a solid plan to sabotage the vessels.

Two days before the ships were to leave Dung Quat, a team of British divers—similar to the British Z Special Unit frogmen, who operated in Borneo and the islands of the former Dutch East Indies during World War Two—went to work. At two in the morning, four divers attached a quartet of limpet mines, in two clusters, to each Liberty ship's hull. This was accomplished by using magnets, seven feet below the waterline. Each mine contained eight pounds of high explosives. And each mine was fitted with a small turbine detonator. After the ship sailed one hundred and sixty miles out to sea, each turbine would detonate a mine and blow an eight-foot hole in the hull where the mine was placed. The other two ship detonators were set at one hundred and forty and one hundred and twenty miles. Three days earlier, another team of frogmen performed a similar job at the Nam Trieu shipyard in Haiphong. Due to the length of the Bach Dang River, their detonators were set at a greater distance.

The captain of each Liberty ship was instructed to maintain radio silence until reaching Japanese waters. However, those instructions were disregarded when the limpet mines began exploding and the crews could not contain the hull breaches. Instead, distress calls were broadcast over the airwaves. Every available cargo ship and fishing vessel within a hundred-mile radius rushed to help the fifty merchant sailors abandon each ship. Unfortunately, only the first ship that sailed from Dung Quat survived the trip due to a malfunction in the detonator.

It took ten days before word of eleven of the twelve vessels sinking reached Tsukuda in Tokyo. This time, Tsukuda was sure that one or two foreign powers—the British or the Americans—were responsible. The most likely culprit was Jon Preston and his team of operatives. Tsukuda vowed to spare no expense eliminating each and every one, including Preston's wife and child.

Unfortunately, Tsukuda was in the middle of his sword heist and not in a position to strike back. He was scheduled to attend the Kabuki Theater the following evening, and one of his trucks broke down. It would have to be repaired or replaced. Despite the setback, his men worked through the night and were ready by the following day. By 5 p.m., the team was deployed to an abandoned warehouse that Tsukuda owned, two blocks from the Azuma Bridge. Because of the previous mechanical issues, Tsukuda had two extra heavy trucks on standby.

# CHAPTER 54

*Hanoi, Vietnam*

Once a month, Yul Butler drove his 1942 Citroën, Type 45, flatbed truck into the *Bac Bo* area—the Vietnamese term for north—purchasing gemstones at a village called Bac Cuong. It was a central location to a dozen surrounding villages. Butler had established relations with the villagers and village chiefs. Bac Cuong was only five miles from the Chinese border. However, most villages were controlled by the Viet Minh. They were ordered by General Giap to sell to the American entrepreneur. Giap did this to control Butler's movements and limit the intelligence that the general suspected Butler was supplying to the American CIA.

On each trip back south, Butler would stop at the village market and the French army post on Route 6 and reach out to Binh Phan. Binh would confirm whether Raizo Hata and his Japanese sidekick had followed Butler. On most trips, they had. However, they had stopped at the market on this last trip, purchased food, and rode their bicycles back south.

"I think they have all the information they need to take over your gemstone operation, Yul. Unfortunately, this will probably be the trip where you get ambushed and killed," Binh explained.

"I think you're right. However, I need updated intelligence before I leave for Hanoi. Can you help?" Butler asked.

"Yes, I can help. Let me hire some of the kids who have bicycles. They can travel the road and come back after they discover where the Japs are waiting."

"I can't let you use kids. What if they get caught? This Raizo character would kill them."

"Trust me, Yul, these kids are smart as well as deceptive. They won't even be suspected. Plus, they travel this road all the time to visit their grandparents in the next village. I'm certain the Japs have seen them on many occasions. The kids will notice if something is amiss, ride on another thirty minutes, turn around, and return."

"Alright, do it," Butler said. He then picked up two toy trucks that Phan had just finished making out of butter tins and dropped a handful of bronze two-dong coins and two ten-dong banknotes in the glass jar at his feet. It was a hundred times the amount of money the toy trucks were worth, but Butler knew the information was worth the price. Butler noticed that Binh was having trouble walking and becoming feebler. He suspected the French were not paying him, and the cost of food was on the rise. From his thin frame, it was evident that his toy trucks were not providing enough income to buy chicken and fish.

Favoring his right leg, Binh walked to the market and talked to several boys in their early teens. After two of the boys nodded, Butler saw Binh give each boy a leather pouch. Ten minutes later, the boys returned on their bicycles. Each had another boy riding on the handlebar. The boys on the handlebars carried slender bamboo tubes in their hands. After watching the boys ride south, Binh returned to his seat beneath the French tricolor flag at the army post.

"What was in the leather pouches?" Butler asked.

"Poisonous darts," Binh replied.

"For crying out loud, Binh, are you serious? You're sending kids out to attack trained assassins!"

"They hunt monkeys all the time. It's the same principle. They will locate the Japs, sneak up behind them, and put two darts into them before they know what's happening."

"I wish I had your confidence, Binh. What type of poison are they using?"

"It's called devil's weed. In a high enough dose, it causes respiratory failure. The ones they are carrying have enough poison to kill ten men. The Japs will have trouble breathing within seconds and be dead within two minutes."

Two miles south of the French army post, the boys noticed where bicycle tracks led off the dirt road into the thick grass and woods. One led west and the other east. The boys continued another quarter mile until they rounded a curve out of the line of sight where the Japanese assassins exited the road. Duc, the boy steering the lead bike, motioned for the other bike to stop.

"Ha—you and Kim go east. I will take Tinh and go west," Duc said with authority. "As soon as you hit them with your darts, make your way back to your bike and wait for us. Do not go near the men. We'll continue south and visit my grandfather at Hung Canh, then return in two hours."

"You said we could take their bikes," Kim said.

"We'll get them on the way back."

Ha and Kim found one of the Japanese men after forty minutes. They each put a dart in their twenty-inch blowgun and placed two darts in the man's back. The assassin swatted at his back, thinking a wasp was stinging him. Within seconds, the man was having difficulty breathing. He tried to say something before he fell backward but had no air in his lungs to project his voice.

Raizo Hata was hiding in a thick clump of elephant grass. From across the road, he heard his fellow assassin swear and then a soft thump. Raizo called, but Itsuki didn't answer. He was about to edge his way out of the grass and cross the road when he felt a sting on his back and shoulder. He used his long arms to swat what he thought was a bee or wasp. But, instead, he felt the slender projectile in his low back. He pulled the dart loose and looked at it. Then, swearing at what he knew were his final seconds on earth, Raizo's breathing became erratic, and he collapsed forward.

Four hours after the boys left the village market, they returned. Kim and Tinh were riding on separate bikes. Duc stopped where Binh was still sitting under the French flag, making another toy truck while Yul Butler watched in admiration.

"I see you succeeded in your mission," Binh said.

"Yes, both Japs are dead," Duc replied. "Were they really the men who had tortured you when you were a prisoner of war?"

"Yes, the taller of them was."

"Then I'm glad I killed him."

Binh grabbed a large handful of coins from his jar. He handed them to Duc and said, "Share these with you fellow soldiers."

Binh turned to Butler and asked, "Is there anything else I can do for you, Yul?"

"No, Binh. You've done enough. Thank you, friend."

Butler pulled a dozen cut rubies from his pants pocket, handed them to Binh, and walked to his truck. If and when Binh sold them in Hanoi, they would bring enough cash to last him a lifetime.


When Butler returned to his office that evening, Jacob and Renate Clairoux were sitting on a sofa in the reception area drinking coffee. Butler looked at the pair and asked how their father was doing and what brought them to Hanoi.

"We brought a message from Brigadier MacKenzie, the head of British SIS in Hong Kong. You'll have to decode it using the codebook that Jon Preston gave you," Renate replied, handing the message to Butler.

Butler took the message and excused himself. Then, he went into his private office, closed the door, and retrieved a black codebook from his safe. After deciphering the message, he returned to the reception area.

"It seems that I'm being temporarily reassigned to the British SIS. I'm to accompany you all to Singapore. It looks like I will be traveling on an Air Force C-54 to Yokota Air Base and then meeting up with Brigadier MacKenzie and Jon Preston. Apparently, you two are accompanying me. Do you have any idea what this is about?" Butler asked.

"Something to do with a Japanese general named Uchito Tsukuda."

"He's one bad character."

"We have a seaplane waiting for us on Lake Ho Tay. How soon can you be ready?" Renate asked.

"Be right back," Yul replied as he turned and went into his office.

A short time later, Butler walked out of the office carrying two bags. He looked at Renate and Jacob and said, "I am always prepared to leave at a moment's notice. We'd better hurry if we're going make it to Japan in three days."

# CHAPTER 55

*Tokyo, Japan*

Nobutake Kojima sat in a chair while Uchito Tsukuda paced his office. Tsukuda had summoned the former admiral to discuss what happened to his ships. Losing all but one of the retrofitted ships during their voyage to Japan was incomprehensible. It was another unexpected disaster for Tsukuda—one he couldn't let go, unpunished.

"You were supposed to deliver those vessels to Japan, Admiral," Tsukuda declared accusingly.

"Actually, General, my job was to purchase the ships and have them delivered to the shipyards to be retrofitted. Once they arrived at the shipyards at Dung Quat and Haiphong, they were under the control of your crews and captains, and were your responsibility," Nobutake replied with authority.

"Then, you should have arranged for better security at the ship-yards," Tsukuda argued.

"General, you hired me to procure and have the ships delivered to be retrofitted with armament. Nothing more, nothing less. Nothing was mentioned in our conversation about security. Plus, the shipyards have their own security. We won't even know what happened to the ships until the surviving ship docks in Osaka. The SOS that the ship sent out only stated that there were two explosions below the water-line. Since the ships departed at one-hour intervals, they could have been sunk by torpedoes from a submarine. If you recall our initial conversation, I told you that this could end up coming back on you in a horrible way. And now it has."

"They were probably sabotaged with limpet mines while still in the shipyard or harbor. Both the British and the Americans used those during the war. Hell, we had something similar. Regardless, I need another dozen ships to keep my shipping business going. This time, Admiral, I'll forgo any retrofits to keep the American and Brits off my back. The money will be transferred into your account tomorrow afternoon. Only this time, I want you to provide security while the ships are readied in Manila. And make sure my kamon is not painted on the bow of the ship. I also want you to register them in Panama under Maritime Shipping of Panama, Ltd. I'm sure you have contacts there," Tsukuda stated, handing him the company address on a piece of stationary.

Nobutake Kojima responded, "As you wish, General. They should be ready to sail in forty-five days. First, however, I recommend you let me provide foreign crews to deliver them to several different locations across Asia. Once they arrive safely, my crews can train yours and get them acquainted with the ships' equipment."

Tsukuda nodded, but he didn't like the admiral's contemptuous arrogance. He briefly considered having him killed but decided his services were too valuable. Plus, someone in his family would surely know that Nobutake was visiting his castle. The Kojima family was too powerful to have as enemies.


After Admiral Kojima left, Tsukuda was still upset. He was about to throw a stack of papers across the office—when a sharp knock on his door interrupted him.

Tsukuda yelled, "Who is it?"

When his security chief poked his head through the door, Tsukuda asked, "What is it, Fuji?"

Fuji Takahashi responded, "The communications officer wanted me to tell you that Raizo has not made his weekly report, General."

"His last report said that he has all the information he needs to take over the gemstone business in Indochina. He's probably not back from taking care of the American business owner. Give him another week. If he doesn't report, contact our agent in Haiphong to look into the matter. Nevertheless, he's probably delayed because he's going from village to village, solidifying his position as the new buyer."

Earlier that morning, Fuji had briefed that there was no progress on finding the traitor that Tsukuda suspected was passing information to the Americans or British. As Fuji turned to leave, Tsukuda handed him a note.

Tsukuda whispered as he handed Fuji the folded note, "Take care of this task and tell no one."

As Fuji left, Tsukuda wondered if Raizo was okay. *Of course, he is*, Tsukuda thought. *He was the best field agent in French Indochina during the war.*

Fuji went to his office, pulled the note from his pocket, and read it. "Yareyareda ze!" Fuji exclaimed, which meant *Good grief!*

Tsukuda wanted him to shadow Nozomi when she went shopping. But why? According to the security files on her, she was as loyal as they come. Plus, Fuji had checked her out with her previous employer, Minister Yano. Yano gave him a glowing report from when she had worked for him on the General Staff during the war. But, orders were orders.

Later that day, Nozomi went shopping for fresh vegetables, chicken, and fish at a market near Tomisato, a six-mile drive. She drove from the castle in one of the small sedans, a 1947 Ohta PA, provided by Tsukuda. Fuji knew where she was going, so he waited ten minutes and drove to a mercantile store two blocks from the market. After a short walk, he stopped in a heavily crowded part of the market and waited. She was carrying several packages of what he thought was fish or chicken. Then Fuji saw Nozomi checking out the fresh mountain yams. She chose a dozen. When the merchant was through putting them in Nozomi's canvas bag, Fuji saw Nozomi hand him a folded piece of paper. He nodded and casually put the paper in his pants pocket and moved to wait on another shopper.

Fuji was stunned. Was Nozomi passing information about Tsukuda to the grocer? If so, she was the traitor. He prayed that she wasn't because he was enamored with her. Since he had assumed his duties as chief of security, he took time to talk to her several times a day. She was kind and knowledgeable. When she spoke with Fuji, it seemed that her eyes would sparkle as she told him about her childhood and her future dreams. Furthermore, she took a genuine interest in what he was saying.

Over the last ten weeks, Fuji gradually fell in love with Nozomi. Last week, he had decided he was going to ask her out on a date for this Friday. The following Monday, Fuji approached Nozomi and complimented her on the colorful kimono. After some small talk, Fuji asked her out. To his surprise, Nozomi accepted. She said she would love to, but Fuji would have to pick her up at her mother's house in Tokyo. She was taking a week's vacation beginning Friday, which included going to a Kabuki play on Saturday evening with her mother.

Despite his delight, Fuji was conflicted. *Maybe she had given the grocer a list of the vegetables for next week. That had to be it*, Fuji thought. Regardless, he would have to clarify what he had seen, which meant confronting Nozomi. Maybe she would be more open if she were to drink a fair amount of sake. Nevertheless, Fuji had a dilemma to solve. The woman of his dreams might be a traitor. If she was, Tsukuda would order him to kill her and dump her body into the bay. He didn't know if he could go through with it. But, if he didn't, Tsukuda would have him killed.


Following Nozomi's directions, Fuji drove his 1937 Datsun Type 16 to the address she had provided, in Yotsukaido—a small city located ten miles east of Tokyo. Her mother lived in a small one-story house that had been built by her husband in 1920. Despite being old, it was well kept and sparsely furnished. Even the tiny garden in the back was immaturely groomed.

Nozomi's mom, Sakura, was a kind and gentle woman in her early fifties. Her husband had been shot and killed by the *Kenpeitai*—the Japanese secret police force—while controlling a food shortage riot in 1944. Fuji suspected Nozomi was bitter from the ordeal but he didn't say anything. After sitting down and having tea, Sakura recommended a small restaurant for them to go to. It was within walking distance, and Sakura had already made reservations for them.

The restaurant was a small family-owned establishment. It had ten low tables. The owners had a small farm nearby where they grew sweet potatoes, onions, pumpkins, squash, and lotus roots. They also raised chickens. And with the harbor so close, they always had fresh fish.

After they finished their meal, Fuji ordered another flash of sake. He was hoping that Nozomi would open up about the note she passed to the sweet potato merchant. However, when he pressed her about the note, Nozomi was not surprised.

"I saw you at the market. You were in a crowd of people, three stalls away. You were trying to hide, but I noticed you. I'm like that. I have a great memory and a mind for detail. Is that why you asked me on a date?" Nozomi asked.

"No, I asked you before General Tsukuda gave me the assignment to spy on you. But to tell the truth, I'm in love with you, Nozomi. Even if you are a spy, I couldn't turn you in. I am fed up with Tsukuda. He's cruel, ruthless, and paranoid. And what he's doing to help the communists in North Korea is beyond my comprehension. It's anti-Japanese."

Nozomi was shocked at his statement that he loved her. She had lost all hope of finding another husband. In the spy business, she didn't want one. However, since George and his American team were about to take Tsukuda down, it might be feasible. She did like Fuji a lot.

The note you passed the merchant. What was it?" Fuji asked.

"Information on Tsukuda having Admiral Kojima procure another twelve Liberty ships," Nozomi said.

"Why are you spying on Tsukuda?"

"Because I hate the Japanese military. The Kenpeitai murdered my father. He was at a peaceful demonstration protesting the food shortage. It only became a riot after the Kenpeitai showed up and started beating people who were only hungry and wanted food."

"What are you planning to do now that Tsukuda suspects you?"

"My mother and I were planning to disappear on Sunday."

"I want to marry you, Nozomi. I want to spend the rest of my life with you. With that in mind, what will you do *now*?"

"I'll have to kill Tsukuda, of course."

"In that case, I want to help you."

# CHAPTER 56

*Tokyo, Japan*

Jacob and Renate Clairoux, and Yul Butler arrived at Yokota Air Base at two in the morning. They were immediately hustled to their quarters in one of the British SIS billets. The British paratrooper who drove the staff car told them he would pick them up at nine for a team briefing with Brigadier MacKenzie and Colonel Preston.

Butler had met Brigadier MacKenzie when he commanded the SIS unit that Jon Preston had been assigned to in Calcutta, in 1945. MacKenzie had been a colonel then. After the war, Butler had the opportunity to work with Jon Preston and George Linka when they needed his help at Pea Island, North Carolina. Butler had helped put together a group of coastal watchers to monitor the coast for a rogue Japanese submarine. The coastal watchers ended up rescuing most Japanese sailors from the Japanese submarine *I-405* after it had struck a rock shoal and foundered near the Pea Island Life-Saving Station. Instead of dwelling on why the CIA wanted him to team up with the British SIS, Butler closed his eyes and went to sleep.

The following day, Jacob, Renate, and Yul were escorted into the SIS headquarters building and then into a large briefing room. They were the first to arrive. A dozen tables at the back of the room contained steaming trays of scrambled and boiled eggs, bacon, ham, and sausage. A half dozen different pastries and a choice of hot coffee or tea were also available.

A steward in a white coat, who spoke with a heavy British accent, greeted them at the first table. There were five more stewards spread out along the other tables. There were two tables, and one steward at the far edge of the room who catered to a Japanese breakfast. The menu included rice with *ikura,* which is cured salmon roe; eggs with *furikake,* a savory Japanese condiment; pickled vegetables; grilled fish; miso soup; and *natto,* a popular fermented soybean food with a unique flavor, strong smell, and sticky texture.

Jacob, Renate, and Yul chose the first line and then went to sit at a table with plates filled. Before they had a chance to start eating, Preston and Linka entered the room. The three got up to greet them.

"Sit down and eat while it's hot," Preston said. "We'll join you in a minute. Then, after we all eat, we'll let you know why you're here."

Ten minutes later, Jim Ballangy joined the group. Before he sat down with the others, he said, "The other American agents will join us in a few minutes. Their bus broke down at the barracks, and a replacement had to be sent. The Brigadier wants everyone to eat and get plenty of caffeine before he starts the briefing."

Kim Jung, Jake Ikestead, and Scott Bayless walked in, followed by Kumiko Fujiwara and a dozen American agents whom Butler didn't know. They were followed by another dozen British paratroopers, and behind them, Miles Murphy and Henri Morreau.

As Butler surveyed the room, he realized how big an operation this would be. With this many operatives, he didn't know how it could possibly be kept covert. However, having worked with Jon Preston and George Linka, anything was possible, no matter how improbable it appeared.

"Damn, it's like a CBI reunion," Butler remarked as he recognized and acknowledged everyone he had worked with while in India, Burma, and French Indochina.

Before Butler could make the rounds and shake hands, Scott Bayless jumped up and yelled, "Room, ten hut!"

As Brigadier Michael Patrick MacKenzie entered the room, everyone stood at attention. He was followed by Lieutenant General Lew Miller and Guy Wong.

"Take your seats, please," MacKenzie expressed rather loudly. "General Miller arrived from the U.S. only an hour ago. Major Wong flew in last night from Formosa."

Jon and George were surprised to see General Miller. However, Kumiko appeared as if she had expected to see the general. *A secret kept remains a secret*, Jon thought. *No harm, no foul.*

"As you can see, this will be a large operation. In addition to you people, there are another forty Lin Kuei warriors we will be using when we attack Tsukuda's castle. They are the remnants of a clan of ninjas that moved from Japan to Hong Kong in the late 1500s. They are also the most violent fighters I have come across. If Tsukuda's castle is well guarded, we're going to need them. But right now, they are just backup. Jon, would you please continue with the briefing," MacKenzie ordered.

For the next three hours, Preston went through the details of the Kabuki play, the expected heist of the two ancient Japanese katanas, and the information obtained from Nozomi on Tsukuda's castle, northeast of Tokyo.

"Colonel Linka, Captain Ikestead, Carol Whitely, Kumiko Fujiwara, Guy Wong, and I will all be at the theater. Kumiko, George, and I are playing characters in the play. Captain Ikestead and Carol Whitely will be part of the lighting crew, and Wong will be the audience. Captain Jung will be stationed near the bridge where we expect Tsukuda's thugs to take the armored vehicle. Jung is there to strictly monitor. If we don't capture Tsukuda at the theater and are forced to attack the castle, Major Bayless and Colonel Ballangy will lead two teams of British paratroopers. They will deploy to their respective areas and cross the rivers before midnight. They will remain concealed until the rest of us arrive.

"We won't attack until Tsukuda's sword heist team returns to the castle. When they arrive, George will lead his team—consisting of Captain Ikestead, Jacob and Renate Clairoux, Yul Butler, Carol Whitely, Hiroki Eguchi, Eizo, and Emon Fujiwara—and will initiate the attack at the main gate. I expect Tsukuda will pull some of the guards from the walls to help out. Regardless, Bayless and Ballangy will initiate their attack and penetrate the west and east sides.

"I will be going with Kumiko Fujiwara, who is leading the remainder of the American CIC agents. We will attempt to enter a secret gate on the southwest side. Any questions?" Preston questioned.

"Okay," Brigadier MacKenzie remarked. "The rest of us will stay at the base until we need to deploy to the castle. Let's hope it doesn't come to that."

Jon pulled the brigadier aside after everyone left, "I would like your five toughest looking and best Lin Kuei warriors stationed outside the theater."

"Can I ask why?" MacKenzie asked.

"I want Tsukuda's men to think a rival Japanese gang is monitoring his movements. The Lin Kuei warriors don't have to do anything except stare at Tsukuda's men."

"What if Tsukuda's men get aggressive?"

"Have them leave and park a hundred yards away. I need Tsukuda to think a rival gang is going to try to take him down. Then I want them to follow the armored truck. After Tsukuda's thugs intercept the vehicle and take the swords, they can become aggressive and feint an attack. It will force Tsukuda's thugs to the castle quicker than expected."

A traditional kabuki theater performance would usually run from mid-morning into the late afternoon. Because of this, many Japanese often attended only for a single act. Therefore, there was always a constant coming and going of people in the theatre. However, *The Legend of the White Samurai* was billed as a three-hour performance to keep the price of admission down, due to the fledgling post-war economy. The play was scheduled to run for three weeks and was the talk of Tokyo. The inaugural performance was by invitation only, and most of Tokyo's elite were planning to show.

By 7 p.m., people were streaming into the Kabuki-za Theater on Chuo-dori Avenue. Most Japanese enjoyed kabuki because it told an entertaining story and allowed actors to demonstrate their many skills—singing, dancing, theatrics, and acrobatics. Furthermore, a kabuki play was always written around a moral ideal and was intended as educational. It was a concept the Japanese called *kanzen-chōaku,* which translates as a reward for the virtuous and punishment of the wicked. This play represented a conflict between a righteous white

European-born samurai and an evil Japanese samurai. Plus, it was the first play about a white samurai in the history of Japan.

The famous kabuki troupe performing the play would guarantee an increased draw over the next three weeks. Nevertheless, many of Tokyo's upper and middle class would attend just to see the famous Masamune and Muramasa katanas. The Muramasa katana was usually described as a demon blade because it was believed to turn the person holding it into a ruthless killer. After Tokugawa Ieyasu's grandfather and his first son were killed by a Muramasa katana, his father was stabbed by one and went insane. Afterward, the Muramasa became regarded as cursed. Eventually, Ieyasu banned the Muramasa katana from his domain.

The hero, in *The Legend of the White Samurai,* was Hiramatsu Buhei, whose Prussian name was Henry Schnell. Buhei was challenged by a Japanese samurai and famous swordsman named Miyamoto Bennosuke—after Buhei rejected a proposal to marry the swordsman's eldest daughter. Despite Buhei having one wife and not wanting another, Bennosuke was disgraced by the rejection and sought revenge. However, because Bennosuke wielded a Muramasa katana, he knew he was guaranteed a victory. Knowing the history of the Muramasa, Buhei's daimyo, Matsudaira Katamori, offered him the use of his Masamune blade.

Fifteen minutes before the play started, a caravan of three cars pulled up outside of the theater. Uchito Tsukuda and two bodyguards exited the middle sedan and made their way into a reserved section of the theater. As Tsukuda looked across the crowd below, he recognized Nozomi and her mother sitting in the fifth row, courtesy of the tickets he had purchased for his secretary. Despite asking Fuji to spy on the woman, he secretly hoped she was not the one betraying his organization.

# CHAPTER 57

*Tokyo, Japan*

The play began with dancers moving from the back of the theater. They streamed, on both sides of the audience, across a walkway called a flower path. It allowed for a majestic entrance, showing off the actors' beautifully tailored, colorful, and flowing costumes. But, at this point, it was all about individual showmanship rather than content. As they merged, onstage, the two dozen dancers celebrated Henry Schnell and his new rank as the head military instructor for the Military Commissioner of Kyoto. Because Schnell was a foreigner, the new title and rank of samurai came with the right to choose a Japanese name, marry a Japanese woman, and carry a sword. One of the samurai in attendance, standing on the periphery, was visibly displeased at the foreigner's elevation.

The second part of the act featured the 9th daimyo of the Aizu Domain, awarding Hiramatsu Buhei his swords and his eldest daughter's hand in marriage. During this part of the play, Jonathan Preston, playing the white samurai, wore a stunning golden kimono with a wig tied in a topknot. His heavy makeup hid his European features. He gestured his thanks to the gathered crowd and new boss. He bowed a lot and spoke no words, to show his humility.

The second act was more dancing, singing, and combat sword tactics that Buhei, now a master swordsman, taught to a group of new recruits. The few words that Preston uttered during this part of the play were either *hai*, meaning yes, or *bango*, meaning no, and an occasional *suiryoku* for thrust, and *surasshu* for slash. Clad in his dark blue kimono and brown pants with his swords thrust through the left side of a heavy black belt wrapped around his waist, Preston was still unrecognizable in his heavy makeup as he grunted instructions and rebukes.

After the second act, there was a forty-five-minute intermission. Most of the first- and second-level audience flooded the tea rooms. The third level was reserved for exclusive clientele. So, Tsukuda stayed in his private box with his bodyguards. One guard pulled a bottle of Tsukuda's favorite sake from a small leather bag and poured a drink. Midway through the intermission, one of the theater troupe members came to Tsukuda's private box and presented him with a gift. It was a bottle of Jack Daniel's Old No. 7 Tennessee Whiskey, courtesy of the troupe's white samurai actor. Tsukuda thought that the bottle had been misdirected until he read a handwritten note that read, *I'm looking forward to meeting you later tonight.*

Now Tsukuda was confused. No one knew that he was coming here tonight. He had kept it a secret from his staff and bodyguards until the last minute. A faint thought crept into the back of his mind. It was his grandmother, saying, *Beware of the white samurai, Uchito.* He shook his head to clear the thought and had his bodyguard open the bottle. Tsukuda asked his bodyguard to taste it to see if it was as mild as he had heard. The bodyguard nodded his approval, and Tsukuda asked for a glass.

After waiting several minutes to see if his bodyguard dropped dead from the whiskey being poisoned, Tsukuda finally put the glass to his lips and tasted the famous American whiskey. "Sumuzu," Tsukuda uttered, which meant *smooth.* The third act began with more dancing and singing and more fabulous costumes. When the white samurai stepped on stage, the audience applauded. Preston bowed to the audience, raised his hand in the direction of Tsukuda's third-level box seat, and saluted—in military fashion—to the general.

Tsukuda saluted back, thinking that the actor was an officer who used to work for him on the general staff. There had been several who had an acting background. So, Tsukuda was beginning to think that a former officer under his command was playing the white samurai and had provided the bottle of whiskey and the salute of recognition. However, he was distracted from the thought by one of his bodyguards from outside the theater, who entered and whispered something in his ear.

"Are you certain they are the communists?" Tsukuda asked.

"No, General. But they are watching our every move. I believe they may make an attempt on your life. So to keep you safe, we should get you back to the castle," the bodyguard stated.

"I will not be intimidated. You have ten heavily armed men. Just run them off. But absolutely no gunplay. The prime minister and most of his cabinet, and several royal family members are in attendance. It would panic the crowd, ruin the play, and tarnish my reputation."


The first scene of the third act started with more singing and dancing, celebrating the birth of the white samurai's first son. The second scene was followed by a dramatic scene between the daimyo of the Aizu Domain, the white samurai, and the samurai and famous swordsman Miyamoto Bennosuke. Bennosuke was trying to negotiate the marriage of his eldest daughter to be the white samurai's second wife.

Hiramatsu Buhei explained that this was a great honor. Still, his Christian religion forbade him from having more than one wife. Bennosuke thought Buhei was lying—because Bennosuke's daughter was not very attractive. Any samurai would be thrilled to have his daughter as a wife and the famous swordsman as a father-in-law. The more he argued his point, the angrier he became. It was as if Buhei had touched Bennosuke's sword and his dignity, which would be interpreted as an act of unpardonable rudeness. In the end, not wanting to insult the daimyo of the Aizu Domain, he bowed and walked away, vowing that he would have his revenge for the snub. He would demand satisfaction and would challenge the arrogant white samurai to a duel.

The third scene of the third act began with Hiramatsu Buhei's wife and her household attendants sobbing and crying over the challenge to the death, issued by Miyamoto Bennosuke. Buhei's wife argued that she wouldn't mind if he were to take a second wife.

However, she was distraught, knowing that if Buhei died, she and her son would be left impoverished. Eventually, Bennosuke would end up killing the child to end her husband's lineage.

The final scene of the third act started on the field where Buhei was training his soldiers. He was dressed in his brown pants and a white shirt and carried his two swords. Buhei's daimyo, Matsudaira Katamori, told him that Bennosuke took pleasure in killing. He attributed it to the man's flawed character rather than the Muramasa katana that he carried. Buhei knew better than to believe in a demon-possessed sword. Only people were possessed by demons, mainly by those they created themselves. However, Katamori told Buhei that Bennosuke loved to duel and had killed over forty men. If anything, he had an uncontrollable desire to kill others. Therefore, Bennosuke's demon was bloodlust.

Before Buhei took the field, Katamori offered him his Masamune sword. Buhei recalled the legend that the only sword that could defeat a Muramasa katana was a Masamune. Katamori mentioned that Bennosuke was very superstitious. Although he knew Buhei probably did not believe in the legend, he was confident that Bennosuke did. Katamori said it would likely create enough doubt in Bennosuke's mind to give Buhei an edge.

Following Japanese custom, Buhei and Bennosuke exchanged names and unsheathed their katanas. Bennosuke was a tall, muscular man with a neatly trimmed beard and piercing eyes as cold as a winter's wind. Bennosuke charged forward and immediately went for a strike at Buhei's neck. The left-handed Buhei parried and, with lightning speed, blocked the sword. Buhei then spun clockwise to Bennosuke's open side. His katana struck Bennosuke on his right shoulder, drawing blood.

George, who was playing Bennosuke, swore that he would decapitate Buhei. Now enraged, Bennosuke charged with a sweeping uppercut, intending to catch Buhei in the throat. Buhei dodged the blow and swung his sword in an overhand, sideways motion at Bennosuke's neck. Buhei thought he had missed. But as he turned and crouched for another parry, he noticed blood gushing from a small cut on Bennosuke's neck. When George turned away from the audience, he pushed several times on a bag of fake blood, which pumped blood from a hidden bag and tube just below his high-necked shirt. When he turned around, the audience gasped. The single stroke from the extremely sharp Masamune katana had barely touched Bennosuke but had ended up cutting his carotid artery.

The cut went unnoticed by Bennosuke, and he prepared to parry again. However, when Bennosuke crouched to begin another charge, he noticed a large amount of blood on his sleeve and the front of his shirt. While staring—without expression or understanding—he began to falter. Then Bennosuke fell to the ground, which was now bathed in his own blood. Buhei stood over the dying swordsman, wiped the blood-stained Masamune on his shirt in the coolest manner imaginable, and returned it to its sheath. The audience erupted in cheers and applause. The applause continued as the lights were dimmed and the actors left the stage. Even Tsukuda was standing and cheering the performance.

Within a minute, the lights came up. The master of ceremony stepped from behind the curtain to thank the audience and introduce the actors. As the curtain came up, all but one actor stood on the stage, in a long row. The last actor introduced was the white samurai. As he moved out of the shadows, the audience gasped. He had removed his makeup. The actor was indeed a white person. As the MC called out his name—Jonathan Preston of the United States— Tsukuda moved toward the door of his private box. As he realized who had been playing the white samurai, Tsukuda nearly tripped over one of the plush seats.

"Get me out of here, immediately," Tsukuda ordered. "To the castle at once. And radio ahead and alert the guards to an imminent attack."

"What about the communist gang? Should we take care of them first?" the guard asked.

"Absolutely not. We must not start a war in front of the prime minister and his cabinet. It would be unforgivable of me."

# CHAPTER 58

*Tokyo, Japan*

Tsukuda ordered his driver to take an alternate route to the castle, taking them east through Chiba before heading north to Yamanosaku and the main gate. When the caravan arrived, Tsukuda could see guards patrolling the walls of the fortress and that the castle was on full alert. As soon as the last car entered the main gate, it was secured.

As Tsukuda strolled casually toward his office down a long corridor, he heard the distinctive chirp of the Japanese bush-warbler coming from his singing floor. It gave him a sense of reassurance that no one could get into the castle's inner sanctum without the guards being alerted. When he approached his office, he saw Nozomi coming with a pot of tea and a flask of warm sake.

"I saw you at the theater with your mother. So why are you here?" Tsukuda asked.

"My mother became ill during the first act, so I took her home. However, she insisted that I leave so I wouldn't catch her illness. So, since I had nowhere else to go, I came back here. I knew you would be coming home soon. There is a little chill in the air tonight, so I prepared a fresh pot of tea and some sake. Would you like something to eat, also?" Nozomi asked as she poured a cup of each beverage.

"Thank you, Nozomi. The tea and sake will be fine."

"Fuji told me the castle is on high alert. Should I be worried?"

"No. A communist Yakuza gang was at the theater tonight trying to intimidate me. It's just a precaution," Tsukuda lied.

As Nozomi left the office, Fuji was approaching. She nodded but didn't say anything. George had left word for her at her mother's house that Preston had planned to reveal himself to Tsukuda at the theater, earlier that night. She knew it would cause Tsukuda to panic because he would wonder whether his grandmother's warning was coming to fruition. If anything, Tsukuda would hole up in his castle until the threat was gone or removed.

As Fuji entered the office to give Tsukuda a report on the defenses, he noticed that the general's hand was shaking as he drank from his cup of sake. The tea was untouched.

"Twenty guards are posted on the walls and inside the watchtowers, General. The remaining guards are in their quarters on standby," Fuji stated.

"Have you noticed any activity outside the castle?"

"Nothing yet, sir."

"Be on alert for our men returning from the armored vehicle heist. They should be returning around 2:30 a.m."

"Yes, General. The guards at the gate are prepared. Is there anything else, General?"

"Yes. What did you find when you carried out my instructions the other day?"

"Nothing, General. She went to the market, completed her shopping, and returned to the castle. No stops in between, whatsoever."

"That's comforting to know. If Nozomi is a spy, I don't think she would have returned tonight."

Before Preston and his team left the theater, they changed into dark clothing. Afterward, they headed directly to Tsukuda's castle. When they arrived at a small hill, a half-mile away, it was nearly 1 a.m. Jon tapped the hand mike on his radio three times. He heard four responses, each with a specific tap sequence. The teams were in place, waiting on the last of Tsukuda's men to return. According to the last transmission from the Lin Kuei warriors' leader, the thugs had intercepted the truck and taken the swords without killing any of the guards.

Once the Lin Kuei warriors made their presence known after the heist, Tsukuda thugs drove toward the castle by the quickest route.

Following, a quarter-mile behind, the Lin Kuei warriors fired several shots but intentionally missed the car ahead. The thugs in the sedan began to panic. Worried that they might lose the swords, they drove faster and radioed the castle for instructions.

"Tell the general that a carload of Japanese males is following us to the castle. We need to know what to do," the guard in the passenger seat radioed.

Fuji replied, "Those swords are priceless. Drive to the castle immediately. Do not engage. They are probably the same communist Yakuza gang that was watching the general at the theater."

Ten minutes later, the sedan skidded to a stop at the main castle gate and radioed, "We are here. Open the gate."

As the gate opened, the Lin Kuei warriors fired at the entrance from a hundred yards away. As the castle guards responded with gunfire, George and his team fired upon the gate and the men on the walls. Two guards, who were attempting to close the gate, fell, leaving the gate half open. George rushed inside the entrance and pushed the gate fully open, while Ikestead, Jacob, and Renate engaged and took down the remaining guards in the gatehouse. Yul Butler, Carol Whitely, Hiroki Eguchi, and Eizo and Emon Fujiwara held off the guards on the walls, wounding or killing six responders. When the lone surviving guard radioed that the gatehouse was being taken by the Yakuza, Tsukuda pulled half of his force from the castle walls to reinforce the guards stationed in the main keep.

When Bayless and Ballangy saw the guards on the wall, running toward the main castle, they immediately ordered the grappling hooks over the walls and their men to begin climbing. Several guards heard the muted clinks and began firing into the darkness. Two British paratroopers were wounded. Then, on both sides of the castle, British snipers began picking off the guards. The few remaining guards were quickly gunned down as the paratrooper made it over the walls and began returning fire.

Preston and his team reached the secret door that Nozomi had said would be unlocked. They quietly penetrated the southeast end under a storehouse where foodstuff was stored. Jon could hear the shuffle of feet and soft crying in the storehouse where Nozomi said the kitchen and maid staff would be hiding. Kumiko Fujiwara and Jon Preston crossed the empty compound while the other CIC agents provided cover. As Jon and Kumiko attempted to penetrate one of the doors into the keep, Tsukuda's guards began firing at the door. Preston pulled Kumiko back before a dozen rounds could have taken her head off. Instead, they splintered the wooden door.

Preston waved the CIC agents to join them. As they crossed the open compound, one agent went down as a guard in the watchtower fired on them. Preston put the radio to his mouth, "Sniper in the watchtower. Take him out."

Seconds later, a British sniper, on a hill outside the west side of the castle, fired. He radioed, "Sniper down."

While one of the agents pulled the door open, several more fired into the keep. When the guards ducked, Jon and Kumiko each tossed a grenade into the keep. Then, from the second level of the castle overlooking the keep, Bayless and Ballangy fired their weapons at the guards not killed by the grenades.

"The keep is clear," Ballangy yelled.

Jon and the others rushed into the keep. When several wounded guards tried to fire on them, the guards were shot and killed.

"Tsukuda is on the second level. Take the eastern hallway, and meet up with George," Preston shouted to Ballangy, as he turned and headed back toward the secret gate.


The news coming into Tsukuda's office was not good. The intruders had captured the main gate. They had scaled the east and west walls and taken the keep. His only option was to flee through the secret exit and get to his boat hidden on the Nekona River.

"Fuji, lead the way to the secret exit. The rest of the men will stay here and cover our retreat."

Fuji gave the orders to the three guards with him—and hustled Tsukuda into the kitchen through a hidden door. When they reached the first level of the castle, Fuji checked the open area they had to cross to get to the exit. It was clear. He then ordered the guards to make sure no intruders followed them. Fuji went first, and Tsukuda followed, holding tightly to a Nambu Model 14 semi-automatic pistol in his right hand. They were ten feet from the outer door that led to the secret exit—when Jon Preston opened the door.

"I told you I would meet you later, General," Preston stated. "How does it feel to be trapped in your own lair?"

"You," Tsukuda shouted. "Now you die!"

Before Tsukuda could raise his weapon, Nozomi stepped from inside the door with a thin bamboo tube to her lips. She blew hard. The projectile from the tube hit the general in the neck. Tsukuda lifted his left hand, felt the dart, and pulled it from his neck. When he realized what it was, he tried to raise his arm, aim his pistol, and fire, but the nerve agent had already taken effect. He couldn't even pull the trigger.

There was a bewildering look on Tsukuda's face. He wanted to ask Nozomi, "Why?" But he couldn't speak. Eventually, his leg gave out, and he slumped to the ground paralyzed, unable to move anything but his eyeballs. Nozomi moved closer and stood over him.

"You're probably wondering why?" Nozomi stated—as Tsukuda struggled to comprehend. "During the war, your storm troopers killed my father during a peaceful protest over food shortages. Over a hundred innocent people died that night. They were loyal Japanese. Their only crime was hunger."

As Nozomi watched Tsukuda struggling, Kumiko Fujiwara walked up. As recognition crossed Tsukuda's face, all he could do was look on as Fuji looked at Kumiko and said, "Hello, cousin."

Kumiko replied, "Fuji! George told me you were one of his agents."

# CHAPTER 59

*Washington, D.C.*

When the message from Brigadier MacKenzie reached General Renick and General Miller, there was an hour-long discussion about what to do with General Uchito Tsukuda. Miller wanted to put him in an American prison for life in the Philippines. Still, Renick reminded him that he was responsible for the deaths of four CIC agents in Washington and the attacks on Guy Wong, Kathleen Lauren, and Camille Dupont. Renick wanted to have him tried by a military tribunal and hung, but that would mean exposing their mission in Japan. Furthermore, he would never get General Bradley's or President Truman's approval.

When General Miller briefed General Bradley, Bradley asked, "Why didn't our agents kill him during the attack on the castle? Hell, they had a Presidential Order to do so."

"One of the agents, planted on Tsukuda's staff, hit him with a tranquilizing dart when he attempted to shoot Colonel Preston. He was paralyzed. Preston put in the report that it would have been murder to kill him after he was incapacitated," General Miller explained.

"For crying out loud, I have a secret agent with values and ethics about eliminating a threat to the security of our nation. So how the hell does Preston get away with this?"

"Jonathan Preston is brilliant and extremely intuitive. He was one of our best recruits in 1939, and he proved himself in the CBI Theater. But, like you, he is also a very strong Catholic."

"What would happen if we gave Tsukuda to the British to handle?"

"The British have more ethics than we do," General Renick replied. "Plus, Brigadier MacKenzie is refusing to take him."

"And we don't dare turn him over to the Japanese," General Bradley stated. "If we did, General MacArthur would know about our secret operation and raise hell with Congress, which would make the President look bad in an election year. MacArthur would love to run for president and have an illegal issue to pound Truman with."

"I'll inform Colonel Preston to come up with another solution," General Miller replied.

As Renick and Miller walked the hallways back to their offices, Renick asked, "What will you recommend, Lew?"

"I'm thinking we give Tsukuda to the South Koreans. To them, he's a criminal involved in the illegal arms trade that is adversely affecting their border security."

"Yes, that might solve our dilemma."

"I'll ask Preston to discuss it with Captain Kim Jong. Despite working for Brigadier MacKenzie, he still has strong ties with the South Korean military. So I'm pretty sure they could come up with a solution to the problem."


Captain Kim Jong listened to Jon Preston as he explained the situation with Uchito Tsukuda. Kim was not as religious as Preston and had no problem dealing with the tyrant. However, since Jong was working for the British SIS, he thought it unwise to deal with Tsukuda himself. He did not want the brigadier to get in trouble with his superiors in London if Jong acted illegally. Jong agreed with Preston that it was best to turn General Tsukuda over to the South Koreans for a final judgment. He knew for a fact that the South Koreans wanted Tsukuda for war crimes extending back to World War Two.

In the end, Brigadier MacKenzie agreed with Captain Jong and arranged for a flight to get Tsukuda to the U.S. Navy base in Fukuoka, where the *Jacqueline* was currently in port. Tsukuda was held prisoner on the yacht for two days before a South Korean fishing boat captained by Kim Jong's cousin, So Jong, slid into a berth next to the sleek spy ship.

At 2 a.m. in the morning, Tsukuda was handcuffed, gagged, blindfolded, and transferred to the fishing boat. Once aboard, Tsukuda's feet were bound together, and he was set on the deck with his back against the wheelhouse. The cold December wind chilled him to the bone. Within minutes the boat was motoring out of Fukuoka Bay. An hour later, when the boat was abeam Shikanoshima Island, it turned to a course of three-zero-five and headed directly for Busan.

Sixty minutes before sunrise, Tsukuda was awakened by two crewmembers threading a heavy chain across his legs and feet. Tsukuda heard someone from the wheelhouse shout an order. Two men caught him under his arms and raised him to his feet, which were so numb from the cold, that he could hardly feel them. Captain So Jung walked down the wheelhouse steps and stood next to the rail of the boat.

"My brother and I were prisoners in one of the camps controlled by the Japanese army and your intelligence agents during the war. To get me to talk, they tortured and killed him before my eyes. I'm not going to torture you, General. Nevertheless, you will die. You might make it to a hundred feet before you suck seawater into your lungs, but I doubt it. I will also see to it that your Shinto god will not be pulling you into Heaven by your ears, General," Captain So Jung stated in fluent Japanese.

When Jung removed the blindfold, he saw the terror in Tsukuda's eyes as the meaning of his words registered in his brain. Jung took his knife and sliced off both of Tsukuda's ears. When he nodded to his two sailors, they picked Tsukuda up and tossed him overboard.

"Jib-e gaja," Jung shouted to his second-in-command in the wheelhouse. Which meant, *Let's go home.*


Colonel Jonathan Preston was sitting in an office, six doors down from Brigadier MacKenzie's—when one of the British paratroopers knocked on his door.

"Begging your pardon, Colonel," the corporal interrupted, "Brigadier MacKenzie wishes to see you in his office."

"Thanks, Corporal. Tell him I will be there in five minutes," Preston answered.

When Preston knocked and entered MacKenzie's office, he said, "What's up, Brigadier?"

Patrick MacKenzie looked at his longtime friend and replied, "The question, Jon, is what's up with you?"

"I don't follow, sir."

"I think you do. You've been sitting in that office for two days. Something is on your mind, and I think it's high time you talk about it to someone."

"And you're that someone?"

"Either me or George, but he's in Tokyo visiting his former martial arts instructor. So, yes. Talk to me. Chances are I've had some of the same questions running through my head after the war."

"Okay. Why did you decide to stay with the Secret Intelligence Service after Japan surrendered?" Jon asked.

"For one, I found something that I was good at. Before the war, my career in the army reserves in Calcutta was lackluster and not very interesting. In addition, I was older than most of my senior officers. With the SIS, however, I found a home. When you were assigned to my SIS detachment, I thought it was the end of my career. I felt that the Americans wanted to take over. Fortunately, it wasn't like that. Even more fortunate was having you on my team. You taught me what teamwork was all about. After that, it was the team that kept me in the SIS. I had built such great relationships with Henri Morreau, Miles Murphy, and Jim Ballangy, that I couldn't abandon them. They became my family."

"That's what I am struggling with, Brigadier. And so is George. I have a beautiful wife and a young son. They need me at home. But, despite what Camille tells me, I know she is constantly worrying that I will come home in a pine box."

"You've got the best foresight and intuition of anyone I know, Jon. What does your gut tell you?"

"It tells me that if I stay, I'll be promoted to a brigadier general in less than two years. Then, I'll be given a job with Army Intelligence to train a new cadre of CIC special agents like myself. But because I'll be the youngest person ever promoted to brigadier general, I'll stay pigeonholed as a one-star for a long time. Eventually, I might get a second star and take over General Miller's position."

"What's wrong with that?"

"You know damn well what's wrong. I'm a field agent. I can't stand to be in an office for more than two days. George might be able to, but not me. I have to be on the front line. It's what I'm great at. It's about taking down the bad guys. It's about solving a problem. It's about detailed planning and flawless execution. It's what I live for."

"And you don't think the army will let you be on the front line as a general?"

"No. It's not like the SIS."

"What about the CIA?"

"All the senior field positions are taken. Plus, most of those guys were Donovan's men. They were grown men playing Cowboys and Indians in World War Two. They were a bunch of Ivy League graduates who had no clue what they were doing. That's why so many died during the war. Now is no different. They will be outwitted every time they face the Chinese, Korean, and Russians, because they don't have the insight into the cultures, nor the field experience, and the street smarts."

"It sounds like you've got your mind pretty well made up."

"Not really. I have to talk to Camille and George. And I owe it to General Miller to discuss it with him. Plus, President Truman asked me not to make a decision about my future until I have talked to him."

# CHAPTER 60

*Washington, D.C.*

George Linka and Kathleen Lauren were finally going to tie the knot and settle down. They had announced their plans to be married in June of 1949, allowing enough time for her mother and father to travel from Australia to the United States. Kathleen didn't talk much about her parents, because they were extremely wealthy. Before the war with Japan, her mother was a university professor in Bangkok. Her father had been a geologist and the top oil executive with Shell-Mex and BP Ltd., in Thailand.

When word reached Bangkok that the Japanese had invaded Hong Kong, her father took the oil company's Boeing, Model 307 Stratoliner, and flew his top six executives and most of his staff to Sydney, Australia. Believing war was imminent, the company had ordered all executives to move their families, a month earlier. Unfortunately, many junior staffers considered Thailand their home and refused to leave, believing the Japanese would leave their country alone. Instead, the Japanese invaded Thailand—five days later.

Now, her father headed up BHP Billiton, the largest mining company in Australia. With his wealth from the oil business, and now from mining, her father was wealthy beyond belief. After moving to Australia, her father purchased a ten-thousand-acre cattle ranch, in the Murrumbidgee region, west of Sydney. He sold beef to the U.S., British, and Australian military during the war, making him even richer. It was embarrassing to Kathleen. And it was one of the reasons that motivated her and her sister to join the OSS when they were recruited in 1942.

George's mother and father were retired and living in Dallas, Texas. They were United Brethren missionaries in Japan for nearly thirty years. George was born in Dallas while they were temporarily assigned to the U.S. for additional missionary training. When George was two, they moved back to Japan and stayed until his father retired in 1940, and then moved back to Dallas. As a young student at a Jesuit university in Tokyo in 1935, George was recruited into U.S. Army intelligence.

After graduating in 1941, George returned to the U.S. After receiving his commission as a second lieutenant, he underwent CIC training; and in 1943, he underwent OSS training in Ceylon. During his training, his skills in martial arts did not go unnoticed. After graduation, he was retained, by the Ceylon detachment, to teach his martial arts to new OSS and army counterintelligence recruits. Within a year, he was promoted to first lieutenant—and a year after that, to captain. With his skills and intelligence, he was placed on a fast track and moved to Calcutta. He began to think he would like to make a career in the army until he met Kathleen Lauren and fell in love.

George and Kathleen had discussed staying in army counterintelligence, but after five years of war and fighting criminals, their hearts were no longer in it. They both wanted children, and with war raging in French Indochina and threatening in Korea, both knew they would be deployed and involved in counterintelligence and clandestine work, very soon. Because of their background in Asia and language skills, George assumed they would be stationed in Hanoi or Saigon before the end of the year, probably mentoring the team of CIC graduates they had returned with from Japan.

While the team stood down from their mission to Japan, General Miller put them to work, training another hundred recruits as special counterintelligence agents like him and Jon. Those who would make it through the thirty-two weeks of training could look forward to assignments in Europe and Asia. It was rewarding seeing the young men and women go through the rigors of training that he, Jon, Camille, Jacqueline, and Kumiko had established over the last year and a half.

Most of the recruits were as bright as he and Jon. One recruit, First Lieutenant Brody Warren, a graduate of Texas A&M University, was as intuitive as Jon Preston, and had a photographic or eidetic memory, like Jon and himself. *This new group of recruits has great potential*, George thought. In a sense, he wished he would be there to mentor them when they went into the field. His heart, however, was elsewhere. Regardless, there were several top NCOs, as well as Alexei and Dimitri Antonov, who would take up the challenge.

Jon Preston knew he was being restless. From time to time, Jon would reflect back over the last seven years—he had been at war most of his adult life. During that time, Jon had suffered pain from the loss of comrades and a gunshot wound. Despite being decisive and focused, he had doubts at times. He felt anxiety over some of his decisions, which resulted in the deaths of thousands of Japanese soldiers during his first mission into Thailand.

Nevertheless, it was also a time of outstanding accomplishments, friendships, joy, and even love when he met Camille. What Jon enjoyed most was his love of life—a love that came with a level of maturity that nearly every young man of his generation, who had fought and survived the war, should be appreciating. Jon acknowledged this joy, and he understood that those who did not fight in a war would never feel what he felt at thirty years of age.

Despite his record of success in army counterintelligence, Jon had not reached the summit of his life, where a person finally matures and looks back on a life of great accomplishments. Jon understood that the greatest difficulties were still ahead. He was still at the bottom of the mountain, looking up, with years of climbing ahead of him. If Jon stayed in the army, there would be many more adversaries to encounter. Most would be fellow officers, jealous or feeling snubbed, as Jon climbed higher in rank. There would also be cliffs to circumvent, valleys to cross, streams to ford, precipices to scale, and slides to avoid—and any of them could spell disaster. Especially if there was another 'General Tsukuda'-like person out there on a power trip.

As a counterintelligence agent, Jon could almost predict what most of the challenges would look like—because wartime enemies were predictable. Because Jon was a hands-on field officer, it would not be an ordinary life of business and personal challenges. New enemies would come at him from all four directions. It would be challenging, but in the end, the death of an enemy always left him empty. Jon also knew that he would come up against someone younger and better than he was, one day, and he would probably not survive. It would break Camille's heart.

Life as a businessman, however, would entail fighting the daily difficulties that arise in business. It would entail coming up with ways to overcome them and then meet the next challenge head-on. On the other hand, there would be no days of sheer horror, wondering whether you would survive an able adversary bent on your destruction. Suppose he succeeded and lived to a ripe old age. In that case, he could look back over his life's efforts and see what he had accomplished, including children and grandchildren—something really important and fulfilling.

The oil business would be challenging and rewarding. According to George's uncle, H. L. Hunt, it was never predictable, and every hole you drilled was a risk. To succeed in the oil business, you had to collect data and outsmart and outthink Nature to find what it was hiding. Jon's greatest strength was outthinking the enemy. He surmised that when he struck oil as a wildcatter, he would be outthinking Nature, who hid its secrets well. Jon imagined what the first strike would be like. *Exhilarating,* Jon thought—*which is what I would want my life to be. I don't want it to be dull and unfulfilling.*

Nature would send problems at him as fast as streaking meteors against a night sky. And those problems in the oil field could be as rash and brutal as those encountered in war. Because nature was bent on hiding the oil and gas hidden below the earth's crust, it would throw surprises at you. Oil rigs could explode from gas pockets igniting, and men could die. Nature would try to defeat anyone who challenged its dominance.

*But, could the constant challenge, of vying for dominance over Nature, provide the fulfilling life he wanted?* Jon wondered. It was time to discuss it with Camille, George, Kathleen, Fitzsimmons, and President Truman.

After weeks of discussions and contemplation, Jon decided that his life lay in a continuous series of unpredictable hardships and struggles that he could find in the oil business. His best friend George was on board. Even Camille and Kathleen agreed. They had all sat down with Elton Fitzsimmons and discussed how the business would be set up. Then, Jon, George, and Elton flew to Dallas and met with George's uncle, H. L. Hunt.

After reviewing the location of Elton Fitzsimmons ten-thousand-acre ranch, Hunt told them they were sitting on a goldmine. When Hunt asked how much money the group had, to invest, he was shocked. Hunt was expecting George and his partners to ask him for a stake, to get started. Instead, they revealed that their pooled resources exceeded five hundred thousand dollars. Plus, they still had money coming in from the gem business. So, Hunt advised them to take a third of the money and buy additional oil leases around Midland and Odessa.

"Nature is fickle," Hunt told them. "One week, the oil is there, and the next, it disappears. So you have to be tenacious and persistent."

If there was one thing Jon Preston knew, he and George Linka were tenacious and persistent. He suspected that Elton Fitzsimmons was the same, or he wouldn't have survived in the smuggling business. Nevertheless, Jon believed he could still be a warrior. It would not be the same as battling Japanese assassins or chasing down a rogue submarine filled with biological weapons. Nor would it entail playing a white samurai to take down a villain.

Nonetheless, unlike the samurai of the 16th century, whose sole pleasures of living were overcoming the multifaceted and dangerous challenges their enemies brought to the battlefield, Jon would be going against the greatest warrior of all time—Mother Nature.

Pleased with his decision, Jon rose from the heavy wood swing hanging from a lone Oak tree in the backyard. He looked west to where the sky was turning from a dim golden yellow to a pale shade of purple. Satisfied with the view, Jon turned and began walking toward the house. Before he took a second step, three shots were fired from inside the house, followed by the extended rat-a-tat-tat of a submachine gun being fired into the home. Then, before the machine gunner could reload a fresh magazine, Jon heard a second round of shots coming from the house.

Jon hit the ground and looked up from his prone position on the grass to see Camille staggering out of the back door with a handgun dangling from her limp, bloody left hand. An M3 submachine gun was in her right.

Shocked by the blood flowing down her arm, Jon jumped up and rushed toward Camille.

"I got the first guy, but there's a second gunman," Camille said, tossing the M3 to Jon as she stumbled and fell to the ground.

Jon caught the M3 in time to see the second assailant inching around the corner of the house. Knowing he had the drop on Jon, the oriental assassin was smiling as he lowered his submachine gun to waist-level.

Before the assailant could fire, the crack of a high-powered rifle rang out from the front of the house. With a puzzled look, the assassin looked down at the large hole in his abdomen before dropping the gun and falling dead to the ground.

Jon was kneeling next to Camille with the M3 ready to fire when Alexei Antonov shouted, "Don't Shoot! It's Alexei."

As Alexei walked around the corner and asked, "Jon, are you alright?"

"Yes, but Camille is hit. Please go in the house and call an ambulance."

"Dimitri is making the call as we speak. He's also calling General Miller."

Jon nodded as he tore a sleeve off his shirt and pressed it against the wound in Camille's shoulder, stopping the bright blood flow.

As Jon held her, Camille opened her eyes and smiled.

"I guess the oil business will have to wait. We need to kill some more bad guys before we leave the army," Camille said.

"Yes. It appears so."

General Miller's staff car came to a screeching halt in front of Jon's house as they loaded Camille's stretcher into the ambulance. The general jumped out of the car, ran to the ambulance, and got in after Jon. Miller ordered the ambulance to Bethesda Naval Hospital.

"I radioed ahead. Bethesda will have their best surgeon waiting."

"Thank you, general," Jon replied.

"How is she?"

"Bullet in the left shoulder. Camille will require extensive therapy before she can come back to work."

"Whatever she needs, Jon. I'll see to it. What do we know?"

"Two Asian assassins."

"Japanese?"

"Alexi believes they are. He heard one mumbling in Japanese before he died."

"Crap! Do you think Tsukuda has a relative bent on revenge? I thought he was the last of his family?"

"The uncle he bought the distillery from is still alive. He was a heavy influence on Tsukuda, so it's possible. But it could also be a relative of Lieutenant General Takaji Sugimoto. His father was a former samurai, and the family might be bent on revenge."

"What do you need from me?"

"Cancel my resignation and reassign me to Brigadier MacKenzie's SIS team."

"Consider it done. What are you planning, Jon?"

"I'm sure you don't want to know, general. But it *will* involve something out of the samurai code of chivalry. I'm going yūrei. I'm going to become a ghost."